One Good Dog
& The Dog
Who Danced

Also by Susan Wilson

The Dog Who Saved Me

A Man of His Own

Summer Harbor

The Fortune Teller's Daughter

Cameo Lake

Hawke's Cove

Beauty

One Good Dog
& The Dog
Who Danced

SUSAN WILSON

ST. MARTIN'S GRIFFIN
NEW YORK

ONE GOOD DOG. Copyright © 2010 by Susan Wilson. THE DOG WHO DANCED. Copyright © 2012 by Susan Wilson. All rights reserved. Printed in the United States of America. For information, address St. Martin's Press, 175 Fifth Avenue, New York, N.Y. 10010.

www.stmartins.com

The Library of Congress Cataloging-in-Publication Data is available upon request.

ISBN 978-1-250-14057-9 (trade paperback)

Our books may be purchased in bulk for promotional, educational, or business use. Please contact your local bookseller or the Macmillan Corporate and Premium Sales Department at 1-800-221-7945, extension 5442, or by email at MacmillanSpecial Markets@macmillan.com.

First Edition: June 2017

10 9 8 7 6 5 4 3 2 1

One Good Dog

Dedicated, as always, to my family—with love.
And in memory of two good men, our fathers:
William Everett Hidler and Frank Gordon Gibson, Jr.

Prologue

He was a rough-looking thing. Big ears, wiry hair. His muzzle just beginning to grizzle. He looked like the sort who'd been living outside of society for a while, maybe never really been a companion. After a long parade of supplicants appearing before me, each wanting me to choose him or her, their noses pressed up to the chain-link fence that separated us, there was something in this one's deep brown eyes, not a pleading—pleading I can overlook—but something else. A quiet dignity, maybe even an aloofness, as if he really didn't need me or my kind being nice to him. Yes. That was it, a haughtiness that declared he needed no one's pity; he shouldn't even be here. Don't look at me; I'm only here by coercion.

Our eyes met and held, but then he turned away. Beta to my alpha. But in that brief gaze, I saw something I recognized. Maybe it was just that I saw my own independent streak, the one that has kept me on top. Or the eyes of a fighter down on his luck, but with memories of recent glory. Maybe I saw that underneath the rough exterior lay a heart, like mine, not entirely hard. You've got to be tough to live in this world, whether your lip is curled in real anger or fear aggression, you have to be willing to carry out the threat. This battle-scarred fella understood that, and on that basis I made my decision. He was the one for me.

So I wagged my tail.

Chapter One

"Sophie." Adam March doesn't look up from the rectangle of paper in his hand. His tone is, as always, even, and no louder than it should be to reach across his executive-size office, through the open mahogany door, and to the ears of his latest personal assistant. On the pink rectangle of a "While You Were Out" memo slip, in Sophie's preferred lilac-colored ink and written in her loopy handwriting, are three simple words that make no sense to Adam March. *Your sister called.* Not possible. Time and date of call: yesterday afternoon, while he was enduring what he hoped was the last of the meetings he was going to have to hold before today's main event. A meeting in which he'd given a combination pep talk and take-no-prisoners mandate to his handpicked team.

Adam flips the pink note back and forth against the knuckles of his left hand. This is a mistake. Sophie has made a mistake. Not her first. Lately he's been noticing these little slips of judgment, of carelessness, of Sophie's slightly less than deferential attitude. As if she's not a subordinate, but a peer. Too many late nights when the jacket comes off, the tie is loosened, and the sleeves are rolled up. Too many weary hours leaning over her as she works on her computer, struggling to make every document perfect. She's made a common mistake: Being in the trenches together doesn't mean that they are friends, that he will overlook sloppiness.

Adam closes his eyes, takes a deep breath. The most important day of his career and it's already started out badly.

His alarm hadn't gone off. Which meant he hadn't had time for his run around the gravel jogging paths of his gated neighborhood, which meant he had lost that thirty minutes of "me time" he needed so desperately before a day filled with meetings, conference calls, at least one confrontation with middle management, and, at the end of the day, a dinner party his wife, Sterling, had planned in order to befriend the newest neighbors, the Van Arlens, before someone else got them. The Van Arlens, it was believed, had connections to the best people. People who were useful to anyone interested in social advancement and really good schools for their children. Which basically summed up Sterling.

Adam had no objection to a get-to-know-you dinner; he just preferred not to have them on the same day as so much else was going on in his life. But then, if they waited until he had a slow day, they'd still be living in Natick and their daughter wouldn't be enjoying the connections that would serve her for the rest of her life. It was hard work, laying the groundwork for social/business/education/recreational pathways for a teenage daughter who greeted him with ill-disguised sullenness when he made the effort to show up for one or another of her endless sports in time for the final score.

When Adam thought about having kids, he'd pictured

himself the Ward Cleaver of his family—wise, loving, adored. Ariel hadn't been wryly mischievous like Beaver, or devoted like Wally. Adam hadn't heard an understandable phrase out of her mouth in years, every mumble directed at the table, or muttered behind her long blond hair. The only time he saw her face was when he attended her horse shows, when her hair was scraped back and under her velvet-covered helmet. But then she blended in with the other girls, all pink cheeks and tight breeches and blue coats. Sometimes he rooted for the wrong girl/horse combination. To say nothing of the fact that all the horses looked alike, too. To Adam, horse shows were a tortuous and endless replication of the same blue coat, black helmet, brown horse racing around the course, and then the girl crying when a rail was knocked or a time fault incurred or because the horse was crazy, lazy, lame, or just plain stupid.

Except for Ariel's drive to become some kind of horse-jumping champion, a goal at which Adam had thrown great handfuls of money, she was an enigma to him. Yet this is why he worked so hard. This and Sterling's four-carat dinner ring and her personal fitness gurus, one at each of the three homes they owned—Sylvan Fields, Wellington, Florida, and Martha's Vineyard—the support of an increasingly large staff and their illegal cousins; and the cadre of financial managers to make sure he didn't pay more taxes than he should. They, unlike most of the rest of the people he employed, were very, very good.

At age forty-six, Adam March had found himself, on this overcast morning, pressing his forehead against the bathroom mirror and wishing he didn't have to go to work. Not only had his alarm failed him but the housekeeper had failed—again—to have the made-to-order granola he needed.

Nowhere in the giant pantry could he put his hands on the imported cereal he preferred. All he could find was the crap Ariel ate. With a childhood fed on cornflakes, now he could afford the best in breakfast food, so was it too much to ask that he find his granola when he wanted it? The sheer cost of importing it from Norway had to be justified by his eating it every day. But beyond that, without it, his bowels wouldn't function, and if that system also failed him, Adam knew that he was in danger of really losing his temper, and it might be that this housekeeper would be the biggest loser once he was done with her. Which, of course, he couldn't even consider until after this dinner party. To fire the stupid bitch today would mean that Sterling's ire would overshadow his, until his temper and his bowels would shrink to a pipsqueak size.

Sterling, blond, whippet-thin, and sleeping the peaceful sleep of the person in charge of everything, was a force to be reckoned with, and Adam wasn't about to unleash that power on a day so patently important to her. Not for her own sake, she so often said, but for his sake. His advancement, their only child's advancement. It was social warfare out there, and Sterling provided the leadership of a general over her troops. "We have to be seen; we have to support the right charities." Their name even appeared as supporters on a PBS documentary series. "We need to attend the right concerts. If you intend to succeed, that's the price you have to pay." That was but one of Sterling's cheerleading themes. Some might say that Adam March had already succeeded. What more could he want? Some men might want strings of letters following their names, others the glory that came from leadership in the arts, the sciences, the political arena. Adam lusted after three letters: C E O. Chief Executive Officer. Such an achievement was no longer dependent on moving up in the ranks of promotions and cultivating years in the same company. It was more of a hopscotch of leaps across and over, one foot down, now two, from corporation to corporation, allowing himself to be seduced away from one major executive role to another. Manager, Vice President of Acquisitions or Division. A rise that came with a move to a bigger house in a better—read: more exclusive—neighborhood, another vacation home where he'd spend most of his time on his phone, too afraid to be out of touch for more than the time it took to use the bathroom, more BlackBerrys. More expense. Some days Adam felt like he didn't have two coins to rub together. All of his salary and bonuses seemed to be absorbed into this machine of ambition. Still, the ripe red cherry of the top post was just out of reach. But not for long. After today, Adam's elevation to the ultimate spot on the ladder at Dynamic Industries would be secure. President and CEO.

But this morning, all Adam had wanted for himself was a bowl of Norwegian granola and a fucking run through the contrived landscape of his most recent gated neighborhood. He wanted his "me time," thirty minutes to call his own, leaving the Bluetooth behind, keeping his head down and his eyes only on the path so that he didn't have to wave at neighbors or their help. His best ideas often came to him during that thirty minutes.

There was only one thing stopping Adam from just taking his run and going into work a bit late. He held himself and his staff to a rigorous standard of punctuality. Adam March entered his office at precisely seven-thirty every day. Not one minute before or after. It was a source of incredible satisfaction to him that people could set their watches by him. Adam believed that timeliness was an art and a science. Despite the ten-mile commute and all the variables of traffic, Adam arrived on time. And woe betide the staffer in his group who wasn't there to greet him. Adam required simple things of people, the sine qua non of his expectation: Be on time. The groups that wandered into the building here and there, untaxed by punctuality, smacked of a basic sloppiness he would not allow in his.

Adam stared at his reflection in the bathroom mirror, looking at an attractively craggy face, his morning shadow of dark beard firming up a jaw that had only just begun to soften. He stared into his own cold brown eyes, eyes that had earned him the nickname, "Dead Eye." A nickname he didn't find offensive, but grudgingly affectionate. A face with gravitas. A face suited to the take-no-prisoners deal maker he had become.

If there was a shadow of an angry, grizzled man in the mirror, Adam swept it away with a brushful of French milled shaving soap.

Adam runs a hand down his silk tie, tucks the strange note into his jacket pocket. Sophie is still AWOL. He stares at her empty chair and, for the first time in many years, wonders about his sister.

Sophie's armless secretary's chair is cocked at an angle, as if its occupant weighs more on one side. Her computer screen with the Microsoft logo drifting around speaks of her having been on the computer opening up the e-mails that she will either forward to him or to his underlings or delete as unworthy. It isn't enough that she's in the building. Sophie needs to be at her desk when he arrives.

Adam lays the offending piece of memo paper down and

opens up his old-fashioned top-loading briefcase. He can't remember what he's looking for. There she is, slinking back to her desk with a giant paper coffee cup in one hand, a pastry in the other. Even from deep in his office, Adam can see that she has a flake of icing on her chin. Now Sophie really is testing him. Instead of dropping everything and grabbing her notebook, she leans over her computer keyboard and taps the mouse. She is checking her e-mail. On his time. Outrageous. Sophie knows this is an important day. What can be more important to her than getting her marching orders from him? He's really getting tired of her insubordination.

Your sister called.

Chapter Two

Adam sits on the floor of a small kitchen. The floor beneath him is sticky, splotched here and there with stains so old, they are part of the geometric pattern of the linoleum. He plays with a Matchbox car, making car noises as he pushes it along and around the cracks in the tile. He is underneath the kitchen table. Four chairs are pushed in; only one has someone sitting in it. His father. Big feet in work boots, one lacing looser than the other. One foot tilted just a little on the rubber edge of its lug sole. Adam runs the little car up and over the feet of his father. His father shifts his foot away, removing the mountain. Adam putters his lips and propels his car around the perimeter of the defined space beneath the table. He can hear the clink of glass on glass, and the rustle of the newspaper being folded. They haven't had supper yet, and there are no sounds of it being prepared. A pair of improbably high-heeled vinyl boots appears. His big sister. From his lair, Adam can see her knees, pale, knobby protuberances peeking out over the top of the white boots, above them a long sweep of skinny leg to the hem of her miniskirt.

"Where do you think you're going?" His father's voice is low, tired.

"I'm going out. I told you."

"You are not. You need to start dinner."

"You promised."

Suddenly, his father scrapes back the chair and stands up. "Veronica." Now all Adam can see is his blue work pants, the too-long pant legs covering the tops of his black steel-toed boots. His sister's legs are obscured by their father's. "No, I didn't. You have responsibilities in this house."

"Fuck my responsibilities."

The sound of the slap is sharp, brief, startling, like the sound of his cap gun, and involuntary tears spark his eyes. His sister makes no sound. "Don't you talk like that, young lady. Who do you think you are?"

"I'm sick of this. I'm sick of you. I'm sick of being the unpaid babysitter. He's your kid; you take care of him."

Adam watches from beneath the table, watches his sister's long legs in those ridiculous boots stride to the back door. They live on the second floor; this door leads to the back stairs, to the dank hallway below with its clutter of empty cans and unused garden tools. She opens the door.

"Don't you walk away from me." His father's voice is authority, dominance, power. Adam is too young at five and a half to think in those words, but he recognizes the hollowness in his chest every time his father speaks. The hollow fear that the troll beneath the bridge is talking to him and that he won't have the answers.

From under his kitchen table cave, Adam watches as his sister's legs come back, coming closer, until her small feet in the vinyl boots point directly at him. He feels a little relief. She's back. She'll stay.

He leans out a little, to see past his father's legs. Veronica speaks, and what she says become the last words he'll ever hear from his sister; the last words he remembers. "Fuck you, old man." The door slams shut. And he is left alone with his father.

"Sophie." A little more insistent. He needs to stop this before it goes any further. Where is that girl? Why isn't she here standing in front of him with her little steno pad, her lilac-colored pen at the ready, waiting for his orders, waiting for his needs to be expressed and acted on. Waiting to hear him say that he, Adam March, has no sister and that whoever left that message should not be given any encouragement. He will not speak to her. Even before he can start the day's critical work, now he has to tell Sophie she's made a mistake, that despite those three innocuous words, despite what some woman has told her, he doesn't have a sister. Sophie needs to be smarter about crank calls.

In more than forty years, he's never had a word from her, not since the day she stormed out of the house, leaving him behind, alone with their widowed father. Veronica has been gone so long that he's never spoken of an older sister, not even to his wife. Why would he bother bringing up a faint memory, a vague recollection of sitting on the couch and sharing a bowl of popcorn, when Veronica's existence has nothing to do with him? With who he is. Who he has become.

Adam has not so much denied his history as created a whole new mythology—that of self-made man, his history beginning not with childhood, but with his summa cum laude graduation from the University of Massachusetts with his B.S., followed by his Harvard M.B.A. He has whitewashed the years of working as a Pioneer Valley Transit driver to pay for college.

He has downplayed his childhood as a virtual orphan, refusing to speak of his past with a firmness that implies a slightly romantic, yet painful experience, not the facts of a father who gave him up to the state. Or the series of foster homes. The degradation of a life in the system. Long ago, Adam March encapsulated his actual childhood as the body will encapsulate a splinter, forming a hard mass of cells to separate the foreign body and dissolve it. In its place, he found ambition. Adam is a man who always catches the gold ring.

Adam folds the pink note. *Veronica. "He's your kid." The sound of a slamming door.*

Adam feels a tiny squeezing of his heart muscles. Not pain, not angina. Something else. Tension. The tension that makes him the tiger he is in the boardroom. Adam closes his eyes for a moment, then opens them and rereads the note. *Your sister called.* That is all that is written on the paper. No number. No address. No name. As if he knew them already.

Certainly this is Sophie's misunderstanding, but what if it's not? What if, in some bizarre circumstance, some unimaginable turn of events, his sister has come back? If so, what does she expect? A tearful reunion? What does she want? Money? That makes some sense, and he makes a mental note to call his lawyer as soon as he can break free from the day's high-pressured activity. He opens the slip once more.

Your sister called. The shaky ground on which he has built his life trembles.

"Sophie." The name spoken in a flat tone, devoid of warmth, as if addressing a dog. A dog that is being disobedient. A dog that needs training.

"Be right there, Mr. March." Adam can see Sophie framed in the open office door as she bends over her computer, tiny dimples forming in the backs of her knees where her slightly too-tight, slightly too-short skirt slides upward in defiance of his dress code. Ties for the men and appropriate office wear for the women. Adam March does not tolerate Ally McBeal wear in his office. Sophie's ample backside wavers from side to side as she taps the keyboard with a response to whatever it is she's finding so amusing at his expense. His expensive time.

Suddenly, his mouth is dry and he is very thirsty. As he reaches for the carafe on his credenza, Adam suddenly feels his blood pressure drop, and with it a swooping dizziness, a sense of being outside of his own head. He touches the edge of his desk for solid contact, but his hands feel disembodied, attached to his wrists by threads. The momentary dizziness stops as his blood pressure begins scaling up, but not the sense of plummeting.

Outside of his office, Sophie laughs. Each note of her musical trill strikes him as increasingly taunting. Adam's thoughts are circling wildly, his razor-sharp thinking suddenly clouded with anxiety. He's got to get back on track; he has important phone calls to make. He doesn't have time for distractions. He doesn't have time to puzzle out what this means. Time for a sister.

Adam crushes the note and tosses it into the receptacle beneath his desk.

His sister, thinking to just walk back in, to pick up a relationship she abandoned when he was a little kid? Leaving him to be passed from one foster home to another? To jeopardize everything he's spent his whole adult life building?

Adam retrieves the note and tears the sheet into halves,

quarters, and eighths. Adam March has no sister. He has a business to run.

"Sophie." Adam says her name again as if it is a dead word, a word that is meaningless, invented. "Sophie." Harder on the second syllable. SoPHIE. Not imploring. Threatening.

The girl stands with her back to him, bending over her computer keyboard, her whole posture mocking his authority.

"Sophie." His voice gone from authoritative mezzo forte to forte, and still the girl doesn't come to him.

Still bent over the keyboard, Sophie raises one hand and waves back at Adam, a casual, dismissive salute, acknowledging his voice but postponing his wishes. Putting him off. Like Sterling puts him off. Time and again, when she stands in front of him in their bedroom, unabashedly naked, slowly lotioning herself, spraying the fine mist of her signature perfume into the air and walking through it, readying herself for whatever social event they are scheduled to attend or host. Untouchable. Her surgically enhanced body nearly unattractive in its rock-hard contours and artificially enhanced breasts, but invoking lust in him anyway. Lust that Sterling allows only afterward.

Waving him away like Ariel does, diminishing his importance in front of her teenage friends.

Sophie's dismissive hand lowers to the keyboard, the importance of her electronic friend subsuming the importance of him. She shifts, the dimples behind her left knee disappearing and the ones on her right deepening, little mocking eyes.

Too much has been invested in this day. This day's anticipated outcome. Too much of Adam's time, effort, reputation, and future is wrapped up in his almost eighteen months of careful analysis, planning, coercing of colleagues to see that he is right, that this takeover is the right thing to do. Too much of his life has been spent in building up to this moment; maybe his whole life has been lived in preparation for this glorious day. With today's launch, he will step into his rightful place as CEO designee, no longer lying in wait to take over Louis Wannamaker's position. The years of building upon the weak foundation of his boyhood, his years of achievement, will come to fruition as heir apparent.

Veronica. He called out her name, then and for years after she slammed through the back door.

And Sophie is seriously challenging his authority. She needs reminding. She needs to remember herself and her place in this corporate pack.

"Don't you talk back to me, young lady."

Your sister called. What idiot believed some raving madwoman?

Adam's mouth is bone-dry; his tongue sticks to the roof of his mouth. His pulse is pounding in his right temple, a curiously painful thumping that seems audible, as if he can listen to the rising of his blood pressure. He is out of breath. Behind him, the morning light casts a yellow square onto his massive black desk, his shadow like a keyhole in the center. He presses his knuckles against his leather blotter. A thin line of ragged pain arcs between his eyes for a single audible pulse beat. Adam presses his knuckles down harder, presses himself against the edge of the black desk, rocks a little to gain momentum, and pushes off. Coming around the wide desk, he knocks the regulation vase of fresh flowers askew; the foot of the fluted glass vase is suspended slightly over the edge, its balance held by the weight of the arrangement. A lily petal loosens and falls to the floor. Adam's shoe crushes it into the carpet, a pink stain like roadkill against the macadam-colored weave.

Even as he reaches the doorway of his office, Adam is amazed at just how angry he is. It is as if the anger is boiling up from some deeper region of himself than he knew he had, that it is transforming him, physically wrenching his bones into another shape, his skin into another species. Adam has known anger; he's shouted at his truculent daughter, at underlings, and even, rarely, at Sterling. But every time he raises his voice, he is reminded of his father, of his father's last words to his escaping sister. His father's voice is the only sound in his head right now. *"Don't defy me, young lady."*

"Sophie." A croaking whisper, as if the anger has him by the throat, squeezing his breath out. The pulse in his temple pounds, and for an instant Adam thinks he is going to faint.

"Fuck you, old man."

Sophie Anderson is riveted to her computer screen, reading through her e-mails, laughing at jokes forwarded from her pal in Consumer Affairs. She stands up only as she feels Adam's breath on her neck. Then his hand on her shoulder as he wrenches her around to slap her full in the face.

Later, those who witnessed the event would claim they didn't know who was attacking Sophie, that they all thought some crazed madman had gotten by security. It took four middle managers and two security guards to wrestle Adam to the floor. Like a beast, he howled. Corporate legend would tag Adam March forever as the Jekyll and Hyde of Dynamic Industries. A man primed for battle in the world of corporate take-no-prisoners management style had slipped his reason, like a steel bear trap sprung accidentally by the touch of a rabbit. Adam March lost his shit, as they said in cafeterias and cocktail parties for years to come. The high-and-mighty top dog was wrestled into submission and never seen again. But his legend, his incomprehensible act of wild self-destruction, lived on.

Chapter Three

I should explain a little about myself to you. A little bio.
A thumbnail—or in my case, a dewclaw—description. I'm a
little over three years old, still young enough to have to vie for
position, old enough to go against only the best. I have good
teeth, set in a strong jaw. One of my ears is sheered off at the
bottom; the other hangs in a three-quarter break, and I keep
it tight against my skull whenever I greet. My tail is as straight
as a stick and I almost never let it rise above my back like some
happy-go-lucky retriever. It's a divining rod of my intentions,
a whip, a warning. Depending on my circumstances, I'm
forty-five or fifty pounds. When I'm on the street, I might
shrink to a mere thirty unless I suss out the best Dumpsters
and get there ahead of my vermin brethren. I don't know what
color I am; it's an unimportant characteristic among my kind.
What is important is that my anal glands describe my authority, my education, and my living arrangements to any who
encounter me—where I've been and where I'm going.

My urine marks a wide territory. I have no testicles. The first time I was nabbed, off they went. I'll come to that part of my history directly, but I will say that by that time I was fully masculine, and I have not given up my boyish ways except for the fulfillment of my genetic destiny. I can do it, but I'm shooting blanks.

From birth, my manifest destiny, as arranged by the young men who kept my parents in cages in a cellar, was to fight. My size and sex determined that I received the best of care from those who had no affection for the animals holed up in the inner-city cellar. I got fed. I got to wear heavy chains around my shoulders to bulk up my body into a mass of rock-solid muscle. I got strong enough that two of these callow young men, boys, pups of their species, had to hold me back. I rarely saw daylight. I was a creature of the night, shuttled from one cellar to another in the darkness, an ill-fitting muzzle all that was between me and their hands. I don't recall ever being touched by them in a nonbusiness way. All jerks and pulls and pushes; the end of a stick, the flat of a board. Had either of those two young men ever dared unmuzzle me and pat my head, I would have licked his hand. They were afraid of me, of what they had created.

As I say, I was born in an inner-city cellar. My parents, unusually, were both on-site, so I got to know them both. So many of my kind are not so lucky. My mom was a full-blood pit bull—whatever that may mean in the lexicon of swaggering young men—descended from a long line of dogs whose survival depended on their prowess in the fight arena. None of them particularly angry, but all able to be incited to destruction; all highly competitive when pitted, no pun intended, against an adversary. Like the gladiators of old, our adversaries aren't of our own choosing, but chosen for us by the men who employ us. Fighting is our livelihood. Our predetermined career. A job. The hours aren't bad, and if you're good at your job, you get to live another day and do it again.

Mom, whom they called "Bitch-dog," was scarred along her lips, even to where there was a half-moon of missing flesh exposing her upper side teeth. Long retired from the pit, she'd become a breeding machine. Her dugs hung limp and wobbly; even after the authorities removed her from the cellar, her teats would never retract to their earlier tightness.

Now, we don't identify one another by the breedist notions of those who cause our creation, but everybody knows that our different shapes and sizes, smells, and tail carriage help us to identify ourselves to one another. So, for convenience sake, I will say Dad was a blend of several types of "breeds" that have power and stamina; Dad was a mix of pit bull and rottweiler or boxer, maybe a little old-fashioned bulldog. Dad's rottie parts gave him his height and bulk. His pit bull parts thinned out his back end but gave him a Bluto disproportion in his front end. He was a tough one in the ring, knew his game well, and he never gave ground. They called him "Fitty," after some rapper they admired. It seemed to me, even as a youngster, that calling a gladiator like Dad "Fitty" was a bit silly. Although Dad and I were neighborhood champs, our boys were not contenders on the real dogfight circuit; thus were able to pass mixed breeds like Fitty and me off on their equally amateurish friends.

Naming conventions have ever puzzled us. If we don't come when called, it's likely that the appellation assigned to us is unacceptable. In my life I've been called many things, some of them not polite. We know one another by the names shouted at us, but more intimately by our scents. I think of my mother not as "Bitch-dog," but by the warm scent of her particular skin, her particular odor nursing my less fortunate littermates. I was the big one. I was the one on the top teat. My lesser sibs perished in the boys' brutal effort at selective breeding, tossed like so many field mice into the training cage.

On the street, my friends, and I've had many, are untethered by spoken names. I can visit them, even if they are out of sight, by their markers. Ah, there's the tough little one. I see that the bitch who mates with big dogs has been hanging around the alley. Maybe I'll wait for her. A further snuffle and I realize that she is now pregnant yet again. I see her in my mind's eye, her teats swelling and her self-satisfied tongue lolling as she seeks out a safe haven for her nest. We think in pictures.

I picture the cellar in which I was born, comforted by the rich, warm scent of my mother's skin and hair; curious at my first whiff of blood, the sweetish scent of it coming to me beyond the partition that separated us from the makeshift ring; not knowing what it was, but equating the smell of it with the sounds that came to me, the sounds of combat. My senses prepared me for my own experience, so that when I first saw blood, first engaged in a fight, it was as familiar to me as if I had studied the textbook.

When it was time to put aside childish things, I left my mother's kennel and moved into isolation. I believe I may have howled on that first solitary night, but I was quickly quieted with a smack. Ever since, I have ducked my head at the sight of a fast-moving hand. My assailant tossed in a hard rubber ring, which I proceeded to gnaw, ingesting the slurry and vomiting in the night before I finally slept.

I picture the heavy chains that were looped over my head and onto my shoulders as I was paraded in the mean streets by the boys. They gave me a strong dog look, and I confess I might have swaggered a bit. I wasn't fettered by the chains; I was proud of them. Around my neck a perfect uniform of tackle suited to controlling an uncontrollable animal. A collar that when jerked pressed prongs of metal into my thick neck. A leather collar fitted out with pointed studs was my dress uniform, the one I got to wear on formal occasions, like when the boys took me out to show off to their crew.

By the time I had reached my full size, the boys had begun my training in earnest.

Though I most resemble my mother—longish body, muzzle like a shoe box, whiplike tail, I am big like Dad. The rottie parts are pretty thinned out, so I'll never weigh in at ninety pounds like those bruisers, but I'm in the heavyweight category for my sport. Fifty pounds, all muscle and bone and spit.

How do we know what to do the minute we're dropped into a pit? We don't. The first time, all we know is that our men expect something from us. Their sweat tells us that they are challenging one another; their voices are sharp, encouraging, cajoling, berating, fierce. In a few moments, we know what to do. We know what they want. We pick up on their agitation; we get into the trash talking. We engage. And, like those old-time gladiators, we know that defeat is not an option. This is what our men want. This is our job.

From the first time my boys put me in the ring, I understood what was expected of me. I fought out of fear. I'm not ashamed to say that. If you didn't fear getting your nose bitten off, you were as crazy as those boys. Be the aggressor and you might not get hurt, or hurt as much. I'll say something else: I didn't always hate it. When you're a little hungry, isolated, when you never get to meet your fellows in any sort of comradely way, your noses never touching the communicating part, only recognizing one another through the scents left on the fence posts, well, you get a little testy. It was my only outlet. I was pretty good at it.

I am and always will be a beast, a man-designed bag of sinew, bone, muscle, and teeth. My ancestors thought it was a good alliance between our kind and man, never dreaming that their physical shapes and proclivities would be so determined by another creature. I am made bestial by the job I was trained to do. Many of my species have lost that bestiality, replacing a heritage of scavenging around the firepit with an attachment to some human who will dote on them.

I never knew about that until the day my boys brought in a mutt from off the street, clean, toenails well clipped, uncollared, but a clearly attached *Canis domesticus*. This happened every now and then. When they'd run out of runts, the boys would bring in involuntary recruits for us to spar with. These draftees were not meant to be real challengers; they were generally short on muscle and low in stamina, often soft from good living. These naïve fellows arrive shamelessly tail-wagging, thinking they've found a new friend, and the next minute some tough-skinned, pale-eyed contender bites into their cheerfully upraised necks.

This one told me his story during the hours we had caged in the cellar of the house, his cage placed close enough to mine that we could talk so quietly that our voices didn't provoke either of the boys to shout down "Shaddup." His scent, even without my being able to sniff around his communicating area, was replete with good food and human touching. He told me that he had a person who took care of his every need, gently, even offering him treats for every silly thing he did. His job was not to roll around in a pit, but to walk without pulling on the leash. No, he didn't wear a collar like mine. His, which the boys removed, was of soft leather, two metal disks declaring who he was and to whom he belonged tinkling merrily from it. He missed the sound; he wasn't sure he could sleep well, not hearing the gentle ding of his tags as they touched while he circled for sleep. They and the collar were the badge of his service. And of them, he was quite proud. I was appalled. The idea of such submission sent an involuntary shiver along my back and I shook hard to rid myself of it. But I was curious, maybe even a little jealous.

I made short work of him in the practice pit, but he stuck in my mind as someone whose story was not singular, but indicative of a whole world beyond my cellar. The idea began to take hold. I spoke to others as we waited our turn, and, yes, they knew of these fellows who lived in houses, who didn't bite for a living. Fellows who owed everything they had to packs of humans. Fellows who were expected to submit at all times like puppies to a grown male, even up into their mature years. They'd seen them, and not just in the arena. They'd seen them as my competitors were walked down the streets of the city, being brought to me on their own chains, they'd seen these others attached to light, meaningless leashes, happily gazing up at the faces of those who held the ends. They were usually dragged away to one side as the gladiators lumbered by, the fear in their people telegraphing caution to those at the end of the leash. The occasional lifted lip, not in challenge, but in submission. They were a hoot. Can you imagine?

I could, and, increasingly, I did. I was good in the pit, but I knew that there would always be the day when I'd be beaten—either by another fellow or by my boys. Beaten as punishment for being beaten. It's what happened to Dad at least twice in my life.

But there was another sort of fellow that I met on a more regular basis, the one that lived an entirely independent life: the street dog. Usually more intelligent than the occasional leash dog, these street dogs were savvy. They understood the freedom of a life lived naturally. If they were often cold, hungry, and in danger of being run over, they lived their lives as they pleased. Unfortunately for them, they were also an easy target; put a plate of food out and, wham bam, they were snagged. Not just by my boys and their ilk but by the authorities, the men or women who made such dogs disappear in exactly the same way as my boys. One minute licking their hindquarters on the sidewalk, the next in a cage. But their stories were the best. High adventure, travel, frequent mating. Oh boy. It was rumored that the street dogs who were captured by the authorities only made it out if they were charming. Those who weren't charming didn't. But it's hard to know charming when your whole life has been directed toward being irascible. No one knew where they went, but it didn't take a standard poodle to figure it out. The odor of charring meat and bones that threaded through the miasma of scents that filled the city air was enough of a clue. Through the diesel and effluvia, doughnuts and wieners, the sweaty population and its overlay of artificial scent, working its way like a winding river of finality, the smoke of oblivion.

I was resting in my cage after a particularly challenging bout. My opponent had nearly prevailed, until by sheer bull force I pushed him over the line that demarcates winning. They thrust the breaking stick between my jaws and the game was over. I was sliced up pretty good, and one of the boys had made a squeamish attempt to stitch up the gash on my chest. The stitches pulled the skin together something like a badly made baseball. I licked at them, tasting the rough edges of my blood-crusted trussed skin, but I couldn't reach the worst of it. My opponent lay on a pile of newspapers, his head flung back like he was baying at the moon. There was still a light in his eye, so I knew he hadn't yet bled to death. I snortled an apology through the bars of my cage and he lifted his head. He snortled back, a kind of absolution for just doing my job. We're a brutish lot, but we don't hate one another. *If we had hands, we could break out of here.* He agreed, then laid his head down, and I watched as his spirit lifted away.

A pounding above our heads. Mom sat up, dispersing her latest litter onto the bottom of her cage. *The men. The men are here.* We'd heard about them, the men who come and our kind disappear. We'd heard they removed us to bigger cages, smaller cages; to fight us with other species, to simply cut our throats. Rumors of the men circulated most often after one of us died. A dime is dropped and things happen.

We heard the percussion of big boys' feet upstairs, dashing toward the back of the apartment, clambering down the back stairs. I knew that there was a door to the outside, to the square of dirt where we were allowed to defecate twice a day. None of the boys ever stepped foot out there in the field of shit. We who used the yard, trotting around the perimeter, sniffing out one another over and over again, raising our legs against one another's mark, we knew how to skirt the worst of the mess. If we lived on the outside, we'd be careful to place our business away from where we lived.

I heard the back door open; I stood and pressed my very sore nose against the wire of my cage and pricked my ears. I sniffed the air, an amalgam of our boys' pungent sweat and the scent of the men. The men and one female. Her female scent lightly mingled with her heat. My mother shoveled her brood against the back of the cage with her nose, a worried gargle in her throat. I shook myself, ready for anything.

Chapter Four

The one-bedroom apartment is his accountant's idea. "Until your lawyer straightens out the alimony and child support, you can't afford to go on living in hotels."

As the months rolled by, Adam had moved from one hotel to another, each one losing a star as the costs of keeping his almost ex-wife and child provided for, writing check after check to keep up with the billable hours of his lawyers fighting on the three fronts of his wife's complaint, Sophie's complaint, and what he determined was Dynamic's illegal firing, drained his nonrenewable resources.

"Get yourself a little place, cook your own meals. Economize a little, Adam."

"Afford?" For some reason, Adam is stuck on that word. It has been thirty-five years since the word *afford* and its ugly stepsister, *economize,* have been used against him, and then by one of his foster fathers with an electric bill in his hand. Not since the early days of their marriage had Adam expressed any concern about finances to Sterling. Maybe even never. By the time they met at a corporate retreat at which her father was keynote speaker, Adam was well on the way to self-made millionaire. A man whom her father, the all-powerful Herbert Carruthers, could admire.

Maybe he even encouraged spending, or at least did nothing to discourage the acquisition of possessions required of their place in life. For Sterling, it was the beautiful fashion-forward clothes, the legitimate designer accessories, the best and most current automobiles—gas consumption be damned—the home entertainment systems, and the luxury vacations. For Ariel, the increasingly more expensive horses, the promised Miata for her sixteenth birthday, and a guarantee that she would never suffer a student loan in her life. His little girl wants for nothing. His little wife had always wanted for nothing, and she intends to keep it that way.

Sterling knows what their marriage is worth and is scooping everything up with both arms. The houses, the portfolios, the cars, except his 2007 Lexus, a car that he would have been trading in this year as outmoded, time for a new one. The real estate investments. Her lawyers are really good. Words like *mental cruelty* are being lobbed at him; he is accused of being threatening, then is threatened himself with a restraining order. The documents chronicle the shadow of fear under which his family now claims to have lived. Adam knows exactly what threat he's levied against Sterling, the threat to her social standing. Her husband is the crazy man who struck his PA. He is the executive whose massive takeover campaign failed to launch.

She can no longer hold her head up in polite society. People like them don't strike underlings, at least not in public. People like them don't fail.

His helpmeet, his partner in life, his Sterling has turned on him.

Adam leans his forehead against the glass of the picture window that looks out onto the street. There are no curtains on the window, and the landlord has yet to install the promised venetian blinds. There is one bedroom, just big enough for his double mattress on its frame and a bureau that he liberated from the attic of the Sylvan Fields house. It might have belonged to Sterling's grandmother, or an aunt. Neither one could recall, and the possession of it was one of the rare moments of noncontention they have enjoyed in the last year and a half. A tiny bathroom with a puke green carpet on the floor opens into the living room. He has a futon, purchased from the same discount furniture place where he bought the mattress, a television on a pressboard stand, a hideous coffee table, a small kitchen table, now tucked against the opposite wall, and two folding chairs. The kitchen is a galley kitchen, barely big enough to turn around in, which makes it surprisingly efficient, especially as he uses only the microwave and the kettle.

The apartment is on the third floor of a four-story building in a row of four-story brick-faced buildings facing west. Not quite town houses, no bay windows or granite steps, these postwar buildings are utilitarian. A line of city trees soften the landscape, promise that this downscale Boston neighborhood is still inhabited by taxpayers who care.

Across the street, a line of small mom-and-pop businesses, a newsagent, a yarn shop, and a store with a jaunty rainbow of colors splashed in an arc across the plate-glass display window: A to Z Tropical Fish and Pet Supply. Little hand-painted fish gambol around the letters.

Standing at the bare rectangle of picture window, Adam stares down onto the early-morning street until he sees a light go on in the hole-in-the-wall paper store. He pulls on his pants, zips the fly but leaves the button undone. His two-day-old T-shirt hangs out, a small hole beginning under the right arm. Adam hasn't taken well to doing laundry. He hasn't figured out the rhythm of keeping a supply of clean underwear and is continually surprised to find none in his dresser drawer a mere week after having dragged his pillowcase of dirty clothes down to the Laundromat that anchors the fleet of businesses across the street from his place.

Adam roots around in his pants pocket for enough change to buy his daily fix of newspapers, *The New York Times*, which once simply appeared at his breakfast table, and *The Wall Street Journal*, which Sophie would leave on his credenza, important articles neatly highlighted in yellow. Nowadays, he adds the local rag to his pile as he scans for news about himself. His loss of control has become a metaphor for the rapacious greed of today's overcompensated executives. If time heals all wounds, the year that the court cases have taken has diluted the amount of coverage. He's old news now.

His sentencing is today. The final chapter for public consumption.

It's pretty amazing at how effective some lawyers can be. Cadres of them. Ranks of men and women in expensive suits, carrying bulky briefcases crammed with the weaponry of law, filing into and out of windowless conference rooms with broad tables and dry-erase boards scarred with the wrong markers. The heavy scent of the knowledge of the law emanating from their very pores. Red-painted lips closed over perfect teeth; rep ties stroked downward, inanimate pets. Adam dreams of them at night. The red lips of the women parting to reveal razor teeth. The rep ties becoming reptiles, hissing and forking at him. Sometimes the faces become those of his adversaries: Wannamaker, Sophie, Sterling. In his scotch-drenched dreams, Adam shrinks as they rise above him like hot-air balloons, and he feels the flames of their anger torch his skin.

The predawn air is thick with humidity, a vaporous scrim obscuring a rising sun that casts no shadow on the street in front of Adam as he crosses over to the newsagent's shop. It's gonna be another hot one. The weather this year has been an example of extremes—miserable cold, nonexistent spring and now a September heat wave that lends credence to the wails of the global warming alarmists he and Dynamic had contradicted with their own cadre of experts. Barely five-thirty, and already Adam feels the slick of sweat coat his underarms, and perspiration trickles down the back of his neck, sliding around in fat drops into the depression of his clavicle. A fast-moving car threatens Adam as he crosses midblock to reach the other side. Adam does not walk any faster, challenging the driver to go around him, or hit him. The car swerves, its honk an afterthought. Adam raises his left hand in comradely salute, a single rude finger extended. It's a gesture he hasn't made since undergraduate days, but it pleases him in some atavistic way.

A man is coming down the street, north to south. He is dressed in the full-dress uniform of a businessman, defying the crack-of-dawn heat with a summer-weight suit, a crisp white shirt that glows in the humid murk, a beautiful yellow print tie done up in a proper Windsor knot, and spit-polished tassel loafers completing his look. Adam sees this man every weekday morning, since he's begun waking so early, and assumes that he is walking to the T, perhaps the only physical exercise he can eke out of a busy day. Adam imagines that he works in one of the law offices, or for a management firm. Instead of a briefcase, he carries one of the modern soft-sided bags that laptops fit into, with a wide strap to carry it over a shoulder. He probably lives in one of the better neighborhoods that abut this one and is taking a shortcut. Not once has the walker acknowledged Adam's presence on the same sidewalk at the same time five days a week. He marches by, his eyes averted. Just the tiniest pursing to his lips to indicate he is aware of Adam standing at the doorway of the newsagent's; a slight acceleration in his pace.

Adam wrenches open the door of the shop, the old-fashioned clanging bell above the door announcing his arrival. There is an old man behind the counter. He perches his wide bum on a stool, an unlit cigar clamped into the corner of his mouth. His apron is newsprint gray, and his hands are black with it. His thin gray hair is highlighted with the ink, as if he's been drawing new hair on his head. He looks up from his crossword puzzle. "Mornin'."

"Mornin'." Those are the only two words of conversation Adam has had since yesterday morning at this same time. Except for his lawyer's secretary's message in his voice mail, reminding him of the time to appear today at the county courthouse, he's heard no human speech save that of the voices on the television, which he keeps on most of the time. Ariel won't return his calls. His friends, plucked from the ranks of people like himself, the self he was for the last twenty years, rich, powerful, well connected, don't return his calls. He is anathema.

It is in the dark of the night when Adam knows the most isolation. In the gray dawn, he shrugs off his self-pity as self-indulgent. But in the night, when the street is silent and the only sound in his apartment is the *tink tink tink* of the leaky bathroom faucet, Adam feels the weight of solitude bearing down on him. He has never cultivated a real friend, someone who knows him well enough to offer the simple support of a shared beer at the local bar. He lacks the quiet comfort of companionship, of sympathy. Strangely enough, the only person who comes to mind in the witching hour of sleepless waiting is Veronica. The only one who might understand his need to move far beyond his upbringing, to forge a new life. Once her existence was reintroduced into his life by accident, she persists in entering his thoughts. He finds himself wondering if she ever thinks of him, the little boy she never even said good-bye to. He could have hated her; instead, he had forgotten her. Denied her.

Adam sorts through the array of newspapers fanned out across the long counter as if he's choosing the right cut of meat. Behind the counter, lottery tickets are on display, the true meat and drink of the small store. There is a coffee service, a double-burner stainless-steel maker offering one glass pot of regular and another of decaf. The regular is fresh—there is profit in being an early riser—and Adam helps himself to a large cup. He picks up a package of peanut butter crackers, which have become his breakfast of choice.

"Four-seventy-five." The proprietor shifts his cigar to the other side of his mouth.

Adam digs out three crumpled bills and makes up the rest in coins—coins he should have saved for his laundry. He's got to make an ATM stop sometime today, see if he can get by on a hundred till next week. Maybe he better do it before the sentencing. The sentencing. A wave of dismay percolates through him; the hand holding the coin trembles slightly, as if Adam is standing on the platform as a train blasts through.

Will the judge send him to jail? It wasn't an outright assault, despite what Sophie kept slipping into the testimony. It was a slap. She wasn't really traumatized; that whole bit about counseling and fear of men is hogwash. He isn't a danger to anyone. He hasn't made it impossible for her to work. Her leave of absence from Dynamic is a sham. The accusations and effect of his, albeit stupid, action had risen in graduated levels of absurdity as the trial went on.

Adam takes in a breath, letting the pain of breathing distract him from his line of thinking. Lately he has experienced pain like that from cracked ribs, as if he'd been the one attacked. "Do you have anything stronger than aspirin?"

The proprietor gestures toward a small display of patent medicines and shrugs. "Tylenol, Advil, the usual stuff. My wife likes Aleve."

Adam studies the boxes, reads the ingredients, thinks back on the various commercial claims each one professes, and then checks the price. "You take credit cards?"

"Ten-dollar limit."

Adam gathers one of each brand into his arms and dumps them on the counter with his paper and the coffee.

"Thanks, pal." The proprietor bags his stuff and hands the plastic bag to him. Outside, Adam shoves his papers under his arm, shifts the plastic bag of drugs. Glancing next door, he sees the tropical fish store woman unlocking her door. She's dressed in low-rise jeans and a tank top that just about touches the waistband. Her hair is still damp from her shower or from the early heat, and it hangs in gentle waves to her shoulders and is the color of molasses. She nods to him, a fellow early bird.

Adam has seen her before, just not this close. He spends a great deal of his day watching the street from his bolt-hole of an apartment. He's watched her perform what seems to be a daily ritual of washing her front window—a willowy undulation side to side, up and down as she squeegees the plate glass with her long-poled blade.

What can he say to her? He feels a little like a voyeur face-to-face with his object. Up close, she's older than he thought, not a girl, despite her youthful clothes, but a woman maybe in her late thirties, early forties.

Adam hesitates too long and she disappears into the shop. Taking a sip of his coffee, Adam waits to take advantage of a lull in the increased morning traffic. A moment later, the woman reappears, her hair bundled back out of the way with an elastic, a bucket of water in hand.

"Morning." There, he's established that he's a human being.

She gives him the wary look of a woman alone on a city sidewalk, and he becomes conscious of his scrappy attire. "Mornin'." Nothing more. She turns to her window washing.

"Hot again." Points for having a conversation, points off for being platitudinal.

"Sure is." Her accent is tipped with some flavor not from here. Southern? Midwestern?

"Keep cool."

"You, too."

Sure, a hot courtroom his destination, an unknown penalty. A life off the rails. He's cool. Absolutely.

Chapter Five

They spotted the dead dog first. The rest of us, Mom, Dad, and two others, were shocked into a momentary silence before coming to our senses and barking invectives at the men, and the woman. She's the one who knelt over the body of my late challenger, running her hand gently down his side as if he might enjoy the feeling. I stopped my noise to watch.

Two uniformed men and one woman stood in our cellar and swore grandly at what they had come to see. It was a little stagy, their response, as if they were pleased to have been proven correct, that they had chosen well. I yarked. Mom and Dad shrank to the back of their cages. One of the others actually growled, catching the attention of the men, who stopped swearing and grimaced with some decision. I yarked some more, a little uncertain and more than curious. What did this visit really mean? The men carried poles with loops of line sticking out of their hollow cores. The woman seemed more confident and unlatched the cage containing my mother and my siblings. Mom shrank back but was silent, which the woman took for a good thing. "Come on, Mommy, I won't hurt you." I stopped my yarking, wanting to hear more of this voice. Fitty, my dad, sat down and did something that was extraordinary in my mind, something I had never seen him do, but I understood immediately the reason for it. He put one paw up against the mesh of his cage front. An imploring "Hey, I'm with you," sort of gesture. The men visibly relaxed. The woman tentatively held out a hand to Mom. Mom wasn't having any of it, and pressed herself even deeper into the cage. In her experience, someone wanting her out of her cage meant only two things, a fight or a fuck. The woman snapped her fingers softly and made a clucking noise with her mouth, a sweet little kissy noise. Mom sighed. Capitulation. Slowly, my mother made her way to the woman's hand, sniffing it with wariness wanting to be trust. Once Mom was out of the cage, a collar around her neck and a man's strong hand hanging on to her leash, the woman gently handed out the six pups into a big box.

I yarked a question to the room: *What's going to happen?* No one answered because no one knew. Mom cast a look in my direction, her tail swinging gently to and fro in a clear message: *Whatever it is has got to be better than this minute.*

Dogs are existentialists. We think of now. But we do have a capacity for learning, which is predicated on our understanding of the past, not as some block of time, but as an action, a pain, a smell. Our idea of the future is limited to hunger pains, I will eat, and anticipation of a walk at a certain time every day. Those of us removed from that cellar that day lacked the imagination to picture a happy place; we knew only that things were going to be different.

Eventually, they came to me. Mom and Dad and the kiddies were all boxed or muzzled, the growling dog had been silenced with a little happy juice, and the other dog was acting all goofy and "happy to see you." I took a hint from him. I didn't want one of those muzzles on me. I suffer a bit from claustrophobia. *Aaah aah aaaah,* I said, cranking the length of my tail into raptures. We gladiator types look amazingly happy when we loll our tongues and split our jaws into grins. The men and the woman bought my act. They slipped a loop around my neck and we all headed up the narrow stairs to the first floor. I'd never been up there. It reeked of boys' sweat and a pungent smoke. Pizza boxes lay on the floor, tantalizingly out of reach from my nose, as I was constrained by the rigid pole one of the men had in his grip. Beer cans were neatly stacked in a pyramid beneath the cracked window in the otherwise-empty room.

I didn't get to look around for very long, as we were quickly hustled out of the place and into the street. A white van with its back doors wide open idled at the sidewalk. One by one, my parents and the other two dogs were hoisted into cages in the back. We were used to cages and didn't protest. Before I was lifted in, another man, one I hadn't seen before, came out bearing the weight of my last competitor, wrapped in a slippery blue tarp. The man's face was grim, as if he was mourning the loss of a friend he'd only just been introduced to, or that he was sad to be right.

There was a moment's inattention as the body of the dead dog wrapped in its slippery shroud slipped out of the man's grasp, thumping to the ground and leaving the empty blue plastic sheet in his arms. The people gasped in unison, and I noticed a lessening of the grip on the pole, a subtle inattention brought on by the clumsy dropping of the dead dog. I bolted.

Chapter Six

Adam sits beside his lawyer on a cold metal folding chair behind a rectangular table in the second-floor courtroom. The veneered surface of the table is lifted here and there, dried out by decades of overheating in winter and summertime humidity. On the floor beside him, faithful to the end, is his old briefcase. His Cartier fountain pen, a parting gift from his coworkers at his last corporation before being lured away to Dynamic, rests fully capped on the untouched lined yellow pad in front of him. Adam wants to cross his legs, to ease the unexplained pain in his ribs, but he knows that he must remain four-square, feet on the floor, forearms gently touching the tabletop, hands reverently clenched. The picture of a martyr.

"All rise."

Adam stands as if a military man. Which is what he might have been had he followed the advice of his guidance counselor in high school, who was impressed enough with his top grades in an underachieving parochial school, but not enough to recommend anything better than a state college, or the military. His last set of foster parents—foster father, really—believed the military was the place to become a man. He'd been to Nam. "Make a man of ya." Whack, then the shoulder jab. "Toughen you up, boy." Jab, jab.

Sophie stands at an identical table with a female lawyer who looks a lot like a college intern. They both wear subdued suits, Sophie's in navy blue and the lawyer's in gray; both have their long blond hair pulled into severe ponytails. They could be sisters.

Sophie. If only she'd added those two critical, essential, defining, unalarming words on that "While You Were Out" slip. *In.* Fucking. *Law.* Sister-in-law. Sterling's sister, who wanted to talk about a surprise party for Sterling's birthday. Then they would be sitting pretty right now, both of them enjoying the fruits of his labors, he as CEO designee of Dynamic, she as the future CEO's PA, which was tantamount to queen bee of the corporate hive.

Instead, they stand side by side in a courtroom after all the words have been said, all the excuses his attorney can make—stress, responsibility, high-powered job—in an attempt to justify the unjustifiable. That the stress of his professional life and the excitement of the anticipated actions of that day had overwhelmed him makes him sound weak, unreliable. The court-ordered shrink has applied the psychobabble of his profession and subpoenaed managers to tout an exemplary work record. Exemplary except for this one egregious mistake. That uncharacteristic moment of loss of control has cost him everything.

And in this corner, Sophie's own militants have presented a compelling story of stress, responsibility, high-powered job, and an equally exemplary work record. Her shrink has rolled out the heavy guns of post-traumatic stress syndrome.

Adam keeps Sophie in his peripheral vision, not turning his head to see her sitting there, her plump mouth pursed in righteousness. Victimhood worn like a mantle. Shoulders back, head held high. Judge Judy, of whom he's seen a lot in the past few months, would send her on her way, telling her to suck it up, saying her inaccuracy was the cause of all this. A seasoned professional staffer, she had made a neophyte's mistake. In-law. All the difference in the world.

The judge enters the courtroom. After him there follows a scent of cooler air coming from an air conditioner placed somewhere a lot more pleasant than this chamber of horrors. He seats himself, and the dozen people in the room are allowed to resume their seats. Behind Sophie are her parents and her boyfriend, a burly fellow with a red-and-green tattoo running up his neck, as if some tropical plant is rooted beneath his black T-shirt. Behind them is a gathering of her friends and supporters. A short line of reporters, press credentials hanging around their necks, sit in the last row of chairs.

Behind Adam, there is no one.

Ted Abramowitz, his lawyer, later shakes his hand and congratulates him. "It could have been worse, lots worse." The pumping hand action of the happy lawyer threatens to turn into a backslap. Worse? Than what, a death sentence? The judge has sentenced Adam to two years probation and one year of community service, plus assigning him court costs, monetary damages, and counseling. Should this end here? Not likely. Sophie's plump lips thin into a dissatisfied line. Her lawyer pats her on the shoulder and a look passes between them; a civil suit will follow.

Abramowitz assures Adam that he should be ecstatic. How so, Adam wonders, with a smear like this on his pristine record? Because he's been unable to defend the takeover plan, the whole thing looks like a colossal mistake. And Wannamaker looks even more godlike, having saved Dynamic's reputation by calling a halt. To say nothing of the fact that he's going to have to fight to get any severance from Dynamic. No golden parachute was offered, just the boot heel of his pension—don't let the door slam on the way out. Seems as though even the most morally suspect of giant corporations have limits. Not only that: Who will hire a top exec with a criminal record, however lightly handled?

To say nothing of his divorce.

His esteemed lawyer licks his lips in anticipation of further business. He's going to be living off the fatted calf for some time at this rate. Although Abramowitz comes from one of the city's better-known legal firms, it is a firm Adam has never used. Quick on the draw, Sterling engaged their personal lawyers, and was rewarded with the services of the best of the best in attorneys, a golfing buddy, a man Adam once thought of as a friend.

"Now we should figure out where you'll do your service. We can get you someplace that won't be too onerous. Maybe tutoring at the community college." Ted Abramowitz stuffs his briefcase with the thick file folders of Adam's case. Adam isn't listening to the second-best lawyer money can buy. He is jobless, convicted of a stupid mistake that wasn't his fault. His wife is poisoning his daughter's mind against him, and his lawyer thinks he's had good news?

Once the verdict has been read, the press clamor for a sound bite. Abramowitz waves them away, fairly easily, as this case isn't that interesting laid against the backdrop of the recent economic woes. Adam's case, and the press's interest in it, has been relegated to an inside page.

"Are you sorry?" One female reporter, a thin, narrow note-book in hand, waits for an answer. She wears jeans, and her dangling credentials identify her as from the local weekly, the giveaway paper. She looks about fifteen years old. Has he gotten so middle-aged that all young women look like teenagers? That they all look like his last memory of Veronica?

Adam's lawyer bleats, "No comment," but the girl catches Adam's eye, holding it with the force of her own question. And for a confused moment, Adam thinks she means about his sister. That's been the strangest thing, this regret that, in the end, it wasn't Veronica after all.

The girl reporter and the disgraced executive stare at each other, she wants an answer to fill out her story; he has no answer. The moment is broken when the bailiff beckons to Adam and his lawyer. The judge wants a word.

As suggested by the breeze that had followed the judge into the courtroom, Judge Frank Johnson's chambers are cool, and after the fuggy warmth of the old courtroom, Adam feels goose bumps rise on his arms. Without his robe, and on a level with them, the judge is whittled down to an ordinary-looking man. A tracery of blond-going-to-white fringe from ear to ear, and a pair of Buddy Holly glasses sliding down his nose. Not as old or as godlike as he had seemed behind the bench.

Adam suppresses a cleansing breath of relief; maybe he's going to be more lenient now that the case is out from under the scrutiny of the public eye, no longer subject to the outrage of Sophie and her lawyer.

"I've asked you in here to talk about your community service." The judge drops into his big swivel chair and points to the visitor chairs opposite his desk, two more cold metal folding chairs. Once again barricaded by his status, the judge lets his momentary benignity evaporate. "I'm placing you myself."

Adam's lawyer bleats a little protest. "We've discussed tutoring."

The judge sits forward, leaning on his desktop and peering at Adam over the top of his big glasses. The effect rucks up the skin of his plain, large forehead, making Adam think of Bozo the clown without whiteface. "March, you may think that you've gotten off lightly, I could have given you jail time. Probably should have. But I think that your biggest issue isn't violence, but arrogance. I've seen the shrink's report, know that you acted out of some sort of emotional self-defense, but the truth is, you're one arrogant son of a bitch and you need to be taken down a peg."

Adam feels the sigh of relief contract into a choke. "I don't know what you mean."

"It's not that you don't have a moral compass; I suppose you do. Despite the opposing lawyer's contention that you're a psychopath, you're not. But your moral compass is way off true north. You're lost, man. You need to eat a little humble pie, and I'm about to serve you a big bite."

Adam looks at Abramowitz, noticing for the first time that the man has a weak chin.

"You will report to Bob Carmondy at the Fort Street Center Monday morning. You will do whatever he requires of you."

Adam nods. He waits for his lawyer to say something, to protest or agree, but the man and his weak chin just sit there.

"Report back to me in six months." The judge pushes himself back, making the giant swivel chair rock. They are dismissed.

Chapter Seven

Ariel Carruthers March greets Adam in the riding school lounge still in tall boots, her helmet still on her head, her scowl reminding Adam of Sterling when she was young enough to permit herself facial expressions. "You don't have to get here so early. You don't have to watch."

The implication is that he never did before, that he always spent the time waiting for her on his laptop or his BlackBerry, so why does he have to stand and watch her now? This is more blatantly expressed by her posture; he is an embarrassment to her. Surely her riding friends know all about him, their parents discussing Adam March and his fall from grace at the dinner table. Adam knows this as certainly as if he were still invited to those dinner tables. Ariel is suffering from acute adolescent mortification. Here stands a father nobody else's parents want to know.

"I like to watch." Neither one of them believes this.

"I have to put Elegance away."

"Okay, hurry up, though." Adam hates the cajoling tone in

his voice, a tone he has only just started using with Ariel, as if he's become afraid of her.

Ariel wrenches open the door that leads to the stalls, letting it slam behind her.

Adam leans against the wall, hesitant to sink down on the tumorous couch or the fur-covered matching chair that serve parents as waiting-area accommodation. The lounge smells of an animal-induced fug, cat pee and wet dog. It doesn't matter how much he spends on Ariel's various training facilities, because to him they always smell bad. Usually, Adam just waits for Ariel in the car, preferring that to sitting in this room with its seventies furniture and stink. But he only gets to see her every other weekend now, and he's taken to watching her interminable lessons simply to be able to see her as much as time permits on these Saturdays foreshortened by scheduled commitments. The riding lesson, the tennis lesson, the important birthday parties. Foreshortened by stalling. Ariel is not happy about spending time with him and she makes sure he knows it.

Adam tries not to think about how, not that long ago, Ariel was Daddy's little girl. She played the part so well. "Take me, Daddy!" When she was little, Ariel wanted to go everywhere with him, cried and tugged at his pant leg as he headed out the door on yet another business trip. He remembers the chirp of her babyish voice on the phone, asking him to remember to bring her something special from Hong Kong or London. When had the pleas for his attention devolved into demands for possessions? At some point, she'd stopped asking him to stay home on weekday mornings until it was time for her to go to school, stopped warbling the kind of endearments to him that some of her friends did with their fathers. He stopped being Daddy and became the Nameless One. And this "situation" hasn't helped. Now they are strangers forced into companionship by the courts. Twenty minutes later, Ariel finally reappears, tiny low-slung breeches pasted to her pipe-stem legs, her T-shirt with its slightly suggestive motto arced over her pubescent breasts, hiked well above her belly button. He says nothing and is still rebuffed when he reaches out to hug her, given the side of her face, her mouth screwed up as far away from his lips as it can get.

Ariel and Adam get into his car without any conversation. His daughter slumps into the passenger seat and plugs herself into her iPod, an effective wall. Do not disturb.

When Ariel was born, Sterling declared that one was enough. And that was okay; he didn't need a big family. Dandling this tiny creature on his knee, Adam was as terrified as he'd ever been. He knew nothing about being a father. Thank God the nanny they hired had been a keeper and so much of his worry vanished as Mrs. Sanchez made sure that Ariel was happy.

"Good lesson?"

Ariel pulls away one ear bud and cocks an eyebrow at him.

"Your lesson? Was it good?" A wisp of something slides across the field of his memory. There is a familiarity he hasn't seen before in Ariel's expression. She is growing up; her facial bones are becoming the structure of the woman she will be. She is adopting expressions that come only with disappointment in men.

"Yeah. It was all right." A flat, expressionless answer. Before his fall from grace, she'd chatter to him about her riding lessons all the way home, often the only conversation they had, and one that he only half-listened to. His shrink, Dr. Stein, tells him to be patient. Ariel's sense of security has been damaged. Everything she ever thought about her father has been compromised by his actions.

Adam tries again. "Oh, come on. What was good about it?" His peripheral view of his daughter's profile reveals a firmly set jaw. She replaces the ear bud. Slowly, her head begins to nod in time with whatever questionable music is pouring into her ear. A sweat-darkened lock of hair falls across her cheek. She loops it back over her ear, and suddenly Adam knows what's familiar to him. She looks like his sister. Ariel is exactly the age Adam remembers his sister best, fifteen, the year she ran away. The year when she was his only ally.

"Hey, little bro, can I help you build your tower?" Adam's sister grabs a handful of red and yellow Legos. He's building a fort, but that's okay. If Veronica wants to build a tower, then that's what they'll build. The idea of ten minutes of her attention warms him, a slight flush of pleasure Adam will never quite experience again in his lifetime. The pleasure of an adored sister spending time with him. Veronica loops a strand of dark blond hair behind her ear. The strand falls back across her cheek as she reaches for another block.

Adam presses his hand against the place over his ribs where he has an inexplicable pain.

Chapter Eight

As usual, Adam is up before dawn. He stands at his one window, staring down onto the quiet street, waiting for the lights to go on in the newsagent's shop. He's in the Harvard sweatpants that he's lived in for the weekend, yesterday's stale T-shirt—an old team-building promotional shirt from his days as division leader for Dynamic's cosmetics division, and is barefoot. He'll slip on his boat shoes to run across the street once the shop opens. The fading streetlights reflect against the jolly little fish dancing across the rainbow of A to Z Tropical Fish, making them luminous in the gray light.

As Adam stares with vacant disinterest at the quiet pre-dawn street scene, his attention is caught by the shadow of something moving rapidly north to south on the sidewalk. It is a dog, its breed and color indistinguishable in the gray light, and it is dragging something behind it—a pole. It would be almost laughable to watch, the way the dog seems to be trying to dodge the object at the same time as move forward, its hind end cantilevering sideways while its front end moves ahead.

The pole is relentless and doesn't give up the chase. From this height, Adam cannot tell if it's a big dog, male or female, black or brown. In a moment, it's gone, vanishing beyond Adam's sight line.

At last, the lights go on in the newsagent's shop. Adam collects the key to his apartment, slides bare feet into Top-Siders, and goes down to get his paper. The businessman walks by, as timely as ever, his eyes resolutely looking anywhere but at Adam. Adam thinks that there should be some sort of gang sign, some arrangement of fingers and fists that would be the sign between men of business, maybe fingers curved into a stylized dollar sign. He'd seen the boys in his former gated community practicing this signing for homies. Outfitted in gargantuan hooded sweatshirts, worn in all weathers, and droopy yet costly jeans, these teens, all boys from Sylvan Fields homes, where the mean income is in the seven figures, get down with their bad selves and do God knows what behind parental backs.

A mere seven blocks from Adam's middle-class bolt-hole, the real deal sailor-walk down the street, greeting one another with complicated hands.

Adam resists the faint urge to call after the guy, throw some business-speak at him and identify himself as a fellow soldier of commerce, lately on the DL. Instead, he goes into the shop and picks up his papers.

"Mornin'." The fat man on the stool shifts his unlit cigar.

And also with you. Adam nods a greeting and helps himself to the coffee.

"How's it goin'?"

"Fine. Nice day."

"Coolin' off."

"Fall's finally here."

This will likely constitute the most pleasant conversation of his day.

Back on the sidewalk Adam sees the tropical fish store lady unlocking her door. Same or similar outfit of jeans and T-shirt, but with a light fleece vest added. Her hair is already pulled back into a workaday ponytail, making her seem plain and unremarkable. She sees him standing there with his papers stuffed under one arm and the paper cup of coffee in the other. "Mornin'."

"Good morning." He raises his plain paper cup to her in a little salute. "Fine day." Adam hears himself repeat the same weatherish small talk he has with the news guy. He would like to say something more interesting.

She smiles at him, erasing the impression that she is either plain or unremarkable. Adam so seldom sees women without the artful application of makeup that it takes him a moment to recognize actual skin, not flawless, but natural. A nice smile. A friendly greeting trumping beauty. The first smile he's received from a woman in a very long time. And just as suddenly as it appears, it disappears.

"Is that a Dynamic Cosmetics T-shirt?"

"Why, yes, it is."

"They test all of their beauty products on rabbits. Did you know that?" Her voice is pitched low, as if she is letting him in on a secret she finds appalling. She presses on the word *beauty* as if it tastes bad. "Where did you get that shirt?"

"I work . . . worked . . . for Dynamic."

"Really." This is a dismissal.

"Awhile ago."

"Did you know that's what they do?"

"Yes. It's so that beautiful women don't suffer damage."

" 'Vanity over humanity.' That's what we called it."

Adam suddenly remembers the campaign against Dynamic that PETA and several other animal rights organizations had lodged six years ago. No Animal Testing Ever—that was the local group who lodged such a successful campaign that Dynamic Industries decided it was important enough to pay lip service to. The one that, as cosmetics division head, *Adam* had paid lip service to. NATE—that was the acronym that had played over the papers for months, along with daily photographs of angry protesters. There were disruptions, editorials, eggs thrown at the offenders.

Adam developed a plan where Dynamic claimed to have ceased all animal testing—well, all rabbit testing. It was a cleverly worded apologia, which satisfied NATE.

"I take it that you are an animal rights person."

"Activist. Yes."

Adam knows when it's a good time to retreat. There is a break in the traffic. "Take care."

"Have a nahss day." A slight southern lilt to her words. Southern for "Fuck you."

Adam drinks his coffee while standing at the window, looking down on the street as it slowly becomes active. It's like watching time-lapse photography, people appearing and disappearing along the sidewalk in clumps of two or three; children skipping alongside adults, doors being pulled open, a steady stream of cars rushing up to stoplights. The door of the tropical fish shop stays propped open, but the NATE woman does not reappear.

Adam thinks of the NATE campaign and how proud he was to have figured out a way to get them off Dynamic's back. Tell 'em what they want to hear. Throw some money at an animal charity. Make "reparations." He doesn't remember this fish store woman from the sea of faces that appeared for almost a month beneath his window at the division headquarters in Westborough, their nonstop chanting becoming like a tune stuck in his head: "What do we want? No animal testing. When do we want it? Now." He and his execs called them "the Free Roger Rabbit mob."

Adam and his team justified what they were doing by promoting a corporate belief that such testing was necessary so that the eyeliner wouldn't damage nerves, so that the mascara wouldn't blind the user. What were a few bunnies compared to that? The bottom line decreed that the products developed by Dynamic for its line called Fraîche Crème, with its inexpensive, oftentimes imported ingredients, be marketed to the high-end users with a 200 percent markup. That didn't allow for lawsuits or unhappy socialites scarred by chemical peels at their luxury spas. The NATE people had to be appeased, but not allowed to be a roadblock to profits.

And Adam March had made that happen and been awarded a rich promotion to corporate headquarters and the penultimate job in the company's hierarchy. His glory days.

As Adam turns away from the window, he sees the stray dog dashing back down the street, the pole still following.

Chapter Nine

I really wasn't panicked. Despite the four feet of aluminum pole dangling like a misplaced tail, I knew I wasn't attached to some demon, but had slipped the grip of the man, who then raced after me, yelling invectives guaranteed to emphasize his mistake rather than my escape. Woo hoo. I was free. Free at last.

Thanks to our boys' relentless training program, which involved a treadmill, I had a lot of stamina. The pole thwacked against immovable objects, ringing hollowly into the sensitive caverns of my ears, but other than that, I was whooping it up. Up the street and down, ducking into narrow alleys with the enticing scent of garbage emanating from Dumpsters soldiered behind restaurants, the ugly backside of sophistication. I knew that freedom was fragile, and that I'd better find a bolt-hole quickly. The men were hot on my trail, and the sight of a fifty-pound dog with a four-foot pole tagging along would certainly catch the attention of even the most oblivious of passersby.

I had to ditch the pole. Unfortunately, my physical limitations being what they are, it was pretty near impossible to get the noose from around my thick neck without opposable thumbs. I tried shaking, ducking, twisting, clawing, and whining. Nothing helped. I needed a friend. Now, this being neither fairy tale nor Disney, no one of my own species was a likely candidate. What's a dog to do?

Being a dog, I sort of forgot about the problem as the amazing scents of the street wafted up to my nose. I began sniffing around, identifying others of my kind and following them on their travels. If females, I quivered. If males with balls, I growled and lifted my leg higher to cover their mark. As I made my way down one narrow alley, I inhaled the scents gathered between the buildings, snuffling in the olfactory stimuli. An experienced street dog would know that it's madness to go down one of these easily blocked passages. But I was, at that time, not well schooled in the lessons of the street. But I was a lucky dog. At the far end of the alley, a form crouched against the wall. At its side, a dog. I meandered along, snuffling and marking, the pole dragging gently behind me on the rough pavement. The form, as I drew closer, smelled human, deliciously unflavored by the foul perfumed scents our boys splashed on themselves.

Here was a human in all his primitive, animal glory. Funky. His true identity was not masked by frequent washing. His dog, a smallish long-haired bitch, growled at me but didn't really mean it. She was just letting me know that he was there and that she wouldn't take kindly to interference. She gave up growling and stood and shook herself, and I saw a flash of metal dangling from a collar. I remembered the leash dog mourning the loss of his disks, but I still couldn't quite

One Good Dog • 59

wrap my mind around their significance. Our kind don't usually revere totems.

I shook myself in reply. *I mean no harm.* We greeted, and I could scent that she was well fed, despite the appearance of her person.

She sat and scratched behind her drooping ear, then stood and sniffed at my pole. *So, they had you and you got away. I know how to get out of those.*

I sat and waited to hear how.

The bitch nudged her person awake. He started; then his head sank back to his chest. He was as furry as a bearded collie. Matted, too. She yipped. He opened his eyes and saw me.

"What have we got here?" His voice was like a load of kibble spilling onto the floor. Rough, interesting. "You bite?"

I walked away, just out of reach of a sitting man.

"I won't hurt you." He didn't move from his crouched position against the warm brick wall.

His companion stalked over to me and sniffed my nose, her tail addressing my doubts. *Okay.* I moved a little closer.

"You want that thing off?"

I danced a little on my front feet, his voice was so calm and kibbley. *Maybe I do.*

He didn't do any of the things I would have expected of a man. He neither lashed out to grab the pole nor stood up to intimidate me. He just kept crouching against his wall and waited for me to decide. I caught the fumes of alcohol when he spoke, his breath more humanized than his skin. I glanced up at his eyes, hooded and hollow. He had no fire in him; he had no fear and no opinions. I moved closer, close enough that he put out one hand for me to sniff, palm flat, no threat.

I inhaled the smell of the city, all the scents that I had been snuffling down as I made my way clear of the men and their van; as I put distance between myself and the cellar where I had spent my life, all of these beautiful, evocative scents were on his hand, as if he'd scooped up whole handfuls of the air and brick and pavement and garbage that made up the world beyond my eyesight. That, plus the very interesting odor of fish chowder. I knew what the guy had had for lunch. Which made me realize I was inordinately hungry and thirsty.

Okay. Take it off.

The man carefully slid the noose from around my neck. Patted my head and slid the pole under a Dumpster without getting out of his crouch. He put his head down again and instantly went back to whatever state it was he'd been in before his companion woke him.

Thanks. I lolled my tongue in gratitude.

No problem. The bitch snuggled back down beside the man and curled her fluffy tail over her nose.

I sloped off in search of sustenance.

All I had to do was follow my nose. I found pizza crusts and an empty ice-cream cone, the dregs of melted ice cream within the cone adhering to my long tongue as I slid it into the conical wafer. Mmmm. Wandering along neighborhood streets, I came across improperly fitted trash can lids, flipped them off with barely a nudge. Within these cylindrical buffets, a host of treats, including, but not limited to, steak tips, french fries, an actual half chicken. And, best of all, a ham bone the likes of which my kind will commit murder to get.

Needless to say, I chucked it all up an hour later, but then I consumed that. Waste not, want not when you're a dog on the street.

Water was a little harder to come by. There was the fountain in the park, but that meant getting too close to people. It hadn't rained in a long time, so puddles were out of the question. A backyard hose with a drip helped. I lapped at it like a gerbil, then went off to find a safe place to bunk down. I wasn't yet streetwise, but I had pretty good instincts. If my objective was to stay out of the hands of people, then I needed to stay out of sight. On the other paw, as it were, I needed what the people had to offer in the way of food and water. Although strong-jawed, I knew hunting wasn't ever going to be my strong suit and that a life beyond the city, in the less populated hills, was out of the question. I needed a little advice.

That there were others loose on the streets was evident on every street corner and against every brick building. I just needed to track a likely mentor down. It wouldn't be hard. The trace left by one male in particular suggested that he'd been on the streets for some time, which meant he knew the ropes, which meant, if I could catch up to him, he might be susceptible to obsequiousness and help me out.

By this time, and it had been since before dawn, I was wrung out. Instead of taking the time to try to find my hoped-for guide, I found a fairly protected niche in the low-growing bushes of the city park. It bore no sign of previous habitation, no circled-down foliage, no nesting, no scent of any other creature within those underslung branches. Like I say, I was a neophyte. I thought that if I couldn't see out, they couldn't see in. It wasn't more than fifteen minutes, just as I was entering that dream sleep we all need, when the sound of soft yelps startled me awake. There was a moment of confusion, when I thought I was back in my cage and my siblings were begging for lunch. The yelps turned into a low, oddly compelling howling.

Apparently, I'd chosen a bush situated behind a very popular human mating area, and suddenly, I was eye-to-eye with a humping human, both of us openmouthed with surprise. I dashed out of my imperfect hidey-hole; he stood up, genitals dangling, and grabbed his pants. I do believe he thought I was going to attack him, the way he yanked his mate up and fled almost as fast in the opposite direction from that of my own flight. Okay, bushes in the park, no good. Another lesson.

Only slightly refreshed, I trotted a zigzag out of the city park and back onto the streets. I had to keep up a steady quick-step, although the pavement was beginning to wear on my pads. I'd never spent much time on pavement. People were everywhere, and I dodged them like a video-game master. No one was going to get a hand on me. I wasn't going back to that cage.

Mostly, I kept to the alleys, having already figured out that my kind kept to those canyons like wolves in the wild. Miraculously, I found a nook ready-made for sleeping, about the size of my cage, which was oddly comforting, beneath a set of back stairs. Yes, it bore the scent of my kind, but the scent was very old, and I had to take a chance that this place was up for lease. There was even a ragged cloth, which I nosed into shape. It felt like a good place, and I was instantly asleep. I'd rest awhile and then go see what else I could find to eat. Maybe see if there were any females around looking for some company.

Before I fell asleep, I licked my paws and thought, This is

extraordinary. Not twelve hours ago, I was cage-bound, my life as circumspect in its routine as a monk's. My battle of the week accomplished, kibble in my dish. My whole life contained in that cellar. Now here I am, making my own plans, eating like a king, thinking already about mating.

The only problem with this living in paradise was that my wound, the jagged rip my late opponent had sliced into me, had begun to hurt.

Chapter Ten

The Fort Street Center is in the worst part of town and serves homeless men, providing a hot meal, a gathering place, and, for twenty of them, a place to sleep out of the elements. Adam knows about the center only because it's one of the hundreds of charities that solicit him every year. He's maybe thrown a few bucks its way, without really thinking about the mission or the nature of the cause.

Homelessness is not a word that Adam thinks about with any degree of interest. To him, a "homeless man" is a bum, a street person, a schizophrenic off his meds. A panhandler. An annoyance. Someone to dodge as he goes down the street, much like a stray dog. Might be diseased or drunk. Shaking empty paper cups, begging for coffee money. Giuliani got rid of the squeegee men in New York, so why couldn't this city find a way to get the street people off the street? That's what Adam thinks whenever some indigent crosses his path on the sidewalk.

If Adam has given any thought to the why of homelessness, it is to believe that as he is a self-made man, these must be self-undone men. Victims of bad habits and bad decisions. Everyone knew of the guy who chose to live on the street rather than in his home, where his abandoned wife or caring children couldn't keep him. Common knowledge. Or the guy who just fucked his life up so badly, no one wanted to be near him, his own violence and temper putting him on the street. The guy who won't even try to hold on to his family.

Adam has spurned his lawyer's offer to go with him. He will report to the Fort Street Center by himself, a man with free will. No hand-holding, no audience. No billable hour. Not sure what to expect, Adam dresses in his usual business attire. Most likely this Bob Carmondy fellow will be overjoyed to have a man familiar with business at his disposal. Maybe the worst that will happen is that he'll hand Adam the books. These nonprofits are so often run on shoestrings, or, worse, like lemonade stands. Adam looks at his freshly shaven face in the mirror as he knots his Harvard tie. He tries not to see the dark circles of restless nights beneath his eyes or the faint yellow color tinging the whites, like pale echoes of the brown of his irises. Or the hollowness of his cheeks. The new gray in his hair. He's even looking forward to putting in some volunteer time. That'll look just fine, with tweaking, on his curriculum vitae. It is no longer enough to have enjoyed the career path he has been on: promotions and bonuses labeling him a man of substance. The ignominious departure from Dynamic has made him less than attractive; in this day and age, corporations are reluctant to hire people fired for such a violation as his. Only embezzlement would have been a harder crime to overcome. Time will help, counsels his lawyer. Get past the headlines, the blogs, the pillory of public discussion. Sit tight. It'll blow over. In the meantime, his bank account, the only one Sterling didn't get, is dribbling away and he is powerless to stop the constant leak. Sterling resolutely refuses to give up any of the houses, the masseuse, the flower arranger. These aren't luxuries, but necessities; she mustn't give up her standard of living, not for her sake, but for their daughter's. Ariel deserves the best-possible everything. She makes it sound like if she doesn't have access to their time-share jet, it will be Ariel who will suffer the humiliation of commercial air travel. Her young life will be ruined.

Lying awake in the middle of the night, Adam realizes that Sterling has never wanted for anything. Not once in her gilded existence has any desire been left wanting. Ever. The basic needs so well met that luxury itself became a basic need.

He has known the want of basic human desires: the pangs of hunger, of real hunger, when his foster mother served only what she thought a growing boy should eat and locked up the rest, the desire for affection; the basic human need to be touched gently.

When his thoughts begin to drift in that direction, Adam finds oblivion in cheap blended scotch.

This will help. In a year or two, working with the homeless will look like philanthropy. A break from high-stakes corporate life; not quite the Peace Corps, but, with the right tweaking, enough to gloss over the empty place on his CV.

Oh yes, it certainly will. Cheered, Adam dusts an invisible speck of lint from the lapel of his charcoal-gray Hugo Boss suit. Just where is that solitary businessman now?

Although Adam lives only six blocks away from the center, he drives his Lexus to Fort Street. It's a world away from his current neighborhood, but Adam is hard-pressed to distinguish much of a difference between his street and Fort Street. A similar group of mom-and-pop businesses line the side of the street opposite the faded brownstones that are home to a host of other nonprofits serving mankind. Maybe the difference is in the check-cashing service rather than a paper store, and the pawnshop with a litter of chintzy lamps and questionable statuary in the window instead of jolly fish cavorting across a rainbow of letters.

Remarkably, Adam finds a parking place right across the street from where he thinks the center is located. There is no sign identifying the center, just an American flag with the ubiquitous MIA/POW flag suspended beneath it, both flags barely moving in the midmorning breeze. Before parking, he wonders briefly if he should find a garage instead. The men gathered on the stoops of the brownstones eye him as he idles, but he shrugs off the worry. It's broad daylight. Getting out of his car, he drops a couple of quarters in the meter, locks his car with an over-the-shoulder flourish, and crosses the street with a "Don't fuck with me" stride.

The Fort Street Center is in a building much prettier than his own, a nineteenth-century town house built in a time when this part of the city was the good part. The bow windows and brownstone stoop are black with grime, but the ornate trim and sturdiness of the building is still evident. Adam checks the address written on the index card handed to him by the judge's law clerk against the black-and-gold number in the transom above the big black door. Number 27. This is it. As Adam puts his foot on the first step, a man swings the door open and stumbles out. He's wearing, despite the warm fall day, a greenish snorkel jacket with bulging pockets, its orange lining exposed by tears under the arm. Even from this distance, Adam can smell the odor of him, the punky, slightly uriney smell of old clothes and unwashed body. The man goes down the three wide steps, pausing for a moment to take Adam in, then meanders down the street, kicking aside an empty plastic bag, muttering in an angry grumble punctuated with a single comprehensible word. Fucking. Fucking. Fucking. Adam slides a moist hand down his tie, shrugs his perfectly tailored jacket into place, and jogs up the steps.

If he expects to be greeted as a visiting dignitary, Adam is mistaken. It takes a few minutes to find the man in charge and he is forced to speak to the indigents hanging around the narrow hallway, who point him to the director's office.

Adam knocks at the open door to a room that might once have been a large room but is now split into two smaller ones. A man Adam presumes to be the director is sitting at a desk, facing the open door. His feet, in the largest shoes Adam thinks he has ever seen, are on the desk, which is piled with manila folders. He's on the phone, the curling cord twisted into a contortion of wire. Seeing Adam there, he waves him in with a wide gesture, mouthing "big donor" and pointing to the phone.

Adam is impatient, not appreciating having to wait to introduce himself and get this over with. The director smiles over the mouthpiece, a helpless "What can you do?" smile.

Rocking slightly on his heels, his hands jammed into trouser pockets, Adam examines the various newspaper-reprint photographs on the wall. Each one pictures the director shaking hands with a familiar politician: Ted Kennedy, John Kerry, Mayor Menino, Bill Weld. Deval Patrick. Each one is a study in two smiling faces, below which, hands are locked in a stagy clasp across bodies.

At last, the director drops the phone into the cradle, further tangling its overstretched cord. "Sorry about that. Potential donor. Gotta listen to their ideas."

"Adam March. I'm here to, uh, volunteer." The word *volunteer* sticks a little in his throat, as if he isn't able to recall the proper verb; he's been thinking of this as a sentence.

"Robert Carmondy." Carmondy is a big man. He knows this and puts it to good use. "They call me 'Big Bob.'" He reaches over the breadth of the desk and cheerfully squeezes the life out of Adam's hand. Whack. A manly Big Bob shoulder slap nearly takes Adam off his feet. "Glad to have you here. Siddown."

Big Bob's office is a tiny space filled mostly with a desk, a file cabinet too full to close the drawers all the way, and Big Bob. Adam turns to the only other chair in the room, the seat of which is filled with even more unfiled folders. Bob makes no move to accommodate his well-dressed visitor, so Adam lifts an armload of folders and sits down; finding no surface available to place the folders, he ends up holding them in his lap. Bob looks at him with a slight smile, and Adam wonders if he's going to be asked to start filing.

"Let me tell you about this place." With that, Big Bob is off on his well-rehearsed narrative on the genesis of the Fort Street Center: the evolution from a crack house to a safe house; his own brush with homelessness, getting off the drugs himself; and the constant need for money.

Adam smiles. This is where he can be of service. "I have some ideas."

Bob cuts him off with a teacher's gesture. "We follow a strict protocol of confidentiality. We don't know what happened to these guys; we don't rehab, counsel, or criticize. We just feed 'em; wash 'em, if they'll have it; bunk 'em, if they want; and street 'em. They don't live here. They can come and stay, but this is a way station. Capice?"

"I do."

"Okay, then." Big Bob rocks back against his chair, which protests like a wounded animal.

"What do you need to know about me?"

"Nothing. You're here and you'll do what I need you to do."

"I have some ideas." Maybe Big Bob hasn't heard him the first time. "I've been looking into some grants—"

Big Bob snaps forward, the back of his chair crying out in relief from the released pressure.

"No ideas necessary. You need to suit up and report to Rafe in the kitchen."

Adam straightens himself on the edge of the chair, realigns the slipping folders on his lap. He clears his throat, finding his executive voice. "I can be of much more use looking into finances, grants."

Big Bob stands up, shoving his desk chair back against the wall. "Let me walk you down."

"Mr. Carmondy, I've got an M.B.A. Surely you can use some help."

Big Bob sets one meaty hand on Adam's shoulder, gives him a friendly squeeze that hurts like a Vulcan pinch. "I'm sure we do." Bob lowers his mouth to Adam's ear. "Judge Johnson is pretty clear about assignments. You will do what we need you to do. And what we need is kitchen help. Ideas are fine; actions are better. And, Adam, it's Big Bob."

Adam March stands in his Hugo Boss trousers, his brand-new Calvin Klein T-shirt, purchased out of a sense that it was easier to buy new underwear than to go to the Laundromat once a week, and a white uniform jacket with a faint gravy stain emblazoning the left side. A paper hat completes his ensemble.

He is humiliated. This is his community service, doling out hot lunch to indigents. Doing whatever the "boss" wants. The boss being Rafe, a wiry black man with a shiny shaven head, hands the size of palm fronds, and a drill sergeant's refinement. Rafe points him to the rack of waiter wear and tells him not to wear good pants again. "Jeans'll do, long as they're clean and not ripped."

Ripped jeans. Just who does this guy think he's speaking to?

"We serve hot lunch from eleven to two. Give 'em as much as they want, but don't get fooled by the greedy ones. Everbody gets enough, but not more than enough. We feed about thirty-five men here a day, sometimes more in winter, less in summer. It ain't cordon bleu, but it ain't junk food, neither." Rafe says *cordon bleu* with a perfect French enunciation. Adam is still hung up on the perfectly pronounced *cordon bleu* linked to the grammatically suspect surrounding of the sentence. Rafe might talk street, but Adam suspects another influence.

"An another thing." Rafe places one of his alien hands on Adam's shoulder. "You treat these men wi' respect. You ain't here 'cause you love 'em. You here 'cause you fucked up. So did they, so that's something you all have in common. Got it?"

Adam straightens his shoulder under Rafe's hand and lifts his chin. He is eye-to-eye with his new boss, his brown eye holding the deeper brown eye of the man, taking the measure of an opponent. Rafe narrows his eyes, sure in his authority. Adam has seen eyes like that before in the boardrooms and back halls of business. Kings of their domains. Men certain of their power and their place in the world.

Adam nods, a curt acquiescence.

"Now I need you to go into the back room and bring out a case of niblets."

And thus Adam March begins his penance.

Adam is put to work as runner, carrying steam trays filled with food from the kitchen into the dining room, then taking the empty bins back to wash them in the industrial sink. The old brownstone has suffered from its change in purpose from elegant home to abandoned crack house to its new life as a shelter. The interior walls have been cut away to open half of the first floor into a large room, filled now with long cafeteria tables no doubt donated from some refurbished high school, the benches fixed to them so that the men have to sling a leg over to get seated. The floor-to-ceiling windows are shrouded even on this warm fall day with industrial-strength curtains, pulled closed so that the men served are protected. No one can stand and stare at them, recognize an old friend or neighbor in straitened circumstances. No one can look out.

Adam hasn't bench-pressed this much since high school. The aluminum trays are filled with slices of meat floating in a thick brown gravy with what appear to be shitake mushrooms folded in. The whipped potatoes are stiff and creamy, real potatoes, really whipped. But they weigh a ton, and Adam fears that his back will go out, and then where will he be? What if he gets hurt on this community-service job? What happens then? Can he sue someone? After fetching the canned corn from the massive stockroom, Adam is put to opening the number-ten cans one after another. What is served to the men is mixed with half as many lima beans and sautéed into a mixture that he might have seen on his plate at any benefit dinner Sterling dragged him to. The lovely odor of cooking food is obscured by the rank scent of the men who line up in front of the steam tables. Even though he isn't—yet—assigned to serving, their smell fills the high-ceilinged room like a miasma, and he gets a whiff every time he comes up behind the man who is ladling out portions onto divided plates. With each customer he greets by name, the server, another middle-aged black man, asks the same question: "One piece or two? You wanna a roll wi' that?"

Adam is reminded of high school, St. Joseph's, where the last two sets of foster parents coincidentally sent him. The ancient cafeteria with its warped floorboards was also the gymnasium. The students passed through an alley, where the food was kept behind glass, pointing to their choices—mac and cheese or hot dog, ziti or a thin slice of overcooked ham steak with a floppy ring of pineapple. Because the cafeteria was also the gym, the odor of unwashed bodies pervaded the air, and the food never tasted good. Most of it was tossed in the massive gray barrels on wheels next to the exits as the kids rushed to get outside to sneak cigarettes or make out in the corners.

When he wheels the big blue plastic barrels to the back dock from the dining room after the meal is over, Adam can't help but notice that there is almost no food in them.

Adam is supposed to put in four hours. It's been four and a half. He's exhausted, wrung out by the unaccustomed physical exercise. He is hungry but has lost his appetite. No one has suggested that he eat. No one has dismissed him. He stands in the doorway of the massive industrial kitchen. Rafe is humming, jigging up and down to some tune on his iPod. He's fixing four plates, heaping up leftover beef, potatoes, and the succotash. He sees Adam in the doorway and beckons him in. "Take one."

Adam can't make himself touch the plate until he washes. He feels extraordinarily filthy, as if he's been handling garbage, as if he hasn't been wearing plastic gloves. "Where do I wash?"

Rafe pulls one ear bud out of his ear. "Men's room out to your left."

Adam sees himself in the speckled mirror over the sink, the ridiculous paper hat tipped over his forehead. He looks like he works at McDonald's. He grabs it off and tosses it in the bin. Gall quickly dissipates into despair.

He has no intention of eating here.

The four plates are now on a freshly wiped table. Someone has folded up the other tables and rolled them all to one side of the room. The floor, no doubt to protect the original hardwood, is covered by a cheap linoleum with a fake wood pattern, and it is filthy with dirt and sand, along with dropped paper napkins and food. It is the single most disgusting place Adam has ever been expected to eat. He is about to say that he's out of there, when Rafe, standing up, waves him over not like a gracious host, but like a commander. *You will sit and eat. This is part of your penance.* "Sit down, man, 'fore this stuff gets colder." The man who has been standing for the last few hours serving up food to the continual flow of men pats the space next to him. Another flashback to high school, the flush of pleasure at being included in a group. But this is no group in which Adam would ever want to be included. "We never got properly introduced. You can call me Ishmael." The black man grins at his well-rehearsed line and sticks out a hand for shaking. He's pulled off his toque, revealing a head full of dreadlock coils. Like Medusa's snakes, the coils bounce around, threatening Adam.

Adam takes Ishmael's hand, a little surprised at its soft warmth. After hours of handling hot implements, Ishmael's hand actually feels feverish.

"March." Adam steps over the fixed bench and sits down to his plate of lunch.

Rafe, opposite him, gestures to the other man of the foursome, an overweight white man with psoriasis covering half of his face. He might be fifty or sixty—it's hard to tell with the disfiguring scales crawling up the side of his face. "This here's Mike."

"Hello, Mike." Adam picks up his fork but is pretty sure he won't be able to eat.

"Adam here is our new CSI."

Adam throws Rafe a puzzled look.

"Community service investigator." He throws his head back and laughs. "Get it? You gonna investigate how the other half live." Rafe chuckles himself into control and starts eating.

Adam flushes with embarrassment. He hasn't expected that his enforced volunteerism would be common knowledge. Where were confidentiality laws when you needed them?

Ishmael entertains them as they eat with a constant stream of chat and jokes, as if hours of asking the same question have warmed him up for the main act. Mike shovels the food into his mouth, gets up, and takes his plate into the kitchen without a word. Big Bob joins them from upstairs, sits down at Mike's vacant spot, tipping the table a little under his weight. "How'd it go, first day?"

"I guess you'll have to ask my boss." Adam has moved the beef around on his plate, nibbled a forkful of potato, which has just a hint of garlic, and a mushroom, which, he's surprised to find, actually is a shitake.

"He'll do. Just has to give up his prissy ways." Rafe scrapes the last of the gravy onto his fork and runs a paper napkin across his mouth. "Damn good, if I do say so myself. Adam, you best get it right now that I'm the best there is, was, and will be in the world of industrial-size cookin'."

Adam politely cuts a piece of beef and puts it into his mouth. Although it's cold by this time, the flavor is good and the meat is tender. A note of some unidentifiable seasoning moves it out of ordinary and into quite nice. Adam eats the rest of it.

Big Bob raps a little drumbeat against the tabletop. "Okay, then. Carry on." As soon as he lifts his weight from the bench, the table relaxes and Adam feels like he and Ishmael are about to tip over. Mike has reappeared with a push broom and is tracing a pattern onto the fake wood back and forth, back and forth, working his way from the far end toward their table. The three men get up and Ishmael fetches a cloth to wipe it down again.

"You can go." Rafe places his huge thin-fingered hand once again on Adam's shoulder. "It gets better."

Adam strips off his white jacket, now dotted with new gravy stains, and jams it into the laundry bin.

Outside, there is a parking ticket under his windshield wiper and a pigeon has crapped on the windshield of his Lexus.

Chapter Eleven

Adam awakens sweating, despite the window open to the freshening fall day. His pulse ticks in his ears, the remnant of nightmare fright. Despite every effort to provide himself with a good night's sleep via Messrs. Walker or Dewar, Adam fights every night with an array of dubious images. If he dreamed of Sophie or Sterling or buildings falling down, that would make sense. Instead, he dreams of city streets and being late. Of not being able to hear what's being said to him. Of not knowing where he is. Cryptic dream messages, or dreams with no meaning.

He wishes he could get away from waking before dawn. It's been months since he's had to be at work at seven-thirty; months since he's thought to go for a run. He has plenty of "me time" now, too much to fill the hours. His job at the center occupies him during the easy part of the day. The mornings and the nights are his burden.

His headhunter isn't returning his phone calls. He hasn't scrounged up any interviews and is apparently sick of having to say so. Adam thinks that consulting is an option. Hang out his shingle, get some business cards, and advise companies on strategic planning or how to plan a takeover. His headhunter hasn't been encouraging there, either, but what stops Adam is the work of pulling it together, of putting the *effort* into an action plan; inertia enfolds him in its cottony warmth. He flips on daytime television.

Dr. Stein hasn't much to say about it, either. He wants Adam to keep a journal, record his feelings. Feelings. Shit. What exactly does the good shrink think Adam might be feeling? Abandoned? Under siege? Mistreated?

Adam takes his place at the window. Just past eight-thirty, the early-morning rush has faded into the workaday flow of traffic, both in the street and on the sidewalks. The dry cleaner is busy. No matter what the economy, people still need their "dry clean only" items cared for. The newsagent's place is active twice a day, early morning and at five o'clock.

Adam rarely sees anyone going into the tropical fish shop; those that do tend toward the little old lady or the ten-year-old picking out his first fish. He's avoided the shop owner since their uncomfortable discovery of a common history. He still watches her wash the window, but he's no longer interested in pleasantries.

The Fort Street Center, whether he likes it or not, has become the centerpiece of Adam's day. It is the only thing, five days a week, that gets him out of the house, and most days it provides the only nourishment he gets. He's forgotten all about the made-to-order Norwegian granola he used to require. Cheese crackers and coffee from the newsagent in the morning, scotch at night.

Adam pulls away from the window, his palm print fading

as his sweat evaporates, a smear of fingerprints at eye level. One of his foster mothers had been a bear on the subject of fingerprints. Adam had spent his eighth and ninth years living in dread of making a mark on polished surfaces or glass. Mrs. Markowitz would have whupped his behind to see the fan of prints marring his curtainless picture window.

He'd had seven in all, seven sets of foster parents from the time he was five and a half, an average of thirteen months with each. The last, the Potters, had kept him the longest, all the way through his last two years at St. Joseph's. The day he turned eighteen, he was emancipated, suddenly outside the protection and purview of the state, magically independent. Even though he'd longed for that moment, the sudden reality of it, three days before his high school graduation, had shocked him with its finality. "You can stay, but we'll have to ask for board." Mrs. Potter, a rake-thin woman just beyond middle age, with enough beds to make something of a living taking in foster kids, needed the bed and needed him out. Nothing personal, just practical. Today you are a man.

They were reluctant at first, as they told him over and over, to take on an unadoptable teenage boy, but his social worker had convinced them to take a chance. What that meant was that he ate more than the others, which practically wiped out his state subsidy, and that they were on top of him about his behavior, always suspicious that he was upstairs smoking dope or hanging out with street gangs, plotting mayhem. That he could have been doing those things but wasn't was no consolation to them.

The Potters were too busy with four other kids, always much younger, all cycling through the foster system, and all into adoptions or reclamation by rehabilitated parents, to pay much attention to his education. They lacked the energy or imagination to prod him into doing his homework. They were just happy never to be robbed or caught in the imagined cross fire of their foster boy's shootout with a rival gang. Adam despised them, and once the door was shut, he never contacted them again.

His college essay, a self-indulgent treatise on life in the Commonwealth's foster system, had earned him a ticket out of that system. A partial scholarship to the University of Massachusetts–Amherst had given him a place to go. An unexpected interest and acuity in finance and economics opened up Adam's world from the narrow confines of the blue-collar, conservative, clannish environment he had lived in up until then. Working nearly full-time as a bus driver for the Pioneer Valley Transit system had financed his schooling and stoked his determination never to go back to Dorchester. He had escaped by virtue of his brains, and by those same virtues, Adam would rise to the top. He would forget his past and forge a future that was unlimited. He didn't entertain himself with visions of returning to one or another of his foster parents with a disdainful "I told you so." It never occured to him. He put his past behind him and never looked back.

Adam made it into Harvard Business School. Three-quarters of the way through his M.B.A. program, he'd been recruited by his first major corporation. Done with the M.B.A., already two rungs up the corporate ladder, and enjoying the first fruits of high pay and glorious benefits, he'd met Sterling. Here was a nymph from another world—no, not another world, a creature of the world Adam intended to inhabit. Her father, the blue-blooded economist guru of the decade, Herbert Carruthers, was the guest speaker at a corporate retreat, and Adam had sat at the edge of his seat to soak in everything the great man could offer. When his boss took him over to introduce him to Carruthers, Sterling stood beside her father with a calm detachment. She was used to young sycophants wanting to touch the hem of his garment.

"You must be very proud of your dad," Adam whispered to Sterling as he waited to be introduced. "Such an inspiration."

Sterling had looked at him with the hauteur he would fall in love with. A look that said, Yeah, so what? Tell me something I don't know.

"Going around with him to these retreats must be a great way to meet eligible men like me." He smiled the toothy smile of his peers. At least his genetics had provided good teeth, despite a spotty dental regimen. Her lips slowly slid into a smile, revealing her own perfect teeth. She was so naturally beautiful then. Tall, slim, her blond hair artfully tossed. She could have had any one of a dozen Park Avenue–raised young men as her choice, but she'd chosen Adam. His glossed-over history mattered less to her than the fact of his wunderkind trajectory. Her father approved of him because of that glossed-over history, liked the idea of a self-made son-in-law. If Adam had cut down the number of foster homes, had implied a decent upbringing grounded in hard work, instead of telling the truth, it was only because the truth had no bearing on who he'd become. No one wanted to hear about the loneliness, the rootless existence of a boyhood spent without a home to call his own. A charity case.

Of Veronica, of their father, he said nothing. They did not exist. They had no hand in the making of Adam March.

Adam hadn't thought a lot about those days until the foundation stone of his reinvention had been uncovered. Dr.

Stein keeps picking at him, wanting him to come to some understanding of his feelings. He prods at Adam to admit some insecurities, to admit weakness. To understand why he has "anger issues."

Adam sits forward on the low chair, resting his elbows on his knees, hands folded and beneath his chin. "In business, in life, it's he who has the most arrows in his quiver who gets ahead—by any means. Sometimes that looks like anger."

"Why was it so important to get ahead?" The shrink fashions air quotes around the words *get ahead*.

"It's what people do," says Adam. "It's how the world works. Even you, Doctor, planned at some point in your life to do something to get ahead. To achieve, to make your mark. To end up somewhere better than where you started. It takes a tough man to do that." Adam sits back, his chin tipped a little forward, pugnacious.

"We're talking about you, Adam, not me." The doctor closes his notebook. "And Adam, until you come to grips with the fact that you have anger issues, abandonment issues, you are not going to heal."

"Heal from what? A lousy childhood? Angry about that? I'm way beyond that. I'm no longer that kid, that punk whose father would show up once a year, take me out to McDonald's, and say nothing about why he couldn't raise me himself. But I knew what it was called. Voluntary surrender. Voluntary." Adam stops himself. The phantom pain pulses in his rib cage. He hears his own breath as it sounds when he wakes before dawn from a nightmare. "It was better when he stopped coming at all." Adam laughs, a little burst of air, mirthless. "I used to pack my stuff in a paper bag on the day I knew he was coming. Just in case he was going to keep me. When I was nine or ten, I sat on the stoop, paper bag beside me like some kind of loyal dog, and waited. And waited. And at some point, my foster mother—can't remember which one—made me come in. Never said a word about why he didn't show. Made me put all my stuff back in the drawer. I think that's when I realized I didn't want to go with him anyway. Why should I? I didn't need him; I could make my own way in the world."

"Are you sure that isn't what you tell yourself now?"

The tiny buzzer indicating their hour is up goes off and the psychiatrist slaps his knees with his yellow pad. "See you next week."

Adam blushes a little, having to ask Stein to cut their sessions down by half an hour. He can't afford a full hour anymore. Dynamic took his health benefits when they fired him and he can't afford the COBRA payments now that Sterling has decided that Ariel needs to have intensive SAT tutoring, with a full professor from Lesley College.

"Against my better judgment, but all right. Thirty minutes twice a week."

Adam is too embarrassed to ask if the psychiatrist offers a sliding scale. Who would believe a man in a thousand-dollar suit would qualify for it?

He's seen him a half dozen times before. Standing on the corner, empty paper coffee cup out. "I just needa cuppa coffee, mister. Can you spare some change?" He's dressed in greasy army pants and a faded army jacket with a bold green empty place where a name badge must have been when the jacket first saw service. Regardless of the weather, the panhandler wears a black wool watch cap, pulled low over straggly gray hair leaking out like seaweed. His cheeks are hollowed out, his eyes bleary above pouches of flesh tinged gray. It seems to Adam that any time he's on the downtown streets, people like this one have their grimy hands outstretched, their jagged teeth hidden, their obsequious begging not compelling, but annoying. This one he sees whenever he comes out of his shrink's building, stationed like a sentry at the corner in front of the Dunkin' Donuts. Adam wonders why the authorities don't just throw him in jail. He's one of the pushy ones, probably crazy. "My dog's hungry." That's his particular refrain. There's a big ugly mutt with him. In the summer, the dog sat in the shade of the buildings as if smarter than his owner. When Adam came across the pair in the winter, they huddled on a cement dust-colored quilt, leaning together against the wind that blew through the canyons of the city, the bum's hand with the ubiquitous Starbucks cup out thrust. The dog, a lantern-jawed pit bull type, sat, but its weepy red eyes followed Adam as he walked by.

Sure enough, pushing through the revolving door as he leaves his shrink's building today, Adam sees the panhandler and his dog at his favorite post. But he's no longer the bum with the dog; by now, Adam knows that the men call him "Jupe," short for Jupiter. The last thing he wants is to be forced to drop a coin in the man's outstretched hand just because he drops mashed potatoes on his plate a couple of times a week. They do not know each other. He does not want even the slightest acknowledgment of acquaintance to pass between them. Adam wears his Armani suit, his "I mean business" Cole Haan shoes. His red silk tie beams authority. He is not the man who wears the McDonald's cap and shovels food out from a steam table. Adam spins around the revolving door one more time, launching himself out in the other direction.

Chapter Twelve

By the third day of my release from captivity, I was a hurtin' puppy. The part of the wound that I couldn't reach with my tongue was swollen and oozing. I was feverish, off my game, and not even hungry. I was in deep trouble for a creature on the street. My reflexes were shot, my nose runny. That's why, when the men came, I put up very little fight.

As docile as a lamb, I went off in the white van, my street adventure over. I cast a longing look at my nest under the back stairs of what turned out to be a tattoo parlor. I suspected that one of the artists inside, who'd come outside for a cigarette or a toke, had spotted me through the metal stair treads and dropped a dime. My sort don't evoke the "Oooh, I found a puppy. Can I keep him?" reaction from people. So the men showed up in their big white van, blocking off one end of the short, narrow alley with it and filling the other end with themselves. It was only prudent to acquiesce.

Maybe I was just a creature of the cage after all. It was cool and comfortable; the docs fixed up the wound, gently poked me with antibiotic-filled IVs until I felt like a new dog. They clipped my toenails and gave me a lovely bath. They also castrated me, but I wasn't initially aware of that, as they did it while they were repairing the chest wound, and I was already knocked out. I ate their food and licked their hands. I'm no dope. The friendly dog gets the best deal.

My kind are notoriously hard to place. Our ferocious reputations and notorious applications preclude us from easy adoptions. No little old lady looking for a companion is likely to choose a pit bull, not even a crossbred like myself. First, we look strong. Second, we look fierce. Third, we ain't all that attractive. Leave the fluffies to them. Then there are the young men who wander in, looking for a manly dog. Forget it. The authorities weren't born yesterday. No used fighters for sale here. That leaves the younger couples willing to take on a dog with a bad rep and a PR problem. Not all that many of them out there, and a lot more of us.

The key is, behave like a Labrador. Let them stick that fake hand into your food dish and not react. Bring the stupid ball back and drop it in their laps. Pretend that fake kid is a real child and all you want to do is lick its face, protect it from harm. Drool a little. Give 'em your best play bow. Oh yeah, I was totally socialized.

So I got my first person. A nice middle-aged lady looking for a watchdog. Living on the edge of town, a block or so from the rough part, she thought she needed a big tough-looking dog with a heart of gold. She would have been all right, too, if she just hadn't persisted in being frightened of me herself. Okay, maybe it didn't help when I greeted every passerby as a threat to the homefront, and nearly took her off her feet when I lunged at passing dogs, but I wasn't sure of protocol. I'd been raised in a cellar. I'd been trained to fight. That was what had been expected of me, and this change of direction was confusing.

I left after a week. I just couldn't take her mincing around, talking to me in that infernally soothing baby talk that did nothing to disguise her fear sweat. Made me want to fulfill her prophesy. She accidentally left the gate open and I took that as a not-so-subtle hint to beat it. I wandered by a few weeks later and saw she'd replaced me with a yapping fluffy. Perfect.

It wasn't long after that when I finally met my mentor. He'd been leaving signposts for me, aware of my desire to meet him. A rangy-looking male, mature in years, and uncontested king of the neighborhood, a gladiator like me, the hallmarks of a fighter's life written in his skin. We came upon each other on the corner, where his territory and my tentative claim conjoined. I knew that he'd been around there from his mark; he knew I had, too. I was surprised to see him with one of those tags dangling from a collar around his thick neck; surprised, too, to find out he was a companion, when his scent described a street dog.

We greeted; I offered submission with a lick of his chops. No sense making the king annoyed right from the get-go. I didn't want to look like a challenger, I just wanted a little advice. He was headed east, so I followed. We walked along an overpass, chatting about where I'd been so far. He snuffled along my spine, checked my genitals, and winked. *You'll miss them less than you think. Otherwise, a little incarceration is sometimes a good thing. The next best thing is a street man. They're not unlike us; we both forage and sleep rough. We are both invisible to the general population, and sometimes we're both rounded up. The difference between being alone and in company with a man is that the food is easier to come by. He shares and he can open things we can't.*

Our DNA is full of the original partnership between us and humans, forged for exactly the same reason this old boy had forged his alliance with his companion. Safety, food, a voice in a speechless world.

You should get one.

I shook, cocked my leg against a lamppost. *I'm not so sure. I think I want to keep solo for a while more.*

Caged? Meaning was I new to freedom.

Yes. I bowed, stretched, and left my new friend as he caught up with his person coming out of a building. Even from a distance, I could smell the scent of hot food on him. I watched from a safe distance as the man slipped his hand out of his pocket and offered a slice of meat to the king of the street. I may want to rethink this solo thing. The man and my mentor made their way down the street, he with his head bowed, a soft mutter coming from his mouth, and my mentor with his nose just at the man's heels. A picture of companionship.

Chapter Thirteen

The idea of standing over the ultraheated water in the industrial sink as he sprays plate after disgusting plate makes Adam slightly nauseous. The smell of food combined with warm dishwater has permeated his skin and he cannot seem to shower it off.

The center is busy when Adam arrives for his shift. Already a dozen men are on the stoop, waiting in the cool air for the dining room doors to open. There is an activity room on the first floor, a television set, a small library of paperbacks, even a computer with Internet access available to the guys, with a lock on porn sites, but the room remains empty, as it has the whole time Adam has been here. The men are like nervous bunnies, willing to eat from the hand of charity, but not willing to spend too much time in its lap.

Adam does not speak to the men. He still doesn't know most of their names, or recognize their individual faces; he doesn't look at them, just at their empty plates when he's assigned to the steam tables. They don't converse much, even with one another. There's a quiet about them, as if each one is solitary in his world, the proximity of others in like circumstances not a bond, but a wall.

Adam hates the fact that Big Bob insists that everyone use the front door, not sneak in the back door via the alley. He's had to tell Adam twice. Everyone here is a man and comes in through the front door.

"What's that supposed to mean? I'm a volunteer, a temporary helper. Why do they need to see me come through the door?"

"It has to do with dignity. It's our way of leveling the playing field."

Adam feels the ache start up again in his ribs. Whose dignity exactly is Big Bob talking about? Wouldn't everyone be happier if he could just come in the kitchen door?

Jupe and his dog wait for the dining room door to open, lined up with the others on the steps, a very few passing the time with quiet conversation, often with only themselves. Adam licks his lips, tilts the ball cap that he's begun wearing lately, and soldiers past the group, which becomes as silent at his approach as teenagers when the principal walks by. As Adam mounts the steps, Jupe's dog bows and yawns; his tail wags. Adam feels the flush of embarrassment, as if he's been caught avoiding someone he knows. He nods to the men.

"March, you gonna work the tables today. Mike's down wi' the flu." Rafe keeps bopping to the rhythm projected into his ears, speaking a little too loudly. He's sauteing onions in a massive frying pan. The scent breaks through the miasma of soapy dish-water and wet industrial-strength mops to tickle Adam's juices. On a stainless-steel cutting table lies an enormous purple-brown slab of liver, waiting for Rafe's knife to carve it into thin slices. Two caldrons the size of oil drums bubble on the range, potatoes on the boil. Liver and onions and fried potatoes for lunch. Despite his intellectual revulsion, Adam tastes the saliva forming. Rafe tosses the mess of onions up and around, up and around, without losing a single thinly sliced ring.

Working the tables means being near the men. Adam's job is to carry a bucket and sponge around, wipe each table off be-tween groups, pick up the detritus left behind, make sure the condiments are full, act, in other words, like a busboy. The men come in as fast as he can make a place ready for them, so he's often wiping as new men sit down, their plates heaped with the luscious-smelling onions and the tender liver. Liver was a frequent item on the menu during his boyhood, a cheap piece of meat with touted values. Not everyone can cook liver without making it tough and indigestible. The idea of it is ab-horrent to Adam. In his adult life, he has never allowed liver on the table. Ariel has never even seen liver and onions. The one housekeeper he and Sterling had early on once suggested it and had her ass handed to her. Liver and onions are the food of pov-erty. Yet the tantalizing smell of it neutralizes his associations. Rafe, he already knows, isn't going to let a lousy piece of liver out of his kitchen; not only are his cooking skills top notch but his pride is equal to any top chef Adam has ever met. Looking at a plate of hand-cut fried potatoes tumbling against the thinly sliced liver with its garnish of perfectly sautéed onions, Adam is surprised to find himself looking forward to his own lunch.

But first he has to walk around the room, where the delicious scent of fried onions is countered with a backwash of dirty clothes, unwashed heads. Instantly, he loses his appetite. Adam keeps refilling the wash bucket with hotter water, more Pine-Sol. Anything to get the smell of the men out of the room before he's expected to sit in here and eat.

"Excuse me, sir. Can I bother you for a clean fork? This one has a bit of food stuck between the tines."

Adam stands behind Jupe, wash bucket in his hand. The phrasing coming out of the old bum's mouth is at such odds to his appearance, to his "Buddy, can you spare some change?" street patter, that for a moment Adam thinks that Jupe has some ventriloquist's hand up his back. "Sure." He takes the offensive fork and dumps it in his wash bucket. Like a good waiter, Adam fetches Jupe a new fork.

"Thank you." Jupe goes back to eating, slicing his meat with fork in left hand, knife in right, daintily cutting one piece at a time, keeping his fork, in the British manner, in his left hand as he eats. Every now and then he slips a piece of meat into his jacket pocket, a bum's sleight of hand.

Adam washes down the other half of the table. As he does, he can't help but glance at Jupe, who is surrounded by men wearing their entire wardrobes. The old man wears his watch cap pulled low, the long gray hair spiking out from beneath the tattered edge and lying against the threadbare collar of the army jacket. Like many of them, Jupe is probably old enough to have served in Vietnam. There are one or two who are still fighting the war, as they jump out of their skins whenever Rafe drops something in the kitchen. Big Bob calls them his "Stressies." As Adam moves to the table behind Jupe, he spots him slipping half of his portion of liver into his pocket. Some of the men are known hoarders, as if the center were going to disappear and they'd be left hungry. But Adam knows that Jupe is sharing his free meal with that dog of his, the one stationed at the bottom of the stairs. Big Bob has told Jupe over and over not to leave the pit bull there; it frightens people, he says. Jupe says the dog does whatever he wants to do. He's an independent thinker.

It's late by the time the last of the men leave the dining room. Adam feels contaminated, like he has spent a lifetime with his hands in hot water, running the sour-smelling sponge over tabletops and seats. His earlier anticipation of lunch has long since been squelched. All he can smell is Pine-Sol and sweat and the peculiar rubbery smell of his own hands after hours encased in Playtex Living Gloves. He's folded the tables and tucked them together, run the wide-headed broom around the floor. At the staff table, Rafe and Ishmael are wound up about the baseball play-offs. Big Bob is heading to the table with his plate loaded. "Go get some lunch, Adam."

Leaving the push broom at ease against the serving counter, Adam goes into the kitchen, whose smell is redolent of the liver and onions. He stares for a minute at the slices of meat left in the warmer, brown now, almost the same color as Rafe.

His third foster mother sits him down in front of a plate of her liver and onions and whacks his head every time he puts his fork down. The liver is dry, forming a nasty paste in his mouth; he can't make it go down. Tears begin to ooze out of his eyes, not from crying exactly, but from the release of frustration. He's only been in this house for a few weeks. By now he understands that he is always going to be temporary. He shouldn't get comfortable in any house he is brought to, just try to behave, try to be unobtrusive. But his foster parents are always finding ways to make him do wrong. At night, he can hear this foster mother arguing with the man who isn't her husband, although the social services people think he is. Sometimes Adam can hear crying; other times, he hears only the slap that silences it. They'd fought last night, and today he is being forced to eat something so vile, he can't swallow it.

Shifting the lump of chewed meat in his mouth, Adam whispers, "Veronicaveronicaveronica." A mantra of protection muttered under his breath. Someday, Veronica will come and punish those who have been cruel to him, unloving. In his narrow bed, or, as here, the den couch that serves as his bedroom, Adam rehearses the heroic return of his half-imagined sister. She didn't mean to leave him behind. She can't find him because he's been moved so many times. Veronica's myth is embellished during wakeful nights. "Veronicaveronicaveronica." Talismanic hope.

The lump of masticated liver slowly works itself down his throat—it's like swallowing a rock—and suddenly is cast up.

Foster mother number three slams a fistful of mashed potatoes into his eight-year-old face.

Adam yanks his catering jacket off and tosses it into the laundry bag. He crumples the paper hat, dropping it into the barrel. He goes out the back door. He's not coming back. Fuck the judge. Later, Abramowicz points out that a contempt-of-court citation will lead to worse things than mopping up after street people. Once again, a judge is in charge of Adam. He is, as much as the men he serves daily, in the system.

Adam stares into the empty night street, waiting for the lights at the newsagent's to come on. Waiting for his life to begin again.

Chapter Fourteen

The one thing about being on the street in the nice weather is that you feel smart. Too smart to depend on anyone, too smart to need anything but an open Dumpster and a leaky faucet. Then it gets cold. I and my kind began to scrap over good nests, the sort that have shelter from the biting wind and some sort of accommodation, a blanket or a dry newspaper. Too many nights, I found myself in the fetal position, with my back against the nominal protection of a wall, the dry culvert or the underpass not already occupied by someone unwilling to have a roommate. My beneath-the-stairs bolthole of the summer had been reclaimed by its former owner. My sublet was over.

My mentor showed me some of the better backyards. His man traveled in the early hours through sleeping neighborhoods, rifling through the heavy plastic trash cans with the kind of lids that defied those of us without thumbs. He'd toss my friend delicacies and take for himself objects, which he thrust into the pockets of his coat. I stayed well behind. My mentor positively forbid me contact with his person, who was a one-dog man, and I wasn't going to screw that up. Instead, he'd point me in the direction of a dryer vent or an air-conditioning unit sequestered behind sheltering bushes, a very comfortable and weather-tight nest.

Except for the remnants my mentor might leave me, food was getting harder to come by as people spent less time out-doors, and my loss of condition made it feel twice as cold to me. The restaurants offered fewer leftovers, as if the human population was bulking up for the cold weather and wasting less food. My water sources were turned off, and that was the hardest challenge, save for the occasional heated birdbath. The park's little lake was sometimes the only water available, and that was frequently under a sheet of ice. My cage-bound upbringing had not educated me in the skill set necessary for carrying out ice breaking. I waited until the geese wore a hole in the ice with their foot action and then ventured out. Risky, I know, but thirst is a powerful motivator.

Cold, hungry, and mostly thirsty, I was still happier out on the street than in that cage in that cellar, waiting for a fight or for my hour on the treadmill, or that blessed ten minutes of backyard relief. Here I defecated and pissed wherever and whenever I wanted to. I'd even begun building up a little ter-ritory for myself. Despite my involuntary neutering, I still liked the girls and introduced myself to a number of them. Sweet. No one was in heat yet, so it was just dating.

All in all, it was okay. That is, until the blizzard.

Chapter Fifteen

It has been snowing since before dawn. Wind-whipped flakes so small, they look like needles slashing down in the street-lights. The snow comes sideways, reverses itself, and swirls in the opposite direction. The media have been prophesying this storm for days, and the gleeful look on the weather lady's face this morning is positively the radiance of a woman who has been proven right. She reminds Adam of Sterling.

They are now officially divorced; the final decree was handed down three days before Christmas. Sterling had signed where she needed to an hour before he arrived. He'd stared at her showy signature, Sterling Madeleine Carruthers. Unwilling to stay married to him, she had abnegated his place in her life by reverting to her powerful maiden name. He no longer existed for her. Just his money. The power and reputation of her father, Herbert Carruthers, had made it easy for the courts to assign Sterling the majority of their joint assets: the houses, the cars, the portfolio. The court has also entailed a percentage of his future earnings in alimony and child support. His fledgling consulting business hasn't taken off—or, to be honest, is nonexistent—and he takes a certain satisfaction in the fact that he has so little income to offer them.

Sterling and her parents took Ariel to Greece for the holidays, citing her distress as a reason to take her out of reach of Adam for even his court-agreed-upon holiday visitation. Somehow the court didn't mind, his rights clearly of a lesser importance than hers. Immediately after they returned, Ariel was kept out of his reach by other obligations. Adam wonders if Sterling lies awake at night making up reasons for him not to see his only daughter. Even when he does manage his Saturday-afternoon visits, Ariel is sullen and uncommunicative, as if he is a stranger to her, someone she's forced to share space with. He excuses her behavior as symptomatic of adolescence, but he's hurt. Like all divorced fathers, he knows that he is trying too hard, making her visits to his small apartment all about fun and nothing about reality, sushi instead of dining in, video games instead of conversation. Ariel stoically resists having fun with him. She comes to visit but refuses to stay overnight; she doesn't want to sleep on the futon and won't swap with him.

It is like hosting a foreign exchange student who speaks no English. The pantomime of good father, devoted child is lost in translation.

Adam stares out, hoping that the newsagent will open despite the weather. Hoping, childishly, that Big Bob will call and tell him to stay home—yippee, a snow day. Ever since the first below-freezing day, the center has hosted twice as many homeless as Adam had seen in the warm weather. Men flock in to grab a little food and a lot of warmth. Many won't stay, but a group of ten or so use the bunks in the dormitory upstairs, mainly guys fairly new to the street, who haven't toughened up yet. Big Bob welcomes them, hands them bedding and a pillow, and points out the rec and dining rooms. He takes their names, offers to receive mail for them, their monthly Social Security checks, their army pension checks. A place to call home.

The light goes on across the street. Adam shrugs on his parka, finds his ski hat tucked into the pocket of his coat and puts it on. He shoves his feet into his boots, laces them loosely, grabs a clean travel mug from the collection he has acquired. The carless street is filled with unsullied snow; the stoplight waves in the wind like a demented flag, threatening to rip loose from its wires and plunge into the intersection. Adam pushes against the wind, the blinding snow making it a dreamlike quest, his objective coming no closer. When he finally makes it across the street, his cheeks are tingling, his eyes watering, and he's breathing like a long-distance runner. Adam has to fight to get the door open, the wind pressing it closed against his pull, a zephyr's game of tug-of-war. As the wind takes a breath, Adam gets the door open. "Mornin', Artie." Adam scoops up his crackers and drains fresh coffee into the travel mug with CUMBERLAND FARMS printed on it. He looks for the papers, but they haven't been delivered.

"Hell of a day." The newsagent shifts the unlit cigar to the other side of his mouth. "Fit for neither man nor beast."

"Or papers, evidently." Adam digs into his pocket for change.

"They'll get here. Don't you worry. Come on back in an hour."

"If I can. Getting worse out there."

"You be careful out there, Adam."

"You, too."

Now it's hard to push the door open, but once he does, Adam stands in the shelter of the doorway, pulling up the hood of his parka, taking what might be the last hot slug of coffee out of his plastic mug. As he's about to step into the storm, a figure appears, another soul out in the storm.

It's the businessman. He trudges along, head down, full-length dress coat buttoned to his throat. Tears are streaming down his cheeks from the wind and cold. Adam feels like he should grab the guy and send him home. Why is he walking? Why is he even trying to go to work? Even Adam would have called it off today. Either this guy is an idiot or his boss is.

"Hey, Buddy . . ." Adam sticks out a hand, the one holding the plastic travel mug, to stop the guy.

"Get away from me, you freak." He thrusts an arm out to fend Adam off, knocking the Cumberland Farms cup out of Adam's hand. "Go get a job."

"Well, fuck you, too." Adam darts to pick up the mug before too much leaks out of the drinking hole. What the fuck? Pulling the strings of his hood tighter, Adam catches sight of his own grainy reflection in the newsagent's plate glass. He starts to laugh. He looks like a Fort Street Center client in this getup. No wonder the guy freaked. *Buddy?* Did he really call the guy "buddy"? He must have picked it up from the men. They all use it, a generic "buddy" directed toward the people they solicit—"Buddy, can you spare some change?" They use it with one another, a dining room filled with buddies.

If the center is closed, where will they go?

. . .

Unbelievably, another figure struggles out of the storm. The aquarium woman. She's bundled in a gigantic parka that makes her look like she's been swallowed by a polar bear. The wind is forcing her back, so that every step taken is a battle won. Adam feels the wind beat against his back as he runs to her. With his ballast, she is finally able to get to her storefront. Adam takes the keys from her hand and unlocks the door, then stands back to let her in.

"Come in. Come in." Inside, she disarms the alarm, stamps her feet to rid them of the snow. Her cheeks are bright pink; a lock of dark hair not captured by her scrunchy is dripping with fast-melting snow. "Thanks for the help. It's windier than I realized."

She shrugs off her parka, revealing a thick fisherman's sweater, corduroys tucked into Uggs. "I'm Gina DeMarco." *Ah'm*. There it is again, that faint coloration of accent. "Welcome to A to Z Tropical Fish and Pet Supply."

Adam pushes his own hood off. "I'm Adam March."

Gina stops smiling. "Adam March. You didn't just work for Dynamic Cosmetics; you were the boss." She says *boss* like it tastes bad.

"Yeah, I was." He's not going to deny it. He ran that division well, even if NATE disagreed with some of its policies.

Adam steps away from the door, looks around at the rows of glowing aquariums full of colorful fish, racks with collars and leashes, shelves with squeaky toys and treats, baskets with tartan pillows, displays with all manner of canine and feline likenesses on coasters, mugs, figurines, place mats. There is a freestanding cage containing the brilliant colors and racket of a pair of parrots, which are happy to see her arrive. A hand-printed sign says NOT FOR SALE.

A gust of supercharged wind bangs against the shop door, rattling the pane of plate glass. "Gina, you can't think that anyone is going to come out on a day like this and buy a fish? This is a 'stay at home, where it's safe' storm. The National Guard is posting warnings against driving. The state—"

She cuts him off. "Electricity goes out and I'm out of business. I've got to be here to get the generator working. Besides, big fish have to eat, or some of them will eat each other."

The center won't be closed. Adam pulls his hood up over his watch cap. "I've got to go."

Gina runs the back of her hand along her forehead to wipe away the moisture from that lock of wet hair and picks up her dripping coat. "Have a nice day." *Nahss.* He is dismissed.

Adam lets go of the door handle, turns back to her. "How will you get home?"

"I won't. Not till the storm ends. I can't take a chance."

Adam debates for a moment whether he should offer to stay, but he can't come up with a reason for doing so. She is obviously capable, and, after all, they are strangers, nodding acquaintances, onetime adversaries, maybe still adversaries in her mind, and not responsible for each other. "Okay. Good luck, then." He pushes hard against the door, putting the force of his shoulder against it, against the wind.

Adam March goes back into the storm, trudging toward Fort Street, hoping he's made the right decision.

Chapter Sixteen

It was a bitch of a storm. I huddled under the culvert with several others, a nominal truce in place. My mentor was there, alone. A little wiry-haired bitch went up to him in submission, obsequiously licking at his muzzle, begging for kindness. I'd scented her before in the neighborhood, a tough little cookie with an underbite.

Two fat Labradors made up the rest of our party. They'd gotten out of their yard; surprised to find the electric fencing neutralized and unable to handle the temptation, they had fled down the street and immediately gotten lost. Nice pets, kinda naïve. We all knew that their people were going to be frantic. Because of that, we knew they posed a real threat. Being leash dogs, not street dogs, the pair of them had left a trail a mile wide and a fathom deep. It would only be a matter of the storm ending before the authorities and a host of volunteers would be rushed out to seek the lost. Signs would be posted. Cunning photos plastered on every telephone pole, smiling, panting yellow Labs, Buffy and Muffy, or whatever their human-given appellations were. Reward!

But for now, the storm kept us squeezed into the tunnel, our body heat protecting us all from the cold, which made the fat Labs a welcome addition for a while. A bite of snow, a quick pee, and we rearranged ourselves to snooze the day away.

My mentor lay back-to-back with me. Out of mild curiosity, I asked him where his man was.

I don't know.

So he just wandered off?

I think he might have been captured.

By the men?

He went into a building and never came out.

The food building?

No, one he's never gone into before. We're not welcome in any building; that's why we stay outside. Buildings aren't for us. Besides, we might be captured if we go into a building. You should remember that, stay out of buildings unless they are empty.

I was surprised then to hear my mentor whine, a plaintive, lonely sound evocative of worry.

I don't know where he is.

You'll find him. After the storm.

He's gone.

As I said, dogs are existentialists. We don't understand the concepts of past or future. My mentor's man might have been gone six days or three hours. In any event, my mentor was uncharacteristically mournful. I rolled over, aligning my back with his for his warmth. But all through the storm, I could feel him shuddering with anxiety.

Chapter Seventeen

By the time Adam makes it to the stoop of the center, he feels as though he is Shackleton reaching his destination. He half-expects seal stew on the menu today. Mike is outside, flailing impotently with a broom against the rising drifts on the steps. He looks at Adam, the angry psoriasis on his face rubbed red in the cold, but he's smiling, the first time Adam has ever warranted a greeting from the notoriously silent man. "Welcome to Fort Street."

"Thanks, Mike. How'd you get here?"

"I never left."

"Wish I'd thought of that." Adam claps a hand on Mike's thickly padded shoulder and goes in.

There are more men in here than Adam has ever seen. Although lunch is an hour off, the dining room is open to accommodate the crowd and they sit at the cafeteria tables, still wearing their soaked jackets, unbuttoned or unzipped. It's something that has long since stopped puzzling Adam. These men take no chances with personal items. The worst fight he's seen, and he's witnessed quite a few, was when a Vietnam vet accused another vet of stealing his pocketknife. Claiming that the object in question was his own similar weapon, the accused hauled off and bashed his accuser in the face, drawing blood and inciting the group into cheering them on. Rafe and Big Bob had pulled the pair apart before the knife became part of the fight.

Knives, Adam has learned, are one of the most highly valued objects a homeless man can have. Protection, threat, a tool, a memento of childhood or war. They are also forbidden inside the center. Everyone knows that a blind eye is turned on pocketknives, like army-surplus store Swiss Army knives, but anything with a blade more than six inches long is immediately confiscated. The knives the men use in the dining room are stainless-steel table knives. This isn't prison, but it is a safe house. Big Bob has rules.

Adam kicks the snow off his boots and pushes his way through the crowd to get to the kitchen. Rafe is there, bebopping to his iPod, skillet in hand, his toque jaunty on his shaven head and his jacket still clean. He glances up and sees Adam in the doorway. "Hey, bro, good of you to come early."

"It's a bitch out there."

"We half-figured you'd bag it today. You a volunteer, man. No cause for life-threatenin' action."

Adam sags against the doorjamb. The effort of walking through the storm has tapped him out. His legs are quivering with the exertion. He's still got his cheese crackers in his pocket, but somewhere along the route he lost his mug. Or maybe he left it at Gina's A to Z Tropical Fish, where she braved the storm for goldfish and parrots. And here's Rafe, telling him that he didn't have to come. For a split second, Adam thinks that he should be mad, that Big Bob should have called him to tell him that. Should have called and said to stay put. Told him to sit there and watch the storm on the television, keep warm, keep dry. A good manager makes sure his people are informed.

Then he thinks, Maybe he did call. He's been walking to work since seven-thirty. The feeling of incipient anger passes. He hasn't seen Ishmael, and the noise from the dining room is unusually loud. "No. I'm here. But I wouldn't mind a cup of coffee before I get started." Rafe adjusts the heat under the skillet and walks to the cupboard. He takes down a mug for Adam and fills it from the Bunn coffeemaker. Adam slides onto a stool; the snow adhering to his jacket trickles onto Rafe's clean floor.

"Here you go, man."

Adam pulls off his wet hat and stuffs it into his pocket before taking the mug from Rafe. "Thanks." Two sets of brown eyes meet, and Adam sees a flash of respect in the other man's eyes. Adam quickly takes a sip of the strong coffee, the flush in his cheek partly the heat and partly wonder. He's never seen respect without fear before.

Today there are women in the center. Fort Street has a sister center two blocks over, but the ferocity of the storm has blurred the divisions. No one cares which center they're in, just happy they're out of the storm. An unofficial attendance is taken by Big Bob as he wanders through the groups, greeting individuals, mentally tallying who is here and who isn't. He'll make a phone call soon to see if some of his people are seeking safety at the Alice Crandall Center. AC, as they call it, is named for its benefactress, the woman who had donated her Victorian brownstone to the city for a shelter for battered, homeless, displaced women. AC is more radical than the Fort Street Center, but an amiable relationship exists between the two managers.

Adam is relieved to see Ishmael come in out of the storm; he's been worried that he might have to serve all these guys alone and run steam trays, too. Like a dog, Ishmael shakes his head with its mass of dreadlocks, spraying the walls of the back hall with droplets. He tucks his dreads up under his toque and sits to change his boots for the shoes he's brought in a plastic bag. Ishmael, too, looks at him with a smile. "You made it, man."

What the fuck? Did everyone expect that he'd shirk his duty? Adam finds himself growing a little annoyed at the suggestion that he's a wuss, a coward, a fair-weather volunteer. He's fucking *walked* all the way here. Six blocks that might as well have been six miles, it took him so long.

He's about to tell Ishmael to stuff it, when he feels Big Bob's hand on his shoulder. "I tried to reach you."

"I got an early start." Adam shrugs. "I'm here."

Big Bob squeezes Adam's shoulder. Like that of a good teacher or a respected scoutmaster, this small manly sign of approval is clear and touches Adam in a place he'd long ago buried. It has been so long since anyone approved of him. He'd been compensated, rewarded for performance with bonuses. He'd enjoyed the claps on the back from upper management for achieving goals. Even once the applause of a roomful of executives for a PowerPoint presentation outlining an acquisition. They had cheered like pirates coming across a gold-laden barque.

The only approval Adam has lusted after for more than two decades is that of his father-in-law. Adam has grieved as much for the withdrawal of Herb Carruthers's esteem as for any other loss. Herb Carruthers had approved of Adam, had, as a sonless man, treated him like an heir. Sterling, Papa's darling, had absorbed the lessons of her socially connected mother and, when Adam asked her to marry him, insisted that he get her father's blessing.

Adam invited Herb to meet him at the Harvard Club. Both were greeted as members, one freshly made, the other a generation ago. Adam loved the club, loved that he was a welcome member, that he had earned the right to sit in this room, an equal among giants even at the age of twenty-six. Over a meal of grilled salmon, Adam carefully laid out his ambitious plans, constructing a vision of the future that his potential father-in-law would approve of. A highly attainable future, particularly with Carruthers's influences, but Adam carefully avoided any presumption of expectation that, as a father-in-law, Carruthers would be of help. Instead, Adam affirmed that he envisioned a good life, one in which Sterling would enjoy all the rights and privileges of her class. The older man never raised his eyes off his plate, shoveling in the food like a longshoreman while Adam laid out his game plan. Finally, Adam paused, waiting for Carruthers to say something.

Plate cleaned, Carruthers sat back, wiped his mouth with his linen napkin, and belched. "That it?" Now his blue marble eyes met Adam's, his pupils tiny pinpricks even in the soft light of the room. Predator's eyes.

"I won't disappoint you, sir." Adam fretted that he'd come across as too pompous, or that Carruthers would detect in his speech the Dorchester of his adolescence, despite his carefully cultivated Harvard accent.

"One question."

"Yes, sir." Adam felt a little pull of anxiety, a shadow of fear that Carruthers might approve of him as a wunderkind but not as a prospective son-in-law. That Carruthers wouldn't approve of him after all.

"Do you sail?"

Adam's little pull of anxiety faded into warm relief. "No, sir." An honest answer.

"You join my family, you'll have to." Herb Carruthers stood up and offered his hand to Adam. Done deal.

Big Bob's hand on his shoulder squeezes a rough emotion out of Adam, a sense of what he has lacked most of his life: someone who genuinely approves of him.

"I should get to work."

An hour later, Big Bob joins the men behind the steam tables. "I'm missing Jupe." Ishmael ladles out a bowl of butternut squash soup, sprinkles a garnish of parsley on top, and slides it on a tray. "He's weird about that dog. Maybe he won't come in if his dog can't."

"I'm not stopping anybody today. Slicker is here with his dog. Course, she's in his pocket, but he knows I know she's here." Big Bob drums his fingers on the metal counter. "No, he's been acting a little off the meds lately. In fact, I don't recall seeing him yesterday, either."

Adam hefts a new tray of potatoes into the steam table. "Check the hospitals?"

"I usually start with the police. Okay, then. If anybody sees him . . ."

"We'll give you a shout." Ishmael fills another bowl.

Adam takes the soup bowl and places it on the ledge. "So, Jupe's mentally ill?"

"We ain't allowed to say, but if I was to make a guess, I'd say that he's one of those brilliant guys whose mind kinda lets loose on 'im. Used to be some kinda professor at MIT or one of them colleges. Rocket science. That's why they call him 'Jupiter.'"

"I figured him for a vet."

"Nah. Got those clothes outta the Army Navy Store. Lotsa guys wear 'em so they don't get hassled. No, he's a professor. You get him talkin' about the stars and you get an earful."

"You think he's out there?"

"I hope not. Freezin' to death ain't pretty."

"You think he's not coming in because of his dog?"

"Could be."

"Why would anyone sacrifice warmth and food for a dog?"

"Like them Katrina people refusin' to get rescued 'cause they wouldn't let 'em take their pets. That's devotion, man."

"That's madness."

"Maybe." Ishmael ladles out the last of today's soup and nods to Adam to remove the pot.

"I hope he gets in."

"Me, too."

Outside, the wind has picked up speed, making a steady high-pitched whistle against the corner of the building. Zephyrs spin down the deserted street. The lights blink, fade, regain strength, and Adam wonders about Gina and her tropical fish.

Chapter Eighteen

The snowstorm had lapsed into stillness by the wee hours of the next day. At full light, I awakened from a running dream and found men standing in front of our culvert. I don't know why none of us heard or scented them. However, the snow packed all around the entrance to our makeshift den announced our presence in the space beneath the road loud and clear to them; they didn't need noses or ears to find us. Those happy Labs had come and gone and come back, all the time leaving big sloppy footprints that just screamed, In here! I should have told them to beat it when I had the chance.

My first instinct, as with the others, was to book it. We turned to the other open end, but these were professionals, and we were trapped, men at both ends, standing in their big boots, poles and lines in their hands, even a dart gun.

The Labs came out, goofy and relieved to see men in charge. I hoped that maybe having recovered the missing pair, the authorities might cut the rest of us a little slack. Not so.

The wiry bitch made a run for it, feinting and ducking between long legs up to the knees in snow. The snow was her undoing; she couldn't run on top of it, and she sank, yapping her disgruntlement. A hand scooped her up and boxed her effortlessly, the yapping muted but not over.

I looked at my mentor. His boxy head was lowered, his grinning mouth open and his teeth showing. He didn't growl, but his lips quivered with warning. I suddenly realized that he was making a mistake. My single incarceration had taught me to play nice. He'd been inside before. He was legal; his tag said so. But for him, incarceration now, with his person missing, was unthinkable. His bold attachment to one man, a man more like us than like his own species, had prejudiced my mentor.

How will I find him? He won't know where I am. My mentor let out a thin whine, a plaintive, weak sound. Aware suddenly of his unseemly show of weakness, my mentor looped the whine into a full-bore growl. Hackles up, teeth bared. Take no prisoners.

They took us instead.

It was okay for me. It was the same shelter where I'd been for my rehab. The food was good, the inside warm and dry. Not exactly a spa, but not a bad place to spend a couple of days out of the weather. I didn't plan to stay long.

I tried to tell my mentor this, but he didn't get it. He was panicked, and nothing I said seemed to make him any more at ease. He just kept growling.

It was his undoing.

Chapter Nineteen

Adam pushes past some of the men squatting in the narrow first-floor hallway of the center; they're full, warm, and reluctant to leave, even though the storm is long over. The snowplows have leveled the ruts in the street, and the sunlight is blinding as it reflects off the pristine drifts. Mike is shoveling the sidewalk in front of the center.

Most of the men had bunked in the dormitory-style bedrooms upstairs; some did not, sleeping crouched against the walls instead, always on the half alert, as if not in the sanctuary of the Fort Street Center, but still out in the mean streets of the city. Adam has been at the center all night, partly because there was no way he was going to fight his way back over that same treacherous six blocks in the bitter, if now snowless, wind, and no way he could get a cab to come fetch him. Even though Rafe and Ishmael happily bedded down in the small office space designated STAFF Adam could not bring himself to flop puppylike among his coworkers on sleeping bags of debatable cleanliness. Big Bob, too, stayed up all night, he and Adam dozing in the chairs in Big Bob's office, their catnaps punctuated by Bob's hourly phone calls to police and other shelters in search of Jupiter.

It's been nearly twenty-four hours since Adam arrived at the center, windblown and frozen. By nine o'clock, he's served morning coffee and doughnuts, courtesy of the local doughnut shop, and he hopes that Big Bob will give him the nod to make his way home now that the streets are plowed and the sidewalks are slowly being shoveled. He's a god-dammed volunteer; he is required to put in only twenty hours a week, and he's put in twenty in one day.

"Do me a favor?" Big Bob covers the mouthpiece of the phone.

"Sure." Adam feels a sinking in his belly. A favor. Two words that, no matter what his position in life, have always had the power to make his mind race with quick reasons to decline. "Shoot."

"Go down to Memorial and see if Jupiter's there." Big Bob's thinning yellow hair sticks straight up, his meaty hands dragging it back and forth like greasy wheat sheaves in a breeze. His pale blue eyes are bloodshot.

"I'd really like to head home." The last thing Adam wants is to go to the local hospital and look for an indigent who's probably frozen to death in an alley due to bad judgment.

"It's on your way." Big Bob's voice isn't unlike his own voice in a previous life—assertive, attention-getting, and brooking no argument.

"How will I know he's there? They aren't going to let me wander the halls. There are rules."

"You talk to Pam Stone; she's the head nurse on six. That's where he'll be if he ended up there. She'll help."

"Can't you just call her and ask her if he's there?"

Big Bob pushes up out of his chair, resting the flat of his hands on his desk. Adam thinks of the Incredible Hulk. "She can't say. HIPAA."

"So I waltz in, asking for a crazy guy in a watch cap who's possibly raving about voices from outer space, and they point me in the right direction?"

"March, we don't use that word here. And he might be unconscious, unable to be identified. A John Doe."

"Or dead."

Big Bob sits heavily in his much-abused chair, reverting back to pre-Hulk condition. "Or dead. Check the morgue."

After the garish cheerfulness of the lobby, the sixth-floor medical ward is an abrupt plunge back into the fifties. Lodged in the oldest wing of the city hospital, it is also the only floor untouched by renovation. It smells precisely like a hospital—a hospital caring for indigents and the poor. It's an odor similar to that of the center: Lysol and unwashed clothing stuffed in plastic bags. The overhead lighting casts a greenish glow on the cracked linoleum. A handrail is mounted at hip level on a beige wall, with not so much as a single fake watercolor to break up the monotony. A lone wheelchair is the only traffic in the hallway, and Adam slips by its occupant without looking at him.

"I'm looking for Nurse Stone." Adam finds the only upright person on the floor to ask, a young volunteer with a resolutely cheerful smile on her stricken face, her braces glinting in the greenish light.

"She's in with a patient."

"I'll wait." There are no chairs nearby, so Adam rests an elbow on the counter of the nurses' station, his cheek against his fist. The slight hum coming from the overhead fixtures seems to have a Doppler effect as he feels himself drifting off. Loud and soft, loud and soft. Drifting on the open ocean of exhaustion, Adam struggles to keep his eyes open.

"Can I help you?"

Startled awake, Adam is embarrassed to feel a slight moistness at the corner of his mouth. A tall middle-aged woman stands in front of him, her hot-pink scrubs a flash of color in the beige hallway. "I'm looking for a man. One of our . . ." Adam hesitates. What's the word Big Bob uses to refer to their people? "One of our guests at the Fort Street Center. He didn't show up during the storm. He's got some mental problems, and Bob Carmondy thought he might be here."

"What's his name?"

Damn Big Bob. He never said what the guy's real name was.

"I'm not sure. They call him Jupiter."

Pamela Stone tightens her crossed arms across her hot-pink midsection. Adam looks down, unable to meet her disapproving glare. She wears soft rubber Crocs on her feet, also hot-pink. "You know that I can't tell you who is a patient here?"

"Yes, of course I do. But Bob suggested that you still might be able to help. We just want to know that he's okay."

"If you were to wander down the hall and notice that a friend is here, there's nothing I can do about that. And you happened to be next of kin . . ."

"But I'm—"

Pam Stone holds up a staying finger, nearly touching

Adam's lips with it. "I never heard you say that you weren't. I have to assume that you are."

Adam leans close to her ear. "I don't even know the guy's real name." Then he's embarrassed, thinking of his unbrushed teeth, his own unwashed state.

"Abernathy. Charles Abernathy." Pam Stone walks away from Adam in a rush of furious pink.

Okay, job done. He's here. I can go home. Adam pulls his cell phone out of his pocket, thinking he'll call Big Bob, and then a taxi.

"No cell phone use here? Interferes with the machines?" The teenage candy striper with the big braces waggles a finger at him, then frowns. "I hate that rule."

Shoving the phone back into his jacket, Adam heads down the hallway toward the elevator bank; a big window at the end of the corridor filters the winter light through a wire-mesh guard, the bright spoke of light making Adam squint. He goes past four wheelchair-wide doorways, each of which opens into occupied patient rooms. The light in his eyes causes him to look away and into the rooms, but the arrangement of beds prevents him from seeing their occupants. The fourth door opens into a larger room, arranged with three beds. Propped at a thirty-five-degree angle in the hospital bed closest to the window, and therefore more visible to the hallway, is the thin form of Jupiter. At least Adam thinks it's Jupiter. This guy is clean-shaven and his hat is gone. The hair against the pillow is yellowish and streaked with gray; it's long, but combed back, as if someone had groomed him. A rush of panic leavens Adam's belly and he can't decide whether to make a run for it or go in to pay a call on a man he doesn't know except from across the steam-table divide.

Jupiter—Charles Abernathy—spots him.

There is an exquisite moment when Adam might be able to keep moving, to pretend that he hasn't seen the man. He can keep going, squinting into the sun at the end of the hall, blinded. He can call Big Bob and go home. Favor fulfilled.

But Jupiter smiles—a reflexive grin on seeing a familiar face. Even from the distance of a room's width, he knows Adam, and, as if panhandling in the street, he calls to him, "Hey, buddy!" Fuck.

Suddenly, his parka weighs a ton. Adam unzips it and shrugs it off, then walks into the room, where he stands at the foot of the bed. "How are you doing?" He smiles like a Welcome Wagon lady, all teeth, no substance.

"A little embarrassed. Sometimes I think I can go without my medications, but each and every time I'm proven wrong. They're going to send me back to the mental hospital to get adjusted." Jupiter fingers air quotes around the word *adjusted*. "But I need to ask you a big favor." It's almost as if Jupiter has been expecting him.

Two favors in one day. Adam grits his teeth and smiles. "I'll see if I can help."

"My dog." Jupiter's pale blue eyes begin to leak tears. "I don't know where he is."

"He'll be fine."

"No, I need to know he's fine. I need to know where he is. He's probably in the pound."

"You've got tags on him; they'll keep him."

"They're old. And they came off another dog. I just have them so that I don't get hassled."

"Well, even so, don't worry about him. You need to worry only about yourself."

Jupiter begins to cry in earnest. "I can't stop worrying, and if I worry, I can't pay attention to my doctors." Suddenly, Jupiter throws himself into a sitting position. "I'm getting out of here. Hand me my pants."

"No. No. Stay put." Shit, now he's going to be responsible for the guy going AWOL, or AMA, or whatever it is when you leave a hospital before you're discharged.

"I can't. Benny is my life." Jupiter is weeping loudly, inconsolable. He swings skinny legs over the edge of the bed. The leads that snake beneath the thin fabric of his johnny pull tight against the monitor that records his vitals. A buzzer goes off down the hall.

"Okay, okay. Simmer down. I'll go. I'll go." Adam wants him back in the bed. The sight of those skinny legs with the topography of lumpy veins and knobby knees is too much intimacy. It's easier to say he'll go than to fight with the guy and get that pink nurse down on him. "Hush, just relax. I'll go to the pound."

"You will? Promise?" The tears stop and a snaggletoothed smile erupts.

"You get back in bed and I'll check."

Jupe does what's asked and Adam makes a run for the elevator.

"Just hang on to him till I get out. It won't be long. I promise. Thank you. Thank you. Thank you."

The elevator door closes off the sound of Jupiter's happy, grateful shouting.

Chapter Twenty

I'm telling you. Shut up. What was that song? When the student becomes the master? I'd had it with my mentor. How had I ever thought this whining, yapping, cowering, fear-aggressive punk was worthy of my adulation, God knows. I kept telling him to play it straight. Not to snap every time one of the people came along to feed him. How dumb animal is that? But he kept it up. His separation from his man was more than he could take. Frankly, I just didn't get it. I know that many of our kind pair-bond with humans, but the slavish devotion beyond the unknown days of their separation seemed a bit much. We're dogs; we aren't supposed to remember much beyond regimented training. Move on.

I, on the other paw, played it like Olivier on the boards. I loooove people. Smooochie smoochie. Yes, kiss my ugly chewed-up nose. Give me a home where the kibble pours free and squeaky toys abound. I fully expected that a reprise of my past performance would win me another easily escapable home. Of course, I'd wait until spring. No more winters on the street. What I hadn't counted on was the lack of interested adopters in February. Seems like everyone wants a spring puppy or isn't considering the daily walk while the temperature is in the thirties and the wind chill makes it feel like an arctic blast. People really only want dogs in the summer. I languished.

The staff were kind, and my prestreet life had enured me to a caged existence, but I was bored. By now I was used to coming and going as I pleased, tooling around my staked-out territory, greeting the neighbors, checking out the Dumpsters. Outside of the daily leash walk up and down the block and being fed twice a day, I didn't have much to keep me occupied. I slept. Which is good fun, but really I wanted to see some old friends, and once my mentor vanished into the door at the end of the hall, from whence no one returns, I had no one around who knew me from my street days.

It was enough to make a grown dog yawn.

Chapter Twenty-one

If Adam thought the hospital reeked, the animal shelter trumps that revulsion with the additional pungency of animal pee. Even in the sparkling clean and bright reception room of the city's animal shelter—the term *pound,* he has learned, is politically incorrect—Adam can smell the lingering odor of overexcited parolees.

"I'm here to find a guy's dog. He's in the hospital." Adam has waited three days before beginning to hunt for Jupiter's dog. Leaving the hospital, Adam had headed straight home and slept the rest of the day. Waking only long enough to eat a bowl of cereal, he'd gone right back to sleep, the first night in months he neither medicated himself with scotch nor dreamed. When the cab pulled up in front of his building, Adam had paid the man off and trotted across the street to the A to Z Tropical Fish and Pet Supply. The door was locked, but he could see the bluish green glow of the aquarium lights. Gina must have weathered the storm and gone home, he thought.

The next two days, Adam had been too busy with appointments, lawyers, psychiatrist, and laundry even to look up the location of the city animal shelter.

"When did he lose his dog?" Yet another in-charge woman in pastel scrubs.

"I don't know, during the storm maybe." He tells this to the youngish woman with yanked-back hair, purple scrubs, and matching Crocs. Does everyone in the quasi-medical profession wear these weird shoes? How can anyone tell the nurses from the aides or the vets from the receptionists these days?

"What kind of dog is it?"

Adam thinks back on encountering Jupe and the dog on the street, or Jupe and the dog waiting on the stoop. "Shorthaired, dark-colored." Adam has paid so little attention to Jupe's dog that it's like trying to remember a detail from someone else's life. "I think he has white on him. About yea high." Adam sketches a line at his knees. "Its name is Benny."

"Terrier?"

"No. More like a boxer, but with a tail." Adam is growing confident, sure of his description now.

"Pit bull?

He shrugs. "I don't know. Maybe. Why?"

The girl pinches her bottom lip with two fingers. "I'll have to talk to the vet in charge about this. Just fill out what you can." She slides a form onto a clipboard that has a pen dangling from a piece of twine. She pushes it across the high counter to Adam. "We have the welfare of the dog first and foremost as our responsibility."

"So, returning a lost dog to his owner is counterintuitive to that?"

The girl looks pained. "Please wait over there." She points to a pair of orange plastic chairs.

Adam's mouth is dry. Dr. Stein says that he can begin to recognize the symptoms of his anger by thinking of his posture and the taste in his mouth. Are his hands shaking? He's supposed to take deep breaths and mentally flick away the disturbance before it grows too big. In the reception area, there is a Poland Spring water dispenser but no cups. Adam is half-tempted to stick his mouth under the spigot and get a mouthful of water that way. He deliberately slumps his shoulders, then rolls them back and down, shaking off the tension. He rotates his head around, then tilts it from side to side. There. Now smile. He prides himself on handling frustration a little better than in the past. Now delays at the post office or being stuck in traffic don't rile him in quite the same way. Adam doesn't attribute this to the slow pace of his days, or the loss of meaningful work; he thinks he's simply making progress toward what Dr. Stein calls "centeredness."

"Mr. . . ." A big man in a ponytail bangs through the swinging door separating the reception area from the rest of the facility. He's wearing blue scrubs and, predictably, blue Crocs.

"March. Adam March."

"Dr. Gil."

The name on his badge says something else, Gilbert Dufrense. *Dr. Gil.* How user-friendly. How he must charm the little old cat ladies.

Adam hands him the clipboard and waits in silence as the vet studies the form Adam has filled out. "This isn't your dog?" For the first time, the vet looks up at him.

"I expect that your staffer has informed you of the situation. I have a sick friend, whose only concern is getting his dog back."

Dr. Gil sets the clipboard down on the high counter and gestures toward the hard plastic chairs. Adam makes no move to sit down. Already this errand has wasted half his morning. "Mr. March. We have a policy."

"You don't have the dog, do you?"

"We did. I think."

"Two things come to mind here. One, how do you know you have or don't have this guy's dog when neither one of us has taken a look? Two, a sick man's civil rights are in jeopardy here." Adam is wishing that he'd shaved before coming, worn something besides his usual jeans and faded Red Sox sweatshirt.

The blue-scrubbed vet fingers his chin contemplatively. Adam notices that his hands are encased in latex gloves, as if he's forgotten the purpose of the gloves is to keep him safe from contamination. "Two pit bull types were brought in. One is familiar to us; we know him. The other was . . . hostile."

Adam shrugs. "Benny is probably not hostile." Adam is trying to think if he's ever seen Jupe's dog being either hostile or, conversely, friendly. He has no recollection, but logic tells him that a street man's dog is probably going to be one way or the other. It's probably significant that he can't recall any of the other men petting the dog. "Why don't we just make this easy and go see if his dog is in there."

Dr. Gil suddenly snaps off the latex gloves, folds them together, and shoots them over the high counter and into a wastebasket as if that's the highlight of his day. "Okay."

They walk down a short corridor past doors labeled SURGERY, EXAM ROOM 1, EXAM ROOM 2.

ADOPTIONS.

At the end of the corridor is an unlabeled door, and Dr. Gil pushes the swinging door open to the cacophony of barks, yelps, whines, growls, ululations, and howls. The noise is like being on a Wall Street trading floor. The vocalizations are accompanied by the sound of wire doors being rattled, metal water bowls tipped, nails tap-dancing on cement and on the metal shelves of the upper cages. Prison movies come to mind.

"Are these dogs up for adoption?"

"Some might be. Some are fostered."

"Meaning?" He knows what it means to kids. It just sounds more humane in reference to animals. Kinder.

"Put in temporary homes, see if they can make it as pets."

"And the others? Adoptable?"

"Not always."

Like him. He remembers his social worker sitting him down and explaining that he had no hope of a real home. "You're a big boy now, Adam"—as if it was good news she offered—"Before you know it, you'll be all grown up, and on your own."

Adam looks around at the faces pressed up against the bars of the cages. Ears are pointed toward him, and he imagines they have no concept of their hopelessness. He is repulsed by the smell, an amalgam of wet newspaper, cleaning fluid, and dog. The vet walks ahead of Adam, pointing into each cage, left, then right, and calling out the closest breed match to the occupant's description.

"German shepard?"

"No." The smallish tan-and-black dog with one upright ear lifts a lip in a halfhearted sneer.

"Beagle?"

A definite hound-dog look. Weepy eyes and a guilty expression. "No."

"Border collie?"

"Look, I said he's a black-and-white shorthaired dog." The fluffy Border collie stares at Adam with one blue eye and one brown eye.

"Describing dogs is more art than science. One man's shorthair is another man's retriever."

They have come to the end of the line. One dog remains, but Adam has already come to the conclusion that Jupe's dog is long gone. He's about to ask if there is another shelter in the city, when he sees the last dog. This one is in a short run instead of a cage. There is nothing in it but the dog and a water bowl, as if he's just in there for a change of scenery. As if he might be leaving shortly. As if he's at the end of the line.

He's a brindle dog, one lop ear, the other a ragged half of an ear; a splash of white on his chest, on which is a long, narrow, still angry-looking scar that glows pinkish in the fluorescent light of the kennel. He sits with a quiet dignity among all these raucous others. Adam stands at the locked cage door, his fingers gripping the diamonds of wire, staring at the dog, willing it to be Jupe's dog. The dog raises its eyes to meet his. His mouth opens; a long, wide tongue lolls out. He stands up and his tail swings mildly from side to side. He has the look of someone with just one last hope in the world.

"This one."

"Are you sure?"

Sure is exactly what Adam isn't. "That's him."

"You can't adopt for someone else."

"So I'll 'foster' him till Charles gets home."

"Look. I know. You're trying to do a favor for a friend. But this is not our policy." Dr. Gil puts his hand on the latch. The dog in question cocks his head, eager to see what comes next. "Especially with these dogs. Pit bulls."

"But you, a vet, would rather destroy him without benefit of judge and jury?"

"He's got the scars. He's been fought. That kind generally don't make it as pets."

"But he's already a pet." Adam feels a surge of anger. He isn't someone who is told no; he is someone who says no. "I'll post bail."

There is a long, uncomfortable moment as the two men eye each other. Finally, Dr. Gil shakes his head. "You need to fill out adoption papers, show us that you either own your own home or that your landlord will allow you to have a dog."

"I have a better idea." There is rack filled with choke chains and leashes. "I'll take him and give you a big donation." Adam pulls down a leash from the rack.

"You'll pay the regular adoption fee of two hundred dollars and sign a paper that says you won't give this dog away."

"Except to his rightful owner."

"That you'll return him to us if you choose not to keep him." The vet folds his arms across a meaty midriff. "That is our policy."

Adam doesn't know why he's arguing with this Dr. Gil, except that he is unwilling to cave in to this pompous guy who probably couldn't make it as a real doctor and so is treating animals instead. Adam is determined to walk out of the shelter with the goddamned dog. He's not going to be told by this Big Bluie that he can't take a stupid dog that's likely going to be destroyed anyway. Adam's not in it for the money; no one will compensate him for taking this dog out of this place. He won't be receiving any state paycheck. No one will hold him up as a humanitarian. No foster father of the year title while all the time he's making life miserable for some innocent kid. Threatening the strap if a towel gets left on the floor.

Adam pulls himself up. What the fuck is he doing? Suddenly, the clipboard is in his hands and he's walking out of the shelter, two hundred dollars deeper in Visa debt, which he has no hope of recovering, and holding the leash of a dog he is fairly certain isn't the right one.

They stand on the sidewalk, waiting to cross the street to his car. Adam glances down at the dog. The mutt is looking up at him, tongue lolling for all the world like he's happy.

"You goddamned better be Benny." Adam jerks the leash and the pair cross the street.

Chapter Twenty-two

"I got his dog." Adam ducks his head into Big Bob's office. "Just what am I supposed to do with him?"

"Jupe's here."

A slight scrim of sweat breaks out on Adam's forehead. Thank God. Despite his assurances to the vet, Adam has no intention of taking the dog home. Right now it sits in the back of his Lexus, the back window cracked open, a towel on the cream-colored leather. He has no idea if the dog will sit quietly or wreck his car. "Is he all right?"

"He's better. More himself. But he'll be happy to see that dog. It's all he's talked about since he walked in, how you're going to find it. Sorry to have put that on you, man, but it's a good-deed merit badge." A euphemism for points earned on his community service. Every hour he works is documented; every hour Adam spends in the center becomes one less he has to serve. A "merit badge," in Big Bob's lexicon, earns him another hour of service. Of course, Adam has just spent several hours and two hundred dollars performing this service, but he decides to let that go. "I'll go get the dog."

The inside of his car smells like a mix of medicated shampoo and dog breath. The blunt-headed animal greets him like a lost friend, tag wagging, tongue drooping out of his split-grin face. "Come on. Your master wants a word with you." Adam hauls the dog up the back stairs of the center.

Jupe is waiting in the empty dining room. It's long after lunch and most of the men are either gone or settled in the activity room. The tables are folded and garaged against the far wall. Jupe has a new watch cap, and his army-surplus jacket is buttoned up to his neck. Adam can see that his eyes are clouded with the comfort of legal drugs. He has the look of a man standing on solid ground for the first time after a long sea voyage.

Adam half-expects that Jupe's drug-induced calmness will abate at the sight of his missing dog, and he is going to hand the leash over and make a run for it before Jupe can give him a grateful hug. The last thing he wants is an embrace. It's late and he just wants to go back to his place, crack open the JW, and relax in front of the television. It's all he wants. The solitude of slow numbness.

"That's not Benny."

"Of course it is." Adam thrusts the leash at Jupe's hand. "Take him."

The dog sits down. He looks from Adam to Jupe and back again.

"I know my own dog. This isn't him. This is some stray."

"Sir. He was the only . . ."

Jupe's tears start down his gunneled cheeks. He doesn't sob, or make a move to wipe them away. "Benny? What's happened to him? Did you look everywhere?"

Adam pokes the leash end against Jupe's fisted hand. "He's a nice dog. Take him."

Suddenly, Jupe's face changes; some older part of himself shows, the professor or the father or the good husband. "Do you think that affection is so easily transferred? Do you think that you could love a stranger child who is given to you as a replacement for your own? Do you have the slightest idea what it means to love someone or something? My dog is my friend, my companion, my protection on the street. I failed to love my family enough, or myself. But I love Benny." And just as suddenly, Jupe reverts to the craggy, hollow-cheeked man of a moment before; then he shrugs back his shoulders and walks away from Adam and the dog.

The dog stands up, shakes, and yawns.

Adam swallows hard. His chest feels as hollow as the Tin Man's. He can hear his pulse in his ears; he knows that he's got to take charge of the moment, but he's stuck, feckless. He feels the dog nudge his leg as if to say, Let's get out of here.

Big Bob has watched the whole scene, as has Rafe, standing in the doorway of the kitchen, his palm-frond hands stroking his cheeks. Adam thinks he hears laughter, faint ripples of amusement at his expense. The familiar knot of frustration twists in his belly, this being thwarted that provokes his just-below-the-surface anger. He has put himself on the line here for some indigent and now he's stuck.

"Hey man, that's a nice dog." Rafe's voice is just one degree to the left of teasing. "Lemme get him somethin' to eat."

Adam is slow to turn around, slow to decide if Rafe is taunting him or sincere.

"Well, you tried." Big Bob doesn't come close enough to slap Adam on the back; in fact, he stays at a distance. "I guess you'll have to take him back."

"Yeah. Great." Adam has an appointment with a potential client in half an hour on the other side of town. "Can you keep him here till I get back?"

"No. Don't think that would be a good idea."

"I can't keep him."

"Take him back on your way across town."

"I don't have time. Come on. I found the goddamn dog, or at least found one like him; the least you can do is keep him here for a couple of hours."

"No. Sorry. It's cold out, he can wait in your car."

Adam yanks the leash attached to the choke chain and hauls the dog out of the dining room and into the back hallway. Rafe is there with a plate of leftovers and a bowl of water. The dog makes noisy, fast work of the mess on the plate and laps water to the bottom of the bowl. Rafe watches with the same self-satisfaction on his face as when he takes a moment to observe the men enjoying his food. "He's a hungry one."

"You want him?"

Rafe makes a little piffle noise. "Can't. No pets allowed where I live."

"Lucky you."

" 'Sides, my wife'd kill me, I bring one of them home."

Adam is nonplussed. Rafe has never mentioned a wife before. Then again, neither has he. It's like their lives begin and end in this old Victorian building. Their conversations revolve around sports or politics, the differences between them offering very little common ground; neither he nor Rafe ever speak of a personal life, or only in a glancing way. "Well, maybe she can change her mind."

Rafe strokes his cheek with his fingertips, as if contemplating the idea. "No."

Adam tightens his grip on the leash and yanks the dog away from the plate he is still licking.

Adam opens the back door of his Lexus. During the hour and a half the big mutt has spent lolling on his backseat while Adam has been doing his dog and pony show for a group of entrepreneurs who don't look a day over twelve, he has managed to stink up the car with his farts and glaze both the door and the back windows with nose prints. His face splits into a grin as he lolls his tongue out at Adam's arrival. His tail wags, slapping the white leather with a tympanic rhythm.

Adam hauls the dog out by the collar and marches to the door of the animal shelter. A strategic retreat is more honorable than a complete defeat. He'll turn the dog over, try to get his money back, and forget the whole debacle.

Closed.

Fuck. It's only four o'clock. What kind of weird hours does this place keep?

Briefly, Adam looks around for a place to tie the dog. Maybe he can just leave him and then put a message on the answering machine why he did; surely someone comes in on weekends to feed the inmates. As quickly as the suggestion occurs to him, Adam shrugs it off. He'd probably get sent up on cruelty charges for doing that. The last thing Adam

March needs is more trouble. He has a date with Judge Johnson next week, and he is harboring a self-indulgent hope that the judge will cut him some slack, maybe even give him a reprieve. "Well, stupid, I guess you're with me." He loads the dog back into his sullied Lexus and heads home.

Chapter Twenty-three

Adam has only a vague notion how to take care of a dog. He's never had one, never allowed one in his house. Although Ariel had clamored for a puppy time and again, a fat black Labrador retriever like the ones that all the other kids whose parents had houses on Martha's Vineyard dragged along from home. "Why not? Why can't we? Why can't we?" Adam's answer was an unequivocal no, with the blame tossed, from time to time, on Sterling's shoulders. "It wouldn't be fair to your mother; she has enough to do." Which, even as a small child, Ariel saw right through. Adam got smarter. "It wouldn't be fair to"— and he'd name the incumbent housekeeper—"she has enough to do." Ariel had to be satisfied with her horses, which at least lived somewhere else.

So to find himself in his small one-bedroom apartment, in a building with no yard, face-to-face with one of the least attractive dogs ever made, Adam thinks he must be out of his mind.

The dog, a rusty brindle with white markings and that weird hacked-off ear, sits staring back at him. Every now and then his mouth opens and that banner of a tongue lolls out. He makes a gasping noise, slips the tongue over his nose, right, then left, and retracts it into his mouth, all the while keeping his eyes on Adam, as if he's waiting for a speech, or a tap dance. Or a fight.

"Don't get too comfortable; you're going back tomorrow." Adam wags a finger at the dog. Swallowing the last of the scotch in his glass, Adam heads into the bedroom, shutting the door behind him. He drops his clothes on the floor, refills the scotch glass with the bottle he keeps on his nightstand, and climbs into bed, exhaustion waving through him and making it impossible even to read to the end of the article in his *Business Week* magazine. He finishes off the scotch and turns out the light.

Instantly, he hears the scratch of claws against the wood. "Go to bed." *Scritch. Scritch.* Like some Stephen King predator. "Knock it off." The scratching becomes rhythmic, persistent. "Stop that." His landlord won't give him back his security deposit on that happy day he moves out of this dump if this mutt has damaged the woodwork. Adam leaps out of bed and wrenches open the door.

The dog is sitting, his tail swishing back and forth on the floor, his mouth gaping. *Aowr. Aowr.* It almost sounds like a syllable. He stands up, all happiness to see Adam back in the room.

Adam slams the door shut, gets back into bed, and pulls the spare pillow over his head.

. . .

For once, he's slept late. Groggy from unaccustomed deep sleep, Adam comes out of his bedroom, and nearly steps in the pile of dog shit laid carefully in front of his door. The dog is sound asleep on the futon.

The screech and cackle of the two parrots inside Gina De-Marco's store grows even more excited as Adam, attached to the dog, walks in. Gina is bent over an aquarium of tropical fish set on a low shelf. Her low-slung jeans gap at the tantalizing space just below the last bump on her spine. She stands up, her mouth crooked in a little surprised smile, which quickly fades. "What have we here?" She stands aside to assess the dog, then looks at Adam. "Would never have pegged you for the pit bull type."

"I'm not." The dog leans against the choke chain, trying to get close to the decorative cage with the parrots.

"Okay. So that's not a pit bull on the end of a leash?"

"It's a long story." Adam snugs the animal back to his side.

"Where did you get him?"

"Shelter."

Gina's disdain suddenly disappears. It is replaced with a grudging approval. "Wow. Good for you. Rescue dogs are the best; it's like they know they've been saved. I've got three greyhounds—"

"It's temporary." Adam isn't interested in rehearsing the whole sorry tale. He just wants some dog food. "I'm not keeping him."

"Fostering is good, too."

Fostering. The word has no heroic connotations for Adam. "No. Not fostering."

Gina ignores his assertion, as if he's a little boy refusing to eat his peas. "What's his name?"

"Doesn't have one. Doesn't need one. I'm taking him back to the shelter as soon as the doors open."

"Why did you get him if you're not keeping him? These are living creatures; you can't decide that they don't fit and then return them like a damned shirt."

"Like I said, it's a long story. I was trying to find a guy's dog, and this isn't it. He goes back."

The dog is leaning against his collar again, his pale brown nose working hard.

"Give him a chance."

Yanked back to Adam's side, the dog sits.

Gina leans over the counter, exposing that crescent of skin above her jeans. She reaches into a jar and pulls out a dog biscuit. She cautiously approaches the dog, whose eyes are fixed on the biscuit in her hand. He lowers his head, swipes his tongue over his lips. "Here, fella." Gina offers the biscuit and the dog shows good manners in taking it gently from her hand. She stands up and smiles. "He seems like a good boy. You should keep him."

The idea is ludicrous, adding an ugly dog to his list of worries. Adam doesn't even know what the pet policy is in his building, but he's willing to guess it's not in favor of dogs like this. "I can't keep him."

Gina reaches out and touches Adam's arm, as if consoling him. "Sure you can." He hears that subtle southern drawl. "He likes you." He likes the feel of her hand on his arm, the persuasive touch of someone who thinks she can change his mind.

"Well, I don't like him."

"You will. He's a beauty."

Adam laughs. "Not really. And he drools. And smells."

"That's normal." Gina runs the same hand that's touched his arm over the dog's head. The dog wriggles beneath her hand. She makes baby-talk noises at him, then looks up at Adam and sighs. "It can be very rewarding, bringing an animal back from a rough beginning to a satisfying life. I've done it with greyhounds, and several friends of mine have adopted pits."

"Doesn't matter. I told you: I'm not keeping him."

"Then why did you bring him in here?"

"I have nothing to feed him."

Now she looks at Adam with a tight-jawed disappointment. "Give him a chance. Haven't you ever needed someone to give you a chance?"

Adam almost laughs at her sincerity, at the storybook ending she's shilling. "I have always made my own chances."

"And see where that's gotten you."

"What do you mean?"

"I see you standing there, staring out your window all day. Too many hours for a guy with something better to do."

Adam feels the flush build, the hum of annoyance vibrating through his skin, the urge to snap.

Gina turns away from Adam, leaving him alone in the shop while she goes into a back room. She comes out with a small bag of dry dog food, two cans of wet food, and a tennis ball. "This'll take care of him for a couple of days. Just remember to give him fresh water, too." She gingerly offers the mutt another biscuit. "I think you're making a mistake."

"You think he's got so much potential, I'll be happy to give him to you."

"I would if I could, but I've got those three greyhounds. They take up a lot of space."

"What do I owe you?" Adam fishes his wallet out of his back pocket.

"It's a gift. For the dog. Throw the ball for him a few times. You both could use the exercise."

"No, no gifts. I'll pay."

"Forget it." Gina's full mouth is drawn into a thin line. She folds her arms across her middle, her hands resolutely not taking any money from him.

He doesn't know exactly what he's done wrong, but he's done something. All women have that ineffable power to transmit disappointment without words, and he's getting a full dose from this woman he barely knows. She bags the food and hands it to him.

"Thank you."

"I guess he's better off dead than unloved."

"Dead? He'll get adopted."

"Not very likely."

"You just told me you have friends who adopt pit bulls. What makes it less likely for this one?"

"Where was he?"

"End cage."

"Nuff said. That's death row. They've given him his last chance with you."

The dog, who has given up pulling on the leash and trying to sniff at every nose-level object in the pet shop, suddenly relaxes the tension on the leash and sits. He looks up at the two humans, his muzzle following the conversation like a line judge. Adam turns away from the counter and nearly trips over the dog. The touch of his knee against the dog's ribs is enough to get a yowl out of the animal. "Hey, that's enough out of you." Adam jerks the leash.

"Who, me or the dog?"

Adam doesn't answer, yanks the dog to his side, and walks out. Really, the woman is too much.

As they wait for the light to change, Adam hears the dog growl, a low, throaty rumble that is aimed up the street. A middle-aged man in a track suit is walking a Labrador retriever. The dog's growl elevates to something more like a roar and Adam is nearly taken off his feet as the dog lunges fiercely at the on-coming dog. The bag of dog food hits the pavement and the tennis ball rolls out. The dog is powerful enough that it takes both hands to keep him from reaching the yellow Lab.

"That dog is dangerous, mister. Put a fucking muzzle on it, will ya?" The Lab's owner pulls his own dog to one side and hurries by, fuming about city ordinances. The pit bull is barking at the top of his lungs, as if the very existence of that Labrador is an insult to him. The Lab glances back at the raging dog and then looks longingly at the rolling tennis ball.

"Knock it off!" Adam pulls on the leash, but the dog is oblivious to the pressure. As soon as the guy and his dog disappear around a corner, the dog sits, licks its lips, and scratches at his half of an ear, then looks up at Adam as if expecting praise.

The dog has to go. Now.

Chapter Twenty-four

I was embarrassed at having to do my business in the house, but then again, I have never been house-trained. I wouldn't have even considered soiling the area—it was, after all, not a lot bigger than my cage back in the cellar—but he didn't give me a clue as to what was appropriate behavior. His language was familiar. I understood the "Shut up" and "Knock it off" bit, but my own attempt at communication was ineffectual; he didn't speak my language. So I crapped where he'd get the message. No furtive behind the furniture for me. Uh-uh. Right there where he'd step in it. I got the reaction I half-expected. Again, familiar words were tossed at me, but he didn't touch me. He also, after a few minutes of diatribe, had the good grace to be embarrassed himself. "You needed to go out? I should have known. Not your fault." Well, he didn't exactly say that, but I understood by his seated posture, his head in his hands, that he had figured it out.

He leashed me and we banged down the three flights of stairs to the outside. The sidewalk was clear, but the grassy divide between sidewalk and street was filled with snow. I hiked my leg up to mark my new territory against a dug-out fireplug but got dragged along before I could finish the job. This guy had no leash manners at all.

Then—oh boy, what fun—we went into that place where the scents of treats and rubber toys was almost narcotic. The female actually touched me with kind fingers. Something I'd never known before, and something I had a sudden and uncharacteristic craving for. The mommy noises from her mouth were enough to make me long for puppyhood. Ah, if only the lug on the other end of my leash had had the brains to leave me here.

And then, would you believe it? One of those Labs from the night of the storm came sauntering down the street, all up in my face, bragging on being somebody's spoiled pet. I guess I showed him. The cur squealed with fear aggression, and I'd have made mincemeat out of him if he'd had the *cojones* to pull away from his man. The guy at the other end of my leash was surprised, but he had a pretty firm grip. Lucky for that Lab.

He yanked on my leash and off we went back to his crib. If I had hoped for a reprise of my first adopted home, with a nice escapable fenced-in yard, this sure wasn't it. Before he could get his entry door unlocked, I squatted. If I wasn't going to be able to enjoy the leisure of a backyard bowel movement, I was going to have to get busy before he dragged me back into the building. I have my standards.

There is a certain comfort in recognizing human male behavior, and this guy's language was completely familiar. He spoke as my boys had spoken. Muttered, yes, not shouted. And no violence, true. I wasn't confined to a cage, but he kept his distance, as if I was. I just knew that my fighting career was going to be revived. Why else bail me out of the shelter? He was tough—nothing namby-pamby about him—and I just knew that he was looking for someone as tough as he was. Right from the get-go, I knew I liked his looks. Hey, I knew that I was out of condition, but I was certain we'd rectify that soon enough. I was even looking forward to the road work and the weights. We'd be a pair. Yes we would.

Inside, he dumped some kibble into a plastic bowl. Good start. I wolfed it, looked for more. He paid no attention, just sat talking to himself with that little toy they all rub on their ears. Suddenly, he stood up and swore. I ducked. I'm not proud of my cringe reflex; I don't speak of it often, but it's there. I ducked and scurried out of reach. The little table afforded me a place to call my own. Chair legs, table legs, like a veritable "cave" of protection. I could look out and see the man's legs pacing back and forth, but he couldn't reach me.

"What's your problem?" He growled like an alpha dog.

Aowr. I acknowledged his position in this pack of two. He had the hands to open cans; I had to be subservient.

"You lucky bastard. You've got a reprieve. Goddamned shelter doesn't do intakes on the weekend. Goddamn it. They need a better business plan."

I laughed. I had no idea what all those words meant, but I do know when things are looking up. *Aowr.* Hunh-hunh.

"Maybe there's another one I can take you to." He scratched at his chin, then said, "Maybe there's a pit bull rescue. Yeah, that's it." He entertained himself for a long time, but at the end, he slammed his toy down. "Fuck it."

More words, but I knew that they were just sounds. I bent to lick my nethers. I was full, and, for the moment, safe.

Chapter Twenty-five

Today is his kid day. His court-approved, Sterling-approved visitation. He's given up trying to get Ariel here; instead, he will meet her at Sylvan Fields, where he will be forced to wait outside in the car until she drags herself down to join him. He'll take her to lunch at a restaurant he can no longer afford, while she texts her friends, no doubt complaining about her wasted afternoon. Then a negotiated trip to the mall, where she will test his patience by going from store to store, leaving him to cool his jets on a bench like some abandoned luggage, then home to Sylvan Fields, where Sterling will berate him for giving in to Ariel's questionable taste in clothing—this after he's bought her something he cannot afford to buy. Any hope of a consulting job, or employment in his field, has so far proven futile

Adam remembers to take the dog downstairs before leaving. The midmorning air is crystal cold, and he's come down with his bare feet tucked into his beat-up L.L. Bean slippers, and his parka is unzipped. "Hurry up."

The dog is happy to comply. Adam bends over with a plastic bag in his hand. He doesn't know if any neighbors are checking out his dog-owner manners, but he doesn't want to take the chance that someone will complain to the super that he has this dog. Even if it is only until the shelter reopens on Monday. No other shelter will take him. In bailing the dog out, Adam has signed a contract agreeing to return him to the same shelter. No bending of rules.

The dog nudges Adam with his nose, letting him know it's time to go in. If he had balls, they'd be frozen off.

"No more crapping in the house."

Aowr.

"Okay."

Adam dumps kibble in the bowl, fills a pot with cold water, and points at the futon. "You stay off."

The dog's mouth breaks open and the tongue lolls out in a gentleman's agreement.

"Yeah, right. Not till my back is turned." Adam locks the door behind him. He has no idea how long a dog can go without getting into trouble, but he figures he can hold on for the six hours or so that Ariel will tolerate Adam's company. Six at the most. He's just been out, he's been fed and watered, and Adam has thoughtfully left the television on so that the dog thinks he's got company. He shrugs back the fact that he has no idea if this dog has the self-control to behave. Then he consoles himself, thinking that, so far, he's crapped on the floor only once. Hasn't chewed anything, and hasn't barked at noises. If he's been hard to handle on the street, lunging at every passing dog, at least he's been good in the apartment.

Ariel saunters out of the house barely dressed. Her skinny rider's legs are encased in tights, which end midway down her shin, a skimpy floral skirt is wrapped around her waist, and her coat is wide open. In a nod to the season, she wears short Uggs on her feet, like Gina wears. Ariel's two thumbs are busy communicating with luckier friends. She gets into his car without a word, ignoring his "hi, honey." As Adam moves down the long shrub-lined driveway, Ariel finishes her texting and looks at him. "This car stinks!"

"You noticed?" He aims at droll, but it comes out weak.

"Whew. Smells like wet dog."

"Interesting that you should mention that. It is wet dog."

Suddenly, Ariel takes notice. Her eyes widen. "You have a dog?" Emphasis on the *you*. As if he had suddenly taken up bungee jumping.

"Temporarily."

"Can I see him?"

Adam recognizes a dilemma when it faces him. If he introduces Ariel to the dog, then gets rid of him, she's going to be as mad at him as ever. If he doesn't show her the dog, she'll be as mad at him as ever. The old "rock and hard place" situation where Adam feels so at home. "I've got him only for a day. No sense getting to know him."

Ariel shoves her hands into the sleeves of her coat, her slump eloquent of his failings. "Fine."

"I've booked us lunch at Trois Chevaliers." He knows this is Ariel's favorite high-end restaurant. He lets her have a little champagne when he takes her there. His pocketbook cries

McDonald's, but his pride and his credit card call for Trois Chevaliers.

"Fine."

"School going okay?"

"Fine."

"Any concerts or plays this year?"

"Not yet."

"How's your old pal Kiki?"

Her eye roll is not charming. "We're at different schools."

"Gran and Granny doing well?

"Guess so."

"Your mom okay?"

"Why do you keep asking me these questions? They're always the same and the answers are always the same. Ask Mom yourself."

Adam swallows back his reply: Unless Sterling wants something, she never answers his calls. Anything of a substantial nature between him and his ex-wife is carried out through intermediaries. Ariel, for good or ill, has become his only connection to his past life. His message board. Poor kid. No wonder she hates these forced dates.

Since he first noticed the shadow of her aunt's gestures in her gestures, Adam has seen more and more of Veronica in Ariel. It's as if the foreshortened memories of his sister overlay the reality of his sullen daughter. Ariel's preferred tone of voice echoes the distant memory of Veronica's angry words. *"I'm outta here, old man."* Not screamed, but enunciated clearly and with a layer of contempt that was nearly physical. Long-dormant thoughts of Veronica leap all too often to mind since his breakdown. He's being haunted by the specter of his sister in the expression on his daughter's face.

He tries again. "How's the horse?"

Ariel doesn't take the opportunity to wax on about her horse's abilities, cute moments, and funny habits as she used to with him. "Fine." She plugs an ear bud in and keeps her gaze on the scenery.

This is more painful to Adam than he thinks he can take. It's been going on so long that he wonders if Ariel will ever mellow toward him. What he's done, by having this meltdown, has forever corrupted him in her eyes. And Sterling is keeping it that way.

Ariel treats him like Veronica treated their father—with disdain. Which the old man deserved. She was right to flee the man who would give up his only son to DSS rather than be a single parent. Who left his five-and-a-half-year-old in the hands of strangers. Adam hasn't committed any sin as egregious as that, and yet he might as well have. Ariel treats him like a man in disgrace, barely concealing her contempt. Is it really a contempt more profound than the usual contempt of an adolescent for her parents, or is he becoming paranoid? It's not as if he'd chosen to leave the family home. He's been asked to leave it by a wife who would not stand by her man.

Veronica may have run away, but his father gave up on Veronica. Adam will not give up trying to stay in Ariel's life. He studies his daughter as they sit at a red light. "Why are you so mad at me?"

Ariel doesn't answer; her iPod blocks out the sound of his voice. He is nothing to her.

Chapter Twenty-six

Adam is startled awake. The dog is facing the door, standing close to where Adam has fallen asleep on the futon. There it is again, a soft knock. Wiping the sleep grizzle from his mouth, Adam drags himself off the futon. The dog barks, one sharp, meaningful yap. "Shut up."

The dog returns to his table cave, his job done.

It has been another week. The shelter is still closed, a water-main break having shut it down indefinitely. The animals have been dispersed to shelters across the state, stretching limited resources, and, no, Dr. Gil says, he can't take the dog to one of them. He'd pushed the rules by letting Adam have the dog in the first place. Adam has to return him to Animal Advocates.

Like a bad houseguest, the dog seems to have extended his stay indefinitely.

"I found this on my book rack and thought you might want it." Gina DeMarco stands outside of Adam's door. Her polar bear parka frames her oval face, the white of the faux fur contrasting with the olive tone of her skin. She's a little breathless, and her cheeks are pinked with the cold.

"Come in. Come in." Adam is embarrassed to be found like some old man in the middle of the day. He's in his undershirt and jeans, his sockless feet in old slippers. He fingers the remote control to shut off Judge Judy. No one has ever come to see him here. His erstwhile adversary in the animal rights wars is the first person to cross his threshold since his landlord handed him the keys. A latent civility awakens in him. "I was just going to make a cup of tea. Would you like one?" He hopes that his breath isn't offensive. Rafe served garlic mashed potatoes at lunch.

"I can't. I've left the store. I just wanted to give this to you." She hands him a thin book: *Your Pit Bull, What to Expect and What to Do.*

"You know that—"

"I know you're not keeping him, but you've got him till that shelter gets back in operation, so you might as well have it." She doesn't sound like a person bearing gifts. "No one who comes into my store is ever looking for a book like that. It was stuck in an order for books on tropical fish. Distributor said to keep it, that it was a mistake. You're welcome to it."

To be polite, Adam opens the thin book, which is filled with color photographs of dogs that sort of look like his dog. Like *this* dog. Except that these are posed and have equal ears. Chapters offer history, breed standards, and training—housebreaking, commands like *sit, stay, heel.* Adam glances down at the dog, who is happily taking Gina's petting; he's rolled over to expose his belly to her fingertips.

"Thanks."

"Read it." Gina flips her hood back up. "You should know

something about the dog if you're going to just foist him off on someone."

"Once the shelter is open—"

"Yeah. I know. And you know that's death row."

Adam sets the book down on the coffee table. "Okay. Thank you for bringing it over."

"No problem." She pulls the front door open, and Adam feels a wash of disappointment.

"Wait, I'll bring you a cup of tea if you want."

Gina folds back the hood. She studies him with eyes the color of olive oil, eyes that suggest she hasn't forgotten his association with the cosmetics industry. Then she softens. "That would be nice." *Nahss.* That soft clue to a previous life. "It's been a slow day."

"Okay, then."

"Bring him."

"Why?"

"Just bring him."

Clutching two travel mugs filled with hot water in one hand and the dog's leash in the other, Adam dashes across the street between cars waiting at the red light. The dog lopes beside him, his satchel mouth open as if this is some kind of game, looking for all the world like a pet out for a romp with its person. Adam doesn't look at the dog, just hopes no other dog appears while he's carrying two cups of hot water.

Inside the pet shop, the air is fuggy with warmth and the scent of aquarium water. Adam is greeted by the squawks of the parrots, his eye caught by the tropical flash of color in a winter world. He sets the travel mugs down on the counter and fishes out two tea bags he's thoughtfully put in a plastic bag. "I couldn't manage the sugar and milk, not with both hands busy, so I'll just go next door and see what he's got."

Gina leans her elbows down on the counter, a posture that elongates her neck. Her molasses-colored hair is loose, and a layer curves against her cheek, framing it. "I've got both here. Don't bother yourself." She chooses a travel mug, one he's picked up at Dunkin' Donuts, and levers the cap off.

"I only have Tetley." Adam proffers the plastic bag, lets Gina choose which sachet of tea she wants. He is still in his coat, still gripping the end of the leash.

"Adam, why don't you let go of him? He can't get into trouble here; there's nothing much he can reach."

Adam drops the end of the leash, but the dog stays put, unaware that he's free to move around.

"How's he doing?"

"Except for taking over the futon, and trying to attack any dog he meets on the street, I guess you can say he's being good."

"Being on a leash does that to some dogs. They feel threatened."

"Seems more like he's the threat."

Gina bobs her tea bag, then scuttles it with a spoon she has produced along with the milk and sugar. "I think he's going to be a good dog. He's quiet."

"I haven't heard any complaints about barking."

"No, I mean his demeanor. Some dogs are all movement. This guy likes to take it all in." Gina looks over the edge of the counter at the dog, who looks up at her with adoration. "He's a good boy." This is addressed to the dog, whose tail ticks left and right.

"Are you sure you don't want him?"

"I would, if I didn't already—"

"Have three greyhounds." Adam takes the spoon from Gina and retrieves his tea bag from the bottom of his Starbucks mug.

The object of the conversation suddenly finds it too hard to remain sitting and flops to the floor, stretching out on his side, releasing a contented grunt.

Gina and Adam pay close attention to their travel mugs. There is nothing else obvious to talk about. This is suddenly like a bad first date. A bad first blind date. There's only one thing they have in common—not the workplace, nor a school, nor a mutual friend, but a dog. The awkwardness of being imperfect strangers. Neither wants to resort to the weather, but no topic presents itself for a prolonged moment. Adam is unaccountably tongue-tied and wonders how fast he can drink his tea and get out of there.

Gina DeMarco sips her tea, grimaces at the scorch of hot water through the small aperture, and asks Adam a question. "If I can find any in the back room, would you like a cookie?"

"Sure, but don't go to any trouble."

Gina disappears and Adam breathes a sigh. What an imbecile he is. Why did he think she'd want his company? When Gina comes back with an opened package of Fig Newtons, he takes one and quickly asks her a question to fill in the silence. "How long have you owned the shop?"

Gina nips a corner off of her cookie and shrugs. "It seems like all my life, but I've only owned it per se since my grandfather passed. About twelve years. Before that, I just worked here. Once he started getting a little confused, he stopped waiting on the customers and just tended the tanks. Then one day, he turned the water temperature up on the angelfish and essentially cooked them. I came in and found him scooping them up in the net and then putting it back in the water and wondering why they were belly-up." Gina shrugs, a delicate gesture. "I couldn't leave him alone in here. But we spent a lot of time together even as he declined, so, in the end, I never had to put him in a nursing home. That's all that I wanted; he'd been so good to me."

"You were responsible for him, not your parents?"

"No. A long time ago, my mother and stepfather sent me up north to live with Grandpa; we haven't been much in touch since." Gina's remark has the worn spots of an old story.

Adam tastes the fig on his tongue, rough and sweet. "Where'd you come from originally?"

"I was born in Louisville, but we lived all around, North and South Carolina, Texas. Any place with an army base, any place hot." Gina leans her elbows on the counter. A barricade of donation jars leaves her a loophole through which to conduct business: greyhound rescue, miniature horse rescue, food bank, breast cancer awareness, therapy dogs, Thoroughbred rescue. Rescue this one; rescue that one; rescue me.

She rearranges the jars, soldiering them. "I have another stool back here if you want."

The space behind the service counter is narrow, an alley between the shelves on the wall behind them and the countertop with its displays of flea and tick remedies, pamphlets on how to feed your gerbil, your Betta fish, how to take care of your saltwater aquarium. Adam sits on the wooden stool he finds tucked under the overhang of the desk and sets down his tea. He pulls another cookie out of the package. "Your dad was in the army?"

"Dad and stepdad. My father was killed in Nam. My stepdad was his buddy."

"A lot of our guys are vets who served in Vietnam."

"Your guys?"

Adam realizes the trap he's set for himself. How to explain his "job" to Gina? Stein would have something to say about this, something along the lines of "Here's your chance. Start with the truth and see where it gets you." Stein is determined that Adam give up his sense that he has any control over history.

"I volunteer at the Fort Street Center."

"Good for you." Gina is looking at him with approval, ratcheting up her estimation.

A fan of dismay colors his cheeks. "Actually, it's not exactly volunteering. It's community service." Adam sees the approval meter slide back down. He hasn't practiced how to tell this story; he doesn't know whether to blurt out the salient facts, or just hope she doesn't want to hear more. Gina is intent on her tea, adding more sugar, a dollop more of the milk from the quart she's found in the back of the store. Intent on not asking the question he can see forming itself as she deliberately pays careful attention to doctoring her tea.

The dog, which has been meandering all around the store, dragging the four-foot leash behind him, suddenly notices that he's on the wrong side of the counter from the people. He figures out how to get back there and comes up to Adam, pressing his blunt nose on Adam's leg.

"Look who's here." Gina reaches across Adam's knees to pet the dog. "You want a cookie, too?" Gina produces a dog biscuit, which the dog gently takes out of her hand. "He's a sweetie, although I'm sure he's been fought." She reaches farther over to scratch the dog on the scar on his chest. Her elbow touches Adam's leg. He thinks he feels the touch of her hair beneath his chin, but he keeps his eye on the dog. "They say once they've done that, there's no saving them. But that's not always true."

Adam sips his tea, doesn't look at the dog or at Gina.

"You could call him Cassius. Or how about George? You know, Clay and Foreman? Good fighters who were good men."

"I don't think it's a good idea to name him."

"Because you're not keeping him?"

"Because I'm not keeping him."

Gina pulls on her bottom lip, crosses her legs. "Let's shoot the gorilla."

"I'm sorry?"

"We've got unfinished business, and I think that if we can just have the conversation, we'll feel better."

Adam is stymied. Is she talking about his community service? Then it hits him. "We sold the division; the Fraîche Crème product was discontinued."

"Yeah, but did you really stop animal testing?"

Adam is wholly unprepared for this. "Experiments were under way. Those were finished. No new experiments were begun. And no more rabbits were used." It's close enough to the truth. "I left the division shortly after your protest."

"I know. You didn't leave the division; you were promoted. I remember reading about it in the *Globe*. Best thing we ever did for you." After all these years, there is still an obvious and righteous anger at Dynamic's policies. The hand not holding the travel mug is shaking slightly, as if adrenaline is pouring through Gina.

Adam feels his own righteous anger simmering. He may have been promoted, which would have happened eventually anyway, but for six weeks Gina and her group made his life a living hell. Eggs thrown at his brand-new Lexus, the predecessor to the one he is still driving; damning signs held by NATE volunteers who lined the public thoroughfare leading to Dynamic's access road; shouts and accusations broadcast every night like clockwork on the local television channels; interviews with talking heads, who condemned him personally. Holed up in his division headquarters eighteen hours a day, consulting with public-relations people and attorneys, he barely got home in time to change for the latest dinner party or benefit; never had time to see Ariel before she was put to bed by the nanny.

A jangle as the pet shop door opens breaks the moment. Gina greets her customer by name. She takes a little while to wait on her customer, a middle-aged man fussing about pH balances in his tank. She discusses this problem with him, her elegant brows arced in concern for his trouble, but once she glances back at Adam, who's still behind the counter, her cold glance tells him the topic isn't finished. The customer pays for his purchases and jangles out the door. Once again they are alone.

"He's a regular. Can't seem to keep his fish alive, but he keeps trying. One of these days, he'll either give up or get it right."

"Sounds like the rest of us." Adam swallows the last of his tea, which is still hot and which burns his throat as it goes down. "You can't dwell on the past. You have to move forward."

Gina nods and turns her attention back to her fast-cooling tea. "I understand. Sometimes there are things you just want to put behind you."

"That's right." Adam sets his empty travel mug beside Gina's on the counter. His is a little taller, a little narrower. The handles touch. "Although I'm learning that even if you put things behind you, they aren't gone. They follow along like a phantom." Unaccountably, the image of the dog running down the street with the pole trailing along behind pops into Adam's mind and he realizes that very possibly this is that dog.

For his part, the dog makes a little *rrrooor rrooor* noise and his tail thumps against the old wooden floor.

Gina remains at the register, fiddling with the arrangement of bills in the drawer, quiet.

"I should go."

"Thanks for the tea." Gina hands him the two empty mugs. Slips the cookies back into their package, busies herself with small tasks.

Adam comes out from behind the counter, the dog behind him, the leash trailing. He feels deflated, disappointed, as if he's failed at something, some attempt.

Adam stops at the doorway. "It's history, Gina. Over and done with."

"Yeah. Ancient history. We were both a lot younger then." A hint of sarcasm.

"We didn't understand what we were doing." He hates that he's defensive.

"Doesn't excuse it."

"Maybe not, but a whole lot more has gone on in the world since then."

"Yeah, Enron, nine-eleven, Iraq, recession. Makes the eyes of a bunny seem somehow frivolous."

"What do you want me to do?"

"I don't know." She sounds just a little defeated. "I guess you could make up for it." She looks at the dog meaningfully. "A little payback?"

Adam tugs on the leash, bringing the dog to heel. The sound of the bells against the plate-glass door hurts his ears.

Chapter Twenty-seven

My man and I have taken to long walks now that the weather is a bit better. Sometimes we even run, although I don't like that quite as much. I prefer an olfactory perambulation to a training-level exercise, but, hey, when in Rome. He's developing some stamina. We go as far now as the outer edges of my old territory. Once in a while, when he slows down enough, I catch a whiff of an old friend still haunting the area. Sometimes, I pick up the scent of one of the boys. I tug on the leash when that happens. I don't want to go back into that cellar.

He still hasn't put me in a pit, nor given me any bouts with sparring partners.

Life here is pretty good. I do spend a fair amount of time alone, but I'm free to wander this crib, stretch, lap water, and sleep the untrammeled sleep of the secure. We go for rides. I am not one of those dogs who hang their heads out the window. I sit with dignity in the backseat, casting my glance right and left, surveying with the utmost authority the cityscape rolling out before me. Sometimes we go to places where I can smell my own kind, places like where we met. I can hear the vocalizations of the lost even from the quiet seclusion of the car, where I jump into the front seat the minute he leaves.

Each time, he comes back out and gets into the car without speaking. Each time, I know enough to scarper over the seat into the back.

After one of these visits, he pulled up to a stretch of sidewalk and left me there, the window rolled down just enough to let the enticing scents of the scene filter down to me, but not far enough for me to get my head out. I glowered at a man in a cap who stuck a bit of paper under the wiper, but I kept my mouth shut. I was bored, so I leapt into the front seat for a change of view. That's when I saw my mentor's man crouched against the wall of the place with the warm foodish smells. His street scent wafted my way, so I was certain of his identity, and I got a little excited, hoping that maybe my mentor was reunited with him. But no. He was alone, unaccompanied on his bundle of blanket, shivering in the cold air, desultorily thrusting out his bare hand with a cup in it at passing humans. "Got any change?" His whimper of submission rarely noted by those other people.

I saw my man come out of the building into which he'd disappeared, watched him coming to the car, walking past my mentor's man without stopping, without acknowledging him. He yanked the piece of paper that the man in the cap had stuck under the wiper, then climbed into his seat. Then he dropped his head like a puppy being scolded. "You should have been his dog."

Suddenly, he pushed open his door and grabbed me by the

leash, pulling me out faster than I could comply. We marched over to the squatting man, and my man started barking at him. The othe guy barked back, and I hunched my shoulders, lowered my head, waited for some clue as to what my man expected me to do.

"Take him," my man barked.

"Fuck you," my mentor's man snarled.

"He needs you," my man snapped.

"I don't need him. He ain't Benny," my mentor's man howled.

The guy on the end of my leash yanked me back off my feet and wrenched open the car door. I jumped in quickly and pressed myself against the opposite door. I might have growled then. A little growl of protest: *What the fuck is the matter with you?* I was a little carried away with the moment. It was as close to a fight as I'd been in a while. Yes, I definitely growled, low and in concert with his vocalizations.

He looked at me with these big human eyes of alarm. We were two alpha males faced off over authority. "Don't you ever do that again." I understood his meaning, if not the exact words. I waited, expecting the strike. It's what my boys would have done. It's what I expected. Maybe I even relished the idea—we'd finally get our cards on the table. But he didn't. He slammed the door shut and climbed into his own seat. I was thrown against the back of the seat as he pulled away from the curb.

Chapter Twenty-eight

Adam is ushered into the judge's chambers. The judge is waiting, standing with his back to the room, his forefinger running along the green spines of the law books soldiered on several shelves. He is intent on his search, says nothing to Adam, who is left standing in the middle of the small room. It's an old technique, one Adam used to employ himself with underlings who had inflated ideas of their worth. Keep them standing just until the silence becomes painful, a reminder that your time is way more important than theirs. A little nonverbal, nonphysical bullying. Even so, Adam is beginning to think the judge is overacting.

The timing of this meeting is not good, squeezed in between sessions in a very full docket, and Adam knows that he won't have a lot of time to impress the judge with his progress. He offered to postpone the meeting, but the judge said no, that if Adam could wait until lunch recess, they could get this over with. Adam doesn't know whether to take that as good news or bad. He wonders now if the judge has had his lunch, or if he's hungry and impatient.

It's been six months. Adam has half a year to go at Fort Street; he's worked his way up to ladling soup. He knows most of the regulars by name. Big Bob likes him. He likes his co-workers. What else can the judge want from him? Delaying his conversation with Adam, the judge is weighting it with more purpose than a simple "checking in" requires. He fully expects the man to spin around, point a finger, and . . . And what, Adam doesn't allow himself to imagine.

"Have you learned any humility yet?" The judge has indeed spun around; although he isn't pointing a finger, he does hold a massive law tome out as if it were a Bible and Adam was expected to swear on it.

Adam flushes with anger. He hears the singing in his ears; he feels the sway of rising blood pressure rock him. He breathes deeply. He breathes again. He tastes the iron on his tongue and swallows. "I believe that Carmondy's report will tell you that I'm performing my duties well and with a good attitude." Big Bob has shared his report with Adam, at least his one-paragraph evaluation. He cites Adam's willingness to help in ways that go beyond his job description, and they both know that's spin on his grumbling obedience to Bob in finding Jupe and at least trying to locate Jupe's dog.

"Hmm." Judge Johnson motions to the folding chair opposite his desk.

Adam lowers himself.

"I suppose you think that I should commute your sentence? That six months of good behavior is enough?"

Adam clears his throat. "No. I don't."

This clearly surprises the judge. "Why?"

"I mean that I don't believe you will." Adam pinches the crease in his trousers, crosses one leg over the other in a deliberately casual manner. He understands this man. He knows that the judge would prefer him to be more of a supplicant, that he kowtow in the manner of a man who has seen the light. As he probably should. There is nothing more Adam wants than to be released from his community service. It's taking up far too much of his time, time he should be spending focusing on the consulting business he believes will lead to a good living. He just has to get his first client, who will then recommend him to more clients. An infinite chain of clients all leading to a new brand of success.

Ishmael and Rafe joked with him yesterday. "Won't see you here again; you'll be outta here faster than Big Brown out the gate on Derby day."

"I'll send you a postcard." He was surprised at the fleeting moment of nostalgia that stung his throat. Adam assuaged his momentary self-indulgence with a mental promise to make sure his charitable giving included the Fort Street Center from now on, or at least once he began to recover from his personal recession. "Besides, it's not even on the table that I get off. Don't take my name off the locker just yet." But, even as he said it, Adam knew that he was whistling through the graveyard.

Which is the same reason he's shown up in the judge's chambers in his best suit, with his Cole Haan oxfords spit-polished and, just for effect, his battered briefcase with the mileage scuffed into its leather. Men like Judge Johnson belong to the same golf club Adam does, or did. Sterling got the membership. Men like Judge Johnson attend the same dinner parties and charity galas as Adam, eat the same hors d'oeuvres and drink the same overpriced wines. Except that Adam hasn't seen an hors d'oeuvre in nearly a year, and his solitary drink of choice remains scotch.

It's why he's challenging the judge, calling his bluff. In any other arena, Adam would be Judge Johnson's peer. They'd laugh over drinks and debate economic strategy. Adam wonders if the judge understands this.

The judge sits heavily into his high-backed black chair. He leans forward, his elbows on the blotter in front of him, studying Adam over the frame of his Buddy Holly glasses. His rheumy eyes are unreadable.

Adam picks a dog hair from his knee. A news brief in the local paper announced that the shelter has reopened. Maybe later today he'll make another attempt at getting rid of the dog. He's tried other shelters, but they don't want what he has. At the only one he got to that would, the staffer was blunt. These dogs don't get adopted out; the ones who have fought, they get a one-way ticket. "The pit bulls who are voluntarily surrendered are humanely euthanized." Voluntarily surrendered. Adam had dragged the dog back to his car, frustrated but not cruel. He doesn't want the dog, but he isn't going to be responsible for its death. Adam thinks about Gina. He saw her walking down the street this morning, a trio of deerlike greyhounds gliding beside her. He got his latest bag of dog food from Stop & Shop; if there's any left over, he'll donate it to the shelter when he takes the dog back.

Adam thinks, or maybe prays, that the judge will free him.

"You're right. You've made an improvement, but you're going to finish out your sentence. I'll see you in September. Make an appointment with my secretary on your way out."

The judge cracks open the massive law book, pushes his glasses up into place, and forgets that Adam was ever in the room.

The foyer door sticks a little and Adam kicks it open with the toe of his three-hundred-dollar shoes. He mounts the stairs, his pace slowing to a trudge by the time he reaches the third-floor landing. The weight of his sentence bears down on him. The seemingly endless months of servile punishment, the complication of trying to get his self-employment up and running, and the grip that the Fort Street Center has on his life bear down on Adam step by step, until he thinks he cannot move. He didn't know how much he was counting on release from his community service until it was denied him. He's been picturing himself a free man, ready to take his rightful place in society. He's learned a lesson; he's working on his humility. He'll be back in the saddle, his powers restored to him fully within the next six months. Except that he'll still be serving swill to the homeless. Well, not swill exactly; Rafe would take great exception to that term. Rafe. Ishmael. Mike and Big Bob. Christ, they all but gave him a going-away party. Even they thought he was rehabilitated.

The dog waits, as always, sitting in the dead center of the room, as if he hasn't spent the intervening hours on the futon. The rearranged throw pillows with the deep depressions in them are enough of a clue, but he always pretends innocence, bowing and yawning like some sort of slave to his potentate. Every day, Adam asks, "Have you been on the couch?" And every day, the dog just wags his spiky tail and grins in a "Who me?" masquerade.

Today, Adam doesn't even look at the dog. He drops his briefcase on the floor, pulls off his fine wool topcoat and drops it on the dog hair–strewn futon, yanks at the tie at his throat, and goes into the galley kitchen. The Dewar's liter is half-empty. There is a dirty glass on the side of the sink and Adam takes it. Without even rinsing out the dregs of last night's drink, he is about to pour two inches of scotch into the glass, when his cell phone rings. Adam sees that it's Ariel and he sets the empty glass down. "Hi, honey."

"Can I skip out on you Saturday? Taylor's having a big birthday party at the Copley and we're all going early to shop. I really want—"

"Okay. Go. Have fun, and tell Taylor happy birthday for me." Adam presses the end key even before his daughter can say thank you. She's adept at finding reasons not to spend Saturdays with him, and this is just one more he won't ever get back.

Then Sterling calls. At some point in the last year, their lawyers have stepped out of the middle and she has found it possible to call and badger him with regularity. Perhaps she is even finding pleasure in it.

There is no preamble, no easing into a conversation with Sterling these days. She simply jumps into the topic, like a missile, allowing him no moment of transition from "Hello" to "I want." It is almost like she doesn't want to allow him to speak, that something in his voice might remind her of their life together. Once upon a time, when they spoke on the phone, they listened to each other. They signed off from every conversation with some affectionate postscript: "Love you," or "I'll be home soon," or "Miss you." Now it's the sound of a dial tone. Dismissed.

Worse, once she's gotten the demands out of the way, Adam knows that she'll start reciting his flaws to him: his temper, his untrustworthiness, his destroying her life. Meaning her social standing, which, as far as he can see, hasn't dipped on the sociometer one bit. She's taken their friends with her. She still has the houses. She still chairs the charity events that make the evening news.

Sterling calls only to arrange things to her own advantage, to demand something of him, to treat him as if he were an underling. He has so disappointed her that she is taking it out on him one phone call at a time.

So it is with great reluctance that Adam presses the answer button. Instead of the woman with whom Adam expected to spend the rest of his life, Sterling has become a sledgehammer, beating him over the head with his sins at every chance.

This time, she belabors Ariel's sudden need for her own car. She's taking her driver's test in a month, and Sterling believes that every sixteen-year-old should be given a car for her birthday, a Miata or a Volvo. Something safe, something prestigious. Something that will be the envy of everyone else's sixteen-year-old daughters.

Somewhere along the line, Adam has tuned Sterling's voice out. She is like a buzzing bee, or the chime of someone else's cell phone. Annoying, but hard to swat away. He holds the cell phone away from his ear and wanders around the small apartment. He straightens up one of the throw pillows the dog has flattened out. He rinses the dirty jelly glass, fills it with water. Little words, miniaturized by the phone held at a distance, like some tiny Sterling trapped in the flat oblong of his phone, keeps *zzzzing* through the instrument. He hears individual words; a phrase here and there comes out of the phone with unexpected clarity. They should consider something that might haul the horse trailer that they should invest in if Ariel is going to attend the major shows.

Adam dumps the glass of water into the dog's bowl and unscrews the cap from the bottle of scotch.

Little Sterling's little buzzing voice is farther and farther away. The cell phone is on the countertop. His glass is filled with scotch. There is a moment of silence. Then he hears her miniature voice calling out from the instrument, wondering if he is still there. He doesn't know. Is he? Still there? The Adam that he once was? He can't afford to buy a full tank of gas, much less a high-priced vehicle for a kid who treats him with as much contempt as Ariel does. She doesn't need the latest status symbol, the latest keeping-up-with-the-Joneses item on the list. The idea that their little princess might be deprived is ludicrous. Adam knows about deprived. Deprived is not getting new sneakers when your toes are coming through the old ones.

Adam presses the end button hard enough to shut the phone off completely. Gently he puts it on the counter, pours another finger of scotch into his almost full jelly glass, and goes into the living room.

The truth is, if things had remained the same, if he hadn't scuttled his own life with the auger of fear and temper, he would have loved shopping for a car for Ariel. He would have relished the delight on her face at the sight of a brand-new Volvo or Miata, or whatever was the coolest ride these days, in the driveway with a big bow on it. He wouldn't have deprived Ariel for all the world.

A bubble of anxiety juxtaposes itself against the lead weight of despair; he's not free of Fort Street. How is he ever going to get beyond this descent into poverty? Not since he was an undergraduate driving buses far into the night in order to pay for his education has Adam debated the cost of national brand cornflakes against the store brand. Not since he was in his first year of graduate school has Adam let a bill sit unopened, or paid the minimum due.

The table, under which the dog has ducked, only the tip of his tail exposed, is covered with unopened bills, along with a laptop he is too tired to open, too tired to use to troll the online job searches. Too tired to think.

Adam sips his jelly glass of scotch. The burn diminishes with each swallow.

Chapter Twenty-nine

It was a little awkward to witness, his whimpering like that. Then the full-blown crying. I'd never witnessed something like that in a human. Plenty of my own kind howl, but this was painful to hear. He'd stopped playing with his toy, after which he began shouting so that I hid myself beneath the table. If he started making sounds like that, I wasn't going to hang around. I knew what an angry human could do. I wasn't committed to being here. First chance, I was going to book it. Frankly, I had no idea why I was here in the first place. We weren't training. He wasn't putting me into the pit. He barely acknowledged my presence. I kept to my side of the room; he kept to his. There was none of that pair-bond stuff going on like I'd seen with my mentor and his man, or the guy and the little bitch that helped me get free of that pole, or even the Labrador and his person.

He got quiet. Very quiet. He sat on the futon with his drink in his hand and stared out at the empty room until I put myself into his view just to give him something to look at. Long tears ran from his open eyes to the edges of his face. He sipped and wept. Sipped and wept. I lay on the rug but kept my eyes on him.

When his glass was empty, he lay down, but the sounds didn't cease. Finally I got up, stretched east and west, shook myself, and then sat. If he'd stopped making the sounds, I might have just wandered off. But the sounds went on, a primal sound of despair, of great anguish. Not like a rabbit in a cat's jaws, or even like the losers in the pit. This was more like the howls of those who ended up in the shelter with me, the ones who were lost, separated from their humans, unable to fend for themselves. The sound of abandonment. Not unlike the sad moan of my mentor when he realized he wasn't going to be reunited with his man. Or even a little like the sound I made myself when he was taken beyond the door at the end of the hall.

What else could I have done? I'm only canine, I had to help. I pushed myself up beside him, nosing his hand until it reached for my ears, until I felt his fingers slide along the edges of my good ear, and then I did it. I nuzzled him. I stuck the tip of my nose against his cheek and touched his face with my tongue. He tasted salty. Not a bad flavor. He didn't push me away, so I pressed myself closer, edging against him until we shared the futon. He draped an arm over my back and pressed his face against mine. And then we slept.

Chapter Thirty

Adam dreams that he is walking through a busy hallway. There is something he has to do, but he can't remember what it is. His arms are heavy with the weight of something he cannot see. He is bumped right and left by the crowd of people walking in the opposite direction. He wakes with a start.

The dog has managed to press him against the back of the futon, his whole body stretched out alongside Adam's, his boxy muzzle tucked into Adam's neck, the moist dog breath tickling him. Adam struggles against the weight of the dog to sit up. Abruptly, the dog dismounts from the futon, stretches, and yawns. "At least one of us has had a decent sleep." The dog, clearly pleased at his piracy, shakes vigorously and sits in front of Adam.

Adam strokes the dog's head, noticing just how soft it is. The bone of his skull is rock-hard beneath his hand, but his short brindled coat is as soft and smooth as silk. Adam does it again. The dog opens his mouth and grins, makes a little chuffing noise; his tail ticks back and forth on the floor. "You are one ugly dog." Adam's tone soothes the dog into raptures. "I should call you Uggie, boy." The dog stands up, whipping his tail in excitement at Adam's compliments.

"The shelter is open again, you know? Dr. Gil left me a message."

The dog begins to dance on his forefeet. Excited at this unusual conversation.

"You ready to go back?"

Hunnha hunnha.

"Maybe tomorrow."

Adam gets to his feet. The sky beyond his window is dark, and Adam is uncertain of the time. It could be evening or the dark of predawn. He feels as if he's been run over. The jelly glass is upended beside the futon. Adam checks the microwave clock. Three in the morning. He hasn't let the dog out. He hasn't fed him.

The last of the February nights is cold, clear, and astoundingly silent. Adam takes the dog for a complete walk around the block, letting the piercingly cold air clear out his own lungs and fuzzy brain. It is so quiet, so still, Adam lets the dog off the leash to sniff around an empty lot. The only traffic is a slow police car; the only other soul, the lone cop. He looks directly at Adam, rolls down the window, appearing almost glad of an interruption in his rounds.

"Just walking the dog." Adam holds up the leash.

"Leash laws here."

"I know. Thought I'd flaunt them a little."

The cop smiles and drives off.

The dog is gone a long time, and suddenly Adam wonders if he'll come back. What if he bolts? What if, having been a street dog, he thinks Adam has just set him free? Adam has never let him off the leash before, and he has no way of knowing if the animal will come even if he calls. Adam strains to listen, to see if he can pinpoint where the dog is in the half-acre empty lot. He's disappeared. Run off. Adam pictures the empty bowls on his kitchen floor.

Adam gathers the leash into a coil. He can't even call the dog; he's nameless. He's had the animal for almost three weeks and has refused to call him anything but "boy" or "buddy" or "you." Refused to consider him anything more than an annoying houseguest. "Come, boy. Here, buddy."

The feel of his soft coat was like satin beneath Adam's fingers. The softest thing he's touched since Ariel's baby skin.

In the distance, the sound of snuffling.

"Hey, boy!"

From out of the darkness comes the dog, tail wagging.

An unaccountable sense of relief flows through Adam, and his hand is shaking a little as he clips the leash to the collar. "Good boy." He pats the dog on the head.

Adam goes into the bathroom and pees, brushes his teeth quickly, and pulls off his sweatshirt and jeans, which he drops into a basket he's stuck in the bathroom for dirty laundry. He climbs into his unmade bed. He lies still, then calls the dog. "You coming?"

His last thought before falling into a deep sleep is that he can't imagine what Gina will say if he tells her he's keeping the dog. The dog that is snoring at the foot of his bed. But, somehow, it comforts him to think that she might approve.

Chapter Thirty-one

I almost didn't come to his call. I was loose for the first time in a long time and I honestly thought that's what he intended when he took off the leash. We'd communicated, him through touching me with his hands, me with touching him with my nose. A piece of the barrier that we both respected lowered a little bit. Like unrelated puppies, we slumbered on, tangled up, one with the other. So when he let me go, I thought that was his way of acknowledging that I should strike out on my own once again. Our time together—for what purpose, I still didn't get—was done.

We went outside in the night, the neighborhood around us quiet as only city neighborhoods can be when the people are inside and the cars are furtive. The night animals, the mouse and rat, the city raccoon and skunk, lurked around every corner, but I ignored them, attached as I was on the end of the leash. Not much point in it.

There were no other dogs around; no scent more recent than that afternoon collided with my searching nose. I marked fresh territory. When we got to the empty place and the man unsnapped the leash, I took it that he was releasing me. Well and good, I thought. Fair enough. He's served me fairly well, and I've behaved myself. Now is the time to scoot. Go find that warm shelter beneath a bush, tuck my nose under my tail, and let go of this soft life of bed and kibble. We're done. Shake hands all around and cheerio.

I headed out into the dark, quartering the empty place, checking for the signs of other dogs, the warm smell of vole, of future meals. I became intoxicated with the odors of free creatures. Feces told me of scavengers and gourmets, of those who fed themselves, and those who enjoyed the servitude of humans, the easy dependability of scheduled meals.

Like I'd been enjoying for this little while. I knew that unlikely show of submission on his part wasn't to be mistaken for subservience. I wasn't going to fall for a pathetic belly-up as total submission. No sirree. We'd kept it simple: He fed me; I was pleasant enough. I didn't owe him anything. Conversely, he didn't owe me anything, either. I felt sorry for him in that moment, that's all. He was grieving, and I offered a momentary solace. That didn't mean we were ever going to be partners.

I heard his voice, understood the meaning, if not the words. A pat on the leg, a low whistle. I continued quartering, but I was torn between freedom and a warm place to sleep. Images of old pals and trash cans insinuated themselves into my thoughts as I found traces of both beneath the hard-packed snow.

He called again, a little louder, a little more concerned. Had I misunderstood? Had he been only allowing me a little privacy, a little decision-making latitude? I raised my head, stood as still as a pointer on mark. A sharpish breeze caught at the scraps of paper nestled among the ragged hills of iced-over snow, lifting them into eddies. I shivered. I really didn't have to sleep rough tonight. I could just go with him. Take the leash.

Come, boy. Here, buddy.

There was nothing in my experience that led me to believe that human beings were ever trustworthy. When I lived in the cellar, the boys who handled us could be pleasant enough, especially when I was winning. Or, with no warning, they could also kick us across the room. Why should I deem a comfortable moment between us a harbinger of a better life and not some anomaly? What did he mean by letting me go and then making those petulant noises? An assertion of pack leadership? No, I'd keep myself to myself. Pick the pack I wanted to belong to.

It was when he went quiet that I heard what he meant. In the absolute stillness of the winter night, I heard him sigh, a sound of capitulation, of disappointment.

I went back to him. Greeted him in the spirit of compromise. Attach your leash to my collar for now. I'll wait till spring to book it.

Good boy.

Chapter Thirty-two

Adam feels a surge of jitters as he snaps the leash to the dog's collar. The hand-painted parrot is turned over to the WELCOME side and the lights are on in Gina's store. It feels as though those little fish that swim across the rainbow of her storefront are in his belly. He's only recently gotten it: the A to Z tropical fish on her window are angelfish and zebra fish. He's tried not to stand in his own window as much, still smarting from Gina's remark about his life. Well, he's about to show her that he can make changes if he wants. He's talked to Stein about this, about this irrational need to explain himself to a woman he has no relationship with, or, worse, who is an antagonistic acquaintance. Stein wants him to examine his motivations.

Gina didn't talk him into keeping the dog. It was his decision, and one he's going to have to live with, or live to regret, for a long time. He wants to make it clear to Gina that while he is committed to keeping the dog, she hasn't shamed him into it; and to get some advice on training. This business of lurching at every passing dog on the street has got to stop. Maybe she can recommend another book.

"Come on." He still hasn't named the animal. Each time a name comes to him, he auditions it to see if the dog will respond. At this point, Boy is the most likely one. The dog neither comes to nor obeys any softly spoken word. Adam has gone through the little book on pit bulls, but it hasn't provided much guidance. So, for now, it's all intuitive. When he picks up the empty bowl, the dog comes. When he rattles the leash, the dog goes to the door. Any sudden movement, like when he cracked his shin on the coffee table and let out a yelp, startles the dog back into his hiding place beneath the table. This is not Rin Tin Tin. This is not Lassie. This isn't even Marmaduke.

"Let's go see Gina."

The year has tripped over into March, but the air is still pure winter. It is just the time of year when warmer weather is impossible to imagine. The men at the Fort Street Center are hardened by this weather, cheeks and lips chapped and noses blue-veined and reddened along the edges. They take the plastic trays hot from the Hobart out of the rack and hold them close. They wear layers of clothing, castoffs donated to the Salvation Army or directly to the center. A big cardboard box sits in the foyer, where donors can drop off unwanted clothing. These days, it's pretty much empty; anything wearable is on someone's body.

Gina is standing framed in the doorway as they cross the street, and for an instant Adam thinks that she's been waiting for him. She turns away; whoever she's been watching for hasn't come. Of course she's not waiting for him.

.   .   .

The parrots squawk a reasonable imitation of a greeting as Adam and the dog enter the shop. Gina is standing with a fishnet in one hand. Despite the cold outside, the shop is warm and she is wearing a short sleeved, button-front white blouse that fits her shape and leaves a lovely triangle at the base of her throat. Her hair is down, softly grazing her shoulders. She doesn't look like a shopgirl; she looks like she may have a date after work. There is a drop of water clinging to her wrist.

When she sees that it is Adam and the dog standing in the middle of her small shop, she hangs the dripping fishnet on a hook and folds her arms across her middle. She doesn't smile, but her expressive brows arc into question marks. "Thought that shelter was open again."

Adam leans over and runs his hand down the length of the dog's body. The dog's tail swings gently side to side, but his eyes are on Gina. "I'm going to keep him." He waits, his own eyes on Gina's face, his lips parted in expectation of her reaction. He waits to see if the hostility with which she usually looks at him will, even for an instant, abate.

"What made you change your mind?" Suspicious, not approving.

Adam shrugs, a gesture nearly lost in the bulk of his jacket. "I don't know. Things." He is disappointed, feels like a kid with an underappreciated crayon drawing. "Got used to him."

Very slowly, reluctantly, a smile comes to Gina's lips. "If you want my opinion, I think you're doing the right thing."

The disappointment lifts; he has no idea why he wants Gina to be nice to him, but he just does, and even this mild approval feels nice. "I was hoping you'd say that. I still think I'm a little crazy." The dog sits, drops his jaw into a cavernous yawn.

"Have you called Dr. Gil? To let him know?"

"No. Why should I?"

"He's going to want to know. Given your"—she hesitates—"peculiar circumstances, you may want to make sure he understands that you're committed to keeping him."

"All right."

Gina reaches for a dog biscuit. "What are you going to call him?" She holds out the biscuit; the dog takes it out of her fingers like a gentleman.

"For the moment, the default name seems to be Boy."

"No. No good. Every male dog on the planet gets called Boy at least half the time. You want something that will distinguish him from the pack."

"Like being a pit bull isn't enough?"

"No. You're giving him a chance at a new life, a new identity."

"Witness protection program for dogs?"

"Something like that. It's not going to be easy, I hope that you're planning on working hard with him."

Adam has not planned any such thing, fairly satisfied with things as they are. Except for the aggression on the street. "I need to get him so he doesn't pull my arms off every time we meet another dog."

"He's been taught that. He can be taught something else."

"I sure hope so."

"I've got a few business cards from dog whisperers. Let me see if I can find them." Gina disappears behind the counter.

"When did trainers become whisperers? This guy is pretty tough; I may need to shout at him."

Gina stands up. "That's something you can't do. Really. He's got to be convinced that gentle is better."

Adam recalls the dog's quick bolt under the kitchen table

every time he raises his voice on the phone, or at the opposing team's interceptions on Sunday afternoon. "Yeah, he's evidently the strong, sensitive type."

"Don't kid. He probably is. These dogs are made, not born, that way."

"I'm not so sure about that, but time will tell." Adam takes the business cards from Gina, flips through the little collection. He knows that he can't afford a dog trainer, but he plays along. "Which one would you recommend?"

"They're all good. But you should start with K-Nine Etiquette. He's very good with problem animals." She sets her olive eyes on Adam. For the first time, there is something besides disdain in them. "I really think that there's hope for him."

Adam can discern a willingness to be nice, or maybe just a willingness to see that he isn't all bad. That maybe there is hope for him.

"Maybe you should call him Chance. You're giving him one. And I think he's maybe giving you a chance, too." Gina blushes a little, a slow pinking of the little exposed triangle at the base of her throat

"Chance of what?"

Gina turns away, picks up the fishnet, and goes back to moving fish. Whatever she is thinking, she's not saying, and Adam wonders if maybe she's embarrassed herself with her presumption.

"Chance. Yeah. Maybe. You like that one? Hey, Chance."

The dog, who has been poking his nose into the fish-food display, cocks his head at Adam and his satchel mouth breaks open in a doggy smile.

"I think he likes it."

Gina hangs up the little net again and comes close enough

to Adam that he can smell the light floral scent of her shampoo. She bends over the dog. "Looks like we have a winner." She strokes the dog on his bulky head and then touches Adam's forearm. "You're doing a good thing."

Now it is his turn to blush. He likes that touch, so simple, so human. It exposes a loneliness that is the central theme of his life.

Chapter Thirty-three

The fur between my shoulder blades rose even before I could thoroughly identify the scent. In a completely instinctive response, I growled. Low and warning. Not my usual style. It wasn't another dog trespassing into the restricted territory defined by the length of my leash; it was them. The boys. The ones who had kept me and my parents in that cellar, dragging us out only to compete, or breed, or train. I could feel the pulse of hostility stir my heart. Was this deliberate, this crossing of paths? Was this when my sojourn living in daylight would end?

Lately, my man had been talking to me, repeating words over and over until I twigged to their meaning. It was quite fun, and the reward of a Milk-Bone was enough to keep me engaged in the process for whole minutes at a time. None of it bore any resemblance to the training of the boys, which required sticks and chains. We did run a bit now that the streets were finally bare of snow. Nothing terribly challenging, a little quarter-mile jog through the park, around the little lake. He huffed and puffed at the end of it, while I had barely begun to pant. Either my stamina was as good as ever or his was poop.

Once in a while I came out from under the table to sit with him while he played with his toys. He'd even become somewhat generous with his own food, a bite of meat here, a lick of the plate there. Just enough to keep me off balance in my estimation of him.

He spoke one of those words to me now. *Chance.* Then *Quiet.* Two words that had been repeated enough I knew that the first identified me to him, or maybe the second one. They were often linked together: *Chancequiet.* I could feel a little tremor in the leash, telegraphing itself down to me. A firmer vibration of concern, of quickening steps.

I didn't want to stop long enough to get reacquainted, so I started to pull on the leash. He didn't pull me back, tighten that collar around my neck with a jerk like he did when I spoke to others on the street. Looked like my man didn't want to stop, either. We both knew that no good could come of it. The scent of the boys, the sound of their feet on the pavement made me nervous. I didn't want to fight their battles anymore.

Then he stopped in his tracks. The boys were in front of us now, their voices and their postures speaking challenge.

Was this guy going to fight me, when he'd done such a poor job of conditioning me? Or hand me over to these boys and let them put me back in the cellar? I'd be hardly better than a bait dog, which made me think of all the bait dogs I'd trained with—okay, savaged. These boys wouldn't be pleased with me when they found out it would only be self-defense in the pit for me, not physical superiority. They'd tape my jaws shut and let the others have me for lunch.

I realized then that I had fallen into the trap of household pets. I was comfortable, and these old caretakers represented a return to a very uncomfortable life. I pressed myself against his legs, imploring—I'm not proud of it—imploring him to keep the leash in his hand. Don't give me back. Maybe I don't want to be a pet, but I sure didn't want to go back to that cellar. I still planned on making a strike for independence, but not till it suited me. Not yet. Not to my old life, but to the life of a free dog.

Chapter Thirty-four

"Hey, man. Where you get that dog?" Two young men come out of a doorway. They are dressed in loose clothing, dwarfed by their massive black sweatshirts, which bear a famous footwear logo. Their hats, also black, are cocked at a jaunty angle, hoods pulled up over those against the chill air. On their feet are dazzlingly white athletic shoes. One boy is wearing sunglasses that give him an Adam Ant look. The other has a chain draped from his belt to his back pocket. It clinks a little as he saunters in Adam's direction, the volume of his pants forcing him to swagger to keep them from falling down.

"Breeder." It's the first thing that comes to mind.

"Look like my dog. My dog was stolen. You know anything about that?"

"No." Adam wonders what the fuck he's doing in this end of town. He's been walking the dog for an hour, mindful of the training book's admonition to keep dogs exercised. He's actually been enjoying the enforced activity, and with his thoughts keeping time to their walking pace, he's ended up six blocks past the demilitarized zone of the center. He's forgotten to turn around. Adam believes that he is not a prejudiced man, but this is beyond his comfort zone. A white man walking a pit bull sticks out in this neighborhood.

"You maybe lookin' for something?" This is spoken sotto voce by the young man not wearing the blocky sunglasses. His face, framed in the giant hood, is tilted. His eyes are almost friendly. "For some action?"

"No. Just taking my dog for a walk."

"Could maybe get you into somethin' if you want."

"I don't want anything." Adam is flanked. The dog is standing with his head lowered, his yellow-brown eyes raised, his hackles raised. His tail stands straight out like the magnetic needle on a compass; his feet are planted on the soiled sidewalk. He makes an intermittent vocalization that might be a growl, or a protest. A chuffing sound of anxiety.

"Hey, fella, how you doin'?" The kid with the sunglasses reaches down toward the dog, fingers snapping. The dog growls, shrinks behind Adam's legs.

"He look like a fighter to me. You sure you doan want a little action?"

"He's a pet."

"Doan look like no pet. Got that scar there."

"He's a pet." Adam squeezes out from between the tall youths. They step closer to the dog.

The dog lowers his head, his eyes on their faces; the soft skin around his muzzle quivers and then curls, exposing his teeth. Both boys back up.

Terrified suddenly that his dog will actually bite, Adam turns on his heel, yanks the dog around to follow.

"Sure look like my dog. Dawg." The boys laugh and enter the convenience store.

"Who were you defending back there?" Adam has covered six blocks in six minutes. A Starbucks is on this block, one with outdoor seating even in the winter. They'll stop there, catch their breath, and calm down with a splurge. Double mocha latte in the largest investment-quality size available. "Me or you? Did you know those kids?"

The dog shakes himself and settles down on the sidewalk. Inscrutable.

It is conceivable that they were telling the truth. Gina has said this dog looks like he'd been fought, but then why did he act nervous in front of them if he knew them? The reason suddenly seems obvious. "Did they hurt you?" Adam kneels down on one knee, draws the dog's face to his own. "Did they make you fight?" The sound of laughter as two people walk out of Starbucks brings Adam back to his feet, embarrassed to be seen talking to a dog. Inside, he buys a biscotti, which he will share with Chance.

As they sit there, Adam's pulse slowly returning to normal, the sweet latte improving his mood, a woman passes by on the street. She looks at Chance. The look on her face is one of nerves, as if the dog might leap out at her. Fear blunts her middle-aged face, fear of a breed's reputation, and her path swings wide of where they sit.

Adam recognizes an expression he has seen before, one that once gave him a secret satisfaction. There is a twinge of the pain in his ribs; he takes in a sharp breath. Was he really so bad, so intimidating? Had he mistaken fear for respect? He had often boasted that he didn't need his people to like him, only to do what he required. When he required it. There wasn't one employee, not peer, but underling, who called him anything but Mr. March. There wasn't one worker who shared baby pictures with him even if he walked by as the new dad was showing them to coworkers. There wasn't one person whose job was owed to Adam's proficiency at his own job who sent him a Christmas card.

The end of the biscotti disappears into the maw of the dog, who crunches it with loud abandon. Adam is chilled, sitting on the metal chair as the temperature falls. He has no doubt that the look on his own face when confronted by those gangstas had shown the same wash of fear, fear of those who have control of the moment, of those who will decide the next action.

The phantom pain twinges again and he takes another shallow breath. The dog looks up at him, his yellow-brown eyes hopeful of another chunk of biscotti, the encounter on the sidewalk forgotten. "Time to go home."

Chapter Thirty-five

Rafe is singing along to Tracy Chapman on his iPod, his voice seriously under pitch. "Talkin' about a revolution, yah yah yah." Today he's concocted a meat loaf with brown gravy, his signature garlic mashed potatoes, and a salad tossed in a bowl the size of a try-pot on a whaling ship. This has become one of Adam's favorite meals, which surprises him, as meat loaf, like liver, was a dish forbidden in the March home. Too many meals in his youth featured meat loaf, extended with fillers of bread or cereal, doctored with ketchup. But Rafe's version of the dish could be served in any of the upscale restaurants Adam once patronized, and he tells Rafe this.

"You say so, man? Go on. This recipe belonged to my granny, who got it from hers and so on, back to when our people brought it over on the slave ship."

"Rafe, your hyperbole is matched only by your skill with a spatula." Adam unties the long white apron from around his waist, tosses it into the laundry bin.

The center's chef plugs his ear bud back into his ear, but he is smiling.

Adam is in a good mood. Two things have cheered him up immensely. The first, a client—his first step toward breaking out from under the crushing debt he has incurred since losing his job and his assets. The second, the fact that Ariel actually initiated a telephone call to him. She wants to come spend the weekend with him, unprompted. This is a first, and Adam is fighting a rising suspicion that it isn't about spending time with him, but about annoying her mother. Lately, Sterling has complained that Ariel is acting out. Her usual friends are absent and the new kids she hangs out with Sterling has deemed quite unsuitable. Adam has defended Ariel, chalking it up to adolescent rebellion, but Sterling, in a rare moment of unguardedness with him, wouldn't shrug it off, fretting that there's something going on, something beyond normal growing pains. Sterling tells Adam that Ariel wants to give up riding all of a sudden. Her grades are falling; she didn't try out for the lacrosse team. And yesterday, she came back from town with a stud through her nose.

Adam thinks about Ariel's form of defiance and Veronica's sixties version. Nose rings versus miniskirts. Normal adolescent disrespect versus complete disappearance.

With everything in the center's kitchen all shipshape, Adam shrugs into his coat, pockets the package of meat loaf Rafe is sending home to Chance, and bids his coworkers to have a good weekend. He's in a hurry; the rest of his day will be spent honing the client's business plan. A start-up company, three baby-faced entrepreneurs who have managed to raise a million dollars from friends and family to start a business designing skateboard parks. They hope to be the Rees Jones of skateboarders, and Adam plans to leave the suit coat and tie at home when he makes this presentation Monday afternoon. Then he has to plan some meals for Ariel's visit. This time, he will resist the temptation to take her to a place he can't afford; he'll cook instead. He's learning a lot from Rafe, although proportions have been a little challenging and he's overdosed more than once on a lasagna that lasted for a week. And Chance needs his daily constitutional.

It's been awhile since Adam watched Judge Judy.

At half-past five, the park is beginning to empty out, and Adam finds this is the best time to take his dog out for some exercise. They run around the man-made lake at the center, then cool out walking along the path that loops gently through the gardens. It is still too early for flowers, but there is a certain tinge of pinky green, a hint of reanimation in the bare branches above their heads. The brindled dog lopes along beside Adam, his lolling tongue giving him a cheerful look. As they slow to a walk, Adam plays out more of the leash and lets Chance do his doggy thing along the freshly edged, if empty, gardens.

As Adam and Chance come up over a short rise, Gina appears with her three greyhounds. They both stop at a distance, uncertain about the dogs, about Chance.

"Let me get them leashed." Gina calls her dogs, who all look like antlerless deer to Adam. He glances down at Chance and is relieved to see the dog's tail wagging ever so slightly. Is he happy to see Gina, or is he okay with the three tall dogs? Very slowly, everyone comes together on the narrow path. Noses are working, tails begin to wag, no hostility. The greyhounds move like dignitaries, circling Chance, winding their leashes into a braid, until Gina has to spin to free herself from the maypole dance of the four dogs, a graceful movement, accompanied by her laughter.

Chance tolerates the inquisition. No lurching. No growling. No lifted lips. "Good boy, Chance." Adam thumps him on the ribs. The tail continues to wag.

"He's coming along, isn't he?"

"Yeah. He's definitely getting better about other dogs."

An awkward moment passes between them. What they have is a lack of definition. They have exchanged harsh words, and shared a cup of tea. She's observed him; he's watched her. But what did that make them: the kind of acquaintances who turn around on a walk to join each other, or the ones who keep going? Passing acquaintances? If circumstances were different, if she hadn't been on the egg-throwing side of a long-ago controversy, would she like him? Adam is flummoxed by the thoughts darting around his head as he looks for something neutral to say.

"Well, nice to see you." Gina gathers the three leashes into her left hand. She looks like a chariot driver, the tall, pale dogs fanned in front of her. "Bye, bye, Chance."

"I'm heading out. Is it okay if I walk with you?" Adam twitches the leash and Chance moves closer to his side. "It's good for him to be around other dogs."

Gina nods. "Sure." Not hostile, not warm. If he was to attribute any adjective to her response, it might be *cautious*. He is disheartened. By this time, she shouldn't be so grudging with her friendship—willing to give him a good reference for Dr. Gil, unwilling to forget about his connection to Dynamic Industries.

They walk in the direction of the entrance to the park with its wrought-iron gates. The silence is not exactly comfortable; neither is it intolerable. They both keep their attention on the dogs. Keep the dogs between them. But it is the lingering memory of her touch on his arm that emboldens him to keep pace with her, not to say "Nice to see you, too" and speed on his way.

Gina is first to break the silence. "Who did you finally decide on as a trainer?"

"No one. The truth is, I can't afford a trainer. At least not at the moment." Adam considers that Gina might think it strange that a man like himself can't afford something like dog training, and he almost adds that his daughter's horse trainer is enough trainer for him. But he doesn't. He waits to hear what Gina might say.

"There are training tapes. You can get them out of the library." If she is curious, Gina doesn't betray it.

"Good idea. Although he's got 'Sit' pretty well learned. And 'Come.' We're definitely doing better on 'Come.' 'Stay off the futon' is not so good."

"But not attacking other dogs is. I see some improvement there."

"Sort of. Today is a good day."

"Lucky for my guys."

"Lucky for me."

They have reached the gates. Gina stops at a Prius parked nearby. "Why don't you come by and pick out a dog bed for him? That may help with the futon issues."

"I will."

"I have some that aren't very expensive."

"I'm sure I can swing a dog bed."

Gina unlocks her car door and the three greyhounds jump in, only to collapse around one another on the backseat. She doesn't offer Adam a lift. Nonetheless, Adam smiles as he picks up the pace for home.

Chapter Thirty-six

If Ariel is disappointed that they are not going out for one of their fancy meals, she has the good grace to hide it. In fact, she's quite agreeable, and there is no sign of her iPod or her cell phone. Adam feels like he should be either suspicious or ecstatic. Maybe she's just growing up, he thinks. Maybe the anger is starting to wear off. She is sixteen, tall and willowy. Her physical resemblance to Veronica is heightened by the way she's wearing her hair, not pulled back into a messy knot, nor in those slightly suggestive little-girl ponytails sported by some of the girls he sees walking to school in his neighborhood. Today her blond hair is loose; ripples of natural wave keep it from being plain. A thick cream-colored scarf is around her neck, and she wears a black lambskin jacket over her designer jeans. He can see the tiny faceted stone in the side of her nose, twinkling in the sunlight like a ruby red mole. It's not as bad as he imagined. Surely the hole will close up once she outgrows this need to mutilate herself in the name of fashion. In the meantime, he's learning how to look at her face without looking at the stud. The effect of all of this is that she doesn't look sixteen. She looks older, and he knows that is precisely what she hopes.

Sterling wants him to talk to Ariel about her friends, behavior, attitude, and blowing off schoolwork and reminded him of that when he picked Ariel up. Adam decides to be the good cop. Why spoil this "so far, so good" afternoon? Maybe when he takes her back to Sylvan Fields tomorrow, he'll say something. But for now, he'll enjoy this air of cooperation, this rare unsullied proximity.

As they pull into the parking lot behind his building, Adam pats Ariel's knee. "I've got someone I want you to meet."

Instantly, Ariel's demeanor tenses. "Who?" She unbuckles her seat belt but doesn't open the door.

"Not going to tell you; it's a surprise." He's a little surprised at her reaction. Adam hasn't told Ariel that he ended up keeping the dog he said was temporary. "You'll like him."

Ariel visibly relaxes, smiles, and twirls a lock of hair behind her ear. Three studs frame the delicate edging of pink ear that he once marveled over while watching her sleep. "Okay. Him. All right." She elides those two words into one odd sound. A'ite.

Clearly, Ariel isn't up to accepting another woman in her father's life. He smiles, then thinks of Gina. If he was ready to date, would she be a likely candidate? He's bought a nice dog bed from her, and she was pleasant enough as he got Chance to try the fit on several of them. They both knew that he could find an equally nice bed at the local pet supply warehouse for a lot less, but he handed over his abused Visa and smiled even as he chided himself for caring if she liked him or not. But there is something about her that lingers like an afterimage every time he encounters her.

Adam and Ariel climb the back stairs to his floor. He tries not to see the place as she must. Despite a perfectly serviceable hallway, no terrible food odors from neighbors, even a few door decorations cheering it up, it still has that worn industrial look about it. Gray carpet, beige walls. Uninspired sconces light the hallway, dim even in broad daylight. The only apartment building she has ever spent time in is on Park Avenue in New York. There is no hallway in that building; the elevator opens into the foyer of her grandparents' floor. They own the entire floor.

Adam hurries to unlock his door.

Chance sits in the middle of the living room, the squashed throw pillows on the futon clear evidence that the new dog bed is a waste of money. At the sight of Ariel, the dog's tail ticks back and forth, his jaw drops open, and his banner tongue rolls out. His eyes squint; he stands and shakes. Then sits again. As with every stranger, the dog is cautious.

"Jesus, Dad. What the f . . . hell is that?"

"My dog."

"A pit bull? You have a pit bull?" She is laughing, though, laughing and patting her knees to beckon the dog to her. "Is this the same dog you had before?"

"The same."

"How come you still have him?"

"It's a long story."

"That's what you always say."

Chance lumbers over to Ariel, tail still swinging. Ariel reaches out a tentative hand, allowing the dog to sniff the back of it before reaching under his chin to scratch. Adam wonders where she's learned this approach to strange dogs. He certainly never taught her that. Never knew it himself. There is so much he doesn't know about this young woman. He wasn't there for the first time the tooth fairy made an appearance. He was in Hong Kong the evening of her first junior high orchestra performance. Even long after she was a toddler, she was asleep most nights before he made it home. He, like the rest of his cohorts, brayed about the quality time they had with their children. The family ski vacations in Aspen; the once-a-year tennis lessons together. Surely that made up for the absences. The preoccupations.

"What's his name?"

"Chance."

"Interesting." Ariel moves her scratching fingers up and over the dog's head, down his spine, which gets him to wriggling. "Whose idea was that?"

"Gina."

Once again, the tension shows in the tightening of her jaw muscles.

"She owns the shop across the street, fancy pet supplies and tropical fish. I bought the dog bed from her." His voice sounds dismissive even to his own ears.

Ariel visibly relaxes again, as if a shop owner isn't someone she imagines her father being interested in. She stands up to remove her coat, looks around the apartment, drops the coat on the futon, and goes to find refreshment in the mostly-empty fridge.

Adam doesn't know how he'll entertain his daughter for the next twenty-four hours.

Adam's meat loaf isn't quite as tasty as Rafe's, although he's followed the recipe exactly. His mashed potatoes are acceptable, and he's cheated with a can of gravy. The salad, however, is very good. Ariel not only hasn't turned her nose up at the plebeian menu; she's helped herself to a second, albeit thin, slice of meat loaf.

"So, Dad?"

"Ariel?" Here it comes, some request he is going to have to deny. A new pair of shoes, a better school. Diamond earrings. He'll let her down with an airy promise of some future acquisition.

"I got invited to a party for tonight."

"Are you saying you want to go back home tonight?" He is disappointed; this is probably a request he can't deny, but why didn't she say something earlier?

"No. It's at MIT. A guy I know—"

"No. Absolutely not. Whatever put that idea in your head?" Adam picks up their plates and drops them into the sink. He bought ice cream for dessert. He sprang for sprinkles, remembering that Ariel always asked for sprinkles on her cones. "I've got Ben and Jerry's. Chunky Monkey or Cherry Garcia?"

"Dad, I promised that I'd go. It's all right. I know the people—"

"No. So, Chunky or Cherry?" Maybe if he talks loudly enough, this ridiculous fantasy of his sixteen-year-old daughter attending an MIT frat party will dissipate like a puff of smoke. He tries not to think that the entire day of good behavior, of cheerful conversation, of her even doing her math homework at this table was all smoke and mirrors, a buttering up of the old man.

"But Dad, everyone will be there, all my friends. If I don't show up, they'll be on my case for a week. I got them invitations to this party and they're all gonna meet me. It's totally safe."

The dog sequesters himself beneath the table. Not even the tip of his tail extends beyond the perimeter. He rests his nose on his paws, but his eyes are darting beneath mobile eyebrows.

Ariel is banging around the small room, her voice petulant, then wheedling. Adam's voice moves from rock-solid to cracking with anger. "No girl of sixteen who's invited to a frat party can expect it's safe. Besides, what kind of college man invites jailbait—"

"Mom said I could go."

Ariel must take him for an idiot. "Yeah. And I'm about to be crowned king of England. Try something more believable."

"I can't believe that you're not letting me go. You always said connections are important."

"No. Now that *is* something your mother would say." Adam yanks the faucet on full and is hit in the face with a backwash of hot water. He drops the pans in, squirts in some dishwashing liquid, and starts scrubbing furiously. The sound of the running water drowns out Ariel's voice. He shuts off the tap. Ariel hasn't taken a breath.

"Courtney's going to be there. It's her cousin's friend's party."

Courtney Bevins. Daughter of the man who took Adam's place at Dynamic. His former protégé. The one who convinced Wannamaker that the takeover shouldn't be launched. Oh yeah, Adam's figured that out.

"Courtney and her parents are no friends of mine."

"Mom likes them."

"Even at your tender age, I'm sure you can see how that loyalty is offensive to me." Adam is quiet now. Ariel is quiet. His pulse is starting to normalize. Episode over; let's move on.

"Dad?"

He turns away from the sink to look at his daughter. She is in her coat, her ruinously expensive handbag—not a knock-off, the real deal which her mother insisted she should have, slung over her shoulder. She's changed out of her jeans and is wearing a tight little skirt, knee-high boots with heels he can't imagine anyone walking in. The little lambskin jacket is open, revealing a low turquoise top that fits like a leotard and accents a cleavage he is shocked to see.

She looks at him with a defiance he might find admirable were it not aimed at him. The set of her jaw, the way she tosses her hair out of her eyes with a shake, the way her lips are parted, all serve to remind Adam of what lies in wait for her at a house full of inebriated postadolescent, horny young men. "I'm going, Dad, and you can't stop me."

"Ariel, don't you dare."

"You don't have custody of me. I'm going. I hate you."

"Don't you talk back to me, young lady."

Ariel wrenches the doorknob, loses control of the door, which bangs hard into the wall.

"Don't you walk away from me."

"Fuck you."

Has she actually said that, or is he hearing an echo from the past? The phantom pain that has tormented Adam less in the past few months bears down now on his chest like a vise.

The door slams.

From beneath the kitchen table, Chance peeks out, but he stays under its cagelike protection.

Adam is frozen in midstep. Dishwater trickles down his wrists under his sleeves. He must stop her, but at the same time he thinks that if she has a few minutes to stand out in the street, where very few cabs travel and where it's a mile to the nearest T stop, she'll be back.

His father did nothing to stop his sister. He stayed in the kitchen. Muttering epithets to himself. He sat back down at the table, opened his paper.

Then he thinks of how she's dressed and imagines who else might stop to pick her up. The dog comes out from under the table, gives Adam a wide berth but keeps his eyes on him. Adam bends over, pressing his wet hands into his sides. Stein has told him to remember to breathe, remember to swallow when the anger comes upon him. One deep breath. Another. Then he can go follow her. The dog sniffs at the overnight case Ariel has brought with her, looks at Adam. "It's okay, boy. It's okay." He is still bent over, eyes closed, gasping for breath like he does when he and Chance circumnavigate the pond at speed.

Chance's nose meets Adam's nose. Startled, Adam stands upright.

And then it strikes him. Maybe his father couldn't pursue Veronica because Adam would have been left alone in the apartment. It isn't epithets he's recalling; it's prayer. He was the reason Veronica got away. There was no one else there to watch over a little boy. His father didn't let her go; maybe he was simply helpless to stop her.

Adam isn't helpless and Ariel's not getting away. Adam grabs his keys and cell phone and slams out the door. He hears Chance bark once as he runs down the front stairs.

Chapter Thirty-seven

Except that they didn't bite each other, this confrontation between my man and his pup was as vicious as any fight in the pit I'd ever seen. Whew. I stayed beneath the cage of the table, my head down low, my ears flat against my head, my eyes on the combatants. Snap and snarl. Woohee.

I watched their legs as they danced around the room, using their voices as weapons. Then the young one banged out the door. He panted, not like victor or vanquished, but like a dog pulled to the sidelines to catch his breath before going in for the kill. I was proud of him and touched his face to let him know he had a partner in the ring.

After he left, I stood for a long time, inhaling the scent of their heated bodies. The room was very quiet, so quiet that I could hear him calling way down on the street. I scratched at the door. Eventually I discerned the sound of a car, its voice as familiar to me as the sound of the man's voice. Then I was left to the ordinary silence of the place. I wandered over to my water bowl, lapped a little, nosed my empty dinner bowl, tried to upend the garbage can with its lovely promise of leftovers, but it was wedged in tight between the counter and the wall and had a diabolically clever top on it, which, so far, had resisted my attempts to open it.

Then I jumped onto the futon, pushed the pillows into a more snug nest, and curled up to await their return. Which turned out to be a very long time, even by dog standards.

Chapter Thirty-eight

In the two minutes it took to follow Ariel out into the street, Adam has lost her, as if she has been absorbed into the evening. The sidewalk is empty, and he cannot believe that she could move so fast on those heels. Or that it had taken him longer than he thought to get himself down the stairs and out. He waits, listening to the pounding of his heart in his chest, trying to decide which direction she might have gone. She doesn't know the neighborhood, doesn't know the area, can't possibly have known in what direction to turn to get to the subway. But *he* does, and heads that way now, jogging, saving himself for a full run once he spots her.

Reaching the station, Adam swipes his Charlie Card and darts toward the inbound platform. Lots of dark coats and short skirts. Not so many blond girls. Then he spots the back of a blonde leaning against a stanchion. Although she is inches shorter than Ariel even without the boots, he tries to convince himself that it is she; that this recent awareness of her mature height is a delusion. Surely she is still small enough to fit in his lap. He makes himself quiet his breathing, moves toward the figure slowly, casually, hopefully. But, of course, it's not Ariel.

Ariel has either gotten lucky and found a cab or had already planned on meeting friends with a car. He goes to fetch his Lexus and make his way to Cambridge. He'll find Ariel if he has to knock on every dorm door, walk into every frat house. There is no way he's going to lose her. He keeps calling her cell phone, his finger on the speed dial. He knows she'll just keep letting it go to voice mail, but he wants her to know he's coming, that his phone is in his hand.

Even as he sails down Memorial Drive too fast, Adam thinks about the frat parties he's been to and realizes something that Ariel, in her high school rebellion, doesn't know. No frat party starts this early. The best start at nearly midnight, not at seven-thirty. So, where will she go? Who will be with her? Maybe he has time to find her and get her home. He begins to relax. Sterling probably has the cell number of that wretched Courtney or one of Ariel's other friends. As a last resort he'll make that call. Right now he has a plan.

Adam pulls into the Trader Joe's parking lot, gives Ariel's phone another try. When it automatically goes to voice mail, he wishes that he'd added text messaging to his cell-phone package, six cents per message be damned. No answer. "Ariel, I want you to meet me at the student center. I won't embarrass you in front of your friends, but I'll take them home, too, if they want. No questions, no consequences."

He believes that, at heart, Ariel is sensible and will come.

This is not the student center of Adam's experience. This is a mall, and instantly he realizes that amid the food venues, bookstore, game room, he might wander all night and never find Ariel if he's not specific about location. He thumbs Ariel's number once again. "I'm in the first-floor seating area. Watching the Mass Ave entrance."

In the student center, Adam feels like a voyeur, or, at the very least, a middle-aged man sitting in a place that makes him suspect. Everyone else looks young, and those who aren't young look appropriately professorial, a little bleary, books tucked under arms, top-loader briefcases in hand. None of them looks like a deranged father on the hunt for a truculent daughter. Adam has swallowed enough coffee to stay awake all night and he's not sure how long he can sit here like a homeless man, observing every girl who walks by in her tight little skirt and her skinny tank top, before a campus cop comes over and strikes up a conversation.

None of them is Ariel. He really thought that she'd be here. That she'd listened to his message. Maybe he's left too many, all with the same invocation to call him, so that she never bothered to listen to the last one with orders to meet him here. Or never listened to any of them.

Adam had been to enough U Mass frat parties to know the damage the young can do to themselves with the heady freedom of supervisionless living. He had seen couches tossed over balconies and set on fire; had witnessed the dumping of an alcohol-poisoned girl at the door of the local hospital. It wasn't that long ago that a student died right here from that. It's a quick progression to thinking about date-rape drugs. His daughter and the sexual predators lurking around every corner. These thoughts send ribbons of anguish through him and his hands shake as if he's been drinking all night. Ariel is his responsibility and he's lost her. The time on his cell phone screen reads 12:30. The student center seems less now like a concourse of activity than a midnight bus station, those still around bent over books or asleep on the couches, satchels and backpacks making up rough pillows or footstools.

He dare not take his eyes off the door. He dare not give up hope. He dare not wait here any longer.

The first student Adam approaches is a big African-American guy wearing a sweatshirt emblazoned with Greek letters he can't identify. He carries a laptop case over one shoulder and has a weary look, as if he's been awake for days and can't wait to fall into bed. He is plodding toward the exit, shoulders hunched and head down, a bull-shaped man who does not look particularly approachable. He looks a bit like the punks who stopped Adam on the street to ask about Chance—his big sweatshirt, his crisp white athletic shoes. If it wasn't for the Greek letters on his chest, Adam would have looked for someone else.

"Can I talk with you a moment?"

The kid stops, altogether surprised to find Adam blocking his way. "I guess." He straightens up, imposing in his height and bulk. He is not hostile, just annoyed. He could brush Adam away with one hand and he knows it. Instead, he waits to hear what Adam has to say.

"I'm trying to find my daughter. She's at some frat party and I have to find her. She's seriously underage." The young man looks at him with some genuine concern and Adam feels that ribbon of anxiety tickle. He is right to be afraid for Ariel.

"Hard to say. There's always something going on. Might even be in Back Bay. Lots of Greeks over there. Are you sure it's at a frat?"

Adam feels the hopelessness of finding Ariel in this city of students.

"But, hey, lemme give a couple of friends a call."

Adam is amazed that the kid's massive thumb is so dextrous, but within a moment he's chatting up someone. "Hey, dawg, yeah, man, look, anything going on at your house?"

The kid looks Adam in the eye and shakes his head, thanks his friend, and snaps his phone shut. "My buddy says there might be something going on at TDC on Memorial."

"Thank you. You've been very helpful."

"Hey, wait, man. What are you going to do?"

"Crash a party."

"Good luck." The big kid in the Alpha Psi Alpha sweatshirt sets his cap on his head, careful to twist it into a fashionable tilt, and heads out the exit.

Adam follows, gets his bearings, and heads off at a jog toward the frat house. The late-night air chills him. He pulls the collar of his coat up higher, regrets that he hadn't taken his scarf out of the car, where it lies on the front seat. Clumps of students bump past him as he goes along the street, oblivious to the solitary man making his way through the Saturday-night crowd. He wants to ask if he's going in the right direction, whether he is getting any closer, but none of these students so much as glance at him. They are safe in their numbers and unconcerned with a harried-looking middle-aged man in a too-light jacket, a man who is trying hard not to be frantic.

The young men who stop him at the door are polite about his request to look for his daughter, and one offers to scout around for him. He will not stay, as told, at the bottom of the stairs, but forges on ahead with his chaperone, looking into every room they pass, despite the guy's assurances that no very young woman would be allowed in on a night for "over twenty-ones." Adam bites his tongue, not mentioning that he doesn't believe that rule for one minute. "She's very mature-looking; she can fool anyone."

"We check IDs. Every now and then some freshman tries to get a high school girlfriend in, but we're pretty diligent." He asks if Adam knows whom Ariel might be visiting.

"No." Courtney Bevin's cousin's friend. Adam thinks as hard as he can, trying to remember if Ariel has mentioned any specific names, boy or girl. What comes to him is the depth of her silence toward him. The lack of any insight he has into her life, despite his interrogations on her visiting days. He has asked, and Ariel has belittled his attempts at piercing the barrier she has built around herself as his daughter and as an adolescent.

The music is deafening; bodies are crammed together in the lounge. A black DJ is scratching records while a hip-hop tune plays for the predominantly white crowd. The ceiling fixture has been fitted out with a strobe light, and the dancers' faces are frightening with a here-there-gone dizzy flicker. Adam strains to pick Ariel's face out of the gyrating group, but the strobing lights make it impossible to fix on any one face.

The smell of vomit rises from the floor. In another room, a table is set up with plastic cups, which someone is filling from a keg. In another, there is an apparent contest to see who can swallow a twelve-ounce cup of beer the fastest. Three young men are already on the floor, and Adam can't tell if they are even breathing. Should he call 911? A small room off to the left holds two men, who are silent over a chess table, oblivious to the racket in the house.

"Upstairs? She could be upstairs with someone."

"I can't let you go up there, man. Privacy."

"This is my sixteen-year-old daughter we're talking about. Anything happens, you and your brothers are up shit creek. Frats have been closed before."

The frat-boy bouncer looks to his partner, who just shrugs. "Okay, but no knocking on closed doors. Open ones only, and I never took you up there."

They wander the length of all the floors, checking into any room with a wide-open door. Most of these have students in them, and Adam's presence startles several into hiding a hand behind a back, or slamming a door. A few are empty.

The hip-hop beat seeps into Adam's bones and he feels as if all of this searching is being done to a rhythm, a weirdly choreographed dance in which he is the soloist and can't remember the steps. "Ariel!" Adam cups his hands around his mouth at every floor and bellows her name.

Adam is back on the street. The boys have suggested a nearby dorm, and one after that. The magnitude of his search is daunting. He can't possibly get to every dorm and frat house on this far-flung campus. He is searching for someone who doesn't want to be found. Adam sinks down on the top step of the old brownstone frat house. He puts his head in his hands. He has to call Sterling, see if she has any ideas about whom Ariel might know here. Suffer her anger and take the well-deserved blame. He takes out his cell phone to call his ex-wife. The missed-call message is on the screen. He didn't hear it ring when he was in the frat house, the hip-hop drowning out any other sound.

His pulse is in his ears as he presses the key to identify the caller. In the instant it takes to see who it is, Adam knows that he is praying, making deals with a God he has all but forgotten. A vestigial belief in a merciful God burns through his heart as he squeezes his eyes shut and waits for the call to connect.

Chapter Thirty-nine

The campus police station is on Vassar Street, not all that far from where Adam is. He can barely remember where he left his car, so he walks the distance, taking the time to reel in his emotions, catch his breath, straighten up. The streetlights dog him. There are only a few people on the streets now: stumbling co-eds, arms linked together, giggling their way back to the safety of their dorm rooms; a lone bicyclist speeding down the center of the street, unthreatened by automotive traffic. A man walking a large dog comes out of the shadows. Adam thinks that he's going to go home to a mess. Poor Chance, abandoned without a backward glance.

Recently, Adam has found himself talking to Chance as if he's a sentient being. At first, he felt silly, embarrassed to think that he'd grown so used to the dog's presence that he'd begun to feel like a pal. "Did you see that play? What was he thinking?" he'd ask. But he didn't stop. It helped, this voicing out loud his train of thoughts, getting nothing more back than a sideways look or a big blocky head in his lap. Once in a while, the dog vocalized a little *rroorr rroorr* sound, agreeing that it was a boneheaded play or concurring with whatever Adam had said. He slipped his arm across the dog's sturdy shoulders when he did that and was rewarded with a quick lick on the cheek. Then they'd both sit back, assured of their masculinity.

Ariel is waiting for her father in a hard-backed chair across from the duty officer who made the call to Adam. She stands up at the sight of him coming through the door. Old tears already blotch her face, and the scent of vomit clings to her. A thin streak mars the perfection of her lambskin jacket. Her panty hose are torn above her boots, as if she'd stumbled and fallen down on her knees. Her hair is tangled. Her expensive purse is gone.

"Mr. March, your daughter is a very lucky girl. She was mugged but not assaulted. We found her alone on the street, although she says she was with friends."

"Ariel?"

"Daddy." It has been years since she's called him that.

"What happened?"

"I'm all right."

"Where are your friends?"

"I don't know."

"What happened?"

Ariel wipes her mouth with the back of her hand. Her nails are chipped and the palms abraded. "I fell down."

"Did someone push you?"

"No. We were going to another party, and I was a little behind everyone because they were moving so fast. Then I tripped. I don't think they knew I was down, because they kept going. They didn't hear me. Then this guy, this guy out of nowhere, was standing over me. I thought he was going to help me up, but he didn't. He swiped my bag. I was so scared, afraid that he'd hurt me, that I just let him. When I got up, I got sick. And then I was alone on the street with no phone and no money and I didn't know what to do."

"How did you end up here?"

"A cop found me. Brought me here and called you."

"And you were drinking?" He can see that she would like to deny that she was, but the evidence is obvious.

"Yes."

"Like the officer says, you were very lucky. You have no idea—"

"I do. You don't have to tell me. Lesson learned." Her tone is sardonic, as if the only lesson she's learned is to expect a lecture from a worry-fraught father.

Her face is tear-streaked and dirty, but she is dry-eyed now. She walks out ahead of him into the predawn darkness. Adam knows that there is more to this story, details that he'll never hear. This is a mishap that she has survived and that will become part of her life story. And maybe someday, when her own child does something equally rebellious, she'll suddenly understand how he feels right now. The panic may have subsided, but the memory of it will last forever.

The gray light of day has faded the long night as they reach Adam's building. The newsagent's door is propped open as he retrieves the bundles of newspapers dropped on the sidewalk. Adam thinks of all the sleepless nights he's spent, waiting for that door to open, those lights to come on. He is nostalgic, although grateful that he no longer awakens in the dark.

Beside him, Ariel is dozing. She's unhurt, except for her scraped knees and bruised ego. For this, he remembers his deal with God and breathes a prayer of thanks. The old words *by the grace of God,* come to mind as he looks at his sleeping daughter. He'll let her keep her nightmare night to herself, as he will. She doesn't need to know the anguish he experienced as he hunted for her. As long as he knows that it was only an injury to her pride and not something more dire that led to her being hauled off to the campus police station, he's satisfied. A lesson learned. Don't hang out with friends who will abandon you to puke in the bushes alone and leave you vulnerable to purse snatching, and be glad it wasn't anything more dire.

Adam wonders if Veronica ever learned her lesson.

Adam rejects the idea that his father could not race after his sister because of him. He could have taken Adam with him, or dropped him with a neighbor—they lived on a street with three family homes; surely some woman would have been willing to watch a little boy while a frantic father chased after a rebellious daughter. Adam knows that he would never have given up looking for Ariel like his father had given up on Veronica, and then on him.

Ariel stirs as Adam shuts off the engine. The short nap has already faded the nightmare result of her defiance toward him. She looks at him with embarrassed contempt. Gone is the "Daddy" of her rescue. He is, once again, the Nameless One.

"I want to go home."

"You're going to bed. I'll take you home when I'm ready to."

Ariel stomps off to shower and Adam snaps the leash on his

dog. They pound down the stairs and Adam feels every tense muscle in his spine and legs revolt. Chance has contained himself and hasn't greeted Adam with anything but gratitude. Adam walks him as far as the empty lot, but he doesn't let him off the leash. He's had enough of runaways already.

"Are you going to tell Mom?"

"Do you want me to?"

"Duh, no." Ariel isn't looking at him; she's looking out her window as the verge along the highway speeds by, guardrail posts spooling out the miles as they head to Sylvan Fields. "Besides, she'll blame you anyway. Save yourself the trouble."

"I can't say you're wrong about that. So, let me get this straight. I protect your butt from your mother, and I benefit somehow. And you've learned . . . what? Not to mix vodka with wine?"

"She's dating, you know."

"She has that right."

"He's a creep. He's younger than she is and she only likes him because he's got a really big . . ."

"What?"

"Portfolio." The corner of Ariel's mouth twitches into a little smile.

The resemblance to Veronica is so vivid that Adam pulls off the road at the next rest stop. "You have an aunt. Her name is Veronica. When she was your age, she disappeared. Ran away. I never saw her again and I have no idea what happened to her. She was just like you. Beautiful and headstrong."

"I'm not running away."

"You did run away."

"That was just to go to a party. I wasn't going to vanish forever."

"Maybe that's what Veronica thought, too."

Adam puts the car into gear and gets back onto the highway.

Chapter Forty

They didn't even have the common decency to call him and tell him over the phone. A fucking e-mail. "Sorry to have to cancel with you, but we've decided that we need to change consultants." Blah, blah, blah. New focus. Different direction. "We really can't take a chance on you. You should have told us. . . ."

His clients have bailed on him. A check will arrive in the mail. Time spent. Maybe two hundred bucks. They've seen his CORI. They've discovered his error. Just like Gina. His criminal offender record information sheet will list A&B—assault and battery. They won't care that he's been sentenced to community service. The lone woman in the group has probably kicked up a fuss. Who would want a consultant like him? A man who has been accused of being a danger to women.

Adam opens up the first draft of the business plan, stares at it, admires how he would have brought the dream to those spineless neophytes, and then deletes the document.

. . .

"Mornin', Artie."

"Mornin', Adam." As has become his habit, Artie wordlessly slides a dog biscuit across the counter, never looking at the dog or at Adam, keeping his eyes on his puzzle. The cookie disappears into Chance's satchel mouth.

"He says thank you."

"If I had one like him, I wouldn't need you know what." Artie waggles his bushy eyebrows, intimating that he has illegal weaponry stowed out of sight.

"Where were you when I was trying to find him a home?"

"I like my freedom. No pets."

Adam and Artie have had this conversation before. In the year or so that Adam has walked through that door seven days a week, Artie has always been on his stool behind the counter, cigar clenched between his teeth, newsprint streaked on his forehead and crossword puzzle under his hand. Adam seriously doubts the man has any freedom at all. If Artie thinks he's unencumbered, it's his delusion.

Adam fills his travel mug, snags a couple of packets of cheese crackers, a *Globe*.

"That's four and a quarter."

Adam hands Artie his last ten, pockets his change, and wonders how soon he'll get his kiss-off money from the skateboarders.

A second dog biscuit comes across the counter. "That's for later."

Gina is unlocking her door as they walk out.

"Morning, Gina." Adam nods to her, is rewarded with one of her smiles. Which he knows is for the dog.

"Hi, Adam. How's it going?"

"Could be better." He just doesn't have the energy to play at civilities with his unpredictable neighbor.

"You look a little ragged. What happened?"

Such small courtesies, a short lifeline tossed in his direction. Although he's certain that she'll snap it back, Adam decides to grab it anyway. "You want a coffee? It's a long story."

Chance is straining against his leash, trying to get closer to Gina. Adam steps forward, loosening the tension. Gina bends to stroke Chance's head, runs her hand along his back, scratches his rump, and then stands up. "Sure. I've got time."

Adam hands Gina the leash and his coffee, goes back into Artie's to get another one for himself. He's smiling and he doesn't know why. His pulse is just a little stronger, as if he's already downed sixteen ounces of dark roast.

The parrots squawk their greeting to Gina, who opens their cage and puts in a breakfast of seed and fruit, changes the water, feeds each one a tidbit by hand. She leaves the door to the cage open, eyeing Chance and wagging a finger at him. "Leave it." Chance wrinkles his brow and flops down on the floor, heaving a great sigh, like a bellows emptying.

Gina sips from her coffee cup while moving from tank to tank, scooping debris, sprinkling in food, checking temperatures as Adam spins out his tale of Ariel and her Saturday-night adventure.

He won't talk about his stillborn consulting job; it would force him to reveal too much about himself that she shouldn't know. It is too shaming.

She says nothing, but her activity doesn't suggest inattention. It's easier to talk about Ariel's attitude toward him, her defiance—her similarity to his sister in looks and attitude—without Gina looking at him. Adam finds himself telling Gina more than he should about his strained relationship with Ariel, and about his sister's more permanent rebellion.

"So where is she now?" Gina's done with the chores and now moves behind the counter.

"I took her home yesterday morning." His coffee has gone tepid.

Gina sets the canister of fish food back on the shelf, hesitating a moment longer than the task should take. She turns to him. "I mean your sister. Whatever happened?"

"I have no idea. She walked out that door and that was it." Adam clears his throat, sniffs a little to suggest that this fact no longer has the power to hurt him. "My father never went after her."

"Well, you did the right thing, going after Ariel."

"What else could I have done? Sat home waiting helplessly? As it was, I was helpless and I did wait helplessly, but at least I was near to hand when the cops called."

"She knows you were looking for her. She knows how much you care."

"I'm not so sure."

One of the parrots has emerged from its cage and has worked its flightless way to where Gina leans against the counter. Cocking its head right and left, it finally launches itself to her shoulder, where it begins to pull gently on her hair.

Adam remembers the packets of cheese crackers in his pocket and pulls one of them out. "Can Polly have a cracker?"

"His name is Fred, and yes. He loves that kind. Just break a piece off for him."

Adam offers the orange-yellow cracker to the bird, who

runs his beak against it, then gingerly takes the offering, keeping his tiny bird eye on Adam while he does this.

"Did you tell Ariel's mother what she did?" Gina lifts the bird off her shoulder and onto her hand.

"Not yet. Sterling wasn't home when I dropped Ariel off, not back from her weekend with her new paramour. The thing is, if I do, they'll both hate me; if I don't, who knows. Maybe Ariel will learn to appreciate my silence."

"I'm sure she appreciates what you did, or tried to do. If not now, she will eventually."

"I hope so." Adam offers another piece of cracker to the parrot. "It's been really hard lately to get the women in my life to cut me some slack." Their eyes meet over the head of the cracker-crunching parrot. In Gina's he sees a flicker of something, something she's keeping back. As if she knows something about him. "What?"

"Nothing." A slight flush touches the apples of her cheeks. He thinks of reaching out and laying a finger on those cheeks to see if they feel warm to the touch. The thought is so compelling that he raises his hand. Suddenly, Gina steps backward; the parrot flaps clipped wings to keep his balance.

"Are you all right?"

"Fine." The warm flush is now scarlet. "Just fine."

And then it hits him. Gina knows about Sophie, about his episode. She's Googled him. There is no burying past sins anymore. Anything and everything is laid out there for public consumption. Newspaper articles and the infinite discussion on blogs all there for the mere typing of his name on a search engine. Potential employers, potential friends can find all the dirt on you. The most personal of stories writ large across the electronic concourse of the Internet.

Adam is powerless. His reputation has been sullied forever by his loss of control that day, that moment. The grinding ambition coupled with the misleading message, exacerbated by hunger and an incipient, if phantom, attack of angina, topped by his personal assistant's increasing and unrepentant ineptitude had triggered a breakdown. A self-immolating act of breathtaking nihilism. He's paid for that error. But all the press or blogs or watercooler conversations ever recall is the act, the unforgivable act, of slapping Sophie.

He sees himself in Gina's eyes and is horrified. To her, he is a man who acts upon a baser impulse. She can't know that it's one driven up from the dark reaches of his background and upbringing. The raised hand. He's watched other foster children younger than he put into closets. He's sat hungry while others ate. He's seen the belt slide out from under the belt loops, the snap of it, halved and threatening. He's been struck. All in the name of good behavior, manners, respect. Mistakes.

But he has conquered this, pulled himself up out of the morass, bettered himself. He has denied himself the self-indulgent practice of remembering the darkness, recalling in his rare stories only the two foster mothers who were kind to him, and even their kindness was of the practical kind. Marge and Mrs. Salter. He's never gone back to see them, these two out of seven. He's pushed them and their kisses on his forehead into the same closet as the five who treated him as a piece of inventory.

Adam wants to tell Gina all of this, to explain himself to her, to get her to stop looking at him with these wary eyes. Eyes that tell him no matter how civil she is to him, how impressed that he's taken on Chance, she will always be aware of his single self-destructive act and judge him by it. The lifeline snatched from his hand.

"I'm not the person you think I am. What happened was an aberration. I'm much better than that. I don't . . ." He is about to say "hurt women," when he hears the anger in his own voice, the rising volume of frustration. Adam startles the dog out of his doze. "Come on, Chance." He leaves his cold coffee and newspaper behind.

Chapter Forty-one

The jagged edge of panic slices through Adam. Daylight demons, far more insidious than those of the night, circle his mind.

With his record, he won't even be able to get a job at McDonald's. He can't even get his old job of bus driving back. He's going to end up in line with the men at the center, being served, not serving.

The savings that the court allowed him to keep, out of which he's been paying child support and every other court-determined expense of his estranged family, has diminished to a laughable amount. He's got maybe three months' worth of rent and car insurance money. When he hears those "get out of debt" commercials saying if he has more than ten grand in credit-card debt, call today, he sometimes thinks he should make the call. He has never been so out of control of his finances. He gets the irony of it. He lost control; therefore, he is out of control. The man for whom the platinum credit card was invented, who had never allowed a balance of two dollars owing at the end of the month: unemployed, unemployable.

Despised by his daughter, his ex-wife. And the woman that he finds he thinks about, whose good opinion is being withheld because of his control issue. A woman who is so unlike Sterling. Who is comfortable with herself, content with her life as it is. Whose ambitions have been realized in the owning of a shop filled with fish and a home filled with rescued dogs. He would call her a simple person, but that would suggest mediocrity. Gina is anything but mediocre, and he feels her disdain more powerfully than even his family's. If his life had been different, if he'd pursued a less ambitious course, he might have found someone like Gina and settled down. Lived his life worrying only about fuel prices, not corporate takeovers. Accepted his rough beginnings and improved on them by being a good husband, a good father. Chosen to get his satisfaction from his family, not his career. Chosen a wife who loved him for who he really was, not for his potential success.

Adam sits on the edge of the futon and puts his head in his hands. He should call Stein, he knows this, knows he needs a voice other than his own in his ears. He needs someone to tell him that he is going to be all right; that this is the dark time, but the light will come.

Absent a comforting voice, Adam's thoughts sink deeper. If he were to disappear, who would miss him? Disappear like Veronica? Unlike his sister, he has no sibling to wish he would come back. His family might even be relieved to have him gone. Adam knows that *disappear* isn't the word for what he's thinking. Oblivion. Release from this black hole that he inhabits. How painful it is to think that his death might bring only a momentary regret to those who know him. *Too bad about Adam March.* Sterling could enjoy a social notoriety as an ex-widow. Ariel would get time off from school. Compassionate leave. Sympathy grades. His life insurance is paid up—a policy that he bought a week before they were married, and then proudly adjusted to designate their newborn daughter as a beneficiary along with Sterling. Adam has the unoriginal thought that he is literally worth more dead than alive.

So it has to look like an accident.

Unless his ultimate revenge is to leave Sterling and Ariel without that money. A slap in the face for their treatment of him, for their rejection of him as a man who is, at heart, not a bad man.

Adam thinks of Sophie. How glad she might be if he were dead. He'd be doing her a favor.

The bottle of scotch has appeared at his hand. The glass is empty. How much scotch would he have to drink to die of alcohol poisoning? There must be a formula. If he weighs 160—okay, maybe 170—and is six feet . . . He's not up to the math. Can he do it with the half liter left in this bottle, or should he run out and buy some more? Would vodka be more efficient? Add a little Tylenol PM?

Adam pours another half glass of scotch. No sense rushing things and vomiting up all his hard work. He has all day. Oops, no, he hasn't. For the first time in his adult life, Adam calls in sick. Rafe takes the call with good grace, "Take it easy, man. Don't worry about it." Rafe's swallowing his story of 'feeling like crap' adds an additional helping of guilt to Adam's quota.

No note. That would screw everything up. Unless he left

one in an unobvious place, to be found later, after the inquest. After the insurance is paid out. After his sorry body is cremated and his ashes are scattered. Or not. He'll probably get left in a box in Sterling's closet, eventually to be discarded with other out-of-fashion possessions. Or left at the crematorium. Unclaimed freight.

This is such a good plan. He has been forcibly disconnected from the world, and now he'll make the disconnection permanent. There is no one who cares about him, or needs him. Or will notice for five days that he's missing. Except Big Bob. Well, that's good. They'll find him before he starts to stink.

Chance walks up to Adam and sits down, lowers his big boxy head and drops something out of his mouth: the tennis ball that Gina gave them, which Adam hasn't seen since that day a month ago. The ball bounces; the dog pounces, scrambles around as if the thing were alive and worthy of capture, then returns to sit in front of Adam. He drops the ball again.

"Who taught you that game?" Adam kicks the ball across the room with his toe.

The dog's tail end is in the air, the ball between his paws. He noses it in Adam's direction, where it clunks up against the scotch bottle. Adam retrieves the ball, tosses it in the air, and catches it a couple of times, then flings it against the opposite wall where it hits with a dull thump. The dog plunges after it ecstatically, tail wagging, barking at Adam to keep up the game. He drops the ball at Adam's feet, looks at him with eager eyes, eyes that declare he is the one who will care. A dog will be the only one to miss him.

And what would happen to Chance if he died? Back to the shelter? Back into the hands of the boys who fought him? Would Gina take him?

Like a rust-stuck wheel, Adam's thoughts begin to loosen and turn. He is the hub of the wheel, his thoughts spokes leading to the faces of Ariel and Sterling. Sophie. Their voices connect to him with the rivets of scorn and accusation. He has failed them; he has frightened them. He has damaged them. They have reacted to him—his behavior, his temper, his unresolved issues.

He is unredeemed, despite the punishment of community service. Loss of job, loss of status, wife, daughter, friends. Most of all, he's lost his humanity.

This conversion from victim to villain is stunning to him. Guilt, embarrassment. Shame. "This isn't who I am." This is what he's said to Gina, and yet it *is*. The person he has become, the person so tightly wound that he can be undone by a minor misunderstanding. The person no one wants to be around. A pariah.

Until and unless he makes amends, he will never regain his humanity. He will never find redemption.

Chance drops the ball. He makes his little *rrooorr* sound, but this time it sounds like speech. This time, it sounds like approval. The dog shoves the damp tennis ball against Adam's closed fist. The two, man and dog, stare at each other for a moment, the man taking great comfort in the reflection of himself in the dog's brown eyes—the only eyes that don't look at him with disappointment.

Chapter Forty-two

Who knows where the tennis ball–playing gene comes from. All I knew was that this object fell to the floor from the counter—perhaps a mild earthquake, or perhaps I nudged it when I was reaching up to snag a half-eaten sandwich from the countertop. At any rate, the ball fell and I hit upon a great way to get my man out of his self-indulgent slump.

He was sitting there with his hand wrapped around a glass and his eyes fixed on the floor, just like the day he sat with his eyes and nose running and first touched me—the first time he acknowledged that I lived alongside him, and from then on it was much better being in this crib. I admit it. So now the sharpish scent of the fluid he was knocking back worried me. He hadn't been indulging in this as much lately, which meant that he'd had more time for me. I was alert to the fact that he was agitated, pacing around, sitting, banging his fists against his skull. Drinking. The odor of his beverage began to seep out of his pores, mingled with an amalgam of fear, anger, grief. He reminded me of a dog I'd known in the cellar who chewed himself with a self-destructive obsession until his skin was a bloody mass of scratches and sores.

I watched him for a long time while he drank and muttered, sinking deeper into a state of anxiety. Even as I grew increasingly fretful about him, I wondered why I was wasting my time observing him, worrying about him. This wasn't something that I came to naturally, this concern about a human. Yes, I knew all about dogs who did, who saved Timmy from the well. But I am not that kind of dog, I told myself firmly, reminding myself that once I was a professional fighter. All along I have been telling myself that I am not a *pet*. My plan had always been to book it for greener pastures in the spring, or early summer at the latest. Not to get attached. If the door opened right now, I reasoned, I would leave. Sayonara, pal.

I had been kind to him once before, but that didn't mean I was a permanent fixture in his life. I was not going to be part of one of those pathetic bonded pairs, man and dog, that I'd been observing a lot lately. Watching the dogs in the park play with their people—undignified romping, tails upright and wagging like out-of-sync metronomes. Happy looks on their faces—dog and man. Lavish face licking. For what? Nothing more than I had right here, a bowl of water, although mine was empty right now, and a twice-a-day meal of dry, crunchy bits and pieces. An occasional pat on the head. No no no. I'm an independent creature, a creature of self-possession, a dog who belongs to no man.

It was nearly dark, and I thought that if I could get him to take me out now and let me off the leash at the empty lot, then maybe it was time to go. To bid farewell to this solitary human.

Even as I thought it, I knew that I wouldn't go. He was talking, but clearly not to me. His speech was slurry, equivalent to the low moan of a defeated champion. I felt a twinge in my heart, a clenching against independence. I went over and stood in the bed that we'd taken away from the woman who liked to give me cookies. Although I frankly preferred the futon, this cushiony substitute curled nicely around my back; snuggling into it felt like a return to puppyhood. This time, I couldn't get comfortable, so I went back to stand and stare at him, urge him to look at me and remember that I had needs, too.

I took a deep sniff, filling my nose with his scent. Beyond the odor of his emotions and his drink, I could still detect the underlying essence of him. For the past days or weeks, or whatever the artificial enumeration of time is for these people, I had been feeling something beyond a normal thanks-for-the-kibble gratitude. Thanks for not hitting me. Thanks for not handing me back to those boys. I was grateful for the times we sat on the couch together and he let me rest my head in his lap. I was grateful that he talked to me, not for his scintillating conversation, but for the sound of companionship. That's the scent that was being overwhelmed, the odor of calm, of partnership, of connection. I was afraid that something very powerful had hold of him, something that mere companionship wasn't going to scare off.

Then the ball dropped. I picked it up and forced him to look beyond his trance to see me. Could I get him to play with me? Could I remind him that I needed him? *I needed him.*

At first, he looked at me as if with someone else's eyes. Me, a critic of play, I urged the ball forward with my nose until it jammed between his feet. Looked at him with a silly dog grin and waited. Something slid away from his eyes and at last he saw me, saw the ball and picked it up.

He threw that ball hard against the wall, where it bounced crazily around the room until I trapped it. Over and over he smashed that ball against the wall, and over and over I pounced after it like some demented retriever until we both collapsed on the futon. I was panting, and so was he. Then he picked up his glass and, with the same violence as throwing the tennis ball, he flung it against that long-suffering wall and it smashed into a thousand shards. I flinched; the sound hurt my ears.

He reached an arm around my shoulders and dropped his head against mine. We might have been littermates snuggling. "Good boy."

I knew then that I might never again entertain the notion of leaving him. Not as long as *he needed me*. I raised my muzzle, lifting my head backward until I could reach his face with my tongue. My own version of "good boy."

Chapter Forty-three

The insistently repeated rhythm of his cell-phone tone penetrates the haze of alcohol-induced sleep. It is an annoying sound that has periodically entered his dreams as voices or objects or touching. Coupled with a full bladder, the sound of his phone ringing finally brings Adam awake. He fumbles for the teeny-weeny button but misses the caller. His missed calls function identifies a number he doesn't recognize. Tossing the instrument on the coffee table, Adam extricates himself from the gravity of the futon and stumbles to the bathroom.

Chance is waiting for him in the kitchen, the empty water bowl an indictment against Adam. He hasn't seen to the essential well-being of this animal. Adam rinses out the bowl, pours in fresh water, and watches as the dog laps up half. Which reminds Adam of his own thirst. Downing two glasses of water and a handful of aspirin, Adam becomes fully conscious of a new day. He looks at the shards of glass and the yellowy streaks of scotch that finger down the bland white wall.

"Ready to go out?"

Rrooorr says the dog, and Adam takes that as an okay.

The dog needs to go out. He needs to start his day. This new day.

Gina's store is open, the parrot sign turned to WELCOME. Adam walks in, Chance at his side. The parrot named Fred squawks a greeting, or an alarm. Gina holds a bucket of water and her window-washing pole. She sets both down, stands still. She doesn't smile at him, and her left hand goes to her throat, an unconscious gesture that makes her appear nervous and at the same time demure, persuadable.

"You've checked me out, haven't you? On the Internet."

"Yes. I was curious. I mean, after I realized who you were, I just wondered why you were living here, why you weren't at Dynamic anymore."

Adam is pleased that Gina isn't denying her curiosity. "Why didn't you ask me?"

Gina's supple mouth purses. "Wouldn't be polite."

"Ask me."

"Will you tell me the truth?"

"What I'll tell you will jibe with what you've read, only it'll be my side of the story. Can you accept that?"

"Yes." Gina locks eyes with Adam. In hers is a glistening of something that urges him on: a desire to believe him, to reconcile the two Adam Marches, the one she's found on the Internet and the one who stands in front of her.

Adam picks up the bucket and the squeegee. Taking Chance's leash, Gina follows him outside. He wrings out the sponge into the warm water, then wipes it in broad strokes across the rainbow and the dancing fish. As he draws the rubber blade down the window, smooth lines of water rushing ahead of the edge, he begins to talk.

The story he tells her spools out from deep within. He hasn't rehearsed, and so his story comes out in chunks, in truths that he has never before voiced. She knows a little bit about his sister, but he tells her about his childhood among strangers, about his father. As he talks, he finds himself elaborating, bringing old memories up from the depths of his subconscious. Stein would say that he was free-associating. He not only tells Gina things he has yet to speak about in therapy; he tells her about therapy. About Fort Street. About his anger at being assigned to serve food to the homeless and now his dependence on that place as the center of his days.

He feels no compunction about discussing a marriage that was more corporate partnership than love affair. About painful and abiding love for a daughter who detests him. About Sophie, what he'd done to her. And why Veronica's sudden reintroduction into his life had triggered his downfall.

"A nervous breakdown?"

"My shrink can't quite fit me into a diagnosis. I'm not quite a conduct disorder, not quite a depressive. A little of both. So we agree only that I had an 'episode.'"

Gina's olive eyes scan his, needing clarification. "But you say that you ran your departments, or divisions, with a firm hand. You were no one's friend. Even choosing your wife was a calculated measure. Everything was about the power."

There is a softening in his chest, a loosening up of the tightness he's felt for months, maybe years. It's as if the urge to cough has suddenly gone away. "Yes. And I now know that you just don't get to control everything. It's not sustainable. I'm not that man anymore."

He is done with the window washing and they go back inside. She takes the bucket of dirty water and disappears into the back room. The fish tanks burble gently, a soothing percolation. Chance wanders around, the leash dragging behind him, sniffing at the chew toys and bottles of homeopathic remedies, stuffed animals and ceramic kittens. Adam leans his elbows on the counter, facing Gina, who has come back but stays behind this barricade.

Gina looks at him, her mouth set in a way that suggests her doubt. She realigns the dozen charity jars. "I don't think that people can change that much just because they want to."

"With practice, you can." Adam lays a palm on the top of the jar designated for the shelter where he found Chance. "I've already changed into a dog owner."

"Why are you telling me this?" Although her words are sharp, Gina's eyes have begun to soften toward him. He can see that she wants to believe him. "Is this some kind of AA task where you have to go around making amends?"

"No. Although AA might not be a bad idea." He thinks of the shattered glass, the streaks of scotch on his wall. The dark terror of failure that plunged him into a soul-deep vortex must not happen again. Despite his proclamation that he is a new man, Adam knows that the vortex is only one bad moment away. Every thought, every action from now on has to keep him from that edge. He likens it to exercise: Every day he will strengthen. "I had a waking nightmare where I was visited by the ghosts of my life as it has been thus far. But today I have awakened to a new day. A new life. You represent the Bob Cratchit of the story, the humble clerk who understands that the good things in life are beyond price."

Adam watches a single tear slide out of the corner of Gina's eye, its contrail glistening in the morning light. He reaches across the counter and touches it, erasing its journey with a thumb. Gina reaches up and cradles the hand touching her face. She leans in and their lips meet over the divide of the counter.

Adam needs to go; Gina needs to get on with her day. He's got to head to the center. "Thanks for listening."

"Can I ask you one question?"

"Of course."

"Your sister. Do you ever wonder why she ran away? What she was running from?"

"I guess I've always believed that she was, like Ariel, rebellious. Maybe a boyfriend."

"Running from your father?"

Adam shrugs his coat on over his shoulders. "Maybe. I don't know, maybe running from me. From the responsibility of a little brother."

"You should find her. Ask her."

Even with all the resources of his former life, Adam has never considered searching for Veronica. She has always been so deeply embedded in a past he had disassociated himself from that the very idea was out of the question. Until now. Until Gina ever so gently has made the idea live.

The parents' waiting area at the barn is empty except for Adam. He sits down on the lumpy couch, pats his knee, and invites Chance up beside him. Asleep on a pile of empty grain bags is a cat. Chance, before jumping up, gazes at the recumbent feline. "Leave it," Adam orders the dog, and is pleased when Chance jumps up onto the couch instead of going after the small animal. Lately, Adam has been devoted to watching Cesar Millan on TV instead of Judge Judy. They are both forthright.

Beyond the viewing window behind him, Ariel, who cannot see that he is there, is jumping a course in the indoor arena. The jumps are not high, but set up so that she has to practice her takeoffs and tight turns. Adam leans against the back of the sprung couch and waits for Ariel to finish. This is not their regular Saturday. He's not here to pick her up, but to corner her into a conversation that is way overdue.

Adam almost dozes off as Ariel goes around and around, the steady thud of Elegance's hooves a melodic tune in four-four time. The little spaces of silence as she leaves the ground are like rests in a musical score. He snaps awake as he hears Ariel's coach call it a day.

In the main aisle of the barn, Ariel is untacking her mare. She sees Adam and doesn't stop what she's doing. She tosses the saddle over the half door of the stall, grabs a curry comb, and sets to work scrubbing the saddle marks off the bay mare.

"Hello, Ellie." Adam runs a hand down the long neck of the horse, something he's never done before; like Chance's, her coat is as soft as silk to the touch. The mare noses his hand for treats, then turns away, disappointed.

"Don't call her 'Ellie,'" Ariel says, but she's giving him a puzzled smile. "And watch that dog."

"He'll be fine."

"Why are you here? I drove here myself. You don't need to pick me up."

"I know. I want to have a conversation and I knew you'd be here."

"If it's about that night, I'm sorry. I said I was and I am. And I'm grateful that you didn't tell Mom."

"It's a little more than that."

"Okay. Just let me put her away."

Adam goes back to the waiting room. Ariel takes so long that he begins to fret that she's slipped out the back and driven off. It seems so odd that his little girl is driving. He's never even been in a car with her at the wheel. He's somehow missed the traditional bonding of parent and child over learner's permit driving hours.

The connecting door to the barn opens and Ariel comes in, flops down on the couch, with Chance between her and her father. She begins to stroke the dog's ears, the good one and the half. "What do you think happened to this ear?"

"I have no idea." Now that she's here, Adam is stumped at how to begin.

"So, what's up?"

"I'm going to let you decide when and where you see me. I'm not going to insist anymore. You're sixteen; you have your own mind. When you want to be in touch, I will always be there for you."

"Dad. Why?" To Adam's complete surprise, Ariel looks hurt.

"Because I can't take the cold shoulder anymore. I think that if it's your idea, you'll come to want to be with me. Why should we both suffer?"

"Are you trying to use reverse psychology on me?"

"No. I'm apologizing for being a crappy, absent, preoccupied, errant father." From somewhere in the barn, a horse whinnies. The sound is piercing, plaintive. "I thought that I could buy your love, but I can't. All I've paid for is contempt."

"That's not true. You don't have to buy me stuff. I thought you liked to."

"If I had the money, yeah, sure. But I don't. And you don't need anything, Ariel. You have more than two-thirds of what anyone else in the country ever gets. The men I work with have nothing, not even a home. And they don't complain. They don't lament their lives; they come up to the serving counter and they thank us. Thank us for serving them the only hot meal they're going to get in a day." Adam is aware that he's lapsing into a polemic, so he shuts up.

"Do you like working there?"

Chance squeezes out from between Adam and Ariel. He walks over to where the cat is still sleeping, gets close, but not too close, sniffs, and then flops down on the floor, leaving a gap between father and daughter.

"I do. I like it very much."

Ariel slides over so that their thighs touch, his in blue jeans, hers in cream-colored breeches. Adam takes her hand. Ariel rests her head on her father's shoulder.

"Tell me about my aunt. About Veronica."

"She looked like you. Or maybe I should say you look like her. I haven't seen her since she was just a little younger than you. She and my father had a fight one day and she walked out. I was little. Around five."

Adam and Ariel sit on the lumpy couch, the dog snoring lightly on the grain bags, and Adam tells Ariel his story.

Chapter Forty-four

Sophie Anderson stands in the cereal aisle of the Stop & Shop. Adam is surprised to see that she is pregnant. When did she get married? Did she marry that guy with the black T-shirt and the tattoos? She could do better, he thinks. She's a smart girl, if a little careless.

Dr. Stein has helped him break the barrier of restraining orders. He's made a phone call and gotten other phone numbers. Introduced the topic to Sophie's lawyer, to her shrink, to her. Sophie has said no, no meeting, however brief and public. She will not give Adam the chance to say he's sorry. Now Stein is cautioning Adam against pushing it. "It's almost enough, Adam, that you know you want Sophie to forgive you. You don't actually have to hear it from her."

Adam disagrees. Unless he gets to ask for her forgiveness, in person, there will always be that unresolved issue haunting him alongside all the others. It's a simple thing to ask, and withholding from him the opportunity to say those words,

"I'm so sorry," is almost as much a punishment as anything else he's suffered.

Stein is proud of him, and encouraging. But Adam isn't going to be put off.

If he's an easy Google target, so is Sophie Anderson. A simple address lookup. Her phone isn't unlisted, and despite the common name, he's able to pinpoint where she lives. If it's quite a distance from where he lives, it's still not inconceivable that he might find himself in that town. He isn't stalking; he's just putting himself in the area, patronizing establishments that she may patronize. Like the Stop & Shop. He needs dog food. He needs milk. It is purely by chance that they both need cereal. It's purely by chance that he's timed this casual drive to coincide with the end of the day at Dynamic, when so many employees who live in this suburb do their errands on the way home. Like Sophie.

"Sophie." She is studying the nutritional values on the side of a box of sugar-coated cereal. Adam speaks softly, gently, so as not to startle her. The way a man might wake up a woman. "Hello, Sophie."

His voice does startle her and her mouth drops into a little O of surprise. Her eyes immediately dart around, looking for someone, anyone, to prevent this meeting. "I said I didn't want to see you. Are you stalking me?"

"No. Not at all. See?" He holds up the bag of dog food, the half gallon of milk. "I just spotted you and . . ." Adam knows he has seconds to make his case. "Sophie, I only want to say how sorry I am for what happened. That's all." Adam bows his head a little, like a courtier to a queen, and turns away, the sound of his athletic shoes squeaky against the flat gray surface of the linoleum floor.

"Mr. March?"

He stops. He is flanked by cartoon characters shilling their confectionary breakfast foods, their leering smiles beckoning. Adam keeps his back to Sophie and waits.

"I know you are."

Adam's shoulders relax; he shifts the weight of the dog food to the other arm.

"But would you be as sorry if you hadn't lost everything?"

It is a crystal moment. Adam is thrust back into the seconds before he picked up the pink memo slip, read the words that triggered his breakdown. If he could go back to the life that he had worked so hard to achieve, a life of long meetings and high anxiety, late nights and a semi-estranged family that wanted ever more from him, go back to doing things that people like Gina despised, all in the futile hope of burying his past deeper and deeper, would he? Adam is unsurprised at the answer that bubbles up. No, he would not want to go back to that life. It no longer appeals to him. He is not that man anymore.

So Adam tells Sophie the truth. "Yes, no matter the outcome."

He walks briskly to the checkout counter. He smiles at the cashier, pulls out his last twenty. In the car, his dog waits for him. It's staying light later now and they'll have time to go to the park on the way home.

Chapter Forty-five

In typical New England fashion, summer has descended abruptly. The wet, cold spring shrugged off the stage, opening the way for the three H's: hazy, hot, humid. The kitchen of the center is a furnace, and Adam works in a clean white T-shirt and Dockers shorts. His apron comes to the bottom of his knees, so from the front, it looks like he's wearing a dress. A blue bandanna is banded around his forehead like Cochise's to keep the sweat from pouring into his eyes. They are all dressed in some variation of this, fighting the heat that comes from outside and within, feeding men who continue to wear their year-round wardrobes, impervious to the swelter.

The air conditioning in Adam's apartment has been broken for a week and his super has yet to replace the antique unit with a new one. The dog is an as-yet-unacknowledged interloper in the apartment complex, tolerated by the neighbors who have seen him, overlooked by the super, who will no longer be able to pretend the dog doesn't exist if he has to enter the apartment while Adam is out. Hence, Chance now comes to the center with Adam. Adam has cobbled together a lean-to shed in the backyard, which is fenced in already. The shed offers shade even at midday, and Rafe offers scraps. Chance seems happy enough out there, and when Adam looks through the back window at him, the dog is usually asleep in the shade. Occasionally, one of the smokers goes out and sits on the back steps and the dog sits with him, making Adam just the tiniest bit jealous. He wants Chance to be friendly but still remain a one-man dog.

Adam is putting in extra hours at the center. Not volunteer hours, but compensated time. He has been given a small stipend to research grant opportunities. Fluent with the language of finance and comfortable with the intensive application questions, Adam has crafted two successful grant applications in the last four months. His pay isn't much, but it keeps Chance in kibble and himself current with his rent. The rest still hangs over him like an anvil, but it's a step in the right direction, and the work is curiously satisfying, gentle as it is.

It is late by the time Adam shuts down Big Bob's computer, pulls off the bandanna, and changes his sweat-soaked T-shirt for a clean one. Chance is doing his "happy to see you" tap dance on the steps, his front legs pumping up and down, his big head swinging side to side, tongue lolling, eyes squinting up at Adam. "Ya wanna go home, big boy?"

Unhnnn unhnnn.

In whimsical moments, Adam thinks that the dog is teaching him a new vocabulary. Different sounds for different occasions. *Unhnnn* meaning "I sure do." *Rrooorr* meaning "I hear you, man." Or "Let's eat." Or maybe "What did you think of the game?"

Adam and Chance emerge onto Fort Street and head east.

The sultry part of the day is past and a slight breeze is coming up off the water miles away. Shadows spike across their path, street signs and buildings, abandoned shopping carts, wheels off, their shadows casting Jurassic figures before them. The sounds of traffic and the commuter train block out voices and birdsong as they walk along. Adam feels more than hears the low growl, telegraphed through the leash to his sweaty hand. He looks down. Chance's hackles are upright, forming a coxcomb of fur between his shoulders. There is no other dog in sight, nor is Chance yanking at the leash. No full-throated barking, just this low growl and the pressure of Chance's body leaning against his legs. There is only an old man standing at the bus stop in front of them. Then Adam realizes that Chance is looking backward.

Without their puffy jackets, Adam isn't sure if these are the same boys he'd encountered before, but Chance's behavior speaks of familiarity. They approach Adam, keeping enough distance that even if he let the leash go slack, the dog wouldn't reach them. "You still got my dog, man." The slenderer of the pair accuses him, pointing at Chance, then at himself. "He's my dog."

"Not anymore." Adam will not be intimidated by these punk kids. In broad daylight, without their massive coats, he realizes that they are just kids a few years older than Ariel. They have no power over him. He's a lone white man in their neighborhood, but, by God, he's got the big dog. He stretches to his full height. "You want him? Try to take him."

The boys look at each other as if daring themselves to reach out and grab the leash out of Adam's hands. They look at Chance, who is snarling and barking, his tail whipping from side to side with the force of aggression. It is all Adam can do to keep his hold on the dog. Part of him wants to keep taunting, "Come on, come and get him." But they aren't going to take Chance; they can't get close enough. They're punks, two kids who act all tough because that's what's expected of them. He was a tough kid once himself. Had to be in order to survive. Maybe his streets weren't as mean as these, but mean enough. Maybe these kids don't have intact families, either. Maybe they are foster kids. Maybe he has more in common with them than the desire to own this dog. "He's my dog. Not yours. Maybe once, but not now. Nuff said?"

The boys simultaneously plug in iPods, turn away from Adam, and disappear.

"Guess we told them." Adam reaches down to touch Chance, calm him down, assure him that everything is all right.

Chapter Forty-six

At first I was a little put off by being left outside to cool my heels in the backyard of the building where the man goes in smelling like himself and comes out smelling like food and other men. I guess I was getting a bit puffed up with myself, what with my status as house dog. Why should I be left out in the backyard like any common cur? Then I realized that being just outside the window where all those good food smells originated was pleasant. Plus, I had the bits and pieces of meat ends and the occasional shinbone to enjoy, courtesy of the man in the big hat. And there was no one around to threaten my possession of such treats. Just me. It was very pleasurable to lie in the shade of the shelter my man had constructed, water bowl topped off, shinbone beneath my chin. Pigeons skulking around, burbling and mating. If there was a fence keeping me in, it also kept out the street dogs that might wander by. Being a dog, I really can't say how long I'd been living this life of leisurely unemployment, but it seemed to me that a whole new generation of street dogs had come of age. In other words, I knew no one. So I acted all territorial about this square of yard defined by a man-made structure. I yarked and growled. Lifted my leg on my fence. Acted all fierce, protective. Sometimes, bitches in particular, they'd ignore my bad manners and come to the fence anyway. A chain-link fence is an obstruction, but not impenetrable, and noses met greeting areas. I wagged my tail in apology. They were all right. Most of them.

There was this one dog. Big fella. Didn't have the look of a fighter, but clearly not someone to be messed with. His tail had been lopped off and he kept the vestigial end of it poked straight out, as if there were a lot more to it. He became a frequent visitor, but he never got over his wanting to challenge me. We'd growl at each other over the fence, him taunting me about my captivity, me throwing back insults at him. *Man, if that gate was ever left open, I'd show you a thing or two.* He was the only one who wandered by that provoked me. I was forced to check the sturdiness of the gate by throwing myself against it. Usually someone came out of the building to put a stop to it. Then the coward would run off, that poky short tail flung down to cover his anus. *Guess I told you, didn't I?*

Most days some of the men in the building would come out and sit with me. Lighting up those sticks that burn, they'd group around the back stairs and puff away. I didn't much like the scent, which reminded me too much of my time in the basement with the boys. They'd often reeked of this odor, or one similar to it. But these guys liked it if I joined them. Once in a while, only one of them might come out. If I sat beside him, the guy might throw an arm over me, talk to me, tell me things I was fairly certain he kept to himself most of the time. These men reminded me a little of the man I lived with. There was a certain fragility to them. The soft voices that they used with me immediately rushed into gruffness whenever someone else came out, as if they were embarrassed to be caught talking to a dog. When they sat with me in a pack, they betrayed none of that fragility. Sometimes on the street, you meet a dog that isn't supposed to be a street dog. He might be lost, or his people lost. Those dogs often make fairly good street dogs, but there is always this core of disbelief that they have ended up this way. That's what these guys were like.

I'd seen the boys more than those times with my man. I'll give him credit: He stood up to them, growled in a very professional way. Good man. What he didn't understand was how much they wanted me back. I don't mean to brag, but I was a top dog for them, a winner. Which made them happy, which meant they wanted to continue to fight me. So when they showed up, leaning against the fence that surrounded the backyard of the building where my man had left me to slumber away the summer days, I got nervous. Which meant that I barked. Which meant that someone from inside looked out and the boys skulked away like half-grown pups lookin' cool.

So every day that he left me in the fenced-in yard, I grew more nervous. I liked the job I had now, giving aid and comfort to the street men, being my man's singles partner with the tennis ball. I just couldn't see myself back in the pit. I was a pacifist now, not a contender. I admit a tiny bit of embarrassment at that admission, but truth isn't always pretty. I once was powerful and feared. Now I was loved. A much bigger deal.

Chapter Forty-seven

Adam has two weeks before his final hearing with Judge Johnson. Labor Day is past; the streets are filled in the morning with schoolchildren. He waits at crosswalks manned by crossing guards who eye a childless man with a fierce-looking dog with a wary expression. He smiles at them, says good morning. Hitches Chance closer to his side. He has been assured of a good report from Big Bob, a real testimony to good behavior and going the extra mile. He has proven himself a tractable volunteer and will keep on with his grant writing even as his time will be filled with his new work.

Even better, Adam has been hired as a consultant for a firm downtown. This one isn't an Internet start-up, or a pie-in-the-sky scheme by recent college graduates; this one is a long-established business looking for someone to head a special project. He sat with two of the three partners and gave them a brief "need to know" about himself. Then hawked his skills so well, they shrugged at the confession. They were getting a very skillful executive at a very reasonable price; his personal failings were his own.

Dr. Stein is pleased with Adam's recent progress, too. And his report will reflect that.

Adam comes out of Stein's building and drops another coin into the meter. There's a gourmet cheese shop nearby, and suddenly Adam has a longing for Wensleydale. They also sell gourmet dog biscuits, and Chance deserves a treat. He deserves a treat. The fresh, dry air ruffles his hair. Tomorrow he'll stop in at the local barbershop for a trim. No more haircuts that cost as much as a car payment.

All the way down the street, across the road, between buildings, Adam looks for Jupe. Jupe has been absent for several weeks. Maybe he's back in a hospital, or maybe he's hitchhiked to Manhattan. Bob doesn't know, but with continuous good weather, he's not all that concerned.

Adam doesn't know why he should be so concerned about Jupe. The old man hasn't spoken to him since the failed dog search, since he tried to give Chance to him. He cuts Adam dead anytime their paths cross. Jupe is one of those who won't go into the backyard and sit with Chance.

Adam understands that in Jupiter's tortured mind, he's responsible for Benny's disappearance because he'd failed to keep the promise the old man exacted from him to find the dog. Jupe can't accept the truth that the dog was doomed the moment he was hospitalized. It wasn't that Adam didn't find the dog; he simply no longer existed. But, like a promise spoken to a child, or a man with a child's grasp of the world, that promise to find Benny was a bond that had no alternate reality. No excuses. But Adam knows how he feels. If anything ever happened to Chance, he'd be devastated. He has become, in a very short time, one of those people who would stay in his house during a nuclear attack if his dog couldn't be evacuated with him.

So now Adam tends to look for Jupe when he's in this area, where Jupe alone or with Benny most often lingered.

Adam decides not to tell Gina yet that he's hired a private investigator, although it was the first impulse he felt after his decision was made, before he'd even met the man in a Denny's to discuss exactly what he wanted to find out, and how much he was willing to pay. To finally act on this lifelong disappointment came with an unforeseen reaction: relief. It was a relief to think that sometime soon he might be able to stop wondering about Veronica, about what had happened to her, and where she'd ended up. He's not even anxious to get the news. He doesn't even try to imagine a reunion, even a nervous phone call to say, "Hi, I'm Adam."

He knows that it could take awhile, and maybe even that the detective will be unable to come up with any results, but that's okay. The important thing is that Adam has taken charge of the situation. Just like problems at work, the first step in handling them is to begin doing something. Inertia is a weight that presses down; action is the removal of that weight.

"Mornin', Adam." The litany of everyday living.

He's not late today. He's been up since dawn, preparing the outline for Stryker, Royal and Martin. He's already taken

Chance around the block. The coffee is brand-new. He's in sweatpants but has shaved. His business clothes are laid out.

Adam fills a second cup, sugars it, dribbles just enough low-fat milk in to suit Gina's taste. He makes his purchases, gives Artie an answer to 46 down—archetype—and goes out the door.

The impeccably dressed businessman is headed his way. Late, unusually late. Adam smiles and steps into his way, armed this time with his name. "Good morning, Mr. Martin."

Augustus Martin of Stryker, Royal and Martin, snaps his head around, his expression one of alarm: How does this bum know my name? Then recognition sets in. Embarrassment. "I thought you looked familiar at that meeting."

Adam thinks, What bullshit. The guy has never looked him in the face in all the months that they have crossed paths on a daily basis. He would put out a hand, but both are occupied. "You, too. Out of context, right?"

"Yes, out of context. I didn't realize you lived in this area. I thought that . . ."

"I know what you thought. Appearances can be deceiving, after all." Adam sips from his cup, decides to let the guy off the hook. In the glory days when he was in Martin's Cole Haan shoes, he would have treated a shabbily dressed, un-shaven early-morning stranger the same way. "I've got some ideas on paper to show you at our meeting. I think that you'll like them."

"I'm sure I will."

There is a moment of awkward parting. They do not know each other at all, but there has been such a long period of morn-ing encounters with prejudice that they don't quite know how to say good-bye.

Gina is washing her front window and watching this little pas de deux between Adam and the man she, too, recognizes from his daily route past her store. She scrapes the squeegee left to right, winks at Adam, and then draws the rubber edge right to left.

"You look pleased with yourself." She scrapes the moisture off the blade with a paper towel.

"Yes, I am."

Gina hears something in his voice and sets down the squeegee and toweling. "Why?"

He tells her about his detective.

At first, Adam doesn't recognize the number illuminated on the screen of his cell phone. He almost lets it go to voice mail, then remembers that the 978 area code belongs to his private investigator. It's been only a week. Surely not enough time, even in today's overexposed electronic Big Brother world, to find someone missing for forty years. Someone who maybe has never wanted to be found, someone whose youthful identity has been made over by marriage or alias into something completely new. Someone Adam has always—and don't ask him why—believed was now on the West Coast, as far away as she could get from her New England beginnings.

"I have some news. Can we meet?" The PI is a small, round man, but on the phone he sounds imposing.

"Can you give it to me over the phone?"

"In person. Denny's, in an hour?" The solemn voice prohibits argument.

Adam swallows against a swirl of nausea. "Are you afraid I won't pay you?"

There is a heartbeat of insulted silence. "I prefer to give my reports in person."

Denny's is mostly empty at eleven o'clock on a workday, just past breakfast, too early for lunch. The lone occupied table has an old couple sitting in silence, mulling over their plates of eggs and red-tinged home fries. It is the perfect backdrop for hearing news of his missing sister, with its massive plastic-coated menus, the slightly sticky tabletop, a garish interior design based on the color of egg yolks. The geometric pattern of the industrial carpet makes Adam feel unsteady on his feet as he follows the middle-aged waitress to his seat. Ron Pascal joins him almost immediately, handing his menu back to the waitress and asking for black coffee. Adam does the same.

"Can I getcha some home fries or a order of toast or some-thin'?"

Ron Pascal meets her eyes, "No. Just coffee. Please." The waitress moves away from the table. "You know why I hate missing person cases so much?"

"You never said that you did." Adam has a packet of sugar in his fingers; he's rotating it around, as if measuring the sides.

"'Cause it almost always isn't good."

"You're telling me . . . what, exactly?"

Ron pulls a thin file folder out of his briefcase, sets it on the table between them. "This is what I found."

The file has a neat green-bordered label on it, VERONICA MARIE MARCH typed in all uppercase Times Roman letters. Solid, real. Not like a missing person at all, but like someone who should have lived enough life to fill this folder. A folder so thin, the edges touch. Thin enough to hold one piece of paper.

"Your sister passed away six weeks after she left home." Ron flips open the file folder; the death certificate is facing Adam, but Pascal knows the line he's looking for. "Cause of death: massive internal injuries consistent with being struck by an automobile."

"Hit by a car? Veronica was killed?"

"I'm afraid so. The two paragraphs of press coverage state that she was either hitchhiking or crossing the street at around two in the morning, when she was struck and killed by a hit-and-run driver." Pascal pulls the newspaper clipping out from under the death certificate, along with the one square inch of obituary.

Adam feels dizzy. He doesn't take the articles from Pascal. His hand is shaking as he reaches for the handle of the coffee mug the waitress has set down in front of him. He's afraid to lift the mug to his lips. It's not that he hasn't steeled himself, considered the idea that Veronica might be dead. It's always been a latent possibility, one that he has from time to time talked himself into expecting. The shock is that she's been dead all this time; that his every childhood dream of how she would someday come rescue him was beyond fantasy, was impossible, an impotent hope. Should he be grateful for not knowing? How could he not have known? Why didn't anyone tell him? He imagines a giant conspiracy of silence keeping the most important fact of his childhood from him. Was it a misguided kindness? Don't say anything and he'll forget all about her?

If he had known that his sister was dead, throughout all those years of foster homes and pullout couches, of bullying, of loneliness, he would have had no hope at all.

Adam pushes himself out of the booth. His knees buckle as he staggers toward the men's room, getting inside just in time to vomit.

"Why didn't my father tell me?"

"I guess you'll have to ask him." Pascal snaps shut his briefcase, pulls a wallet out of his back pocket, and drops a couple of dollars on the table.

"I can't." Adam lifts his eyes from the folder containing his sister's death certificate and looks Pascal in the face. "I have no idea if he's even still alive. I haven't heard from or spoken to the man since I was nine."

Pascal opens the folder again and points to a yellow Post-it Note stuck to the inside. "That's his address and phone number."

Chapter Forty-eight

Because of his unscheduled appointment with Pascal, Adam is an hour late to the Fort Street Center. He's called ahead, gotten Big Bob's dispensation without having to give him any excuse. He's never been late before, a fact that only today occurs to Adam. He's treated this enforced do-gooding as he treats all his responsibilities—with professionalism. Someone should be proud of him. It's not like he's been working for a merit raise. He's just applied his hard-coded work ethic to this situation, exactly as he has always done in all of his positions in his rise up the ladder. Automatically doing his best as an involuntary volunteer.

Adam stops by the apartment to leave the car, get Chance, and walk to the center, despite already being late. His pulse is still pronounced from the effects of his conversation with the investigator and he needs to slow it down, to force the twin facts of his sister's untimely death and his father's unlikely survival into some form of neutral territory, assign them someplace in his mind where they are harmless. He has to make the basic facts lie down and be still. Instead, his mind cavorts with the unanswered questions.

Gina is in her shop, but Adam can't tell her yet. He needs to digest this new truth on his own. He can't speak out loud, can't make the words come out in a way that will make sense to himself, much less to another. He needs time to adjust his entire concept of the past.

Adam latches the gate behind him, unsnaps the leash, and runs cold water into the dog's bowl from the outside faucet. With a quick pat on the head, he leaves Chance to entertain himself for the next few hours. Chance lumbers over to his lean-to and flops down in the shade.

Ishmael is behind the steam table, ladling out the day's soup. Adam grabs a clean apron and a paper toque and settles into serving the main course of pork chops and mashed potatoes. Everything looks gray to Adam, the chops, the gravy, even the soup. Shades of gray, like they say dogs see. Nothing is sharp.

"You okay, man?" Ishmael asks.

"Yeah."

"You seen a ghost or somethin'?"

Adam shakes his head, tries to smile. "I'm okay."

"You sick, you shouldn't be here."

"Not sick."

"Sad." Jupiter is standing in front of Adam. After so many weeks, it is a surprise to see the old man standing in front of him, his watch cap pulled low, his eyes flinty, and Adam notices for the first time how pale they are, not like looking into eyes at all, but into reflectionless mirrors. "Too bad." Jupiter might be addressing them, or himself. His pale eyes flicker from Adam to the plate, then to Ishmael. "So sad your dad. *Sad* is the loneliest word in the world." Adam vaguely recalls that rhyming can be a symptom of some mental disturbance, but he doesn't recall Jupe ever doing it before.

"You want gravy with that?" Ishmael slides the plate across the stainless-steel surface.

Jupe takes the plate, squinting at Adam. "Now you know. Now you know."

Ishmael raises an eyebrow at Adam, mouths, "Woo. Woo."

"At least he's back." Adam lifts the now-empty soup tray out of the steam table. At least he knows where Jupe is. One less disappearance to worry about.

Chapter Forty-nine

I was alone in the backyard, tending to my nethers, waiting, hoping that the man in the hat would come out with a treat, wondering if something interesting might be on the docket for later. Maybe a ride in the car, a walk in the park.

"Hey, boy."

I stopped my ablutions to stand and appraise my visitor. It was the man who once hung around with my former mentor. I hadn't seen him in a long time, not here and not on the street. I sniffed the air. He smelled ripe—of the street, of the untamed, free life. I drew closer.

"Good boy."

Two words of their noisy language that I knew, and agreed with. He wasn't in the yard with me but standing outside the gate. I trotted closer, anxious to meet him, breathe in more nearly that sweet scent of street. Obligingly, he opened the gate. Then he walked away.

The gate swung itself three-quarters shut. Not enough to keep me in. I sat. I am a dog; I do not usually wrestle with the ethics of trust and obedience except as they suit me. My man has trusted that I not jump out of his car if he leaves the windows open. I trust that he will feed me, scratch my belly. That's about as far as I go. This open gate, this invitation to walk out onto the street like a free dog was like a gift from some bountiful deity. Who was I to say no? But I sat. Waited. I have no capacity to debate right and wrong, or the moral dilemmas of faithfulness. I had never been told to stay. Neither did I have any excuse to go.

I was waiting for a reason to push that open gate wider. And along he came, that mutt who loved to challenge me as long as he thought I was behind bars. Boy was he in for a surprise.

Chapter Fifty

Adam has moved in a fog all afternoon. The last time he'd felt like this was after his episode at Dynamic, the light-headed feeling, the sense that his hands are attached to his wrists by thin threads, his feet blocks of stone. Adam goes through the motions of helping Rafe, of serving lunch, of running the dishwasher, of listening to Ishmael's chant of "You want gravy with that?" over and over, until the five words hummed in his head like the catchphrase from a B movie or the chorus to a country-western tune. You Want *Gravy* wi' That? Gravy. Wi'. That? What Do You Want? Ishmael even pushes a little rhythm to the words. Sing along now. Follow the bouncing ball. Where did that come from anyway? Funny how the references faded after a generation or two but the phrases lasted forever.

The last man has been served. The tables are nearly empty. Mike has folded up most of them, letting the stragglers bunch together at one, the other meant for the staff. Right now the smell of food is making Adam queasy. He'll just skip it today.

Get his dog and go home. Big Bob will understand; sometimes a guy just isn't hungry. But when the others grab their plates and cutlery, Adam finds himself joining them. If he goes home, he'll just sit and think. At least the conversation here will provide a slight distraction; maybe he can even summon up the verve to add his two cents to the inevitable discussion about the Red Sox. Anything to avoid thinking about Pascal's report. About Veronica. About the fact that his father is still alive and living within a scarce two miles of him. All this time. All this time she's been dead and he's been alive. It's not that Adam's ever thought about the old man being dead; it's more that he's cast him so far out of his life that he cannot conceive that his father still exists. The pain in his sternum twinges and Adam presses a hand against it.

Rafe drops onto the bench beside Adam. "I got some scraps for Chance. How come you didn't bring him today?"

"I did. He's out back."

"No he ain't."

Adam extricates himself from the fixed bench, banging his knee against the table, nearly kicking Rafe in the process. "Are you sure?"

"Gate's open, man. No dog."

"Fuck." Adam starts for the back door, and suddenly Jupe is in front of him.

"Excuse me." Adam doesn't want to touch the old man, but he's desperate to get outside. "I need to get by." *Some idiot has left the gate open.*

"Now you know." Jupe doesn't move. "Now you know."

Adam has been here for three hours, and he knows that he was careful with the U-bend latch. No one is supposed to come in by the back door, Big Bob's rule, but someone did. Or left that way. The staff are all here; he was the last one in. So which of the men slipped out, careless with the gate, careless with Chance? A panicked notion: His dog may have been on the loose for two hours by now. He could be miles away. Or dead from running in front of a car. Adam pictures Chance running, confused, dismayed. His former street dog panicked like anyone's coddled purebred. Alone.

There is no time to lose, and this old man is in his way. Adam tries to get past Jupe, but Jupe is determined to be in his way and nimbly blocks Adam's route.

"I said, now you know what it feels like." Jupiter grins at Adam, grins and holds his Swiss Army knife at chest level, the blade extended. "Sad. Sad."

"Whoa. Okay, Jupe. Hold on there." Adam hears Big Bob, feels his bulk just behind him, a bulwark against this madness. "You need to put that down."

It's not a very big knife. Not a long blade, but the light touches it in such a way that it reflects a dull shine, an ancient patina, lovingly sharpened. The tip is tilted just so, like a woman's smile. Adam steps back. Jupe follows, a pas de deux. Big Bob, Rafe, and Ishmael circle the dancers.

"You killed my dog."

"No I didn't. I just didn't find your dog."

"Don't engage him, Adam. Just hold on." Big Bob is slowly working his way around behind Jupe. "Mike's calling for help."

Jupe is more dangerous than a man who knows how to use a knife. He slashes wildly, pokes and thrusts the short blade with a jerky rhythm—up and down, from side to side. A manic sign of the cross. The sharp little blade is poking out of the handle like a serpent's tongue.

Adam backs away. Jupe is too fast and too erratic for Big Bob or Rafe or Ishmael to attempt to knock the knife out of his hand. The group moves as one into the middle of the dining room, until Adam feels the bench of the emptied table behind his knees.

"Look, Charles," Adam hopes that using the guy's real name will shock him back into reason. "I'm sorry about your dog. I know how much he meant to you."

"But you tried to foist a fake on me. You didn't know what he meant to me. You think one dog is like another. Didn't even look like Benny."

"I do know what it's like to lose someone you love. I do know. You can't replace them. They aren't interchangeable."

"You promised me."

"I shouldn't have. I didn't know it would be impossible to keep that promise."

Jupe is suddenly still. His flinty, pale eyes are rimmed in pink, the sclera yellowish, and they bore right into Adam's eyes, making him think that this isn't a man they're dealing with at all, but a demon. There is nothing human in those eyes.

Adam forces himself to stare into those eyes. "And now I want to go find my dog. Before it's too late."

Jupe's right hand, the one with the knife in it, begins to relax. It's like watching the demon leave a soul as the flinty look is replaced with confusion, with a mildness. An awakening. In the distance, a police car's siren. Adam thinks that he can ask for the knife, that the demon is gone and Jupe, the man, can be disarmed. That maybe Jupiter has returned to being Charles. Adam puts out his hand, waggles his fingers as if encouraging a small animal to come to him. "Will you give that to me?"

Jupiter lunges.

Chapter Fifty-one

Here I was, on my unexpected ramble, practically intoxicated with the world of street scents, enjoying my leashless freedom, and—wham—trouble. I was as naïve as a newcomer to the street life. My months on the end of a leash had dulled my instincts for self-preservation. For too long I'd been led around, not using my own brain, relying on a human to tell me where to go and how to get there.

After chasing off the poseur, I snuffled along the sidewalk of the neighborhood I had ended up in, a little disoriented, since I had paid no attention to landmarks while I chased the bastard off into traffic, so I was exploring what seemed to be new ground, which, I have to admit, was great fun. Until I hit on a scent that tickled the memory keys in my brain. I imaged the scent, searching for the visuals that would tell me what my nose was trying to. Cage. The filthy backyard redolent of feces. The scent of dried blood. I had somehow ended up on the street where I got my start. This was definitely not in the plan, so I raised my nose, trying to discern the scent of my neighborhood—either the one I shared with the man or the one with the backyard—from the myriad threads that make up the world. Maybe that way? Was that the scent of the coffee place he likes to sit outside? Or that way? Do I smell the street men gathering? Nothing. Nothing I could get a line on.

I was well and truly lost. I'm dog enough to admit it. My fanciful thinking that I'd play a little hooky and be back in time for our walk home turned into being lost. Well, I may have been lost, but I wasn't stupid. Retrace my steps. Logical, huh? But I'm a dog, a male, and one who had clearly challenged the other dogs in these neighborhoods in that I had announced myself on every post, hydrant, and rear tire. Every one of my own markers had been covered by someone else's. And not the same someone. Eventually, I found myself right back on the same block of my former life.

"Looky here, dawg. You b'lieve it?" Since I'd been gone, the fine distinction between potential and corruption in these almost men had disappeared, and in its place, was sheer hostility. They reeked of it. They reeked of dog, of smoke, of malice. Of pizza and beer. Of the blood on their shoes. Of their own fear, which masked itself as anger. I hadn't realized before that they were much like the dogs in their cellar, guided by forces outside their control. Victims of their breeding.

This time, there were four of them. The two I'd known, and two who were bigger, older, and distinctively powerful. Men.

I snarled, snapped, spun around, not wasting my breath on sound but putting it all into action. But I was surrounded. I ducked, made for the gap between legs covered in baggy jeans. The kick hurt; I stumbled. I had never used my teeth on a human before, but I wasn't going to go down with a whimper.

But, of course, they knew how to handle a snapping dog. The last thing I remember is the quick grab of a rope around my muzzle, squeezing my jaws together, then nothing as one of them brained me with a break stick.

I awoke in a cage, my old cage. Deep in the corners, it still bore some trace of me. My parents were gone, replaced by another breeding pair. She eyed me with dull curiosity. He growled. I didn't respond. I wasn't about to get into a shouting match. I was just relieved to have my mouth open, and I drank from the shallow puddle of water in the bowl in the cage. Here I was again, right back where I'd started. I wondered how soon I'd be back in the pit.

Chapter Fifty-two

Adam holds a large, thick square of absorbent material against his face, the ER staffer having taken away the kitchen towel that Rafe had given him to stanch the bleeding. Big Bob sits beside him in the waiting area, thumbing through a dated *Popular Mechanics* magazine and drumming his leg with sausage fingers. Adam had fought the idea of racing to the emergency room, wanting only to get out on the street and look for Chance. Every hour that goes by, and they have been here for over two, means it will be harder to find him. How far can a dog get? By the time Bob and Rafe had convinced Adam that he was well and truly injured, he was faint from the searing pain of a short-bladed slice in his face and was willingly led to Big Bob's car.

Adam gingerly pulls the pad away from his cheek. Has it stopped bleeding? He turns his head to see Big Bob, and feels a fresh drizzle of blood. He'll give them ten more minutes and then he's going to leave, despite his blood-soaked shirt and bleeding face. He's got to find Chance.

"You don't have to stay."

"'Course I do. You got hurt on my watch."

"I'm fine. You should go home." Ten minutes, as soon as he can convince Big Bob to leave, he'll bolt. "Really. Go." He can see Big Bob's temptation to get out of this depressing place, to go home, versus his good nature working against that temptation. Adam pushes. "Face wounds bleed worse than serious wounds. I'll be all right."

"You have anyone to call? Anyone who can come get you?"

"I'll grab a cab."

"Adam, I'm not going to let you do that."

"I need to find Chance."

"You need to get stitched. The dog's fine."

"Gina. Gina DeMarco." Give Bob a name and then get him out of here.

"Okay. What's her number?" Bob, ignoring the NO CELL PHONE USE sign, pulls out his Nokia.

"I don't know."

"Not a close friend?"

A slight dizziness, as if he is standing on the roof of a tall building and looking down. "A neighbor."

"Listed?"

"Try DeMarco's A to Z Tropical Fish."

Bob's massive hand fondles his cell phone and he speaks first to an automated voice, then to a real person. "Okay."

A nurse scowls at Big Bob and he walks outside to make the call. She then beckons Adam.

Gina is sitting by herself in the waiting area when he comes out. Her hand goes to her own cheek in spontaneous reaction to the sight of him, face swathed in bandage and surgical tape, bloody shirt and pants. "Oh sweet Jesus, what happened?"

"Chance is gone. He got out. I need to go look for him. Now." Adam shoves his discharge papers into his back pocket and grabs Gina's hand. "It's almost dark. Can we please start looking?" Adam has inadvertently made a good choice in giving Bob Gina's name. Of all the people he knows, she is the only one who understands his frantic desire to drive around the mean streets of Boston with half of his face numb, looking for a half-eared pit bull.

They drive in slow squares, block by block, radiating outward from the Fort Street Center. As they drive, Adam talks. "It's all tied together; Jupe's attack and Chance's disappearance are two sides of the same coin. Because I failed to find Benny. No, not my failure to find Benny. It was my lack of understanding as to how much the dog meant to the man, that one dog is not like the next. I just didn't get it, and the poor guy has been mourning—" Adam's voice catches with a sudden and powerful dismay.

Gina takes her right hand off the wheel to place it over Adam's. "We'll find him. There are plenty of good ways to locate lost dogs. We'll keep looking until we do."

As dark descends, making the search well nigh impossible, the lidocaine begins to wear off and suddenly Adam's face feels like he is being seared with a hot poker. The pain distorts his thinking, overwhelms him, and he lets Gina take him home. As they make the corner, he prays that his brindled dog will be sitting on the steps, *Lassie Come Home*. There is nothing there. No dog waiting for him.

Adam dreams of Sophie, of his hand on her face, but somehow it is he who feels the pain of the slap. He wakes. He is given only a split second before the pain and worry return.

His face aches with the seventeen stitches that form a neat crescent from the corner of his eye to the corner of his mouth on the left side of his face. He knows that he is lucky. Jupe's blade missed his eye and didn't penetrate through his cheek. The slice is deep, but his plastic surgeon has promised that he'll look piratical, not disfigured.

The hollow space under his ribs aches with emptiness.

Deep in his heart, Adam fears that Chance's fate is going to be the same as Benny's. His breed will be his demise. The prejudice toward his type: the automatic death sentence for animals like him in some cities. A dog can wander a long way, and he may be well away from the Animal Advocate shelter, which has his photo and his description and his tag number. Adam deeply regrets not getting around to microchipping him. Even though there is a better than even chance that no shelter would bother to run a reader over a brindled, half-eared, scarred pit bull.

The hollow place is filled with panic. He keeps losing those he loves. Veronica. Ariel. Now Chance. He presses on his sternum, willing the panic to subside. The panic begins to diminish. He is breathing too hard for someone sitting in a chair. He concentrates on slowing it down. He's back where he started. Alone. The leash hanging on the door mocks him, tells him that he was soft and stupid to let emotional well-being be dependent upon the presence of a mere animal. Animals die; they disappear. Veronica disappeared. She died.

The bolus of grief may be for Veronica; it may be for Chance. It is indistinguishable, these two losses, and he feels guilty about that. He should mourn his sister more, but it is the dog he misses. He is alone again.

Alone with the thought that his father, his abandoning father, lives two miles away.

Adam wasn't even ten when he last saw the man who had turned him over to the state. The visits had winnowed down to once a year, usually in the fall, so that returning to school, usually a new school, became synonymous with being made to dress in too-short dress pants and a short-sleeved dress shirt. A tie would be clipped at his throat. A knock, or sometimes the doorbell. This last time Adam had shot up so much in the previous year that he nearly reached his father's chin. They were almost eye-to-eye, a fact that clearly startled his father. "You've grown some." Adam couldn't read the look in his father's face. Was it concern or pride? His father wore a gray jacket, like the kind mechanics wear. He smelled of cigarettes, his fingertips stained with nicotine; his hair was still dark, slicked back, giving him a wolfish profile.

As usual, they walked to the nearest McDonald's. All around them were families with small children, teenagers banded together, and senior citizens sipping endless cups of coffee to kill the empty hours. "You want a Happy Meal?"

"No. Quarter Pounder with cheese."

"Please."

"Please." Once a year, and his father had to correct his manners.

Adam doesn't remember much of what they talked about. His father asked the usual litany of questions an adult asks of a child he barely knows: school, friends, sports.

School was fine, he told him. He had a couple of friends. He played baseball and basketball.

Just like his exchanges with Ariel. Brief and unadorned.

This time, Adam ate quickly. Did not want to prolong the

interrogation, had nothing to ask of his father but one thing. "Will I see you again?" Meaning, "Are you coming back into my life?"

"Sure. Soon."

The last words his father ever spoke to him. For the first time, Adam wonders why he never asked his father any questions. Why hadn't he asked the important ones? He knows now that by this time Veronica had been dead for four years. Why hadn't he asked about her? Had he known but not known? Suppressed the knowing? Certainly by this time, Stein would have weaseled that out of his subconscious. Along with why he never thought that his father was still alive. That after all these years, he's never imagined him as still alive. And yet he'd never truly imagined that Veronica was dead.

A knock on his door, purposeful. At once, Adam jumps up; the hopeful grin hurts, as he wants to believe that someone has found his dog, maybe someone in the building who has been generously quiet about the illegal tenant in 3A. Adam wrenches open the door. Gina stands there, a gentle, empathetic smile on her face. A mourner's smile. She carries a casserole dish, a carry bag full of bread and cheese and all the comfort food that she will press on him.

Adam wants to take her in his arms; instead, he goes into hers. The panic is gone. The hollow place is slowly filled as he tells Gina about Veronica being dead all these years, about his father living almost in the same neighborhood where Adam has been living since his expulsion from Sylvan Fields. She sits with him, holding his hand, rubbing his back. He doesn't know if she'll stay in his life, but right now, she's here, and he is so grateful.

Gina is slowly knitting Adam back together. She takes care of his wounded face, applications of vitamin E and gentle cleansing. She feeds him, turning his inadequate kitchen into a source of delight. She lets him hope. She lets him howl. She lets him talk. She lets him be silent. She finds his phone, which has fallen behind the futon. She makes up a list of shelters and calls in her animal-activist troops. She promises that if Chance is to be found, they will find him.

She calls Ariel for him, recruits his daughter into helping. Day by day, they scour the neighborhoods, the good ones and the bad, hanging lost-dog posters, making calls. Ariel holds Adam's hand as they walk the streets. Maybe it's the fact that she's simply growing up a little that has changed the dynamic of their relationship to something that, if not perfect, at least has the seeds of hope in it. Sometimes Adam thinks that, even absent, Chance has brought them together.

Ariel has Photoshopped a picture of a brindled pit bull into a reasonable resemblance of Chance. Adam can't bear looking at the picture. Sometimes he wonders how he ever came to lay so much human emotion at the feet of a dog. Wonders if this is normal. Gina has lent him a plaque from her store with Rudyard Kipling's poem "The Power of the Dog," the last line of each stanza warning against giving your heart to a dog to tear.

Chapter Fifty-three

The only light that works its way into the cellar is a thin border of gleam surrounding the cardboard squares set against the rectangular windows. I can judge day from night only by the strength of that thin line as it goes from bright sunshine to dull streetlight glow. I'm not taken outside even to defecate. My cage grows ever smaller as I try to keep the mess to one side. I am fed, watered. Talked to in low mutters, but not the kind that means sweetness, but which indicates a surliness at my mess, at having to feed and water me. All too clearly, I understand what is coming. I'd left this place a champion; now I'm the underdog. Upstairs, the sound of toenails on linoleum. Men's voices, challenging each other. Laughter. A sharp bark followed by the sound of a hand on flesh. Shaddup.

The cellar is divided into two spaces—the space where we live and the space where we fight. When I hear the sound of feet on the stairs, I look at the other two dogs in residence. The male lowers his head, his eyes barely reflecting in the dim light. He raises a lip at the scent of the challenger. This is someone he knows, someone he's fought. A soft growl. *He's a tough one. Lost to him last time.* The female circles three times and lies down. This isn't her game.

I am on my feet. The idea of impending battle sends the adrenaline coursing through my body. I fill the room with my voice. *Hey, pal, you just wait and see. Better look to your hind end.* All sorts of flimsy challenges. Bravado. The truth is that I no longer want to obey the orders of these boys. The game that I once was compelled to play, that once was my job, has been supplanted by a new and better job. I am no longer a gladiator. I am a pet, a leash dog. I miss my man. I didn't think that was possible, but that is the image that fills my mind, my man. Why hasn't he come to get me? What is taking him so long? I stop barking and start howling.

One of the boys pokes me with a break stick to get me to shuddup. In one smooth action, he opens my cage and slips a muzzle over my mouth, then a pinch collar over my head. Good. Let them take me seriously, let them understand that I'm a danger to them, and maybe they'll let me go. He doesn't have to drag me from the cage; I leap, roaring and twisting in an attempt to intimidate him into letting go. He just laughs, and the pinch collar obstructs my breathing until my roar is squeezed off into a pitiful choking sound.

I will not be dragged. I pull against the one holding the short chain attached to the pinch collar, pull him toward the other half of the cellar. Pull toward the pit. Okay. Let's do it. I may be out of shape, soft from good living and affection, but I'm still a dog. I'm still a fighter. Maybe a lesser challenger than this mass of muscle on feet in front of me, but I am. Woe betide the gladiator who doesn't understand that there is a better life away from this pit. I want that life back, and the

only way to it is through this moment. Then the boy not holding my chain, he does it: wraps my jaws together with silver
tape. I am not a fighter; I am bait.

I will not describe what happens. A dogfight is best left to
the imagination. Suffice it to say that it will be my last fight.

Chapter Fifty-four

It has been a very long time since Adam was with a woman. Even longer since he touched one who didn't counter his efforts with instructions, with time limits, or with conditions. Adam knows that comparisons are madness, yet he can't help but compare the soft curves of Gina with the exercise-hardened ridges of his former wife. Gina isn't self-conscious about the shape of her hips, or the full, swinging weight of her breasts once released from her brassiere—breasts that are natural, unaugmented, soft and sweet. She doesn't make excuses; she makes love.

In the end, Adam feels as though he's been borne away.

They have left a side lamp on in the bedroom and have dozed beneath its gentle light. They wake and nuzzle and Gina reaches over to turn off the lamp. The streetlights outside his bedroom window keep the room flooded in a pale light; he hadn't pulled the curtains, too hurried when they slipped into his room, drew back the heavy corduroy bedspread, and lay for the first time together. It wasn't inevitable, this act. Like their friendship, this moment has never been a foregone conclusion.

Adam flops backward on the mounded pillows and pulls Gina to him upside down across his lap. He's told her so much about himself, his life and troubles, that he's ashamed he's asked so little about hers. She's come to him whole, not in pieces, and that's how he imagines she's always been. But that can't be true. There are photographs on the shelf in her store; an elderly man and a set of twins—her grandfather, with whom she lived from the time she was seventeen, and her siblings from her mother's second marriage, no longer little kids, now young married people themselves. There are other people in her life. Certainly other men. Surely, Gina would have had someone besides lovers, surely someone better than damaged goods like him. "So why hasn't some smarter guy than me snapped you up?"

Gina raises a hand and touches Adam's face gently, tracing the route of his fresh scar. "I was married for two years. A long time ago."

Adam begins to stroke Gina's hair back from her face. Waits. He wants to know that she isn't grieving for a lost love. "What happened?"

"I told him to get out."

Adam shifts a little under Gina's weight. "And did he?"

"Went without a protest. Easiest thing I ever did."

"You are a very strong woman." Adam bends and kisses her on the forehead.

Gina moves off him, sits up, and takes his face in her hands. "So are you, a strong man, even when it hurts."

They lay quietly for a time, until Gina moves away from

him, turning in the bed to look at him, putting her hand on the cheek without the slash. "Adam."

"Yes?"

"You're doing the right thing."

Chapter Fifty-five

Adam has chosen his clothing carefully. Chinos, not jeans. A light blue dress shirt, but one that has been retired from business, demoted to weekend wear. No tie. A golf jacket, not a sports coat. On his feet a pair of Reeboks. At first, Adam thought that he'd wear his best suit, his most expensive shoes, his favorite understated tie, but when he took them out of the closet, they looked wrong, formal wear at the diner. The statement he wants to make needs to be spoken, not bespoke.

Adam has circled the block twice, ostensibly looking for a parking place, but there are several to choose from on this residential street. He finally parks directly in front of the house.

The three-decker house looms over an empty lot on one side and a more recent two-family house on the left. It is painted in graduated shades of brown, tan, and yellow, so that the third floor seems less substantial than the first two. A double driveway takes up the space between the houses, a thin grass strip of border between them; a light gold Marquis sits alone on the right side. The porch steps lead to twin front doors. He knows that one will lead to a stairwell, the other to the first-floor apartment. Adam checks the address in his hand—42 A, first floor. A fence encircles the property, rhododendron bushes softening the chain link. Adam opens the gate, careful to replace the latch. There is a small round table on the porch, tucked into the corner, a citronella candle full of dead matches in the middle of it. The last few nights have been cold, and a pair of chairs are folded up, leaning against the porch rail as if done for the season.

The door on the left is the one he wants. A brass plate with *March* written in script adorns the doorbell. All Adam has to do is push the white button. He shoves one hand into his jacket pocket, runs the other through his hair, over his face, forgetting that his cheek is quite tender even though the stitches are out. Adam feels a light scrim of sweat prickle against his exposed neck, beneath his arms. This is ridiculous, he thinks. He's performed far greater acts of courage in the business arena, boldly facing down naysayers and enemies to prove his point. Asking Sterling Carruthers to marry him; asking for her hand from one of the most powerful men he's ever known. Adam suddenly realizes that he'd either better push the damned doorbell or retreat before someone notices him standing out here like some anxious adolescent on his first date.

None of the other brave moments of his life ever felt so fragile. All the other times, he was absolute in his vision of the outcome. This time, this once, he has no idea what resolution he wants.

Adam presses his forefinger into the bell. Twice.

A woman opens the solid wood door, leaving the storm door latched. The screens are still in, and she looks at him through the fine mesh. She studies him, looks past him to determine if he's alone. "You're not a Jehovah, are you?"

"No." Adam has forgotten to rehearse what he might say, fully expecting his father to be the one to answer the door. He hasn't considered this, that there might be a wife.

They study each other through the door.

"I'm Adam March. John's son."

She nods slowly, considering this bit of information. "Yes. Yes, you are. Come in." She unlatches the storm door and stands aside to let him in. The small foyer with an empty hat stand leads to the front parlor. He can smell something baking, brownies or maybe a cake, the aroma coming from beyond the parlor. The room is tidy, uncluttered. Old-fashioned furniture: a sofa and matching wing chairs, a mahogany occasional table with a pair of silver candlesticks on either end, a Revere bowl in the center. "Wait here." She doesn't invite him to sit.

He looks around the room but remains standing in the middle of the Oriental area rug. The pattern is worn in the center, but still beautiful in reds, blues, and yellows. Adam realizes he's looking for something, some item that will connect him to this home. He walks over to the fireplace, where there are three matching silver frames. He studies the photos: a wedding picture, a baby picture, and a family group.

He is still studying the photo when the woman comes back into the room.

"That's my family. My son, Carl, his wife, Jennifer, and their kids." She doesn't take the picture down, doesn't touch it. "I'm Bea. John's wife."

"I'm Adam. And this is awkward."

Bea March smiles at him. "I know it is."

"Is he here?"

"Yes. I'll take you to him. I have to warn you: He's not well. Bedridden." She looks away, studies the pattern in the rug. "It's lung cancer. Couldn't get him to give them up." Bea pulls her gaze from the floor to meet Adam's eyes. "I don't want him riled up, and he's already riled up knowing that you're here. You probably have a million questions, but if you can keep it to a few, that would be best. I won't have him tired out."

"Just one. Just one question."

"Okay. One question."

Bea leads Adam through the dining room and down a short hallway. The scent of baking is now mingled with a mild pungency beneath an overlay of air freshener. She knocks on the door with a single knuckle and Adam can see how nervous she is. "Johnny, he's here."

There is a sound, a hissing susurration of air accented by an audible blip, like the sound made by someone clearing a piece of tobacco off his tongue. Bea doesn't wait for an answer, but swings the dark-stained door open to let Adam in. John March is in a hospital bed, the head cranked up so that he is sitting at an angle, the foot bent slightly so that his legs are elevated. A white sheet is pulled up to his waist, folded down, and straightened over an orange thermal blanket, and Adam knows that Bea has just tidied him up for company. The gray face that looks at him is hollow-cheeked, a nasal cannula fitted under the nose. The eyes, deep brown, stare at him, assessing him, quite obviously reconciling this man with the boy he last saw nearly forty years ago. The boy he left behind, the boy he gave to the state. Adam swallows. The shape in the bed raises a hand, reaches out. That hand is shaking, trembling with nerves or with palsy. Adam can't tell which, but his own hand is equally tremulous. There is a folding chair placed beside the bed. Bea touches Adam on the shoulder and points to it, then walks out of the tiny, claustrophobic room and shuts the door behind her.

Adam is close enough now to see the places where Bea has missed when shaving his father. His hair is steel gray, slicked back from his forehead and longish in back. Adam remembers that his father always wore his hair in what used to be called a pompadour, a style that required an application of Brylcreem. He remembers the tube on the sink in the bathroom, the smell of it. It comes back to him in a flood of recollection. His father, standing at the bathroom mirror, black comb sweeping this way and that. His dark brown hair turned jet black, glistening from the hair cream. He'd sing the slogan: "A little dab'll do ya." Adam would sing it, too, ask for a dab of Brylcreem.

It's the first time he's thought of that, ever. All the thoughts he's ever had about his father have been of his temper, his fighting with Veronica, of her leaving. A little dab'll do ya.

"Hello, Dad."

His father smiles, and over the sound of the oxygen machine, his own voice a breathy susurration, he answers. "Hello, son." He taps the covers with a hand that is bruised from the permanent line in his vein, and Adam wonders if he's supposed to take it.

Adam gets one question, if he's to play by Bea's rules. One question after a lifetime.

John March licks his dry lips. "How you been?"

His father's first question after a lifetime.

"Why, Dad? Why did you let me go?"

His father reaches up for the cannula, pulls it away from

his nose. "I had no choice. I was alone." He puts the cannula back but misses one nostril.

"Why didn't you come back? When I was old enough? Why did you leave me in the system?" Adam reaches over and helps replace the tube.

"Complicated."

Adam knows that he's used up his allotted question, and he still has no answer. The old man is struggling to remove the cannula again, and Adam presses his hand away from his face. "I know it is. I just don't understand why you stopped contacting me even once a year. But you know what? I managed. I succeeded. I have a daughter. You have a grandchild. You missed knowing her. You missed knowing me."

There are tears in the old man's eyes, but they seem less like tears of regret than tears of defiance. Adam sits back, taking a deep breath that is filled with the smells of illness and old man. Two eight-by-ten framed photographs sit on the bureau. For a moment, Adam thinks that one is a picture of Ariel that has somehow come into his father's possession. The long blond hair, the angle of the chin to eye, the closed-lip Mona Lisa smile. Veronica. The other is of him, a gap-toothed five-year-old with a crew cut and wearing a plaid shirt. Sears portraits. The photographer had him hold a toy train. Adam remembers this. And the swoop of recognition, of memory, threatens to force him to run from the room. His father has kept those studio portraits, taken weeks before Veronica was dead and he was placed into the foster system.

"Why did you—" Adam stops. There are no answers to his questions. None that he wants to hear; none that will make forty years of anger go away. He stands and opens the bedroom door. "Good-bye."

John March raises his hand again, struggles against his disease to speak. "Will I see you again?"

Adam is aware of the irony. He has turned the tables on his father; he has the upper hand, the ability to choose to see him or not. The choice to get even. The last time he asked his father that question, "Will I see you again?" his father had said, "Sure. Soon." And then he disappeared from his life. The hurt, the anger, the grief eventually mellowed into a dissonant memory. Adam turned his sights to a future that he would have control of. That he thought he had control of. One that turned out to be beyond his control.

"Sure. Soon."

Beatrice March is waiting for him. She takes him into the kitchen, despite Adam's protests that he has to go. She sits him down and puts a cup of coffee in front of him; a plate with warm brownies cools in the middle of the kitchen table. She is wearing an old-fashioned apron, the kind that slips over the shoulders and crisscrosses in back. She doesn't sit down, stands to one side instead, her hands busy with wiping the counter, her back to him. He feels like a little boy waiting in a neighbor's kitchen. Waiting quietly for a parent to return to fetch him, or a pal to burst into the room. Waiting for an adult to take over the moment.

"He told me about you." Bea wrings the sponge out into the sink. She doesn't look at him as she says this. "About having a child he had to give up. Broke his heart. I will tell you that."

"If it broke his heart so badly, why didn't he keep in touch with me? He did, you know, for a few years. Come see me, take me out to lunch. Then, when I was maybe ten, he didn't come. No contact. No one ever told me why. I began to assume he was dead."

Bea turns to Adam, pulls out the chair opposite, and sits down. "No one ever said what happened?"

Adam's heart does a tricky little quickstep. "No."

Bea presses her hand to her forehead. "Men don't admit failure easily. John doesn't admit failure easily. He'd failed with poor Veronica. He was adrift with a five-year-old, couldn't work enough hours to make a living. Right after Veronica left, he was offered a job doing long-distance trucking. It was good money, but he knew that he would never be home. He had no prospects of being able to offer a kid a consistent home life. It was the best choice he could make at the time. To put you in state care. He wanted you to have a family, to be adopted. As painful as that was, it's what he saw as the best choice for you."

"You're excusing him."

"Damn right I am. The first thing he told me about himself when we met, and we've been married twenty-five years, is that he'd lost his family. And how it had been his fault. He's rarely spoken of it since. It's too painful."

The quickstep has settled into an arrhythmic thumping.

"Then they told him you were unadoptable as long as there was a parent in the picture. He wanted a better chance for you, a chance at a stable home. He had no family to help. He thought that if you were adoptable, you'd finally have that stability. He anguished over it until he finally gave you up."

"And I was never adopted."

"He never knew that. The belief that you had a happy home was all that cheered him when he got despondent about the past. The belief that you had ended up with a better life than that of the son of a transient."

"He doesn't look very transient to me. You've got a nice home. You raised kids together."

"No. I raised Carl, in this house, by myself. I met your father after he retired. Course, he wasn't a trucker anymore; he retired as a mechanic, so, yes, he wasn't transient anymore. He lived next door. Rented from the Garritys. Turned their backyard into a vegetable garden. I used to watch him from the kitchen window. I knew who you were in a minute because you look just like he did back then. Handsome." Bea covers her mouth with one hand, then reaches for her coffee cup. "Since he's been sick, he's been talking a lot about you. Wondering about you."

"Did he never imagine that I might have wondered about him? About what happened to Veronica? I've only just found out that she was killed. Why didn't anyone tell me that?"

Bea shakes her head. "People weren't so—what's the word nowadays? Up front with kids. Some things weren't meant for little pitchers' ears. They believed that ignorance was bliss. I'm sorry. If I'd been around then, well, it would have been different. I'm sorry you never knew that the poor girl was run down like a dog in the street."

A dog in the street.

"I have to go."

Bea nods. "He hasn't got long now. It would be a wonderful thing if you'd . . ." She puts her hand back over her mouth, unable to say the words.

"Forgive him."

Adam lets himself out of the house.

Adam sits in his car, which still smells faintly of Chance. A leash is on the floor on the passenger side. He hopes that Bea

March isn't looking out the window, seeing him still sitting there as he waits for his heartbeat to level off, waits for the shaking in his hands to subside. His phone is in the console, and he picks it up out of habit, checking to see if anyone has called while he was in the house. Two missed calls. He goes to voice mail.

The first is Ariel, calling again to see if he's found Chance. As if she wouldn't be the first call he'd make once he does. If he does. In her message he hears a faded optimism that someone will spot Chance, that miracles do occur. The only good to have come out of Chance's disappearance, besides Gina, is that Ariel has found her way back to being his daughter.

The second message is brief.

"Mr. March, this is Dr. Gil at the shelter. I think we may have your dog."

The expression "emotionally overwrought" comes to mind as Adam copes with the juxtaposition of his strained reunion with his father and the joy of getting Chance back. In one hour, he has been emotionally flayed alive. Every feeling has come into play, but right now he is enjoying the pounding heartbeat of hope. If Chance is back, then things will be all right. That bugger, how could he disappear like this for so long? He'll take him right over to Gina. Get him some new chew toys. This is ridiculous thinking. He's a grown man. Why is he weeping with relief over a dog?

There is one parking space left near the shelter and Adam pulls in, drops quarters on the sidewalk in an effort to feed the meter, and bursts through the shelter doors, trotting to the reception area. "I'm here for my dog."

The receptionist looks a little puzzled.

"The dog Dr. Gil called me about. The brindled dog, half an ear?"

"Oh. Right. Let me get the doctor."

The scrubs are green today, the Crocs lime-colored. Gil's ponytail is slightly askew. "March, okay, man. Here's the thing."

Gil goes on to describe the dog: mauled, crushed bones, loss of blood. Found in an alley, dumped. Except for the fact that Adam had been pestering the shelter for ten days, Gil would have euthanized the animal immediately. The half ear was the only resemblance to Adam's description, and it was then that Gil remembered him, remembered the unorthodox adoption and put two and two together. "I'm asking that you not be alarmed. And that you make the right choice."

Adam hasn't said a word. He's listened to the doctor and begun to pray that this poor battered animal isn't Chance. He wants to call Gina. To have her opinion. To have her hand on his shoulder.

"All right."

The swinging door leads to the hallway of doors. This time, the vet takes Adam through one that leads to the infirmary. The walls are stacked on two sides with cages, one up and one down. Some are small and contain small sleeping animals; others are occupied by silent creatures looking like science experiments with bandages and tubes. Other cages are doubled for larger animals, and all but one are empty. Gil leads Adam to the cage and squats. "Hey, boy."

Adam kneels beside the cage, fingers looped through the wire mesh. Inside is a brindled hulk. White gauze interrupts the brown striping. The hulk's head is swathed, one foreleg is splinted right down to the end of the paw, making it look like a prizefighter's hand wrapped for the glove. It lies with its back toward the front of the cage, so Adam cannot see its eyes. Nothing moves. Adam looks at the veterinarian. "Is it too late?"

"He's been given a little happy juice."

"I don't understand."

"Something to make him rest. Not too much. Not until you say so."

"Can I have a minute?"

"Take as long as you want." Gil rises to his feet, presses a hand on Adam's shoulder. "As long as you want. I'll be in my office when you're ready."

Adam unlatches the door, reaches in and strokes Chance along his shoulder, between the lines of gauze continents. "Hey, buddy. It's me." Adam doesn't feel self-conscious whispering to the recumbent dog. His knees hurt a little against the tile floor, so he sits, leans in awkwardly, and rests his scarred cheek against the dog's side. He can hear Chance's heartbeat. "You wouldn't believe who I met today. My father. My absent father. He's as banged up as you are, but from the inside out. He's dying, too, and there's no one who will put him out of his misery. Are you miserable? Do you want to die? Do you want me to do it? To say 'Do it'? I've missed you. The place is pretty empty without you, except that now Gina is there. Oh Chance, where have you been? How did you get into such trouble?"

Adam feels the dog stirring under his sore cheek. He lifts his head and two sets of brown eyes meet. A tail thumps against the cage floor. *Thump. Thump. Thump.*

Rroorr. Chance puts his head down and is still.

Chapter Fifty-six

Bea has filled in some gaps in his father's life, things that have helped to move the old man from contemptible to comprehensible in Adam's mind. A man with a high school education and few prospects; a suddenly single dad with no living relatives; a man who had grieved for a wife lost to cancer. Circumstances that had made his father seem an angry man, a man whose temper lost him his teenage daughter, lost him his son.

It's too hard for John to talk, so Adam does. One day, he brought pictures of Ariel to show his father. Now he has brought her to meet the grandfather she never knew she had. They don't stay long, he and Ariel, and at the end Adam feels washed out, drained of the substance that has been keeping him upright for years. Most of his life has been spent in defiance of his upbringing. He sits with the fragile shape that was once his powerful and angry father and understands that he is just like him. But Adam knows that he has been given a chance, a chance to regain the happiness lost by his own actions. Maybe not regain what he once believed constituted happiness, but to appreciate a simpler, more profound contentment with what has become his life.

Judge Frank Johnson stares at Adam's face for a moment longer than is polite. "Bob told me what happened. Tough."

Reflexively, Adam touches his cheek, touching the groove that is still carmine. Gina insists vitamin E will soften the scar. "It's all right."

"He also told me that you've done well." The judge motions toward a side chair. "Sit."

This time, Adam is confident that his sentence is complete, that his term of community service has been served, and he is no longer nervous that the judge will tack on more time. As long as he doesn't ask if Adam has learned a lesson. That would be too paternal for Adam's taste. And yet he isn't embarrassed to admit that, yes, he has learned something. Adam takes a seat, runs his slightly sweaty hands against his legs. "Frankly, it's turned out to be a very good thing."

The judge slides his Buddy Holly glasses to his forehead. "You've taken on grant searches. Are you going to keep doing that?"

"I am. I've found a couple of foundations that award funds to purchase needed equipment, like a new computer, and one whose grant will allow us to bring in a visiting nurse once a month."

Johnson sits back, squeezes his chin with one hand. He nods slowly. "Good. Case dismissed."

And just like that, Adam March is a free man.

. . .

Adam is startled awake by his cell phone playing the overture to Rossini's *Barber of Seville*. He answers the phone, then leaves his bed to go to his father's house.

Adam and Ariel stand in the cemetery, arms linked, the first real chill of fall nipping at their ungloved hands. "She was my age."

"Yes. And just as rebellious."

Ariel shoves him a little, her shoulder against his arm. "Not quite. I haven't run away lately, but I will if Mom marries that a-hole Troy."

"She has a right to be happy."

"Can I come live with you?"

"Yes. But not out of anger. You have to come live with me because I'm your favorite."

"Okay."

They have just buried his father. The rest of the mourners have already gone back to Bea's house for refreshments—her son, Carl, and his wife and kids, the neighbors, friends from church. Adam and Ariel have hung behind so that he can tell her what happened to Veronica. And more about her grandfather, who has been in her life only briefly and is now gone. It was painful to see his father's eyes light up at the sight of this girl who resembles the long dead Veronica so completely that she is a gift.

"Why did she run away?"

"I don't know. I asked my father, mostly because I wanted to blame him, but he didn't know, either. She was looking for a better life." Adam squeezes Ariel's hand. "I always thought that she was running away from me, from having to take care of a little brother when she was just a young woman, ready to start her own life. Wanting freedom and fun, not be a housekeeper and surrogate mother."

"That's so cheesy. I'd never do that."

"You've never been responsible for a little brother."

They are quiet for a moment, both lost in their own thoughts.

"I've been thinking about taking a year off between high school and college and doing City Year."

Adam slides his arm around her shoulders, surprised that she comes up to his shoulder. "That would be fine with me."

"Mom's flipping out."

Adam smiles at the image. "You have to do what you feel is right for you."

"It does feel right. I've been listening to you talk about Fort Street and it got me to thinking. You went back even though you didn't need to anymore."

"It's a lot nicer volunteering than being ordered to do good works." Once his face no longer pulsed with every movement, the hole in his days was deep, and he'd missed the structure. He'd gone back a few weeks ago. With a second consulting job, he is finally able to make ends meet, and that is enough. Jupe, medicated, more Charles than Jupiter now, has apologized to Adam. Strings were pulled and he is living in a halfway house nearby but still takes a noontime meal at the center. He wants Adam to go with him to the animal shelter to find a new companion.

Ariel pulls the sleeves of her cashmere sweater down over her hands. "I'm cold. Let's get out of here. Do we have to stay long at Bea's?"

"You don't. Just come through and have a nibble. I'll make your excuses."

Adam and Ariel link hands and walk to his Lexus. Despite their flawed history, Adam is deeply saddened by his father's passing. These last few weeks have been hard and yet the sweetest that he has known. Reconciliation. Renewed affection. Recovery. A new love.

Gina, wanting Adam and Ariel to have some private time, waits for them in the car.

And in the backseat, boxy chin resting on the open window, Chance waits for them, too.

Epilogue

I walk with the swagger of a champion, but I know that is only because I limp. My foreleg aches on cold mornings, a reminder of the long weeks in which it was splinted, the miserable days of wearing that ridiculous plastic cone over my head. There were moments when I was crazed, mad to chew that splint off and lick the multiple wounds along my chest and on my belly that itched and ached simultaneously. My man scratched them for me, allowed me a brief respite of coneless sleeping when he was around. He gave me canned food to accommodate my sore mouth. He fed me bits of cheese that he pretended didn't contain sharp-tasting pills. He carried me downstairs to do my business, and carried me back up.

They say that a dog cannot know about its own death because it doesn't really know about its own existence, but I can tell you that simply isn't so. I knew that I was headed for oblivion as I lay drugged in that hospital cage. One cage is much like another, the one in the cellar or the one in the shelter. They both restrict and protect. The one in the cellar had been a prison, but the one in the shelter a haven. I was waiting for the moment when I could let go of life. It isn't something you can do at will; you have to be patient. I'd had a good run. Adventure, travel, a little romance. A good man. As I lay there, I realized that I wasn't just waiting for my end, but for him.

As I lay dying, I thought about him, about how I knew his kind said "Adam" when he was called. That he depended on me to keep him happy. I lay facing my death, and if dogs can wish, I wished that he would come to me, to be there as I let go of life.

And, lo and behold, out of my too-deep sleep, I awoke and found him there.

I pushed the desire for death into a corner as his face pressed against my side, his voice rumbling into my center. I could feel the slow moistening of the tears he shed and I knew that his crying wasn't for me alone. A profound sadness transmitted itself from him into my racked body. I'd awakened with the thought that now he was there, I could let go. Join my ancestors, give up the ghost. But when I felt those tremors, heard his raspy voice, I realized that I was still needed, maybe as much as ever. I had chosen this one and I owed it to him to see him through this new pain. It's my job; I'm a pet. We're a pack of two.

So I wagged my tail.

Acknowledgments

If it takes a village to raise a child, it certainly takes a team to write a book. This book could never have happened without the guidance, insight, crystal-ball gazing, and friendship of Andrea Cirillo. Thanks, too, to the gang at the Jane Rotrosen Agency, who patiently read every iteration of this book; and, to my copy editor, Carol Edwards, who smoothed things out.

To Jennifer Enderlin, who had the vision and imagination to see this as a "big" story—thank you isn't saying enough.

To Jane Rotrosen Berkey and Bernice Clifford, CPDT, of Animal Farm Foundation, who opened my eyes to the charms of the much maligned pit bull. Thank you.

Thanks Kevin, for being my non-pro, yet eagle-eyed, reader.

Bonnie, Hunter, Sprout—you are all good dogs.

1. What explains Adam March's outrageous attack on Sophie?

2. Why do you think the author used the first person in telling Chance's story?

3. There are two protagonists in this story. How would the reading experience change if we saw only one side?

4. What is Adam's initial attitude toward Chance?

5. How does that attitude reflect his attitude in general and the situation he's in?

6. When Adam breaks down, what motivates Chance to approach him?

7. What does Chance think of his "career" as a fighter?

8. Should Adam forgive his father?

9. What role does Gina play in Adam's personal growth?

10. Describe Adam's relationship with his daughter Ariel. Does his childhood impact this relationship, and if so, how?

11. Does Adam relate at all to the boys he encounters on the street? How so?

12. What are Adam's three sins and does he overcome them?

13. In this story, men are living on the streets as well as dogs. Are you more likely to support animal shelters or homeless shelters?

14. Conventional wisdom believes that fighting pit bulls cannot be rehabilitated. In many cities, a dog that has been known to fight is automatically put down. Do you think that a character like Chance is realistic? Does he change your mind about pit bulls?

15. In the end, has Adam been redeemed?

For more reading group suggestions, visit www.readinggroupgold.com.

A Reading Group Guide

St. Martin's
Griffin

The Dog Who Danced

Dedicated with love to our mothers,
Dorothy Geer Hidler and Claire Darling Gibson

Part 1

Prologue

Nothing was ever handed to me. My old man taught me the value of never expecting kindness. My stepmother taught me that the only way you get to be first in life is to stand alone. I've managed. I've never gone hungry, or worn anything I was ashamed of because it was threadbare, at least not since I left home at seventeen and a half. I've never sold myself in order to eat; I've met women like that. It's true I've had living arrangements that might be looked at as nearly that bad, but that's only if you're looking in. I have done some things I'm not proud of, but each one was the result of wanting something I was willing to make a hard choice to get. And, yes, I've made those "bad" choices along the way. Even if you don't grow up with religion, you still know right from wrong, and the difference between good and not so good.

My name is Justine Meade, and in my forty-three years, there have only been a handful of people I have loved. No, that's an exaggeration. Two. Two whom I lost because of stupidity and selfishness. One was my son. The other was my dog.

1

You gonna finish that?" Artie stubs a blunt finger in the direction of my English muffin. We're sitting in a Travel America rest stop, one of the several that we've visited on this west-to-east run. He likes to keep on schedule; I like to pause for an hour and get the blood flowing in my legs again after hours in the cab of the eighteen-wheeler, inhaling Artie's cigarette smoke and drinking warm, flat Coke. TAs are little shopping centers, catering to folks who live on the road, modern Gypsies, with anything you can think of for your vehicle from oil to mud flaps to little bobblehead dashboard figures of football players and Jesus. The restaurants offer big man's meals, all-you-can-eats—chicken-fried steak, biscuits, apple pie. How hungry can a man be who has sat in a rig all day, keeping busy with radio and Red Bull?

"No. Take it." Unlike the majority of the people jammed into the booths and bellied up to the counter, I have no appetite, no desire to heap my plate with eggs and sausages. The good hot coffee is enough for me. I'm hoping that Artie will stay put long enough for me to visit the ladies' shower room.

I'm riding shotgun with Artie Schmidt because I need to get back to the East Coast. He comes into my bar pretty regularly when he's not on the road. It was Candy's idea, hitching the ride instead of flying. She knew that round-trip airfare would make me have to choose between rent and food; and a one-way ticket might mean that she would have to find another girl. Besides, this way I could take Mack with me. The idea of being in my stepmother's presence without an ally was unthinkable. Going with Artie meant that I could take my dog with me, and there is no way I'd subject my Sheltie to being cargo.

Frankly, it was Candy who convinced me that I had to go east in the first place. My stepmother didn't reach out often, or at all, so when she called to say my father was failing, it was almost impossible to get past the fact that it was Adele on the phone, rather than take in the fact of my father's dying. Wicked stepmothers are only in fairy stories, right? I'm here to tell you that Cinderella had it good compared to what that woman put me through. But Candy said I should go, that it was important. Family is important. Right. Despite my better instincts, I set my course eastward and signed on with Artie Schmidt. Mack, my blue merle Sheltie, right alongside me. The boyfriend who gave Mack to me is long gone, but my little man stays, keeping his long, pointy nose at my heels wherever I go.

Candy Kane—and that's her real name—runs a decent tavern just outside the city limits of Seattle. I've lived pretty much everywhere. Starting when I walked out of the house the day after high school graduation, getting as far as Somerville, where I bunked in with a pair of roommates I found on a message board in a coffee shop. Then down Interstate 95 to Brooklyn, where I might have stayed; then Florida, then Louisiana and Texas. I have made my way as far west as California, and as far north as Washington State, where I've stayed put longer than anywhere else. When I look at a map of the United States, touch all those big cities and little towns that I've spent time in, I see that I've been moving in a slow clockwise circle around the country. When we're getting the place ready to open, before the first happy-hour customers come in and want to watch ESPN or CNN, Candy calls me over when *Jeopardy* is on; I can nail the geography questions.

My point was never to return to my starting place, New Bedford, Massachusetts. I'm like the old-time whalers, seeking my fortune far from home. Instead of the ocean, I travel along major highways. Instead of ships, I own clunkers good for only a few thousand miles. Instead of whales, I'm not sure what I'm seeking. Ahab had revenge in mind. I just haven't found the one place that will hold me still. When I was young, I thought that there would be a man to tie me down, but it never worked out that way. And no job was ever lifelong interesting; not one has ever gotten me to sign on for the retirement plan.

You might think that having a kid would have kept me in one place, or at least slowed me down, but even that failed to root me. Every time I pulled up stakes, I told my son that no matter where we were, we were at home as long as we were together. For a long time, that was true, but then, well, it wasn't.

So, here I am, circling back to my starting point in a direct run down Interstate 90, New Bedford–bound.

"I'd like a shower."

"And I'd like to keep on schedule. You've already slowed me down with twice as many pee breaks as I take."

"You pee in a bottle."

Artie pulls off his greasy Tractor Supply cap and runs his fingers through his stringy hair, resettles the cap, and drags a long breath. "Five minutes, or I swear to God I'll leave without you."

Artie has said this before. I smile and grab my duffel bag, which nestles at my feet. It contains everything I need and nothing that I don't. That bag and I have a longer relationship than most married couples. I pull a couple of dollars out of my back pocket and drop them on the check. "Give me seven and I'll meet you at the truck. Go buy yourself a pack of gum."

"Justine. I mean it. I come in late with this load and I'm fucked."

"Then don't hold me up talking to me." I shoulder my duffel and stride off to the showers.

Once Artie figured out that I meant it, that I was paying him three hundred bucks to let me ride east with him, and that didn't include any physical stuff, he'd turned sullen. It's funny how the barroom personality can be so different from that of the real person. Mr. How's My Girl quickly became Mr. Cranky. Tough. I'm not taking this ride for the company. I keep Mack between us, and get out of the cab while Artie catches a few hours' sleep—walking Mack around quiet parking lots, sitting at empty picnic tables and sipping cold coffee—then unroll my sleeping bag and crawl into Artie's man-smelly bunk to catch my own z's. Artie doesn't want Mack in his bed, but that's okay. The dog curls up on my seat, his little ears twisted in my direction, so I know he's not really sleeping. On guard. Shelties, miniature collies, are guard dogs by breeding. His instincts are to watch the hills for wolves. Artie is on notice every time Mack stares at him with his eagle eyes.

There are three shower stalls. One is broken, and the other two are in use. I should forget about it. I wash my face and brush my teeth. Whoever those two women are, they are flipping taking a long time. I floss. I wait. I know that Artie is getting pissed. Finally, the shower turns off. Now I have to wait for Miss America to dry off and get dressed. "People waiting out here!" I shove my washcloth and toothbrush back into my bag.

No answer. The second shower shuts off. The room is suddenly quiet except for the sound of towel against skin. I look at my watch. My time is done. I pick up my duffel, and, miraculously, Shower Queen exits the booth. I can do this in one minute. I can't stand the feeling of dirty hair. I hate that I smell like day-old sweat and Artie's cigarettes. I can get in and under and out in two minutes, tops. I won't dry my hair.

Artie will be pissed, but I'm confident that he'll just bitch, not leave. I strip.

Five minutes later—it can't have been more than five minutes—I emerge from the shower room, wet towel rolled up under my arm, duffel over my shoulder, and my hair, wet and unstyled, hanging to my shoulders. I'm in the second of three T-shirts I've brought and the same jeans I started out with. But I feel better. I'll finish the job in the truck, put on the mascara and finger-wave my hair.

As I promised, and only a couple of minutes late, I head out the automatic doors, making straight for the truck lot. Maybe thirty semis are lined up in rows, Roadway, Bemis, UPS, May-flower Movers, and independents with family names on the cabs and unmarked trailers behind. Rigs with full berths above, rigs with shiny red and chrome, fancy lettering, rigs with more lights than a carnival midway. And campers. Campers snuggled up between the big guys, tagalongs and fifth wheels; double-axle motor homes. Four-wheel-drive trucks with engines that rival those powering the big rigs.

I don't see Artie's truck. I look to the diesel pumps and then the line for the truck wash, but he's not there. I start to trot down the lane between trucks. His rig isn't distinctive, a plain dull green. He's hand-lettered his name, Arthur B. Schmidt, on the driver's door in an uneven attempt at block letters—the Schmidt is narrower than the Arthur. He's hauling a trailer that he was hired to haul. Nothing to distinguish it from the others. But I can't have missed it. It's been my home for the past two days.

"Artie, for God's sake, stop teasing." I say this under my breath, but the panic is rising, a sour taste in my freshly brushed mouth, the taste of trouble. I stop looking for Artie. I know that he's gone. The mean SOB has called my bluff. He's taken my three hundred bucks and abandoned me in Ohio.

Then it hits me, like someone has punched me in the stomach. Mack was in the cab. My dog was in the truck, where I'd left him after giving him a quick walk in the doggy rest area. He's been waiting for us to come out and give him a little treat of Artie's leftovers, a bowl of fresh water. I can't believe that Artie would have driven off with him. There's no chance Artie would keep him. He's dumped him into the middle of this parking lot of bulls.

I call and whistle. Mack won't know where I am, and he'll be frantic. *I* am frantic as I begin to run, my wet towel lost on the pavement, my duffel banging against my back. "Mack! Mack! Come, boy. Mack!" My mouth dries out and I can't whistle anymore.

Mack is obedient; if he hears me, he'll come like a shot. He's not the type of dog that would wander around; he'll be looking for me, his nose to the ground, maybe heedless of the danger of being in this active parking lot. All of a sudden, it seems like every truck in this parking lot starts its motor in a cacophony of diesel. Mack can't hear me over the noise; I bend to peer beneath the behemoths, looking and looking for the flash of white and gray that will be Mack. I can't find him. I stop dead in the path of a moving truck. The driver slides a hand out his window, waving me across the lane.

Okay. If Mack isn't here, then Artie still has him. I circle the TA building. Artie's yanking my chain. If he's still got Mack, then Artie hasn't gone anywhere. He's not going to do that. He's got to be here. If he's back on the road, there's no way he's going to turn around and come back; the time he'd lose in playing me would be too precious.

But there are no trucks on the other side of the building, just family cars, a horse trailer, and a Harley with a one-legged rider parked in a handicapped spot.

"Have you seen a dog? A Sheltie? Gray with black streaks. White ruff? One blue eye and one brown eye?" I keep talking, as if adding to the description will make the answer become yes.

The one-legged rider shakes his head, which is swathed in a filthy red bandanna. "Nope. Sorry. This is a tough place to lose a dog." Like a lot of the rugged men I meet, he has a sympathetic voice, which does not match his tough appearance.

I collapse onto a bench in front of the building, all the strength in my legs gone, my heart thumping with a disconcerting loudness. I fight back the tears. In my experience, tears have never been useful, neither relieving pain nor offering comfort once shed. What I need is a plan. I need to stop Artie.

Artie has driven off with Mack.

Mack sleeps with his brushy tail curled up over his pointy nose. Tucked up like this, he's a small package of dog, burrowed into the sleeping bag Justine has left unrolled on the bunk behind the driver's seat. He's quite pleased to wait, dozing, waking, dozing, for the people to return to the truck. There might be a taste of something good as a reward for being quiet and patient.

This mobile living is a bit boring, but he is satisfied with the almost constant presence of his Justine. Usually he has to doze, wake, doze for a long time every day until Justine comes back from her day away from him, smelling of beer and fried food. He loves that smell; once, when she took him with her to work, just to pick up her check, he immediately recognized the place as where she went during the day. The lovely odors defining her away time and making it comprehensible to him. Who wouldn't want to be in a place that smelled like burgers?

When only Artie got back into the cab, Mack merely opened

one eye. He isn't a big fan of the guy, but that's mostly because of the stink of his cigarettes and the fact that the man ignores him. Mack is more accustomed to having Justine's males be friendly, sometimes even presenting offerings. Good stuff, like rawhide chews and squeaky toys. This guy just talks and smokes and, once in a while, gets too close to Justine. That's when Mack will find a reason to squeeze himself onto Justine's lap. No need to show teeth, just be there, a reminder that he is in charge, that she is his person.

Artie lights up another cigarette, not even rolling the window down to release the smoke. Mack tucks his nose deeper under his tail, his jack-in-the-pulpit ears turning like miniature radar detectors to catch the sound of Justine's feet on the pavement. Artie drums on the steering wheel, fidgets with the arrangement of knickknacks on the dashboard, cranks down his window, and ejects the butt of his cigarette. "Goddamn. She's pushin' me."

Mack keeps still. He wishes Artie would be quiet so that he can listen better for Justine. The dog lifts his head to sniff the air as the window goes down, but the cigarette stink is an impenetrable barrier, obscuring even the fresh air outside, and Artie's head blocks his view. She'll come. Justine will be back. She always comes back.

The first day that he lived with Justine, he learned that lesson. A mere baby, a pup of few weeks, he'd been taken away from his mother, his littermates, and the only human hands he'd ever known. He was boxed and carried to Justine. When she took him up and rubbed her inadequate human nose against his pointy one, he fell in love. And then she left him, putting him back in the box that would be his cave, his home, until he outgrew it. Then she came back and let him out. Fed him, cuddled him on the couch, named him. He never worried about her absence again.

Mack is startled back into full awareness as Artie hollers a stream of tongue language that Mack doesn't recognize word for word, but he gets the meaning. The man is angry. There is no one here for him to be angry at, unless he's angry at him, so Mack shrinks even more into the dim closet of a bunk. Suddenly, Artie starts the truck, and the rumbling vibration of the big engine fills the air. The gears grind and the truck moves forward. Justine isn't here. Maybe Artie is going to find her. Mack's soft whine is shadowed by the sound of the diesel engine. They pull away from the other trucks and shoot down the TA access road. In a minute, they are back on the highway. Justine is not there.

2

You don't have his plate number? I can't have every truck with a green cab stopped before it leaves Ohio. I'm sorry about your dog. If the guy gets pulled over, we can maybe get the dog."

I hang up before the state trooper can give me any more bad news. They can't, or won't, help track down Artie. I've called Artie's cell eighteen times, but he won't answer. If he did, I wouldn't ask him to do anything but leave Mack where I can pick him up, maybe at another TA, or a vet not far off the road. But Artie sees my number and ignores me. I don't exist for him anymore.

I need a ride. I need to catch up with Artie. Feeling like a tramp, I start talking to the truckers arrayed around the counter like piglets on a sow. "No can do." "Against the rules of my company." "Back off; I'm a family man."

Soon enough, I attract the attention of the center's manager, who gives me the look. I hold my hands up in the universal sign of "no harm" and move away from the truckers.

Families are tucking into the all-you-can-eat brunch. I sit alone at a table a mere three feet from a likely-looking group: mom and dad, two chunky preschoolers, and a grandma. "Nice day. Where you headed?" Nice, ordinary midwestern friendliness, nothing scary here.

"We're headed down to Disney."

That's east enough for me. Maybe they can get me as far as New York before they head south down 95.

"What'll you have?" The waitress is looming over me. The seventeen-inch-tall multipage plastic menu is still flat on the table.

Hungry I'm not, but I need to look like a customer. I order two eggs and bacon, white toast, coffee. I think that I'm going to hurl. I smile at the family beside me. "I'm heading east, too. Any chance you've got room for a passenger? I'll pay your gas."

The father twitches his mustache-covered lip like an old-time movie Lothario. His wife's eyes open in that wifely "Don't you dare" look I've seen on the wives who sometimes come looking for their husbands in my bar. He holds his hands palm up. "I don't think so. We're pretty full." Grandma, intent on her biscuits, suddenly gets what's going on. From her corner of the table, she sets an eye on me, and I nod and go back to playing with the sugar packets in their little white box on my table.

Before my food can arrive, I drop a dollar on the table and leave the building.

"You need some help?" It's the one-legged Harley rider. He leans on a single crutch, resting on a leg that ends in a traditional motorcycle boot, the leather beneath his left knee vacant, moving slightly in the Ohio air.

"I guess I do."

"Your boyfriend dump you?"

"No. My ride east abandoned me. But, worse"—I swallow to gain control of my voice—"he's got my dog. He took off with my dog."

"Bastard."

"I need to catch up with him." I hate that my voice cracks.

"Where's he headed?"

With those few words, I feel a flicker of hope, as tiny as the flame on a Bic, but a flicker nonetheless. "Boston."

"No stops on the way?"

"No. Nonstop."

"Down Ninety?"

"Yeah. He'll keep going straight through. He can do twenty hours with enough Red Bull."

"I can get you to Erie."

"That'll help."

"Climb on board." My one-legged Harley rider ships his crutch into a special hanger and slings his bad leg over the saddle. "There's a helmet in the pannier, and a headset. Put it on and we'll be able to talk."

I find both, a turtle-shell helmet that scarcely looks like it would protect me, and only if I fell directly on my head, and the headset. I stow my duffel in the pannier, fishing out my sunglasses first. I slide onto the seat behind him, careful not to kick him.

Using his one good leg, my new friend backs the Harley out of the space, then carefully removes the handicapped placard from the handlebars and places it in his jacket pocket. "I'm Mitch." His voice in my ear startles me.

I bring the mouthpiece up. "Justine Meade." As I'm about to embrace this stranger for the better part of the day, I offer him my hand.

He takes my hand in his leather-gloved mitt, an oyster in a black shell, then brings my hands around his middle. "Hang on tight. We'll catch that son of a bitch."

Mack doesn't know how long they have been going. He only knows that it is time for dinner. His dinner. His kibble, which he can see in its plastic bag on the floor of the side of the cab where Justine should be, is tantalizingly out of reach. It would be nice to have a lap of water. His Shetland sheepdog ancestors knew about privation as they rounded up sheep on the rocky hillside, but he's a domestic house dog and quite used to routine. Dinner at six. Water all day long. If he were any other dog, he might take himself down from the bunk and go help himself, ripping into the flimsy plastic with sharp teeth. But Mack is not just any other dog. He is a well-trained dog. One of his first lessons was in *don'touch*. Stare at that kibble in the bowl all you want, but *don'touch* it until given the word. *Don'touch* the garbage pail, despite its temptations. Justine once left a package of cold cuts on the kitchen table, an easy reach from his back legs, but he disdained touching it, although he spent the day staring at it in futile hope that it would fall off the table and become fair game. Justine hadn't said *don'touch*, but he'd never reach for anything on a table anyway.

Artie keeps staring at his cell. Mack knows that it's called *cell* because Justine has taught him to fetch it when she's in one room and the cell is singing in another. Artie's cell doesn't sing; it makes a sound like a miniature truck horn: *blat blat blat; blat blat blat*. Artie thumbs it quiet. He doesn't speak to it. But each time it honks, Artie looks at it.

3

We've been on the road for twenty minutes. My only thoughts are the calculation between a fast-moving semi and a faster-moving Harley. It's like one of those math problems in junior high that I could never wrap my mind around: If vehicle A is traveling at sixty-five mph and vehicle B is traveling at seventy-five mph, how long will it take for vehicle B to catch up to vehicle A, and will Artie even stop in Erie? Mitch pulls me out of my mathematical reverie. "So where are you from?"

"I've been living in Washington."

"State or D.C.?"

"State. Seattle."

Our conversation is bulleted, quick phrases spoken through tiny mouthpieces directly into ears. A weird intimacy. Can he hear my breath in his ear? Once, I was a telemarketer for a male-enhancement product. We were encouraged to be breathy.

"Where you from?" I'm not sure what I'm expecting. He has the look of a man who might not be from anywhere.

"Cleveland Heights."

"So you were just starting out on your trip?" The travel center is only a few miles from Cleveland Heights.

"Not going anywhere. I was just buying coffee. Taking the bike out for a spin."

I feel a little flush of embarrassment. "Look, I'll pay for your gas when we stop."

"Not to worry. I was looking for an excuse to take a good ride."

"Don't Harley riders tend to ride in packs?"

"Only on weekends." His chuckle actually tickles my ear.

We drive in silence for a few more miles. Even though I know we're traveling over the speed limit, it feels too slow. The scenery flowing past seems too distinct, as if it should be a blur, a mass of green and brown and white. Instead, I can pick out individual trees and houses and farms that take forever to move behind us. I want to tap Mitch on the shoulder and beg him to go faster. I am secure behind him, his body protecting me against the cold slipstream. Billboards advertising attractions one hundred miles away tick off the miles in tortoise slowness. Annie's Café one hundred miles. Annie's Café ninety miles. Eighty miles. Will we never reach Annie's Café?

The road trips of my childhood in the memory of another person might come across as a good thing. Dad, stepmother, stepbrother and me, looking for all the world like the average family. Dad married the wicked one six months after Mom died. Six months in the life of a fourth grader isn't the length of time it is to an infant, or a toddler. I was still moving around like a zombie, waiting for someone to come along who could explain to me why this had happened and tell me that I would someday be okay. Instead, Dad married our divorced next-door-neighbor, Adele Rose.

Adele had aggressively courted Dad, supplying us with casseroles long after my mother was in her winter grave and the daffodils were coming up in the backyard. She had him going next door to fix things—lightbulbs, loose hinges, the clock on her microwave after a power outage. The first time I heard my father laugh after my mother's death was in the company of Mrs. Rose. Even a nine-year-old could figure out what was happening.

It wasn't enough that Dad married her; in some bizarre decision, he moved us into her house. We lived on a typical New Bedford street of three-deckers, built in the heyday of small manufacturing, as the whaling industry petered out and the textile industry grew. As owners, we lived on the first floor and rented out the other two three-bedroom flats. Mrs. Rose lived in the only single-family house on the block, a modern ranch house built on an empty lot where once there had been a three-family that had burned down in the sixties. Dad rented out our flat, and I was literally given a tiny closet of a room, the walk-in closet they'd turned into my bedroom by moving the door. It came with one rectangular window placed so high that all I could see was sky. Living in a closet, I didn't have one, so my clothes were stored in a series of cheap cardboard storage boxes piled one on top of the other in order of the prevailing season. My bed and bureau from our old house occupied most of the floor space. When Adele screamed at me to clean my room, it took barely four sweeps of the vacuum.

My new stepbrother, Paul Scott Rose, Jr., exactly two years older than me, slept in the real second bedroom of this two-bedroom ranch house. A room that was filled with his stuff—model airplanes, hockey equipment, stinky clothes.

Paul, as it turned out, could do no wrong, not just in his mother's eye but also in my father's. He was the son he'd never had, a reprieve from being the father of an only daughter. Paul, bright and precocious, was the sun around which this pair revolved, and woe was me if I didn't see Paul in that light. Paul was mean. Paul set me up for trouble. When Paul lied, I was the one who got punished. The more I protested, the worse it got. I was no longer Daddy's little girl; I was a stepchild. I had inherited my mother's Portuguese coloring, brown eyes and a unibrow; my only Meade quality was that my hair wasn't dark brown, but dirty blond. Adele never avoided an opportunity to remind me of my Azorean heritage: "Don't dress like that; you look like a little Portagee." A slur that puzzled me until I understood that Adele had been brought up to think that any vivid color combination was somehow low-class. And, from her lofty position as a WASP, everyone who had been baptized in the Catholic Church was low-class. I was an adult when it finally occurred to me that she lived in New Bedford, too. What made her so high-and-mighty? Her first husband, a nice-enough guy, smart enough to bail on Adele, was Portuguese, which made Paul as Portuguese as I was, but somehow that didn't sully him as it did me. A Rose in New Bedford, by any other name, is Portuguese.

Once a year, we traveled to some exotic location: Atlantic City, Myrtle Beach, Kennebunkport, in that peculiar way of seaboard people who always venture to someone else's coast to enjoy themselves. When I was fourteen and Paul sixteen, we made the pilgrimage to Disney World. Which meant two days in the backseat of the Chevy Citation with Paul. Two days for him to torture me with farting and shoving. Adele and my father would trade driving in five-hour increments. We spent one night in South Carolina before forging on to Orlando in a manic race against the clock. Getting there late meant losing out on one of our three days in this mecca of American fun.

While Paul wasn't particularly interested in Disney, I was excited to be going. We had both reached that chill of adolescence that didn't allow enthusiasm for anything faintly resembling family togetherness, but I couldn't hide my excitement about going to the place where so many of my peers had already been. If only my mother had been the woman in the front seat, and a real brother, a younger one, beside me, it would have been perfect. But Adele was in the front, Paul beside me, and a curiously quiet father in the driver's seat. Adele talked. It was her thing, her right, and her most killing attribute. The woman never shut up.

She had recently taken to expecting me to become a slut. What I remember most about that family trip to Florida was Adele's reaction when I came out of the hotel bathroom with my eyebrows plucked. I had found her tweezers and gone to town, weeding through the thicket that was my most embarrassing feature. Following the recommendations in a teen magazine, I had spent an hour "shaping" my unruly brows. They had gone from overhang to slender silkworms poised over my suddenly enhanced brown eyes. It was like raising a shade to a sunny day.

Needing no further evidence of my inevitable downslide into slutdom, Adele punished me in the way she saw as the most convenient. I spent the entire vacation in the hotel room, the television my only entertainment. My father didn't make a single protest. Not once did he assert himself and overrule Adele. Not then, and certainly not later, when the stakes were so much higher.

When I left home at seventeen, a stolen fifty-dollar bill tucked in my pocket and an overstuffed suitcase dragging behind me, I wasn't leaving because of Adele's miserable treatment; I was leaving because my father had finally proved that he didn't love me.

The daylight in the cab has faded; the late-September sun behind them slips away into a pale sunset. Artie has mostly stopped his muttering. The cell has also stopped honking. Justine has not appeared, and Mack is less certain that she will be able to. The forward motion of the truck has been steady except for those places where Artie brakes and dances on the pedals and they slow down through little doorways where men or women stand and wave at them. Mack lifts his head at each of these, with the fleeting hope that Justine will be there, waving from one of those little doors. Waiting for them to find her.

From his nest in the bunk, Mack decides that he is hungry enough to mention it to Artie. As a dog used to long stretches of waiting, he has an internal clock that is on Greenwich dog time. He's well past his usual dinnertime; he is well past his usual outside time. He knows this and has allowed that these couple of days on the road have changed his routine significantly. But he was still getting fed and walked at regular intervals. If he could tell time, he'd know that it had been nearly seven hours without a break. If he could read an odometer, he'd know that there were about five hundred miles between himself and Justine. If he could read a map, he'd know that he was in New York State, bearing down on Albany. The only thing Mack can read is his hunger and his thirst.

Mack stands and stretches, loosening the limbs that have been curled up all day. He yawns, a long jaw loosening to settle his anxiety. Artie is unaware of him, eyes on the road, cigarette burning between fingers gripped on the wheel. He's turned on the radio, and a man's voice is barely audible above the engine noise. The cell suddenly commences its honking again. Mack sits down, waiting until Artie attends to the object's needs. Once again, Artie silences the cell without speaking at it. He lets loose with a stream of volatile tongue language. Mack decides he can wait a little while longer before asking for dinner. Artie's voice sounds like a kick in the ribs.

4

"What takes you east?" Mitch's voice in my ear yanks me out of my reverie.

"Sick father. Duty call."

"How far east?"

"New Bedford, Massachusetts."

"Far enough. Whaling capital, right?"

"That's what the sign says." I try not to shout, even though I can barely hear my own voice over the slip of the wind. I know that I can whisper over this mic and Mitch will hear me, but I still feel the temptation to shout. "What about you? What takes you on the road on a Wednesday?" Because I can't see his face, I don't register that this might be a rude question until it takes him a minute or two to answer. I've been embracing this stranger for the better part of an hour, the scent of his leather jacket so deep into my nose that I could pick it out of a crowd, the age-softened leather like chamois beneath my fingers. I don't even know his last name and I've trusted him to take me across a state line. "How come you're free?" Maybe my question isn't about why he's free on a weekday to ride his Harley, but why he's free to help me pursue Artie.

"Felt like taking a day off."

"What do you do?"

"Tap dancer."

I don't know whether to laugh or not, sort of like laughing at an off-color joke, but it was his joke, so I do. "Really? Tap dancer."

"I wear a peg."

"Okay. I believe you." I'm willing to let him keep himself to himself. I get it.

"Actually, I'm a musician." This makes sense, I can see him behind a guitar.

"In a band?"

"Symphony orchestra. Cleveland SO."

This is one of those moments that makes me nervous. Is he still joking around, or could this rather large, unshaven, but not in a good way, Harley rider really be telling me the truth? I decide to let myself be strung along. "What do you play?"

"Violin. First chair."

This is so specific that it sounds plausible. "You must have to practice a lot."

"That's what I'm taking the day off from. I'm skipping out on rehearsal. Being rebellious."

"You look the part for that."

"Thanks. I've cultivated the look."

"A Harley-riding violinist. That's a first for me." Ahead of us, for the tenth time, is a semi that might be Artie's. I tap Mitch on the shoulder and point. He speeds up, overtaking the truck easily. It's not Artie. A skinny guy in a Raiders cap salutes from the driver's seat.

"Here's the thing—I've got to be back for tonight's performance."

If I had any hope that he'd be my knight until we caught up to Artie, this shatters it. We'll go to Erie and he'll turn around and go back, transform himself from shaggy Hell's Angel into this longhair classical musician and forget about the woman he let ride on his bike, whispering over his microphone, urging him to catch up with the rat who stole her dog.

"So why take me to Erie?"

"Like I said, nothing better to do. Wanted to feel a little wind on my face."

"Well, I appreciate it. Maybe Erie will be far enough."

"Do you think he'll stop so soon? It's less than a hundred miles."

One hundred miles doesn't sound like a lot. Not after two days of making five or six or even seven hundred miles. Back in the day, when I was more of a rambler, I could do that much all by myself. But I'm out of practice. I'm not hopeful that Artie will stop at all, not without me beside him, reminding him that Mack needs to get out and stretch, or I need to pee. Besides, where he might stop is an open question. There's no TA near Erie, no Interstate 90 rest stop anywhere near Erie. I want Mitch to just keep going all the way to Boston, but that's not going to happen. I wonder if I have enough credit on my card to rent a car.

"Maybe you should just drop me at a car-rental place. There's no telling where Artie might stop, or even if he will stop."

"There's a gas station popular with truckers just off the highway. We can check there first; then I'll find you an Enterprise or an Avis."

"Thank you, Mitch. I really do appreciate what you've done for me." I fight the urge to rest my forehead against that soft leather jacket. I'm pretty sure I've maxed out my credit card. I have no idea what I'm going to do.

It is such a familiar place, this pennilessness, this hopelessness. I have been so often on the edge of out of control that it has a bizarre comfort to it.

Abruptly, the truck swings off the highway and into a rest stop. Artie jumps out of the cab, slamming the heavy door behind him. Alone again in the cab, Mack stands and shakes, stretching himself fore and aft, yawning. Relief starts his tail wagging. Justine will be here. In a minute, she'll come and let him out, then give him what he is beginning to need desperately—water. Then dinner. Then she'll climb up and let him sit on her lap, running his brushy tail through her fingers. She'll apologize for being gone, whispering little words in his ears so that it tickles. He'll give her a forgiving lick of his tongue. He's not like some dogs, perpetually trying to lap a human's face, but once in a while he'll give her a quick reminder that she belongs to him.

As abruptly as he'd left the truck, Artie reappears, holding a bag of food, which he tosses onto the empty seat beside him. A rich amalgam of meat and cheese, grease, and salt filters out of the bag, making Mack, patiently waiting on the bunk, salivate. He whines, but the sound of the engine turning over veils the noise. He considers pressing his nose into the back of Artie's neck, but the idea of touching this man is repellent to him and he sits down. Justine will be along, and she'd be plenty unhappy with him if he was to be caught begging like some common cur.

But Justine doesn't come. Artie wheels the rig out of the parking lot and, stuffing a cheeseburger into his mouth, where it dangles like a kill in a cat's jaws, strong-arms the truck back onto the highway.

The cell honks again. This time, Artie doesn't even bother to shut it off. Eventually, the honking ceases and the cab is filled only with the sound of the radio voice and the undertone of the engine.

Mack curls up on the sleeping bag without further consideration of food. Sometimes it's just best to sleep, to let hunger and thirst be forgotten. Suppressing his discomfort, Mack lets the sanctuary of sleep press him deeper into the folds of Justine's sleeping bag, where he takes a deep breath of her scent. Maybe Justine will be there when he wakes up.

5

Answer, you bastard." I have been calling Artie's cell once every five minutes since Mitch and I landed safely at the Crossroads Convenience Mart. My behind is numb from the hour and a half spent riding pillion. Mitch had to grab my hand as I dismounted. With a grace I wouldn't have expected, Mitch was off the bike and into the store ahead of me. By the time I'd phoned Artie the first time, Mitch was in line, a travel mug with the Harley-Davison insignia on it in one hand and a packet of peanut butter crackers in the other.

"I should buy you a meal."

"I'll have dinner at home."

"Then let me get your snack. And your gas."

"What, and cheat me out of being a gentleman? No. I was going to be doing this or something like it today anyway."

"Artie isn't answering his phone."

"Let me try."

"What do you mean?"

"He won't recognize the number."

I hold my phone steady while Mitch reads Artie's number off the contact list. He pulls off his right glove, punches in the number. "Voice mail." Artie has shut his phone off. "Schmidt, if you don't want some serious trouble, get off the road and get the dog back to Justine Meade. If you don't, you'll be looking in your rearview mirror for the rest of your life." My soft-voiced violin player has become a Hell's Angel. "You see a Harley, you'd better hope your life insurance is paid up." Mitch snaps his phone shut with a flourish. "Sorry, that's the best I can do. Empty threats."

"Thanks for trying."

The look on my face is pretty telling, because he pats my shoulder with a hand that is improbably large for a man who fingers violin strings for a living.

"You weren't playing hooky, were you?"

"I was thinking about it. Then you came along and I gave in to temptation. I just wish I could help you further, but I can't. I have to go back pretty soon. This is as far as I can take you. I'm really sorry."

"I can't thank you enough." I thrust a couple of dollars at the cashier, blocking Mitch's attempt to pay for his coffee.

Mitch propels himself back outside, sitting sidesaddle on the Harley while I hunt down a phone book to find a nearby car-rental agent.

I know that this is going to prove an exercise in futility. I have maybe a couple hundred bucks available on my credit card, probably not enough to rent a car to take out of state. I'm not one of those spendthrift people. I haven't run my credit card up on the temptation of using it for day-to-day living. I don't own a flat-screen TV. I don't even own a decent pair of shoes. No one had to teach me that using credit cards willy-nilly was bad. I didn't go to college, so I wasn't one of those kids who got handed a card at freshman orientation, then jacked it up, confident that Mom and Dad would cover the bill. I have lived by a pay-as-you-go policy all my life. Until Mack got sick.

It doesn't take much to run up a vet bill. A simple well-care visit can set me back half a paycheck. But when Mack needed emergency surgery for an intestinal blockage, I never hesitated. The credit card was always for emergencies, and this one was a big one. I've been paying it down for a long time, but the balance remains stubbornly high. It was scary enough to have a $2,500-plus balance on a $2,500-limit card. It didn't help that my day job at the health center ended when they lost funding and I was left to living on my job at the tavern. I've only been able to chip away at a little of that bill, a fact that sits on my shoulders like a ten-ton dollar sign. It colors every decision I make, even the one that has cost me my dog. I should have said no. I should have said I couldn't afford to fly, I couldn't get there. I should never have taken Artie up on his offer of a cheap ride to Boston.

I don't regret the expense of that surgery. Mack is more than a dog to me. He's my partner. We dance.

From the very beginning, Mack was easy to train. We aced puppy training and quickly got into obedience. But all that *sit-stay, down-stay* just didn't showcase my Sheltie's personality. Agility was more his style. Here's the thing. I'm not a joiner; I'm not a performer. I'm the woman behind the desk, or the cash register. I've been so transient that I've never felt that belonging to anything made sense. A year here, a few months there. The need to keep moving is like an itch. Usually, I feel that urge after a breakup, or if a job has just gotten too annoying. My résumé, if I had one, would be a long list of short-term jobs. I've thought about training as a dental hygienist. Or a nurse's aide. I like the health-care field. I've even taken a few courses as an EMT, but never finished. But we joined the Agility Club, and that is what's held me in Washington for longer than any other place I've lived. And when Saundra Livingbrook introduced me to canine freestyle, I knew that Mack and I had found our game. Canine freestyle, dog dancing, is not obedience or field trials; it's not a beauty pageant. It is egalitarian, open to all dogs, regardless of breed. The beauty comes from the enthusiasm of the dog for its work. All dogs that show a devotion to work and are easily trained are welcome. Trained, not like dogs, but like ballerinas. The talent coaxed out with hand signals and repetition, praise and bits of bacon. Lots of hard work. Mack took to it like the natural athlete he is. I could make my signals as subtle as could be and he'd see them. Those herd-dog eyes, mismatched though they are—one blue and one brown—catching my slightest movement. Hand up, palm out, spin; hand up palm out, one finger cocked, back up. Depending on the music, those movements look like a waltz or a rumba, like we are dancing, when, in fact, I am giving him signals, his eyes on me with such focus, the world could drop away. Mack never tires of it.

Mack waits for me to fasten his little tuxedo front on. His little white feet dance in place, happy that we're getting ready to strut our stuff. He shakes himself from the tip of his little black nose down through his magnificent white ruff, along his silver-and-black body to the tip of his plumed tail tipped in white. He's ready; he's got his game face on. I adjust my own costume, a white jumpsuit embellished with silver sequins, a white top hat finishing the look for "Puttin' on the Ritz." There we were, in this high school gymnasium in Seattle, costumes on, Saundra doing a last-minute adjustment to the straps of my jumpsuit, my blue merle Shetland sheepdog already pumped to get out there. An announcer speaking our names: "Please welcome Justine Meade and her dog Maksim." The spotlight is on us.

Mitch finishes his coffee and watches me as I write down the number of the only car-rental agency in this area. "They'll pick me up; that's what it says. You can head back now."

"That's okay. Let me drop you off."

I really don't want him to. I'm that certain that I'm not going to be renting a car, and I don't want him to be a witness to it. My alternate plan is to get one of these truckers to take my last hundred dollars and let me ride with him. I'm trying not to think of how poorly that plan had worked before.

"I'm fine, Mitch. You need to get back home."

Mitch swings his bad leg over the saddle but makes no move to start the motor. "I really don't like just leaving you here." I can't see his eyes behind the aviator-style sunglasses he's wearing. His red bandanna has slipped forward over his forehead. He looks tough, and can sound tough, but I know that he's not. He didn't have to tell me that he was a musician; he could have kept the Hell's Angel persona, stuck with the impression he seems to want to make. We exchange cell numbers, carefully punching in the digits and saving, as if we're going to stay in touch.

"Don't you worry. I'll be fine." I step away from the motorcycle, give him space to maneuver.

He starts the engine, which comes to life with a heavy rumble, deafening beneath the gas station canopy. "Let me know what happens."

"I will." He's got the bike pointed back the way we came.

"Wait." I almost have to shout to be heard over the sound of the motorcycle's roar.

Mitch wheels around to come back to my side.

"What happened? Your leg, I mean." I'm not usually this rude, but given the circumstances of our meeting, this seems like a fact I should know about him, something as personal to him as the raw facts I've given him about myself are to me.

He doesn't say anything at first, and I wonder if I've offended him with my sudden curiosity, or if he's trying to come up with some smart remark like he's done before.

"Nothing terribly interesting. Bone cancer. I was fifteen."

"I'm sorry."

"Don't be. If I'd been able to play football, I probably wouldn't have played violin. Things happen. Things happen for a reason."

"I guess." But to me, losing a leg seems a harsh price to pay for discovering a musical talent. I don't add that I can't see the reason for my particular situation, because it seems childish to compare losing a dog to losing a leg, but it's what I'm thinking.

Impulsively, I hug him, and then he's gone.

Mack and I step into the spotlight. The music begins. I tap my cane against the floor and Mack rises to his hind legs and, in perfect time with the music, turns in a clockwise circle, then extends his right front paw to me and I take it, bowing to him. By the time he leaps into my arms three minutes later, the crowd is clapping wildly.

6

It's worth a try, calling the car-rental agency, so I do. Get a nice young man to pick me up, just as promised. He takes me back to the office, and as soon as he runs the card through, I know that I'm cooked. As I feared, they want a lot of money to take a car one-way out of state. More than is available on my abused credit card. He looks at me with a sheepish face. "Sorry, ma'am. I can give you a car for the day."

"No. Thank you anyway." I shoulder my duffel, jam the offended credit card into my back pocket, and walk out of there with as much dignity as I can muster.

I have no idea where I am. There is a bench outside of the rental place, and I sit on it. No sense walking off into the unknown. I should go in and ask the nice young man for directions. But to where? To what? The ride from the Crossroads Convenience Mart wasn't long or complicated. I'll walk back there and go back to plan B. Surely some nice trucker with Mass. plates will want a quiet rider.

"Ma'am?" The nice young man, really not so young—he's old enough to have a day job and not be in school—is standing beside me.

"Yes?"

"The bus station is about half a mile from here. I bet you can get one to Boston."

I am touched by his concern. "That's a good idea."

"I'll take you."

Twice in one day, I've been rescued by unlikely heroes. I want to find my dog, but I know that a bus to Boston is really my only hope of getting where I'm going. In all of this, I've forgotten that I have a destination.

I don't let him see that I have been defeated. I shake my head against that thought. Oh no, I'm not giving up hope of catching up with Artie. This is just a better way to find him. When I get to Boston, I'll locate Artie easily. I know I will; I'm certain I'll remember where he was going with his cargo. Once I catch up, I know that I'll find him. He won't turn around and head back immediately. He said something about a relative. I try to think back on Artie's conversations. Mostly, I had tuned them out, since they were the kind of brash manly-man nonsense so many men like to think they impress me with. But I'm sure, mixed in with the hero-in-his-own-life stories, that he'd mentioned a sister or a cousin he would see when in Boston. I'll find him. I have to.

Artie has my dog.

"That would be nice."

The young man spins a key ring around his forefinger like a gunslinger. "We can take this one." He holds the passenger door open for me, a gesture that makes me feel old, or at least old enough that he sees me as requiring courtly behavior. He's got to be around twenty-one or twenty-two, about the same age as my son. Which makes me think, as I am actually old enough to be his mother, that's how this young man sees me.

"What's your name?"

"Tyler. Tyler Schmidt." This boy still has that adolescent gawk about him that will diminish as age thickens his neck and bulks up his skinny chest.

"Justine Meade."

We don't shake hands. "You said Schmidt?" Artie is Schmidt.

"Uh-huh."

"I'm trying to find a guy named Schmidt. I guess it's a common-enough name."

"Millions of us. Some related, most not. Where's your guy from?"

"I have no idea. I met him in Washington State, but he's got relatives in Massachusetts, I think." This is a silly conversation, like asking if all the Smiths in the world are related. "Arthur Schmidt."

"Doesn't ring a bell. Why are you looking for him? You a bounty hunter?"

I catch the look in his eye; this entry-level boy has a sense of humor. "Something like that. He's got my dog and I want him back."

"Isn't dognapping against the law? Can you get him arrested?"

"I'd like to try."

The bus station is nothing more than a convenience store. Tyler pulls up into a bus lane and hops out as if he's my taxi driver and is going to repeat his chivalry of a few minutes ago, but I swing the door open and we end up facing each other on the cracked sidewalk. He is just the height of my son, and I resist the urge to give him a quick hug good-bye, if only for the feeling of holding a son, in my arms again, even if not my particular son. It has been a very long time since I've had that privilege.

"Thank you, Tyler." I try to give him a couple of bucks.

He quickly forces the folded-up dollars back into my hand. "It's part of the service."

I feel the chill sweat of embarrassment dampen my shirt. This boy has me pegged. He knows I need every penny I have on me. "Do you have a card?"

Tyler fishes a company card out of his wallet, hands it to me as if he, too, believes that I might rent a car from him someday. I'm just thinking that I'll send him a nice note he can have put in his personnel folder—service above and beyond, rescuing maidens. Then I wonder if he'll get in trouble for being my taxi. Then I do hug him. And, strangely enough, he hugs me back.

"I hope you find your dog."

"Me, too."

He drives off, leaving me standing on the filthy sidewalk, thinking about my son.

I was so young when he was born. Not unreasonably so—plenty of girls have babies at twenty. But then choosing to raise him alone, without help, comes back to me now as the sort of reckless hubris of the very young. I named him Anthony, like his father and grandfather, but called him "Tony" from the moment he was born. Every mother thinks her baby is the most beautiful, but Tony really was: curly dark hair still wet against his tiny skull, murky dark eyes that would become chocolate brown in a few weeks. Starfish hands reaching out for me.

What girl doesn't believe that the guy who is her first real lover is the one who will remain the love of her life? At least back then. Not like now, when girls take up partners as if they're making sandwiches. Two bites and you're done. Move on. Meaningless. Anthony wasn't meaningless to me.

Every girl who worked at Marcone's Grill had a crush on him, the youngest son of the Marcone family. I was working there, taking courses at the local community college, and definitely not interested in complicating my life—at the tender age of twenty— by falling in love. It's probably because I didn't pursue him that Anthony began to pay attention to me. Long talks as we closed the place up for the night, then coffee in the all-night diner that was their nearest competition. Very platonic, very sweet, and this sweet, unthreatening attention made me fall in love with him.

But, in the end, I was meaningless to him. He married me

because he had to, but he never loved me. Not the way a woman wants to be loved.

"Anthony, I can't do this anymore." I face my husband of three and a half years. His face is a mask of indifference, which is how he is treating me, with indifference. He goes out every night with his friends; he rarely plays with his son. The sweet, gentle nature of our friendship has become silence and avoidance. I no longer delight in his physical beauty; I cannot see it anymore. His fastidiousness has gone from endearing to unbearable; his loyalty to his friends undermines our marriage. Our marriage, clearly, is not important to him. Maybe even abhorrent. "I can't stay if things keep on the way they have."

Anthony shrugs, as if his wife's telling him she's leaving is of no consequence. I wonder if he's calling my bluff, but the relief in his eyes is clear. I have been the braver partner; he's been waiting for me to pull the plug so he won't have to. "So go."

When I left his father, Tony was almost three, just young enough to think this was a normal life; just old enough to ask, every now and then, where Daddy was.

"When's Daddy coming?"

"He's not coming, baby. He lives in Brooklyn."

"Why don't we live in Brooklyn?"

I have no answer for that. How do you tell a little boy that his father won't love his mother?

If I thought that Tony would keep me tied to one spot, I was wrong. But he did give me a different reason for moving on: I was pursuing the better life for him, one that didn't mean living in a motel by the week or taking a shit job just because it came with some benefits. I wanted to give him a home, one he could be proud of. I always told him that the next place would be better, bigger, cleaner, safer. The next place we lived would be where he could play with kids in the neighborhood, ride his bike. Heck, own a bike. The next town or the next city, the next state, would be better. What I didn't realize was that in order to have a stable home, there must be some permanence. It isn't enough to have a loving mother. You need a place to call home.

I'm a little puzzled by the seeming lack of a bus station, until I figure out that this is a stop, not a station. The storefront has high windows, plastered with beer advertisements and lottery signs. To the left of the Budweiser ad is a smallish placard stating the place's secondary function as a bus agency. Outside the place is a single bench, occupied by a large black man wearing an old-fashioned fedora. Inside, the place is tiny, tight, with too closely arranged displays of potato chips and lager beer. It smells like spilled beer; it smells a little like my bar. The wood floor is littered with a healthy scattering of abandoned lottery tickets.

I wait in line to buy a ticket to Boston from a cashier who may be Pakistani or Sri Lankan. On the counter, tucked between Slim Jims and condoms, is a cardboard box with bus schedules in it. I grab one and stand aside to let the line move forward. The lottery must be big tonight. The line keeps forming, filled with quiet people, fruitless dreams of a new life playing behind downturned eyes.

The next bus from Erie is at 8:40 tonight. It will take thirteen-plus hours to make it to Boston.

"One way to Boston, please." I fish out my credit card and hand it to him.

"No credit card. Cash only."

"You have a terminal, so why won't you take credit cards?"

"Not for bus. Store policy." He doesn't even have the good grace to look sorry. "You go to Erie to use credit card."

"I thought I was in Erie."

This does get me a crooked smile, like the kind you'd expect from somebody who enjoys other people's troubles because they make him feel momentarily superior. "No. You have to go to Erie."

Suddenly, the logic of a bus ride fails me. By the time I limp into Boston, Artie will surely have turned around and headed home. I wonder if there's a cheap flight, one of those thirty-nine-dollar specials. If I could fly, I might even beat him there.

My cashier friend offers no help, just shrugs and waits with a feigned patience for me to decide what to do. I move out of line again. The sun is setting as I sit beside the old black man on the bench outside the store. I hold my duffel on my lap and fight the urge to rest my head on it. In the fading September light, the shadows pool at my feet.

"Nice evening." My bench companion says this quietly, as if afraid to mention it.

"Yeah. I guess so."

"Don't sound convinced."

"How far is the Erie bus station?"

"You're in Conneautville. Erie's thirty miles away."

"Then I guess I'm not walking there."

"That's why there's buses."

I know that I'm going to have to go back into the store, use some of my dwindling cash reserve to buy a ticket for a bus to get to a bus. I suddenly feel the lack of food and the exhaustion of defeat. I want to lie down. Mitch has failed me; he didn't get as far as Erie. I'm in Erie County. I've been fooled by the same generalization that people from Boston suburbs use when they say they're from Boston.

"Going home?"

"No. Well, my father's home."

"Not your home?"

"Hasn't been for a long time."

"But you don't live around here."

"No. I just found myself here. A long story."

We sit quietly for a time, watching the gradual lengthening of those shadows. I study the bus schedule as if it's tea leaves. I look in vain for a faster, cheaper, more convenient bus that will magically transport me to Boston.

"So, where is home?" His voice is still just above a whisper, making his question seem far more philosophical than the simple words would suggest.

And then it hits me. Why not just go back? Turn around and wait for Artie to come back to town and show up at the bar. And then I will kill him. The logic of this is breathtaking. In the next breath, I realize that the chance that Artie will show up in that bar without my dog is a chance I do not want to take. No, I've got to catch up with him.

I finally answer the old man. "Where my dog is."

"I had a good dog once. Saw me through a lot of years of hard times. Never once complained."

"They rarely do." I shoulder my duffel and go back into the store. When I come out, the old man is gone.

I hunker down in the bus seat, sitting toward the rear, left side, against the window, which is streaked with the dried paths of raindrops from some past storm. I am bone-tired. My dinner of microwaved burrito is sitting uncomfortably mid-belly. I've smuggled a can of Coke onto the bus to wash away the metallic taste of prepackaged food. Thirty miles is far enough to catch a quick nap, and I close my eyes. But the image of my dog rests behind them and all I see is his little silver-and-white face, with the dollops of black eyebrows over those mismatched eyes. I named him Maksim after that ballroom dancer on *Dancing with the Stars*. I am an unabashed fan of that show, although the only ballroom dancing I ever did was in junior high when the phys ed teachers made us all learn the box step, even though disco was the rage. Everyone thinks I named him that because we dance together, but the truth is, canine freestyle came well after I'd named my puppy.

Rodney Parris gave me the puppy. He was a nice guy with an unfortunate handicap—he was married. I didn't know that, of course. I've never dated married men, and have been cautious around those who claim to be "separated." But he was married, and that was a very disappointing fact to me, because I really liked him. He was the first guy in a long time to make me glad he was around. Having discovered the wife—or rather, she discovered me—I told him good-bye. I shut the door in his face, turned my back to it, and slid to the floor. I've broken up too many times to forget that the pain does go away, but in that moment I was crushed. My little puppy, maybe four months old at this point, dashed over to where I sat on the floor and dropped his teddy bear in my lap. I burst into tears, me, a noncrier, and he looked at me with such worry. Sniffing back the momentary deluge, I hugged him and swore then that he was all the man I'd ever need.

And, so far, he has been.

I feel that long-ago dammed-up deluge working its way up from just above where that burrito is sitting. I bunch my fists up under my closed eyes, hoping that no one sits next to me, that no one hears me sniffle like some brokenhearted teenager. Stifling the urge to cry, I pull my phone out of my pocket.

My cell has only a tiny percent of battery left. I close the cover, praying that Artie will call me before I run out of juice. I have no idea when I'll be able to recharge it.

By the time the bus pulls into the bus station in Erie, it's full dark. I have a long night ahead of me.

7

I manage to recharge my cell phone while waiting for the 8:40 bus to leave from Erie—the city, not the county. I'm leaning against the wet counter in the ladies' room, my charger plugged into a random outlet beside the hand dryer, when the phone rings with my "Puttin' on the Ritz" ringtone, startling the bejesus out of me as the music bounces off the tile walls of the hollow room. My hand literally shakes as I flip the phone open, praying that Artie's number is on the display. It isn't.

"Where are you?" My stepmother doesn't even begin by saying hello.

"Erie. Waiting for a bus."

"I don't know how much time you think you have to get here, but you should hurry up. This isn't a drill. I thought you'd be here by now."

"It's a long story."

"It always is with you."

"I'll be there tomorrow."

"Why didn't you fly? You could have been here two days ago. I could use the help."

"You know why."

"Because you had to bring that dog?" Adele smacks the word *dog*.

"No. Because I couldn't afford it." I say this loudly enough in the echoing rest room that my voice is amplified and the woman just shaking the wet off her hands and hunting for the dryer that I'm blocking stops and walks out of the room, wiping her hands on her pants.

"It's not that expensive. You should have just done it." Good old Adele. Wanting something and not being able to have it just isn't part of her world. I find it slightly curious that she doesn't even suggest that they might have helped me get home, not even as an afterthought.

"I'll be there tomorrow." I would like nothing better than to hang up, but I don't. I wait. I listen. When the silence builds, I finally ask what she should have been offering. "How is he?"

"Dying. How else do you think he is?" Adele sounds royally pissed off that she's going to be a widow.

"Please don't."

Adele finally drops the outdated angry-stepmother role. "He had a good night last night. The pain is manageable with the morphine, but he's not very talkative."

I bite back the obvious jab—that she never let him talk anyway, so why should he start now. "Can you still keep him home?" I'll give her that; she hasn't opted out for hospitalization or a nursing home. Last spring, when my father was diagnosed with prostate cancer, no one seemed overly concerned; it was treatable and I didn't get the feeling that there was a time bomb ticking. So when it metastasized into his bones, it was a complete surprise to me. Adele's call last week to say I should come home really did come out of the blue. She didn't bother me with "details," as she liked to say. She waited until it was almost too late to have me come. But he was still at home.

There is another silence. I lean toward the wall, press the charger cord deeper into the phone. Wait.

"I hope so. That's why I need you here."

I fled that house as soon as I could, bitter and heartbroken. And yet I am going back, dutiful daughter to a man who turned his back on me when I needed him most.

"Tomorrow. I get into Boston at about nine-thirty. I'll grab the first bus to New Bedford I can and be there maybe around noontime."

"Good." She never says hello and she certainly doesn't say good-bye.

It doesn't escape me that I am faced with making a choice. My desire is to find my dog. My self-imposed obligation is to go to my father. In both situations, timing is going to be everything. I could abandon my journey to New Bedford and focus on finding Mack, except that I hold on to a childish hope that, in showing up, in facing my father, I might get an apology, an acknowledgment that what he did to me when I was seventeen was wrong. I'm not sure if I want him to have the opportunity to clear his conscience; or is it more that I want the opportunity to forgive him? Ever since Adele called, I have run little dramatic scenes in my head. Deathbed hand-holding, my father begging my forgiveness for betraying me so long ago. My saying something that would bring us both peace. Some might call it a desire for closure. I guess so. You can't live most of your life with anger your primary emotion.

I pull the phone-charger cord out of the wall and coil it around the plug. I have a half-full battery now, so at the very least I can keep dialing Artie. By this time, he must be close to his destination. It's been over seven hours since he abandoned me and stole my dog. Without stops, going seventy—my math fails me again and I can only imagine that the distance between us is growing minute by minute and a thirteen-hour bus ride will never catch me up to him.

Fully armed with a recharged phone, I dial Candy. When she answers in her usual businesslike "Candy's Place, proprietress speaking," I almost burst into tears. With Candy, you always get the feeling she'll fix the problem, whether it's the leak under the sink or a customer complaint, a staff member's broken heart or the need to get an ordinance against sticking advertising flyers under windshield wipers voted in. "Oh Candy, I'm in a fix."

She listens without interruption. There's a pause before she weighs in, a gentle, thoughtful pause. "Okay. Let's see what we can do." I lean back against the wet apron of the sink and allow a flutter of relief. "I'll make a call or two, see if I can find out where Artie is going. You get on that bus and keep your phone on. Once we know where he's going, we can call and have him held up there."

"Do you think you can find out? I've been with him for two days and I can't remember what he said or even what he was hauling. I'm not sure if he ever said, just told me Boston." Which, if my recent experience of Erie is any indicator, could mean anywhere in the vicinity.

"I can't make any promises. But I'll do my best. Just get on the bus. I'll call you later."

Unlike my stepmother, Candy leaves me with a "Good-bye" and a softly spoken "God bless."

Candy Kane is maybe ten years older than I am, but that doesn't stop her from treating me like she does all the women who work for her—as her child. Not *like* a child, but with the same care and concern that a good parent shows a daughter. I sound mushy, and I don't mean to. It's just that her quick call to arms has me emotional. Maybe it's just that her instinctive mothering skills have always left me jealous. Lacking a good example, turned out not to be such a good one myself. In my experience, mothers either died or preferred other children. Having grown up pitted against two people who saw me as an inconvenience, I swore I'd be a better mother to my son. I wanted to lavish attention on him, but, young, single, and poor, I'm not sure I lavished the right kind. Late at night while he slept, I would crawl into his bed and press my weary body around his, sorry that when he was awake, I was more stressed than loving, more impatient than playful—the daily fear of not being able to keep him in sneakers and cereal making me short-tempered and unable to take pleasure in him. I wanted to make him feel as though he was the most important thing in my life, but that was harder than it sounds.

Tony sits very still on the daybed that I convert from my bed back into the couch in the living room of the efficiency apartment. He clutches his special pillow, the one that ensures that wherever he sleeps, he has his own pillow with its singular Donald Duck motif. A sitter is coming in a minute, but she's late and I'm beginning to get nervous that then I'll be late. Late again, and I might not get the extra shifts at the restaurant where I've waitressed for the past six months.

Tony has already spent the entire week in day care, and he is so stoic about being left again so that I can work a Saturday shift. He never gives me fits about leaving; he understands, even at four years old, that I have to do whatever it takes to keep him in juice boxes. I never promise to bring him treats; I never make promises I can't keep. But the juice boxes, little individual servings of grape or apple or mixed-berry juice, are his special treat for his lunch box. Just like all the other kids have.

The sitter finally arrives, a scrawny teenage girl with braces that look like they could tune in Mars. I bend down to give Tony a kiss good-bye. "Be good for . . ."

"Molly." The girl has the good grace not to roll her eyes at me. All these Mollies and Shannons and Morgans blend together, an unending supply, courtesy of the local high school.

"Mom?"

"What, sweetie? Mommy has to go; I'm late."

"I don't need juice boxes."

I still have a few minutes before boarding the bus bound for Boston, so I thumb the number for my pal Saundra Livingbrook. Saundra is the one who got me involved in canine freestyle, and she is the sole support of six dogs, all rescues. I can hear them in the background as she answers my call, sounding like children clamoring for mom's attention when she's on the phone.

"He is chipped, isn't he?" Saundra is talking about the microchip embedded beneath the skin between Mack's shoulders that identifies him as my dog to anyone with a reader.

"He is." I take small comfort from that fact. He's with Artie, and who knows what Artie will do with him. If Mack is picked up by a dog officer or dropped with a vet, then I have hope. But I simply can't imagine that Artie will do anything thoughtful like that.

"Let's think about this. I'll post the story on my Facebook page and get the word out to as many rescues as I can. It'll be like putting up posters all over the country. He's a Sheltie, so I'll make sure that Sheltie rescues have his information." Saundra has to control a pack of dogs, so she's no stranger to getting things done.

"If you could do that, it would be great. Candy is trying to find out specifically where Artie is going and see if she can get help at that end. I'm boarding a bus and won't get to Boston till tomorrow morning. And I've got my father to deal with."

"How is he?"

"If my stepmother is to be believed, on death's doorstep."

Saundra has known me long enough that I've let her in on some of my history. I don't do that too often; usually, I speak of my past in safe generalities. It's not that my story is particularly interesting or rare, but I don't really want to think about it. I prefer talking about the now. The past is like a series of black curtains; each one covers the essential scenes of a life that only in the last half decade has become less damaged. A tough childhood, single motherhood. Bad choices and better ones. Just like everyone else. So, I keep myself to myself except with certain people, friends like Saundra, whose life hasn't been that famous bowl of cherries, either.

Mack awakens from his wolf sleep with a jolt. The truck is moving; there is no light but the stars that flee past in the night sky. They are climbing, and Artie shifts the lumbering vehicle to gain more power. The cab is fetid with the miasma of greasy, farting man and cigarettes; the driver's window is down a crack, not enough to let in sufficient fresh air, only a vague trickle of breeze. Then the truck levels off and almost immediately noses down the long incline they have just climbed. Just as Mack feels the truck speed up, Artie downshifts to slow the pace.

Artie lights another cigarette, inhales deeply, then blows the smoke out of the side of his mouth into the moving air, which catches it, pushing the drift of smoke into the bunk.

Mack sneezes.

"What the . . ." Artie's head swivels and dog and man look each other in the eye. "Shit."

Mack braces himself against the sudden lurch of the truck, shakes from head to tail, and jumps into the passenger seat, where he fixes his eye on Artie, giving him his best I'm-a-good-dog look. This is more like it; now things will improve. A quick glance at the bag of kibble on the floor, just to remind Artie that dinner is late. A soft whine to emphasize the need to go out.

Artie grabs his mute cell phone and scrambles his fingers over its face to find the right buttons to listen to his messages. "Nothin' but trouble. I need this like a hole in the head. Goddamned bitch. I knew this was a bad idea. Freakin' dog. Twenty-seven unheard messages!"

Artie keeps up the tongue language and Mack sits confidently in the seat, where Justine's scent lingers on the cracked plastic. He should have come down sooner; he just didn't believe that Artie hadn't known he was there. How can a man not scent a dog lying close by? Now that the man knows he's here, things must improve. Anytime that Justine has left him, which is rare, the person he's left with knows about the basics: food, water, toys, go-out. It is inconceivable to him that Artie doesn't speak enough dog to get those basics attended to. But the man just keeps yakking and flailing the cell around. The truck is picking up speed, and if the dog could see over the hood, he would notice that they are too close to the little car in front of them.

The truck banks left, then right as Artie drops the phone and pays attention to the road. He's still grumbling, tossing sideways glances at Mack every now and then. He rubs his sandpaper chin with rough hands, making a whiskery sound. Mack sits in the passenger seat, never taking his eyes off of Artie. Artie hasn't used any tongue language to let Mack know where Justine is. He's only used the more subtle but highly legible body language of a man powerfully annoyed. There was a dog in agility class with the same pissed-off demeanor. No one wanted to be near him, always afraid that the next growl would be followed by a bite. Everybody else loved the free playtime they were given after class, chasing each other, wrestling, or simply standing side by side. Not this guy. He left as soon as the class was over, his human keeping his leash in both hands.

Artie holds the cell in front of him, resting it on the steering wheel. Mack hears the distorted sound of Justine's voice emanating from the tiny rectangle as Artie listens to the stream of messages. One word is recognizable: *Mack*. He wags the tip of his tail at the sound of it. Yawns and swallows to show Artie that he knows that word. If he can hear that word, and recognize Justine's voice, she must be close by. Just out of sight.

Then there is the sound of another voice leaking out of the tiny speaker.

"Shit." Artie glances at his side mirror with the expression of a squirrel being chased. "Goddamn it." Artie pitches the cell phone into the back, where it lands with a silent thud in Justine's vacant sleeping bag. "Freakin' A. Hell's Angels?" He guns the motor and picks up speed.

Artie continues to mutter. Mack remains upright on the seat that bears so much of Justine's scent. He gives Artie sideways glances, the tenor of that voice keeping him alert and wary. He won't go back to sleep. Not now. Mack will stay alert until Justine comes back.

The dog knows that it is deep night, the time of day when a good dog is tucked into his bed, nose under tail. A good dog who sleeps only lightly, one part of him always at the ready to defend the house against intruders. Skunks. Possum. Nightmares. One of Mack's jobs is to comfort Justine when she wakes at night.

Artie downshifts and brakes, the truck slowly coming to a halt. Mack wags his tail. At last! He even whines, just a little, to let Artie know he's happy. Artie has stopped talking. The truck idles and Artie sits still. Mack peers at the window but sees nothing.

This wasn't like any of the places where they'd stopped before. This was just the side of the road. The cars zoom past them, the headlights streaming together like something liquid; other semis rush by, making even the weight of the truck vibrate a little.

Artie pushes open his door and drops to the ground. He comes around to the passenger side. The door swings open and man and dog are face-to-face. "Get the fuck out." Artie grabs for Mack's ruff. The dog instinctively pulls back and the man is left holding the dog's collar, not the dog. He makes another lunge and this time gets a fistful of fur and skin. Artie drags Mack across the seat, yanking him out the open door so hard that the dog falls to the ground before he can get his feet under him, landing hard on his side, pushing the air out in an audible *whuff.* Mack gets up, shakes, and waits. Artie is on the ground now, feet planted, hands in fists. "Get out of here. Go on, git."

Mack growls; this is too much. Even a well-behaved dog has limits. Artie steps closer. Mack pins his ears back and lowers his head, but he doesn't growl again. He knows that this man is his last connection to Justine. He keeps his head down, his eyes pinned on Artie's eyes, like his sheep-herding forebears.

"They can't prove nothing, if you ain't here." The flashers are beating a hectic rhythm against the dark. Artie swings a leg over the guardrail. "Come here, boy." His voice is all sweetness, a gooey sound that doesn't fool the dog.

Mack keeps to his side of the metal rail. Artie pats his knee. "Come on."

Mack is still skeptical, but the man is his only connection to Justine. Then Artie utters the magic words. "Let's go find Justine."

At once, Mack leaps over the rail as if it's one of his agility obstacles and lands at Artie's feet. Artie is taking him to Justine. Finally!

Then one well-aimed kick sends him down the steep grade. Stones and twigs catch in his coat as he rolls out of control and lands at the bottom of the slope, his breath knocked out of him. By the time Mack is back on his feet and up the embankment, the truck is gone.

8

I am wide-awake to Buffalo, drowsy by Rochester, and sound asleep by Syracuse. I miss Albany altogether. I wake cotton-mouthed and cramped in a window seat. I need to pee, and the person beside me has stretched out her legs and sleeps with her cheek propped up against her hand. If I try to slip out, I know I'll step on her. We haven't spoken and I can't remember when she got on; the bus has gone on and off the highway so many times, I can't remember each little town or hole-in-the-wall bus stop we've pulled up in. The whole of New York State is a tangle of sodium-lighted pauses along the way, each one a delay in my pursuit, and I try not to think about how much longer this ride is taking than if I could have rented a car. I would have been there by now. I would have found Artie by now.

I guess I can hold on for a little while longer. I'd like to go back to sleep myself, but now I am wide-awake. The dim interior light of the bus turns everything a vague green and I feel like I'm underwater. Outside, the pinpricks of light from houses un-fortunate enough to be located along a highway remind me that I am not home, tucked beneath the patchwork quilt that I have moved with me everywhere I have been. The quilt that Tony peed on as a baby, and that Mack inevitably chooses to lie on when he's wet. This quilt that is the only possession I have that came from my mother, who, by being blessed by sudden death, is forever my ideal of motherhood. An ideal I was never able to achieve. I've sorted through my memories of her, and keep only those that appeal to me. Each of my recollections corresponds to one of the four pictures I have of her: Easter morning, Christmas morning, my fourth birthday where she bends over me helping me to blow out candles, and the random photograph that isn't of her, but of my father. She is caught in the background, but it is the only one of her pregnant. In each photo she is idealized and that's how I like to keep it.

The house lights move by and the bus moves back into deep countryside. I have no idea where I am.

Dawn creeps up on me. Maybe I've slept again, because suddenly the trees and fences, the barns, and the cattle standing in the fields are distinct. Color eases its way into the landscape. I still don't know where I am, but it's pretty. I'm on the wrong side of the bus to read the signs that might let me know how much farther I have to go.

The woman beside me suddenly startles herself awake with a violent jerk of her legs and hands. "Oh!" She looks at me sheepishly and wipes the drool from her chin with the back of her hand. "Where are we?"

"Don't know. Not there yet." I excuse myself, climb over her, and make for the stinky rest room.

When I get back, my seat companion stands up to let me climb back into my place. She's a large woman, in her fifties, if I was to guess. She wears a loose dress clearly chosen for its traveling comfort and not the fact that it makes her look nine times bigger than she is. She fumbles around in a cloth grocery bag until she extracts a can of Coke and a banana. "I got more. Want one?"

I'm not proud. I'm really thirsty, so I say yes. The Coke is sweet and hardly my morning drink of choice, but it burns through the cotton in my mouth and makes me feel less gross.

"I'm heading for Springfield, going to see my grandkids. Where you heading?"

We haven't even exchanged names, but the rules of the road are clear: story time.

"New Bedford."

"Never been there. Went to the Cape once. But mostly we go to Canada for vacation." My companion needs nothing further from me. She chatters happily on and on. I wonder how close we are to Springfield. I wonder if this is her normal way, or whether she's quiet at home, keeping to herself, baking those pies for the church supper, minding her own business. But traveling by herself to visit kids she probably rarely sees opens something up in her and the floodgates of talk gush open. Kids, grandkids, little Mikey's First Communion. I'm not even listening when she tires of herself and asks me the inevitable woman-to-woman question: "You got kids?"

The question is a normal one. She's handed the deck to me. My turn to deal story now. "A son. He's grown." I don't say grown and gone. He was gone and then grown. "Tony."

"Where's your boy now?"

This is a hard question. Before I have to answer with some tepid reply, my phone plays its little tune and I fish it out of my pocket, that little compulsive prayer that it be Artie singing along with the tune: Let it be Art-tie. Please be Art-tie. I don't even look at the display to see who it is. The woman beside me presses back against her seat, as if that gives me privacy.

"He's going to a warehouse to leave the trailer." Candy gives me the address, and I know Boston well enough to recognize a street along the harbor, near or even in Southie. Not terribly far from South Station. A cab ride, a good walk. I thank her and promise to keep her posted. I can't find any paper in my duffel, so I write the address down on the palm of my hand. The bus schedule I have doesn't tell me anything about buses from Boston to New Bedford, but I know they must be fairly frequent. We're entering Springfield now. Boston is at most two hours away. At the least, Artie got there at night and may still be asleep in his cab. I press a hand to my chest to feel the impulsive beating of my racing heart. I feel like this is that TV show, *The Amazing Race*. I'm closing in. Maybe I'll catch him. Maybe this will all fade to a bad dream in a few hours. I'll have my boy back. My Mack. He'll jump into my arms like he does at the end of our performances, overjoyed. A furry bundle of wiggles and kisses.

"Are you okay?"

Funny how so many people have asked me that question in one form or another in the past twenty-four hours. I look at my companion, who is gathering up her Coke cans and bundles of presents for the grandkids. We're at the Springfield station, her stop.

"Yeah, I'm fine. You enjoy your family."

She looks at me for a long moment. Her chubby face doesn't hide the fact that she has beautiful eyes. I expect that it was those eyes that drew her husband to her, those eyes that have kept him despite the baby weight that didn't disappear, but settled in; despite the years of caring for children, caring for his house, settling for a life lived in terms of vacations to Canada and First Communions. "You, too."

She struggles to make her way down the narrow bus aisle. I can see a woman who must be her daughter, a little kid clasped by one hand. Simultaneously, they both open their arms to the woman as she lumbers down the bus steps.

Yeah, I'll be enjoying my family all right.

The points of the compass are not nominal values, but instinctive. Standing on the verge of the highway, he raises his muzzle to the air, orients himself, and begins to walk. Cars bullet past him, flattening his coat by the force of their passing. He keeps to a westerly course but moves into the protection of the tree line, keeping up a businesslike trot despite the ache in his ribs. This takes him under the highway and into a culvert that has only a sluggish trickle of water running through it. Inside the culvert is the scent of ground animal, possum or raccoon. Mack is fiercely thirsty and laps gratefully at the shallow stream as if he could lap it dry.

As he emerges from the culvert, Mack pauses, listens. Justine must be somewhere. He heard her voice. He's not ignorant enough to believe that she was trapped in the cell, but he has a vague idea that if he could hear her voice, she can't be far off. If he wanders too far, she won't find him. Even so, he keeps moving, instinct telling him that she won't find him here in this wild place.

The highway is a distant susurration; the slow passing of cars on a back road is closer. One at a time, slow enough that he can discern the sound of their radios, smell the waft of cigarette smoke exhaled through cracked windows, the voices of couples arguing late at night.

Justine will expect him to wait for her someplace. He needs to find that place. In their life together, she often tells him *down-stay*, leaving him waiting outside doors, or gates, or on sidewalks. He needs to find a place where Justine might ask him to down-stay. And then wait for her.

Part 2

9

Alice spots the dog first.

She mentions to Edward that she noticed this furry little dog sitting quietly between the twin painted brick pillars of the cemetery. "I thought about stopping." Alice Parmalee pulls a can of tuna out of the carrier bag, studies it for a moment. "I sort of wish I had. I hope he doesn't get hit by a car."

Edward grunts, shakes his newspaper in half, peers at her over his glasses. "Best not to approach strange dogs. He'll go home."

"I don't think he had a collar." Alice doesn't know why she says this; the dog has a thick ruff, which certainly would obscure any collar. "He was just sitting there, like he was waiting."

"He probably was. Maybe his owners were tourists looking for ancestors." Ed slides his glasses back up onto the bridge of his nose, the box scores regaining his full attention.

Alice finishes emptying the green cloth grocery sacks, lining her cupboards with the same cans of peas, corn, and Campbell's Chunky soup, the same boxes of cereal that she replenishes every few weeks from the Big Y. For the most part, she shops at Potter's General Store—150 years and still going strong—which offers basics like milk and bread, eggs if she wants to make omelettes for dinner, as well as things Ed calls "gourmet," although she buys nothing more exotic than guacamole. Anything with a pretty label and Ed scoffs that she's paying for packaging.

Alice can no longer raise any enthusiasm for cooking. Edward is happy with "plain fare," and it isn't any fun to have a new recipe consumed with the same unappreciative haste as a meal of hot dogs and beans. Alice doesn't mind, not really. It's easier, in some respects, not to have to think about meals, not to have to care.

Once upon a time, she imagined that in her middle years she'd take up tai chi or go back to college and finish her degree. That was when she thought her life would travel along a smoother road. She also expected to have children while still in her twenties. She never expected that it would take a miracle to have the one child in her fortieth year. She certainly never expected that, as hard as it was to get her, it would be so easy to lose her.

When Stacy was born, the folks at the plant chipped in and bought Ed and Alice a video camera. Ed got quite adept at using it, and for years they filmed every significant moment of Stacy's life, from crawling to tap dancing; from T-ball to her first day of high school. She was used to it, although as she got older she tended toward foolish faces and rude gestures whenever Ed fired up the recorder. They almost never watched those videos, not then, and certainly not now. Then, they were too busy raising her; now it is out of the question.

Stored in sleeves, labeled carefully with years and events, the rows of boxes remain untouched. A video collection of Anastasia Marie Parmalee's life. They could have her back at any point in her short life, relive the moments preserved on VHS tape, but they never open the glass doors of the breakfront, never do more than run a dust cloth over the labels. Neither Ed nor Alice can allow the emotion that lives just beneath the surface to get out. They dealt with it then, and opening the doors now would only serve to start the process over again. They aren't like the other families they met at grief counseling, scrapbooks and albums opened and reopened so many times that the bindings were worn; grief-stricken parents making you look at the faces of lost children, acting like those children weren't lost, but just out of sight. Talking about their children, as if whatever tragedy had taken them was merely a part of growing up—cancer, car wrecks. Iraq.

Ed and Alice closed the doors and kept the evidence of Stacy's short, active life inside that cupboard. They never speak of what might have been, nor of what is past.

Alice keeps busy with her little cutting garden, her yoga classes, and her part-time job at the library. She fills her days up with housework and chores enough for any woman. Who has time for anything more?

The dog had looked so forlorn. Maybe *forlorn* wasn't the right word. The way it looked at her car as she drove slowly out of the cemetery, ears pricked in her direction, and then lowered, as if, well, as if it was disappointed. Maybe after dinner she'll go see if it's still hanging around the cemetery. Besides, she should check on the russet and gold chrysanthemums she planted earlier today to see if they need a little more water.

10

Edward Parmalee sees the dog as he heads out in the morning to gas up the Cutlass. Can't miss it. The dog is sitting just where Alice saw it, between the cemetery gates. It carefully studies Ed's car as he slowly drives by. He probably belongs to some neighbor who lets his dog loose to roam the countryside. Don't see much of that nowadays, not like when he was a kid and everyone knew everyone else's dogs because they were allowed to wander—as were the kids. You didn't worry about leash laws or child molesters in those days. Didn't neuter male dogs, and bike helmets hadn't been invented. Ed rolls his window down, slows enough to lock eyes with the dog. "Go home!" Didn't worry about drugs and AIDS and terrorists. Well, maybe they worried about the Russians, but by and large, they didn't worry about the things that he and Alice had to worry about with Stacy, the dangers of perverts lurking in malls or poisoned Halloween candy. Not wearing a seat belt, or easy access to drugs.

"Go home!" Ed stares at the dog that sits outside the cemetery gates. No. It's always been tough to raise kids. His parents had to cope with potentially fatal childhood diseases that they were lucky enough to have vaccines for by the time Stacy arrived.

But sometimes the threat isn't external at all. It doesn't come from outside, but from the inside.

The dog doesn't move.

Like Alice said, no visible collar, but that doesn't mean anything; he might have slipped it, or maybe it's buried beneath the fur of its ruff. If Moodyville had a dog officer, he'd probably get a call. Lacking one, what can be done?

It's unlikely that the resident state trooper will come by and collect it. He barely responded that time the gas station alarm went off. Meandered over from the MassPike half an hour after Tooley figured out it was a bird that had gotten caught in the garage, its panicked fluttering in the bay triggering the motion alarms that the tire distributor had insisted Tooley install if he was to sell that brand of tire. Goddamned statie took so long that a tire thief could have taken the whole inventory and been all the way to Hartford by the time he showed up. It's a different guy now; the former trooper, the one they knew, had moved on.

Ed cranks the car window back up, thinking, He'll find his way home. Thinking that he'll mention the dog to the guys at Lil's, where he's going after he gasses up the Cutlass. It isn't a planned thing, this coffee with Joe and Chuck nearly every morning. Joe calls it "the early retirees club." Stupid, really. They barely knew one another at the plant, and now, forced into retirement five years earlier than any of them planned, they meet like a clutch of old hens to knock politics and weather around, tell bad jokes, talk about their wives as if the women are really the tough old bats they make them out to be. *My old lady.* Christ, they sound like yokels or, worse, toughs. But it is the time of day Ed Parmalee looks forward to the most. He says it gives Alice time to vacuum without having to make him pick up his feet. It means a little time out of each other's hair. Out of the silence. Maybe it's the only thing he looks forward to these days.

Being cut loose from his job of thirty-five years has left Edward Parmalee rootless. He lives in this town only because of the job. He met Alice because of the job. His daughter grew up with dozens of other kids, attending the annual holiday party, sitting on Santa's lap in the evergreen and construction-paper chain–decorated cafeteria. The "old man" of the plant, the owner himself, ho-ho-hoing and handing over the bubble makers and coloring books as each child perched on his knee, along with a big candy cane, which would later show up under the seat of the car or end up sticky on the kitchen counter. Then the old man sold up, caved in to progress. And then some fucking Japanese company swooped in and everything was about efficiency and function, the bottom line. Pride and longevity were no longer hallmarks. The old man is living in Florida now; word is that he found himself a new young wife.

So now Ed looks forward to killing some time with the guys at the diner. Killing time.

Ed does a Uie from the gas station driveway, going across Route 146, which serves as Moodyville's main street, and directly into an angled parking space in front of Lil's. He gets out and nods to Chuck, who is pointing his remote key lock at his 2007 Tundra. "How ya doin', pal?"

"Can't complain."

"Won't help."

Same old greeting, more like code words than sentiment. Friend or enemy? The Lil's Coffee Shop Secret Society.

Joe has claimed the counter, his big butt drooping over the old-fashioned canister-style stool, the tumor of his overstuffed wallet protruding from his back pocket. Ed and Chuck flank him, nod, and simultaneously reach for the folded sections of the *Boston Globe* in front of him. Ed scores the sports page; Chuck is left with the "Styles" section. Lil pours coffee into the thick ceramic mugs in front of them and walks away. This is most likely all any of them will order. Ed is perfectly aware that, arrayed along the counter, these three don't have to face one another, look one another in the eye. All conversation can be spoken out of the side of the mouth. "Sox are going to be out of it."

"Maybe. They can still get the wild card if they pull it together." Chuck positions the sugar dispenser over his mug and lets it pour freely.

"Remember the pools?" Ed sips his black coffee, winces at the temperature, and sets it back down. If he were at home, he'd blow into it, but here he just pretends he's taking his time.

"Office pools?" Joe hands the front-page section to Chuck.

"Yeah, the betting that we'd do on the Sox or the Pats."

"I remember the year we got to betting on the pregnant women. Remember, there were three of them at once?" Joe swallows the last of his coffee and holds his mug out to Lil.

"Hey, Ed, didn't you win one of them?" Setting the sugar dispenser down, Chuck pours half-and-half from the little metal pitcher.

"Fifty bucks." Ed makes another attempt at drinking his coffee. He doesn't add that he gave the money to the new mother, one of the secretaries. Or that he never told Alice he was betting on delivery dates and baby weights. That was the bet; You had to get two out of three—date, time, and weight. He'd managed to pick the right time and weight, and was only a day off on the trifecta. It was when they were still trying to get pregnant. Alice was in a weepy stage and any mention of someone else's success sent her into a funk.

"Good times," Joe says, his lumpy hands embracing the curve of the mug.

"Yeah." Ed's coffee is finally cool enough to drink. He handed the cash to the new mother, who had come into the plant to show off the baby. He put the fifty bucks in her hand, admired the child, and told himself that it didn't matter, them not being parents, that it just wasn't meant to be. You couldn't dwell on it. You couldn't let it ruin your life.

The dog is still waiting by the cemetery gates. Once again, its eyes follow him as he slows down. Ed won't stop, won't turn into the cemetery road. Not for this dog, not ever. But he slows down enough to see that the dog's eyes are two different color—one blue, one brown. "Go home."

The dog merely cocks his ears at Ed's words, unimpressed.

It's a fanciful notion, but Ed thinks that the dog is waiting for someone.

Mack positions himself at the cemetery gates. In his mind, this seems like the likeliest spot for Justine to find him. His scent won't be mingled with that of other dogs. Besides, it looks like the place near home where they go when Justine decides that walking isn't enough exercise. It's not the park. It's like the park, but not the park. She puts him into a down-stay position at a spot that looks like this one, stone pillars that cast enough shade that it's a comfortable wait while she runs. So Mack decides that if he stays here, Justine will come back for him.

He's found the brook that runs alongside the western perimeter of the graveyard, so he is no longer thirsty. He's discovered acorns and roots beneath the massive oak trees that border this little plot of grass and stones. They crunch in his mouth, unappealing, but are a little something to put in his belly, although he throws them up a little while later. There are field mice; he can hear them in the tangle of briars and in the grass, but he has yet to capture one. He imagines snapping his jaws down on the fragile bones of the rodents, savoring the wild meat, being true to his distant ancestors, but the field mice are too quick even for a dog that dances. That's the word that Justine uses: *dance*. "Want to dance, little man?" He always keeps his eagle eye on Justine's face and hands, watching for the subtle signals of weave and bow, prance and spin. And, finally, his favorite—leap into her arms as she laughs and cuddles him close, proud and pleased with their performance. He has learned to like applause.

11

The second time she sees the dog, still at his post between the cemetery gates, Alice pulls her fifteen-year-old Dodge Caravan to the narrow shoulder of the road, a few yards from where the dog waits. "Here, boy." She clucks at him from the safety of her car. A half a pound of sliced roast beef is in the sack beside her on the seat, Ed's lunch. The dog stands up, then sits again, but his eyes remain on her, odd eyes, one blue and one brown, clearly skeptical. Why should he trust her? Alice climbs out of the van. The dog watches with interest as Alice pulls the meat out of the plastic deli bag. Ed won't miss one slice. The dog does not approach her, nor does he move away; the unmatched eyes focus on what's in her hand. The skeptical look has become that of wishful thinking. Gingerly holding the floppy piece of roast beef where it stains her fingers pink, she proffers it. "Come on, boy. It's okay."

Suddenly, the dog trots over, as if he's made his mind up about her, that she is trustworthy, and all hesitation is gone. She holds out the meat and he takes it from her fingertips with surprising gentleness, swallowing the slice without chewing. He licks his muzzle, cocks his head with its jack-in-the-pulpit-shaped ears, and waits for more.

"Oh, what the heck." Alice takes another slice of roast beef out of the deli bag. Now the dog's tail end wriggles from side to side, his eyes on her hand, and his tongue, pink and narrow, appears. She can't just leave him here on the side of the road, now, can she? He's been here long enough that she knows he must be homeless. Just waiting outside the cemetery gates like that Scottish dog, Greyfriar's Bobby, keeping his dead master company. Maybe the dog belongs to someone recently deceased. Alice can't think of anyone who's recently passed. Mrs. Fontaine died a couple of weeks ago, but she was in a nursing home, so this can't be her pet. Besides, nowadays most everyone gets planted in the new cemetery, closer to town. In an old-fashioned way, this place is still called "the graveyard." No one but those with old Moodyville names buried here. Moody, Thompson, Pierce. Her family names, dating back to when her great-great-grandfather came from England with a young bride, bringing his skills as a metal smith to the new factory.

Four generations of Alice's family before her. And one after. Their daughter. All here.

Alice thinks of Ed's warning about approaching strange dogs. This one isn't so strange, except for his eyes. He is now fully engaged in rump wagging and whining for more roast beef. He prances on tiny Muppet paws, making little chuffing noises of hope. His plumy tail gracefully waves in the warm September air. He's an unusual color, deep gray, with a white ruff and black streaks here and there in his coat, like someone with a wet paint brush got too close. He looks like a miniature Lassie painted all the wrong colors.

"Ed'll kill me for sure." Using the last piece of beef, Alice entices the dog to the sliding door on the passenger side of the van and opens it up. "Get in." As if he expected nothing less, the dog hops right onto the middle bench, turns around three times, and curls up. Alice slams the door shut and goes around to the driver's side. A car passes her, slowing down to see if she needs help. It's their next-door neighbor, Mr. Fry. Alice waves him on. No problem here.

Not yet.

The woman gives him meat. From her fingers. He wants a slice of the cheese he can smell in its plastic wrapper, but she doesn't offer him that. As a dog, he seldom gets to choose. Usually, things are just the way they are. Out now. Eat then. If offered meat and cheese, take both. Maybe there is choosing in where to bed down for the night—in his bed or in Justine's. Snooze on the couch or in front of the sliding glass door where the sun beats in at noon on cold days. But other than that, Mack has never made a deliberate, meaningful choice in his life. Even living with Justine wasn't a choice. It wasn't his choice that she disappeared.

When the woman talks to him, Mack feels soothed, a little of the anxiety smoothed over by a woman's voice. He is lonely. He's never spent more than a few hours alone. No one is here to tell him what to do, and he is nervous. Justine hasn't come, and he's been here, in this down-stay spot, for what even a dog knows is a long time. So when this woman speaks sweetly to him, calling him "doggy," Mack knows that he has a real choice. If he jumps into the van, he is leaving Justine behind. She won't be able to follow his scent. But if he stays here, waiting for her to find him, he will die.

He stands at the open door, nerves making him yawn.

"Go on, then, hop in." The woman's voice is gentle. Maybe she knows where Justine is and is taking him there. With that thought, Mack leaps into the car.

12

A lice, this is not a good idea." Ed leans over to place both palms on the kitchen table, pressing his weight against the surface. The dog stands in the center of the room, tongue lolling out, almond-shaped eyes focused firmly on Ed's face. Ed can't decide if the gaze is friendly or judgmental; the odd eyes study him, minute flickers of movement at Ed's changes of expression, as if they're having a subtle conversation without words. When Ed straightens up, the dog's muzzle lifts, his blue-and-brown focus penetrating. Little smudgy circles of black against the silvery fur of his forehead act like tiny eyebrows, giving him a quizzical expression that is very nearly human.

"He's been standing outside the cemetery gates since yesterday, and he's starved." Alice has made tuna fish sandwiches for Ed's lunch. "You should have seen him drinking the water I gave him, like he was parched. If anybody has lost him, they aren't looking for him very hard." Ed Parmalee has been married long enough that he knows when to sit down and eat his sandwich and put the conversation aside. Alice has always been a tough fighter for things she wants—a new couch, when he knew the old one had years of life left in it; a deck on the back of the house, when he couldn't see the point of sitting outside slapping mosquitoes and staring out over the neighbor's backyard. Theirs was the first development carved out of cheap farmland when the plant was running at full capacity and new people were coming into the area, swelling the class size at the elementary school. Now half the houses on their street are up for sale and no one wants these little raised ranches with one and a half baths on half an acre of lawn, and the student population has diminished so much, teacher layoffs have been threatened.

He watches as Alice places the plastic bowl back down, the fresh water swirling a little but somehow not slopping over the edge. The dog waits patiently until she straightens up, then laps politely at the new water, clearly sated, but willing to be grateful. Alice trails a hand down the length of the dog's body, picking out bits of leaf and twig. She is smiling, and she reminds Ed suddenly of her younger self, the one who smiled down on the baby as she nursed, holding to herself a singularly female satisfaction in having this ability. As if the child belonged more fully to her.

"Well, don't get any ideas about keeping him. We don't want a dog."

"I never said anything about keeping him." Alice turns her back to him, busying herself with cleaning up the counter. "If this one-horse town had a dog officer, I'd have called. What else can we do until someone claims him?"

"How long do you expect that's going to take? We don't need the bother of a dog. You don't need the extra work. And what if we want to travel?" Ed fists half of the tuna sandwich, taking a large bite.

Alice laughs, a sharp, humorless laugh. "Ed Parmalee, when was the last time we traveled anywhere but to my sister's for Christmas?"

"It would be that much harder if we had a dog."

"I never said I wanted him." Alice holds out the empty tuna

can for the dog to lick. He does so daintily, his facile tongue sliding along the smooth interior of the can. "But please don't make travel an argument against it."

Once upon a time, travel was the grail at the end of child rearing and mortgage payments. Once Stacy was launched, they dreamed of Europe or a Caribbean island. Looking back now, the only travel they ever did of a recreational nature were the trips they took to Disney World and camping in the White Mountains. The occasional weekends they spent in Boston with Ed's relatives, wanting to give Stacy some culture: the BSO, the MFA, Faneuil Hall and Quincy Market. Once Stacy had gotten busy with Girl Scouts and sports, ballet lessons and band concerts, they had a hard time finding a free weekend. Eventually, they traveled east only for the day, paid their duty call, and came home. Now with Ed's parents gone and his siblings scattered as far away as Poughkeepsie, they haven't been east in years. The idea of a European vacation or the winter visit to a warm island has been not so much abandoned as simply forgotten.

Can cleaned, the dog goes back to sitting in the middle of the kitchen, as if he's waiting for something, some action on their part.

Ed gets up from the table with his empty plate in hand. He has to pass the dog as he goes to the sink. A pat on the head is only a pat on the head. Not capitulation. The fur beneath his hand is as soft as down. The dog presses his skull up into Ed's palm. The eyebrow spots lift, making Ed think of Stacy when she saw him coming home from one of his rare trips, maybe a union gathering in Springfield or training on a new machine out in the Midwest. The eager anticipation of *presents* writ large on her face, the hope for a new board game or the next book in The Babysitter's Club series, nothing exotic.

Ed looks down on the dog. "What do you want, fella?"

The dog suddenly yawns, his sharp muzzle widening, his tongue curling up in a lingual arc. He emits an elastic vocalization that ends in a sound that could have been words: *Home-home-home.*

Ed and Alice Parmalee laugh simultaneously. They keep their eyes on the dog, where he absorbs their surprise at the sound of it.

He watches these two new people carefully. Food, water, and gentle touches are very welcome, but what he really wants is for them to take him home. He's tried to tell them, but, like most humans, they are single-language speakers. For now, though, this is all right. He is satisfied with his decision. He is safe, fed, and watered. The woman has tidied up his coat. There is a tension in the man, not like Artie and his solid hostility, but a withholding. Like some dogs who refuse to sniff and get acquainted. That's okay; Mack can handle aloofness, even respect it. He also enjoys a challenge. Just accepting the man's grudging pat on the head is a start.

The woman takes him outside at night, fastening a length of clothesline around his neck, walking him around the grass until he squats. He keeps to his training, staying close to her side until he needs to do his business, which she picks up with a plastic bag and a squeamish look on her face. She praises him with words he knows: *good boy.*

He is Maksim, although Justine mostly calls him Mack. This person just calls him "boy." He's been called that before; it's okay. If she calls, he'll come to it.

The important thing is that maybe they will know how to find Justine.

13

This morning, after coffee with the guys, Ed Parmalee points the Cutlass toward Aubuchon Hardware. He's out of 3-in-One oil and could use some shop rags. The towel bar in the bathroom is pulling away from the Sheetrock. Maybe he should pick up molly bolts. Oh, and he should get some poster board, too; start tacking up FOUND DOG posters in the area. It's starting to sound like a Wal-Mart run, so if he can't get what he needs at Aubuchon, he'll keep going. Alice won't miss him till lunchtime, if then.

He knows that he drives her crazy. Alice never says anything, but it's there, this annoyance, evident in the angle of her chin when she wipes the counter after he makes a sandwich, or when she has to ask him to move his feet so she can vacuum. It hasn't always been there, this perpetual annoyance; it's something that has evolved out of the long period when they didn't know what to say to each other, or what they might have said would have been too toxic for their marriage to survive.

Ed doesn't imagine for a minute that Alice would worry about him if he didn't show up at noon. She'd put his sandwich in the fridge and keep moving. She might scold him about not using the cell phone to say he was going to be late, but she'd never complain that he was. It's as if she longs for time by herself. Too much time alone, Ed knows, was a problem back then, back in those hard days when she'd become inert, as unmoving as a portrait, just the artist's imitation of light, illuminating the idea of movement. The stillness eventually gave way to the movement of chores and purpose, but it was always under the surface, always a possibility that someday he'd come home and find her frozen in place again.

His answer to those black days had been to throw himself into work, returning to the double shifts of his youth, expending his energy in walking the floor of the machine shop, monitoring the workers whose job he once did, approving, chiding, goading, joshing the men and women, most of whom spoke little English, feeling like a shark, the reputed need to keep moving the only way for him to stay alive. When Ed realized that Alice wasn't moving, he stopped working as much. Now he isn't sure anymore if that helped, or if she just had to move out of that fugue state on her own schedule. He knows of some couples whose troubles have made them closer. Theirs haven't. They both know it and have no idea what to do about it. So they go on with their day-to-day lives, living in tandem but not in companionship.

Ed squeezes the Cutlass between a Prius and a Volvo. It's strange, this going to the hardware store on a weekday. Typically, it was the favorite errand of chore-filled Saturdays, scheduled after the dump and before the barbershop; now he just goes whenever he thinks of something he needs. It's the result of having all this unoccupied time, time he should be putting to better use, but he hasn't found anything that interests him enough to commit to. He isn't keen to volunteer at the regional hospital or join the group of retired volunteers that do people's taxes, or substitute-teach at the high school. Maybe he suffers from his own kind of inertia, which is contradictory to the fact that, in being retired so early, he still has plenty of energy. Ed reads the want ads every week, but nothing ever appears that attracts him. He doesn't want to end up behind the counter at a McDonald's, although he knows a couple of guys who have and seem to like it well enough. Management is management, they say. Product is product. Instead, he fills the middle of his days with made-up errands.

Ed wanders the aisles, sliding his readers on and off as he examines the molly bolts; ponders the wisdom of the larger can of 3-in-One. Even so, it takes only minutes to find everything he needs. As he heads between aisles to get to the register, he spots the pet supplies.

There are fluorescent collars, nylon collars in pink, purple, blue, and black; varying widths of collars, choke chains, and something that looks like a tiny halter. They've been using a length of clothesline to walk the dog, but maybe they should at least buy him a collar and leash. He's going to be with them only until his rightful people are found, but still, a proper leash and collar wouldn't suggest that if they *don't* find his people, he's staying.

Ed stands long enough over the selection of leashes and collars that a salesperson finally takes notice. "Do you need help?" The clerk says this with the same voice she likely uses on her kids when they reach for the cereal. This is probably her job while they're in school. Mother's hours. Where are the men? When did hardware stores become a woman's domain?

"No. I'm good."

There are collars with gingham patterns, collars with little paw prints. Whatever happened to simple leather collars adorned with metal buttons? Here there are spike collars, thick macho ones.

"Are you looking for a training collar, or just something to hang his tags on?" The clerk, persistent, strums her fingers along the array of collars hanging by plastic hooks. They move like a rainbow-colored curtain.

"We've got him only until his owner is found. I guess I won't be hanging any tags on him, but I'm sure not going to be training him, either. I just need something we can use to walk him."

The saleswoman taps a finger to her lips, then pulls down a flat red nylon collar. "This'll do, and it's cheap. And the chain leashes are a bargain." With that, she walks away to greet a woman gripping a list.

Ed looks at the collars for another minute, puts the red one back and picks out a black collar with a rolled edge. He finds a matching black nylon leash. The dog, wherever he came from, isn't a red collar kind of dog. Then Ed pulls a dog brush off the rack. This one says it's meant for longhaired, double-coated breeds. Alice has been brushing the mats out of the dog's coat with an old hairbrush of hers. She still wears her hair bundled in a twist, a light fringe of bangs framing her face. In that way of random thoughts, Ed thinks of the nights when Alice pulled the pins out of her hair and let it fall like it did when they courted, curtaining them as they kissed. That stopped happening a long time ago.

As an afterthought, Ed selects a squeaky toy shaped like a hydrant.

His route home takes him along the Moody River, but Ed'll turn off before coming to the old pistol factory, where a two-hundred-year-old dam holds back the Moody River, at one time forcing it into powering the old factory. Alice's great-great-grandfather came from England to work in that factory. Just like Ed migrated west from Boston to work in the screw-machine plant 150 years later. This late in the year, a day or so before the autumn equinox, the stream is shallow and hardly looks to be moving. It bifurcates around rocks littering the streambed. In the spring, the river is high with snowmelt and the rushing water can be dangerous even when the fishing is the best. In a moment, Ed sees the ruins of the old factory and signals his turn.

Mack thinks about going, leaving the comfort of this way station; pointing his nose in the direction from which they came and walking home. Justine must be there. He has only two places he can picture her: here and home. But he's not been given an opportunity to choose to do that. Every moment he's been with these people, Alice and Ed, he's been in their charge.

They don't understand his basic request. All Mack wants is for them to open the door and let Justine in. Each time he goes to the door, they tie a piece of rope around his neck and walk him around the perimeter of the house. Every time Ed leaves the house and Mack whines to follow, the woman calls him back to sit with her. When she's busy with her tasks, he stares out the sliding door into the empty backyard, glimpses of the local cat prowling the hedges the only entertainment. It isn't his house, so he doesn't bother sending up the alarm. He's not here to protect their territory. He is a guest and he will behave like one. Grateful for the rather tasteless kibble poured into a bowl, happy to be allowed on the couch to sleep beside the woman. She isn't Justine, but she is generous with the belly rubs.

She talks to him when the man isn't there. Tells him all sorts of tongue-language things that Mack doesn't interpret as particularly meaningful. Her language has some of the nuances of Justine's, although the words are unfamiliar. The pitch is the same as when Justine chats to him, higher and softer than when people talk to other humans. Humans have this need to express themselves through their mouths, and he supposes that this is because they are so poor with their noses.

There was that moment when he followed her into a bedroom that did not hold much human scent in it; an overlay of cleaner like Justine used on her furniture, almost, but not quite, masking a vestigial odor of some other person. Not so much the scent of a human as of the objects belonging to that human, an old scent lingering beneath the chemical. If she'd opened the drawers, he could have gotten a clearer picture of the room's absent human.

That's when she said the only meaningful thing, when he followed her in there. She said it clearly and in words he understood: "Get out."

14

"Let's see how this fits." Ed holds the collar out with both hands. The dog trots over to take a good sniff. "Can you sit?" The dog sits. Ed fastens the black collar.

"Make sure that it isn't too tight, or too loose. We don't know if he'll walk without pulling, or if he'll try to pull out of the collar. Clearly, he's escaped once. How foolish would we look if he takes off on me?" Alice takes the new brush and smoothes the dog's ruff over the collar so that it doesn't show. "Let's see the leash."

Ed hands his wife the leash with the tiniest reluctance. Alice snaps the clip onto the ring. Ed takes it out of her hand. "I'll take him out."

Alice takes the leash back. "No. I will." She doesn't even make it sound like she's doing him a favor. "I'm going to take him for a proper walk."

"Where?"

"I should take a plastic bag, I guess. I don't think I want him soiling the neighbors' yards."

Ed snags a plastic grocery bag out of the calico sleeve they stuff them into. "Guess we'd better stop using the green bags at the store for a while."

The dog is dancing on his little front feet, his tail swinging in anticipation of a walk. He looks from one to the other, a little furry linesman.

"He might be a little strong on that leash. You don't want him pulling you down the street."

"I'll be fine." Alice gathers the leash in her hands.

"Be careful on the road. It's getting dark earlier."

"I won't be long."

Ed asks again, "Where are you going?"

Alice knows what he's driving at. He's holding her up, questioning her decision-making abilities. "To the old path."

The old path is an ancient way that begins at the end of their dead-end road, which takes its name, Old Path Road, from it. It wends through the woods for a mile or so, to the rocky banks of the Moody River. The path meanders along the top of the escarpment, following the river, until it ends at the ruins of the old pistol factory. A set of steps lead down the steep grade to the quarter-acre millpond, where the Moody River was once harnessed for power. Alice and Ed courted along that path, holding hands, dreaming their future, walking to the place where there once was a footbridge, now a pair of stone abutments facing each other, separated by the river water that cascades over the dam in the spring. The slippery rocks are the perfect place to fish for the trout that the conservation commission stock in the millpond of dammed water. It was the place where Ed taught Stacy how to fish. They practiced mostly catch and release. Like him, Stacy preferred the hunt to the kill, and frankly, nobody in the house really liked freshwater fish all that much. In late summer, after dinner, he and Stacy would grab the poles and walk the path to the south abutment, where they would drop in their lines and call it fishing. That time of year, the Moody River no longer cascaded over the edge of the dam, escaping gently through the ancient sluice gates, so they might walk single file along the narrow lip of the dam to get to the north-side abutment, where the big trout were rumored to live,

Ed holding Stacy's shoulder in front of him. Stacy was warned over and over never to go there alone. Ever.

Because the path also branches off to Alice's mother's house, they used to let Stacy use it to go to her grandmother's, because she wouldn't have to cross any roads. She wouldn't be in danger.

"Where else can I take him?"

"But why there?"

"Anywhere else, I'll have to drive to, and that's just silly. Besides, I'm not going all the way." Not going all the way to the millpond, she means. Not there.

It's been seven years. And still the thought of the old path hurts. Ed drops into the kitchen chair, the stony weight of his memory bearing down on him.

Ed runs the length of the old path, uselessly calling out Stacy's name, hearing his own voice echo against the newly leafed trees ringing the still surface of the still pond. There is no sign of her, and the relief is pounding in his chest. He runs home, believing that she must have gone to her grandmother's house, not come this way after all.

The dog, giving up hope that the leash means anything, rests his head on Ed's knee. "I guess he deserves a good walk." Ed turns away from Alice, but she sees that he has hurt himself with remembering. He strokes the dog's head, keeping his face from her.

Alice hands Ed the leash. "Do you want to take him?"

Ed shakes his head. "I forgot to get the poster board. For the 'Found' signs."

"That's all right. There's no hurry, is there?"

"His people could be looking for him. Panicked, don't you think?"

"If he's meant to be found, he will be."

This place reminds Mack of go-to-the-park. The tall squirrel-bearing trees, the enticing bolt-holes of ground vermin, the twitter of bird life above his head. The scents. Oh, the scents of a primeval wood on the nose of a dog long removed from his ancestral purpose. Justine would encourage him with a whispered: "Get it!" and then laugh when he couldn't. They never tired of the game.

Today, his new female, Alice, has linked him to the leash and led him to this equally glorious patch of nature. Above the scent of rodents lies the even more welcome scent of other dogs. He breathes in the calling cards of a variety of canines, all of which indicate they thought this was their territory. He covers their marks with his own. The only spoiler to this perfect outing is the fact that this Alice does not let him run off leash. She clings tenaciously to the other end, keeping up a soft patter of tongue language that Mack interprets as a request not to pull her off her feet. As if he'd ever do such a thing. From birth, Mack has known better than to pull on the leash. From earliest training, he has kept to the side of his person, his long nose just at the crook of the knee. Justine believes that he has genius. He may have, but he also has a Sheltie's proclivity for obedience, as well as a superior sense of dignity. He has always prided himself on being a perfect gentleman. So he lets this new woman, Alice, keep him close without argument. He accepts her restraint with equanimity. He listens to her voice as she speaks of what a good boy he is and cheerfully looks up at her, his herd-dog eyes locked on hers. In catching her eye as a good sheepdog does, he gets a glimpse of her own intelligence. She doesn't look away from his gaze; she looks deeper into it. And with that look comes a thin line of connection, of partnership. Alice strokes his muzzle and lifts it to her face. Just like Justine sometimes has on her face, this woman has tears streaming. Clearly, Alice, like Justine, needs him. He licks at the salty tears.

15

I feel like a whaler reaching port after a four-year voyage as my feet hit the pavement in Boston. The morning commotion of traffic, and the pedestrians all vying for dominance as they stream toward office buildings and shops, catches me by surprise as I come out of the bus terminal. I have a ticket to New Bedford in my back pocket and exactly forty-five minutes to find the warehouse and Artie. And if not Artie himself, at least another clue as to where he might be. I have decided that he is still here. That there's no way he'd simply turn around and head back west. He'll need another job, another truck loaded with something needed west of the Mississippi. And surely that will take time, time enough for me to catch up with him.

I go in the opposite direction of the human current, heading away from downtown and toward the street where the warehouse is located. I'm lucky; it really is fairly close to South Station. But not that close. I still have a good walk ahead of me, over a bridge, down an unpopulated side street flanked by windowless warehouses. From the bridge, I can see the interstate highway with its thrombosis of cars working their way into the tunnel beneath the city. Overhead, a near-constant stream of jets coming in and taking off from Logan. A traffic helicopter makes a wide swing over the scene, hunting for accidents. I've lived in cities all over: Brooklyn, Louisville, Los Angeles, but I always think of Boston as the best. I guess everyone who grows up in eastern Massachusetts thinks that way. I shove my duffel behind me and pick up the pace. My nostalgia is costing me time.

By the time I actually reach the street where the warehouses are, I've got about fifteen minutes to locate Artie. Two long warehouses opposite each other have at least a dozen trailers backed up to loading docks. Men driving forklifts and other men watching them crowd the open bays. The trailers are in such perfect alignment, if I stand in the right position, it looks like there is only one. But there are no trucks attached to these trailers. I need to find the truck lot to find Artie's dull green cab. I don't have time to do this; I'm running out of time if I'm going to catch the bus to New Bedford this morning as I promised. But I have to find Artie. The urgency literally squeezes my heart.

"You lost?"

I turn to see a big black guy wearing a gray uniform, a yellow and black security badge sewn onto the right breast pocket of his shirt. He has a nightstick holstered in a belt that squeezes him so that he plumps up over it and below it. He has the look of a guy who has found a legitimate way to be a badass.

"I'm looking for someone."

"You need to check in at the office."

"I didn't see an office."

He slides the nightstick out of its loop and uses it like a professor using a pointer, as if his forefinger wouldn't be enough. "Over there, three doors down. Big sign. Somebody will help you."

"Thanks. I appreciate it."

"No problem."

I am aware of him watching me as I jog toward my destination. I assume it's to make sure I get there and don't cause some daytime mayhem on the way. Maybe it's that he's appreciating my ass. Either way, I'm glad when I reach the open office door, where, predictably, there is no one just sitting there waiting to help me.

I scan the company names printed over each of the bay doors, an array with a few familiar names, but mostly names of companies I've never heard of. I struggle to make Ra-Mar or De-Light-ly the name of the company Artie was hauling for. He was hauling a load of seed; that much I finally remember. Maybe one of the more floral-sounding names is where he backed up the truck. Or agricultural. Are there any farmers here? My mind is racing as the moments slip by and with them my chance to track down Artie. I start walking along the apron, skipping past skids loaded with shrink-wrapped goods. I look for any trailer that might have Colorado, Washington, or Iowa plates. I ask every worker there if he knows Artie Schmidt. "Did a guy driving from Washington State pull in last night?" They call into cavernous spaces, consult with one another, shift their yellow hard hats, but none of them has heard of Artie Schmidt. And no one has seen a dog.

I get down the length of one of the warehouses and realize that each building is two-sided; another whole lineup of trailers is backed up on the other side. As I reach the end of the line, I see my friend the guard. He is not smiling at me.

"You find the boss?" The guard is on the ground, looking up at me as I stand on the loading dock.

"No, and I don't have time to wait."

"Then come back when you can. Only authorized visitors can be here." Viewed from above, he's a little less scary.

"Do I look like I'm going to run off with a load of machine parts?" I've really had enough. The frustration of the past day and night feels like an elastic band in my gut. It is wound as tight as it can go and in the next second it could snap, and I won't be responsible for the outcome. The big guy needs to back off. "I'm looking for Artie Schmidt. He's the thief. He's stolen my dog. I have to find him now."

The guard is older than he looked to be at first. There is a little round bald spot that is clearly visible as he drops his gaze to the ground. He looks up at me. "You want to file a report?"

"How long will that take? I have to catch a bus for New Bedford in . . ." I look at my watch and the elastic band in my gut takes one more twist. "In fifteen minutes."

"Ten minutes. I'll get someone to take you to South Station."

In my life, I have come to the realization that time really doesn't stand still and that there is no way I'll make that bus if I stop to fill out a report on a man who will never be found. I don't know if the bus ticket is transferable to another time, but I do know that if I don't show up at noon, I will endure the wrath of Adele. "Will filing a report help catch him?"

The guard shrugs. "It's a start. It's the only thing I can do."

"Okay." I walk down the cement steps to the ground. The guard now towers over me, and I feel like a captive as we head toward his little office. As we walk, I tell him my story. About being left, about Artie driving off with my dog. About trying to get to New Bedford before my father dies. About wanting my dog back and Artie drawn and quartered. He listens, and once inside, he's quick to call a cab to whisk me back to South Station even before he pulls out a form.

"Name, address, cell number or number where we can reach you." He's moving as fast as he can. "Theft of dog valued at?"

How can you put a value on Mack? What he means to me. He may be a puppy-mill dog, but he is everything to me. "Ten thousand dollars." What I mean is, priceless. I wouldn't take a million for him. But if I don't exaggerate his value in terms that mean something to a guy sitting in a guard's booth all day, can I trust that he'll take me seriously?

The guard looks me in the eye, weighing my exaggeration. "Have you gotten a ransom note?"

"No." I start to explain that I don't think Artie would think of that and then stop. If it's a clear case of dognapping, then maybe the authorities will do something. "I've been on the road, so how could he send a ransom note?"

"Okay. His name? Address? Make of truck? Rig?" The guard peppers me with questions I cannot answer. I sound like a jerk. I can tell him that the guy likes Camels, that he drinks Red Bull like it's orange juice, that he prefers redheads to blondes, and that when he's not on the road, he hangs out at Candy Kane's bar, bragging about his string of ex-wives. No, I don't know who his agent is. If I did, I'd know how to find Artie. I think this but don't say it. I need this guy. Getting snippy now won't do me any good.

The cab pulls up. I dig into my pocket to find my last ten. "You have my number. Please don't hesitate to call me, even if you don't think it matters."

"I can do one more thing. I'll talk to the drivers. They may know something, and they may be able to help. They talk to each other over the CB all day long. If they spot him, they can stop him."

The elastic in my belly snaps. Why didn't I ask a trucker to do that before? Artie was on the CB constantly. If I'd just used my head. "He has a name, a handle. When he talks to other drivers, he calls himself 'Rockin' Roadie.'" I am almost embarrassed at saying that out loud. Artie wouldn't tell me how he acquired such a nickname, just leered at me, implying a suggestive origin.

"That will help."

I have three minutes to make my bus.

This time, I am alone, no curious seatmate to ask me innocuous but challenging questions about my life.

When I left Anthony, I really thought that he would come after me, apologize, make things better. But he didn't, proving that he was relieved with my decision. At the very least, I thought that he would demand that I bring back his son. Instead, he was relieved to have dodged the responsibility of parenthood at age twenty-three. Maybe it was an accidental conception, but one I never regretted. Maybe ours was a forced marriage—a self-fulfilling prophesy, in my stepmother's eyes—but one I intended to make perfect. But when lovelessness becomes betrayal, the answer for me is to move on.

When I left home, I had fifty bucks and a suitcase. When I left Anthony, I had a thousand dollars and our car. I drove off with Tony, a suitcase full of his little clothes and a duffel bag with my essentials.

Tony and I sang songs all the way down Route 95. *Sesame Street* songs, Raffi songs, silly made-up songs, just to keep him from asking questions. We were on the road, on an adventure. Another chapter in the story of me.

"Where's Daddy?" Tony is in the back, in his car seat, playing with a magnetic puzzle that I've found in a rest stop convenience store.

I have rehearsed an answer for this inevitable question. "Daddy has sent us on a voyage like the old-time whalers. We're out to make our fortune."

"What's a fortune?" He lisps the word, making it sound like four-thune. I laugh, a bubbling sensation forcing its way up into my mouth. I'm laughing because if I don't, I'll cry.

16

When I was a kid doing homework at the kitchen table, Adele would come up behind me and press one finger into my neck at the place where skull and vertebrae meet, forcing me to look down at my papers.

"Are you going to pass that mess in?"

I'd look at the math work sheet with the gray smears across the work space from the too-hard eraser at the end of my stubby pencil, testimony to my struggles with the subject.

"Use scrap paper if you can't do it neatly."

She never offered to help me figure out the arithmetic.

I often wonder where my father was when she was jabbing me with a finger or shoving me ahead of her to my room. Or chastising me for not closing the peanut butter jar tight enough or the bread wrapper secure enough. Or slapping me because she interpreted my response to some demand or question as impertinent. "I will not have impertinence." I thought impertinence was a venal sin. I would have confessed it had she ever taken me to confession. I'm not making it up, remembering it wrong, when I believe that Paul never suffered any of these physical and verbal assaults. He fluttered in and out of the kitchen, on his way to a practice or a game, or to meet up with friends, leaving the jars open and the bread hanging out of the wrapper like a tongue. He wasn't expected to sit at the kitchen table to do his homework; his homework was done in the privacy of his room. A gentle knock and reminder not to stay up too late, the only words his mother ever said to him on the subject. I know for a fact he wasn't burning the candle on his homework. He was doing other things, things that I could hear through the thin wall of my former walk-in closet.

I wonder if Paul will be there today. As the Bonanza bus nears the transportation center in New Bedford, I notice that my hands are shaking in a barely visible tremor. Nerves. I haven't seen any of these people, my *family*, in years. I might not even recognize Paul. The last time I saw him was maybe ten years ago. I really can't recall. I came back for his wedding. I had received an invitation and I have no doubt that it was the subject of great debate, whether or not to waste an invitation on me. I was long gone. Paul and I had never kept in touch. I knew that it was a courtesy invitation, probably sent because the poor bride had foolishly insisted that I get one, harboring some prebridal expectation that she'd be able to heal family rifts out of kindness. I was just contrary enough to tick off "Yes, I will attend" on the tiny RSVP card. I mailed it to the bride's mother, wondering if she had any idea who Justine Meade was. I'd gone back to my maiden name a couple of years after leaving Anthony. In a further act of defiance, I changed Tony's name to Meade, too. He was young enough that changing his name seemed like a normal thing to do. Another new school, another new neighborhood. Another name. Simple.

Maybe it was more like eighteen years ago. Time has a way of zipping by, the mile markers racking up so fast, whole decades disappear from sight in the rearview mirror.

Having spent my last ten bucks on the Boston cab, I sling my duffel over my shoulders and begin to walk. I have to climb Johnnycake Hill, New Bedford's best-known street, with its cobbles and whaling museum, and work my way under route 195 to the other side of town, where the double- and triple-deckers, built back when the city had industry, line residential streets. It is a perfect September day, warm and dry, with a high thin veil of cloud in the southwest, portending lousy weather in the next twenty-four hours. It's a nice day for a walk. If I had my dog with me, he'd be hoping that we would come to a park, where I could slip off his leash and toss the tennis ball for him. I actually have a tennis ball in my duffel. I brought one with me, as if they might not have them in New Bedford. I have the ball but not the dog. The hope that I had when the guard, Troy, told me about the CBs and how the drivers would put the word out is already fading into the more familiar sense of despair. I'm not a child, too easily inclined to hope for magic. I'm an adult whose life has pretty much been magic-free. The idea of a convoy of truck drivers caring enough to help find Artie is pretty far-fetched. Why should a group of anonymous drivers moving from one side of the country to the other care about my stolen dog? I wipe the "cavalry to the rescue" image out of my head.

I am at the corner of Lawton and Green. The house that I grew up in is half a block away. I can see the triple-decker that still belongs to my father looming over the ranch-style single family house that we crammed into for the eight years I lived there. It must suit Adele and my father so much better now. It's really a house meant for two. Before I make that final turn, I pull out my phone and call Saundra.

It is ominously quiet behind Saundra's voice. No barking. "I've got it posted online and I've contacted all the Sheltie rescues I can find from Cincinnati to Boston. Any word at all? Where are you?"

"No word. And I'm almost to the house."

"You need to focus on your dad. We'll keep going here. Do you need anything?"

"Just to find Mack."

"We're praying for you." And just like that, the background is filled with Saundra's pack barking joyously at being let in.

No one, to my knowledge, has ever prayed for me before. Tears prick at my eyes, but I don't let them fall. I can't let them start, because they might never end.

Swallowing against the lump in my throat, I march myself to the middle of the block and face my childhood home. It is the same vinyl white that it has always been, grimy now with decades of street dust. A pair of plastic shutters flank the picture window that looks out on the street and the neighbors' houses, no view worth such a large window, and one that had to have custom-made drapes to keep those neighbors from looking in. The foundation plantings have grown from shrubs into bushes and need a good trimming. *Unkempt*—that's the word that comes to mind, and I am a little surprised. Adele is a house-proud woman. This place doesn't look like anyone has taken care of more than getting the grass cut in years. I wonder how long my father has been sick.

I don't know which door to use. Should I mount the three cement steps to the front door and ring the doorbell like a guest? Should I go through the one-car carport and open the side door and call out: "I'm home!" like a family member? As it turns out, Adele spots me and opens the front door, pushes wide the complaining screen door and stares at me. "It took you long enough. Come on in."

Now I know I'm home.

17

W ipe your feet. I've just had the rugs cleaned." The front
door opens directly into the living room. It's different
from my memory of white walls and fake Colonial-style furniture. Three of the walls are a pale pink and the fourth—the
narrowest, at the far end of the room—is the designated accent
wall, as it's painted a weird persimmon color. The furniture is
modern; the couch and chairs have huge soft cushions that could
swallow a child. The only thing in this room that I recognize is
the antique oak sideboard, which is too big for the dining area in
this house, but which once fit perfectly in the dining room in
my mother's house. It's placed against the persimmon wall, with
a collection of photographs in chunky frames displayed on it.
Even from a distance I can see that all of the pictures are of
Paul's kids. It looks like he has a dozen, but I realize that they're
the same two, replicated over and over at different stages of their
lives—as infants, as toddlers, in grade school photos, in middle
school graduation pictures. There's no picture of Tony. Perhaps
I've never sent one.

Adele is standing in the archway that leads into the kitchen,
waiting for me.

"Shall I put my stuff in my room?"

Adele looks at me like I've asked for money. "I assumed you'd be staying in a hotel. We don't have room here. I never suggested . . ."

"I can't afford a hotel."

She doesn't answer me.

I drop my duffel bag, travel-worn and grubby, right on her cream-colored sofa. I want to ask why I can't use Paul's room. I know that the closet that was my space has long since been retrofitted into the walk-in closet it originally was designed to be. I decide to drop the subject for the moment. There are far more important questions to ask. "Where's Dad?"

My stepmother pins a look on me. "Paul's in with him now. When he comes out, you can go in."

"I'll go in now. I just came two thousand miles to see him."

"You will wait here."

I've been through the tortures of the damned to get here to see my father and this woman is going to prevent me with four words? "Give me one good reason I can't go in. He's my father."

"He gets upset if too many people are in there."

"You mean that you do." I turn around and go through the living room to the short hallway that leads to the two bedrooms. As provoked as I am, I hesitate before entering the hallway. I stand in the archway and listen to the voices coming from one of the bedrooms. I realize that my father isn't in his bedroom at all, but in what was once Paul's. The voices aren't live; they're coming from a television show. The canned laughter gives it away. I listen harder. If Paul is in there, he isn't saying anything. Then I hear a pair of chuckles, a shared amusement at whatever's on the screen, and I have a flash of childish jealousy.

Why should this stepson be there in the first place? Oh, yeah. I know why. Because his stepfather always treated him like a son—apple of his eye if not child of his loins. If Paul had been a wolf cub and my father the pack leader, Dad would have made sure Paul got the best chunks of the kill. If there was one life preserver in the boat and we were sinking, I know who would have gotten it. It wasn't normal. Weren't young men supposed to hate their stepfathers? I guess when the stepfather in question is treating you like the son he never had, you don't have to hate him. The laughter again. I march down the hallway and push open the bedroom door.

Because the television is on the same wall as the door, they are facing me as I enter the room. I am shocked at the sight of both of them. I know I should have been anticipating seeing my father as a dying man, but I am more shocked at the sight of Paul. He is huge, bald, and dressed in a Bridgewater State College sweatshirt that has seen better days. There is one brief, crystal moment when all three of us stare at one another, trying hard to reconcile this version of ourselves to those of our memories.

My father speaks first. "Justine? You're here." It almost sounds like a question.

"I got here a few minutes ago." I can't get near to him because Paul's bulk takes up the space beside the twin bed, which is shoved up against the wall and the bureau. "Didn't Adele tell you I was coming?"

"No. I guess she wanted it to be a surprise."

More like she didn't want him disappointed if I failed to show up. I sort of respect that.

"Well, I'm here now." I take a step toward the bed and Paul gets the message. He rises and squeezes himself out of the alley formed by the bed and the bureau.

"Hey, Justy, it's good to see you." He opens his arms wide and scoops me into an embrace I'm not looking for. The nickname reminds me of his taunting me with "Busty Justy" when puberty hit me like an invasion of the body snatchers. I've grown into them, but the girls are still worth a glance.

"Yeah, you, too." I hope that it doesn't show on my face just how startled I am by him, but he knows.

"My wife's a great cook." He's obviously had to explain before how he was a star athlete turned blimp.

Once Paul leaves the bedroom, I am alone with my father for the first time in decades. We are both silent for a moment, taking it in, figuring it out. Not just about the fact that I'm here only because he's dying but by the larger gorilla of our history—his failure to love me. His failure to make me an equal in an unequal house. His failure to stand up to that woman when I most needed him to, if only that once. I step to the side of the bed. He is sitting up, the thin blanket spread neatly over his lower half, with the top of his *Father Knows Best* pajamas buttoned right up to the top button. A glass of water is on the nightstand, a newspaper folded up neatly beside it. The television is blaring out a commercial for adult diapers, and my father points to it. "That's me. How about that? Just like a baby."

I wonder what I want from him, this desiccated remnant of the father who bowed to every opinion Adele voiced. I sit in the chair beside the bed and wait for him to say something of worth to me. What do I want? A deathbed confession of wrongdoing? I want him to tell me that he was wrong not to take my side. Wrong to be sucked into the lie that I had made the whole thing up. Isn't blood thicker than water?

I am trembling with the desire to hear his confession. Get an apology.

My father says nothing. He is attached to a morphine drip, and I excuse him again for his silence.

18

Adele is sitting in a kitchen chair. Paul is gone. She says nothing to me, so that the silence of the sickroom and the silence of the kitchen make me think that no one will speak in this house until I go away. But I'm not going anywhere. She asked me to come, I'm here, and she'd damn well better like it. I've lost my dog because of this, so giving me the silent treatment is not acceptable.

I've lost my dog, my Mack. The thought keeps returning to me, fresh in its intensity each time.

"Got any tuna?" I suddenly realize that I'm really hungry and I'm not going to wait for an invitation.

Adele looks up from studying the pattern in the old table-cloth. "Yes. In the cupboard."

I don't move for a moment, just look at her. I'm having trouble recognizing this stranger as the same person who tortured me enough that I bolted from home as a girl; the one who gave me no choice but to strike out on my own as soon as I could. She traces the pattern of the flowers with her sharp nail and sighs. Should I feel sorry for her? She's remained my father's wife, taken care of him. Presumably loved him in some way. She doesn't look at me, doesn't tell me anything, and I don't know if she's expecting me to ask her questions or if she is so absorbed in her thoughts that she's forgotten I'm standing here. I look at Adele and see her as she really is, an old woman facing widowhood. The upright posture and the Wicked Witch of the West scrawniness have melted into a dowager's hump and a midriff roundness. Her hair is the yellowy white of faded blondes and the skin on her hands looks like paper that's been crumpled and then flattened. I try to think how old she is and am shocked to think that she's at least seventy-five. She's been a part of my life for over thirty years. I think that when I was a kid, I held out some hope that eventually she'd go away, or that my father would come to his senses and we'd go away.

Now she looks at me. "Well, are you going to stand there or are you going make us some lunch?"

I laugh out loud. The relief is amazing. She's still Adele.

She directs my making of the tuna sandwiches from the amount of mayonnaise to the way I cut the sandwiches. I ignore her and make it my way, lots of pepper. I plate the sandwiches, find an open bag of chips, and wrench open the antique avocado-colored refrigerator to hunt down something to drink. The first shelf is filled with some sort of protein drink, chocolate- or vanilla-flavored. Something intended to supply calories to a person with no appetite. I slam the door shut and fill two glasses with tap water.

How do you make small talk with someone who has always seen you as a burden, a pain in the neck, an unfortunate price to pay for happiness? Am I such an outcast that she can't bring herself to talk to me? Then I wonder if it is simply hard for her to talk about my father, to tell me what's been going on. She called me, called me here. But now she has nothing to say to me?

It's up to me to get things started. "How long will he sleep?"

"I don't know"

"Is he in pain?"

"Sometimes." She looks at me as if I have asked the most personal of questions. The hostility coming from this withered apple doll is less frightening than it was when she would focus her pale eyes on me when I was a teenager. Those looks were sharp and hurt as much as it did when she grabbed me by the bare arm and dug her fingernails into my flesh. "The morphine helps."

That's about as much conversation as either of us wants. So we eat in relative silence, politely passing the chip bag back and forth.

My cell rings. The sound of it startles both of us. A quick glance at an unfamiliar number and my heart starts to beat. It's a 617 area code. Boston. It's Troy.

"No one has seen a dog, but a couple of the guys recognize the Rockin' Roadie handle." Troy has been as good as his word. He's talked to truckers from all over, asking about the dog with Arthur Schmidt. I have to be satisfied that Artie or his road moniker is at least known, even if no one has seen Mack.

"Thanks for trying." I'm certain that the disappointment shows in my voice.

"Truckers do not take kindly to men who mistreat women or animals. No they don't. Word gets out, he's a dead man." He sounds vaguely like a cowboy, and I kind of think that he's not correct in this estimation. I can hardly believe that these hardworking drivers are that interested in my problem.

But I do appreciate what he's saying and tell him so, wondering why this stranger is doing this for me. I wonder enough to ask him.

"I have a dog, ma'am. If anyone ever stole her I'd kill the fucker. Pardon my French."

"No apology necessary. It's what I intend to do if I ever catch up with Artie."

We both laugh a little—that humorless chuckle people give when the next sound might be a cry.

I clear off the lunch plates while Adele goes into my father's room to check on him. They are the same Corelle plates that served as our everyday ware back when I was a kid. I am a little surprised that they have survived all these years. Why is it that a visit to a childhood home turns common objects into jarring memory? The sight of a white glass plate with a seventies orange pattern has the power to drag me into my childhood. Sitting here in Adele's kitchen, I am thrust backward in time. I have been gone so long, it should have changed utterly, but instead I see the same plates, the familiar cookie jar with the very same chip out of the lid. The clock on the wall is a three-dimensional memory, bringing me back to the hours spent watching it as I struggled through homework or sat there, being forced to consume some hard green vegetable left on my plate. Or to the night that I waited while my father and Adele argued over the story that I was telling them; argued over whether or not to act. I waited for them to do something the night I came home from my date with Paul's best friend. Waited for them to finally decide that I was being a big baby and order me to take a shower and go to bed. Nothing had happened that didn't happen on a date with a college boy, a grown man. A man with a good upbringing. A man whose father was my father's employer.

I pull myself out of this self-indulgent funk. The clock becomes just a clock. I wash and dry the plates and put them away, noting that they are the last two of the set. That's all they need anyway. They have managed to grow old together, my father and our neighbor. They have more than doubled the number of years that my father was with my mother.

It was as if my mother vanished. One moment, we were sitting in our kitchen; the next, she was on the floor. I can't remember anything more except the way the ambulance driver took me by the shoulder and made me sit on the kitchen chair, out of the way. We'd been baking cookies; it was almost Christmas and my mother was trying out a recipe for a new kind. I don't know who called the ambulance. I don't remember my father's being there, but I guess he was. It is a seamless memory, going from hoping my mother would let me have the leftover cookie dough to standing in a line at the funeral home.

I flop onto that creamy white couch beside my grubby duffel bag and listen to the soft murmur of conversation coming from Paul's old room. I'm here, but who cares? Adele demanded that I come, and now she acts like I've invaded her home. Again. For the first time, I wonder whose idea it was for me to be here. Who convinced Adele and my father that I should be a member of the club that will witness his slow slide into death when I haven't been a meaningful part of their lives in years? I'm clearly an unwanted guest, and my father has nothing to say to me.

Mack would love this couch. If he were here, as he should be, I could tuck his body up close to mine. I would tuck his body up close and rest my head on the fine triangle of his skull. He would sigh and be happy to be held. I press a hand against my chest, where I can feel my heart squeeze down on itself each time I realize that Mack could be anywhere and that I may never find him. Or nowhere and that there's no point in searching for him. I can't think that way. I just can't.

I flip my phone open, hoping that by some quirk I have missed the call that will tell me where my dog is. No missed calls. No voice mails. No answers.

I hear the murmuring and the sound of a toilet flushing, then the click-roll of a walker being pushed down the short hallway.

My father always prided himself on his height and his posture, but the glimpse I have of him now is that of a hunched-over old man who is gripping the handles of the walker and eking his way down the threadbare wall-to-wall carpet of the hall. This disease has reduced him to an old man even though I know he's not more than seventy. Isn't seventy the new fifty? It's what I tell myself when I think of going over the crest of forty-five, the short descent to fifty. If Adele, five years older than my father, looks her age, my father looks like someone else's idea of an old man.

There is a moment of suspension as the pair of them, father and stepmother, simultaneously look at me without smiling and then continue on their way down the narrow hall.

"Do you need my help?" I call out to them as I push off the couch.

"No." Adele, as always, answers for both of them.

Did I mistake the desire for my presence with what was only a courtesy call? Fulfilling the social expectation that a daughter be notified of her father's impending death? Was the truth of it that I risked everything on what amounted to manners? Or that Adele was calling my bluff?

The air in this living room is stifling, close. The windows are closed against the mild September day. Suddenly, I can't breathe in here. I bolt out of the front door and stand on the chipped front step, sucking in breath after breath. I can't make myself go back in there. I have come all this way, and sacrificed the being I love best next to my absent son—for what? To be revisited by every bad memory I've worked so hard to grow beyond? This is a haunted house, and I don't have to be here.

19

I have no place to go, so I sit on the front steps and wish that I smoked, so that it would look at least like I'm outside for a purpose. I pick at the weeds that are growing at the base of the steps. Ugly, unwanted things, more green than the summer-burned grass. Hardy fools. Thinking that they are welcome.

I can call Candy and see if she'll buy me a plane ticket home. I know that she will, but I also know that she'll try and talk me out of leaving. I guess I haven't been as honest with her as I might have been. She just thinks that our family suffered the normal range of conflict. She thinks, like good people do, that a tearful and heart-felt make-up session will occur before my father's last breath and I will feel better, or relieved or something, so that this trip will help "heal" me. I know. I've seen her pull that Oprah shit on other friends.

But even if I call Candy and convince her that staying is a bad idea, I still don't have Mack. How can I leave without knowing where he is, without finding him? Even as I think this, I know that each hour that goes by lessens my chances of locating my dog. I still have no idea where he is. Any thin hope that I had squirreled away against the worst thoughts is gone. Artie isn't driving west now with my Mack alongside, riding shotgun. The unanswerable question is, Where did he abandon my dog? Ohio? Pennsylvania? New York? Massachusetts? How long would he have kept the dog with him before ditching him?

Did he at least leave Mack somewhere that a kind person might find him?

Did my impulsive ride on the back of Mitch's Harley take me *away* from Mack? Was he simply waiting for me by the exit? I feel that burn in my eyes, the hollow ache in my throat, and squeeze my eyes shut.

"I didn't realize how much you cared." Paul Rose, Jr., casts a broad shadow over me; the sudden shade makes me shiver.

"I don't. Not really." The urge to cry vanishes, replaced by the leaden taste of old anger.

"Then why did you come? You think that he'll leave you an inheritance?"

"Oh, he has. Just not the kind that's worth anything." An inheritance of bitterness.

"May I sit?"

"It's your mother's house." I don't move over until I realize he really intends to lower his bulk next to me. I squeeze against the wrought-iron railing.

He sits with a huff, as if even sitting is a form of exercise for the once-athletic Paul. "Hey, this is hard on all of us."

"Why? Why would you think that?"

Paul tugs a little at his sweatpants, loosening the obvious constriction of his crotch. "I know things got weird back then, but that's history. Old, old history."

I twist my head to get a better look at him. "Some things are always present. I don't care how many years go by."

He turns his fat face to meet mine and for an instant I see the other boy, the thin, popular boy whose best friend was Ronnie Markham.

I remember Ronnie Markham even before my father married

Adele, when we went to the annual Markham Motors Christmas party with my mother. Ronnie always seemed to be crying at those parties, overtired and oversugared. By the time we were in our teens, Ronnie had stopped crying and turned into a golden boy. Girls fluttered around him. Boys like Paul simply surrounded him, an uneven admiration society. I did neither. I hung in the shadows and nearly died anytime Golden Boy cast his eye on me, as accidental as it might have been, like my being in the sight line between Ronnie and the cool girls, the popular girls he dated. I was not worthy of notice, but, like all the other girls, I daydreamed that someday he might.

"Hey kid." Ronnie Markham acknowledges my presence there in the kitchen and I feel like a god has spoken. In high school terms, he is a divinity, a god of sports. I am two years younger and tongue-tied. I grip a glass of milk and my hand trembles with the effort not to drop it. I blush, throw a look at Paul, who is oblivious as he ransacks the cupboards for snacks for himself and his buddy. Does he notice that Ronnie has spoken to me? Somehow validated my existence?

They disappear into the basement rec room, where they will play Ping-Pong, talk about girls, and drink endless Cokes. As he pushes past me, Paul gives me a fraternal shove, making me spill the milk down the front of my shirt. I am mortified, but Ronnie doesn't seem to notice. I am already forgotten.

Ronnie Markham was the reason I plucked those damned eyebrows.

Paul turns his face away from mine. "Anyway, we're here for Dad now."

"Dad. Right." My father, not yours. I have never called Adele "Mom." The word would have burned a hole in my mouth.

It is too hard to keep going with this conversation, so I shift it aside. "How's the family?"

Paul brightens, pulls a grin, and begins to recite his kids' achievements.

I don't have to listen, just nod here and there. I am worn out with worry and travel; it is easier to let him talk and think that I'm an interested stepaunt than to keep up the volley of verbal gunfire. He can never expect me to forgive him, but at least he can relax and chat with me as if we are two strangers meeting on a bus. I'm too tired right now to care. Maybe Paul's right. Maybe it is ancient history.

"So, where are you staying? Which hotel?"

"Right here at the Hotel Meade. Nonsmoking single couch."

"That's no good. Come to my house. I can offer you a bottom bunk."

"As tempting an offer as that is, I came to be here. I've slept on worse couches."

"I don't think that Mom can keep this up. This nursing. It's why we thought you should come."

I didn't expect candor and I'm surprised that Paul is so open with the truth that I wasn't called because I was the daughter; I was called to serve. "Now it makes sense."

"But for heaven's sake, you don't have to sleep on a couch."

"Thanks. Let's just see how it goes." I guess I mean how long it takes, but that seems a weird way to put it. I also don't say that I'm not likely to stick around too long. I have a life. I know that death comes in its own time, and most likely will take longer than anyone thinks. My father is up and using a toilet, which, to me, proves that the direness of the situation was overstated. So I may not be around for the final curtain. I haven't come here to be a nurse, just to say good-bye. Not to make peace, but because Candy persuaded me to come, pushing me out the door and into

Artie's rig with those rose-colored words: "So you won't live to regret it."

But while I'm here, I'll help the best I can. I won't say that I owe it to anyone; I don't owe anyone anything. I'll do it because I know how.

20

Alice and the dog come in from their morning walk. She hangs the leash on one of the back door pegs they use for keys, raincoats, and grocery bags, as if it had always hung there. "He really is a good boy. He never pulls."

Ed looks up from the eight-and-a-half-by-fourteen-inch poster board that he's working on. In nearly perfect block lettering, he's written: FOUND, GRAY-AND-WHITE LONGHAIRED DOG. NO COLLAR. ONE BLUE EYE AND ONE BROWN EYE. He turns the poster so that Alice can see it. "What do you think?"

Alice thinks that she hates him. "I don't know. I guess it's all right." Her good mood of the morning is gone.

"We should try to get a picture of him to put on it."

"He's so beautiful—how will we prevent people from just claiming him?"

Ed shrugs. "I doubt that anyone would actually do that, but even so, won't we be able to tell by the way he reacts when his old owner shows up?"

"Not he if was abused."

"Alice. Really. Does he strike you as an abused dog?" Ed waves a hand toward the dog, who is daintily licking his forepaws like a cat.

"He got left by the side of the road, hungry and thirsty. That's abuse enough." Alice knows that her tone is verging on hostile. She doesn't mean to be, but it's an easy tone to take instead of just saying what she wants to say. Instead of just telling Ed that, goddamn it, they're going to keep the dog because she wants him and she takes care of the house and, like everything else, it will be her responsibility. But she doesn't. Instead, she wrenches open the refrigerator door and begins shoving GladWare containers around, trying to assemble an idea for supper hours before anyone wants it.

"I'm going to go hang these." Ed scrapes back the kitchen chair, a sound that makes Alice grind her teeth. There are permanent tracks burned into the tile. As soon as Ed pulls his keys off the pegs, the dog gets to his feet and dances to the back door as if planning on taking the ride with Ed.

"You want to go?"

The dog tap-dances, front paws doing a high step.

"Think I should?"

Alice shuts the refrigerator door, leans back against it, and studies the pair. "He looks like he wants to go. Maybe he likes car rides."

Ed pats his leg. "Let's go."

The dog yips, an easily translatable *Yippee* sort of sound.

"Leash him." Alice says that exactly as she might have reminded him to fasten a child's seat belt. A reflexive maternal remark, unnecessary but vital to say so that the protective charms of ritual are in effect.

Equally reflexive, Ed replies, "Of course."

And to their mutual amazement, the dog pulls the leash off the peg himself and brings it to Ed, sits in front of him with the black nylon leash dangling from his sharp muzzle, his plumed tail swishing back and forth on the tile.

"Wow. That's a little scary."

Alice nods. "He really is smart."

"A real one of a kind, I'd say." Ed snaps the leash on the dog's new collar. "Someone must really miss him."

"I know."

"We have to advertise him."

"I've put the ad in the *Press*." Alice has missed this week's deadline, so the ad won't appear until next Thursday's edition of the weekly town newspaper. *Found, small collielike dog. Gray and white, one blue eye, one brown. Near Old Path Road. Call* . . . Alice wishes she hadn't been so specific.

Ed retrieves his hat from one of the pegs. "Maybe no one will see it."

Alice covers her mouth with one hand. She knows, and Edward knows, that doing the right thing might mean a loss; but not to do the right thing—in this case, to properly advertise the dog—isn't an option. It's not how either of them was raised. Ed was a Boy Scout. She was a Girl Scout.

Alice Rae Thompson saw Ed Parmalee for the first time when he was standing in line at the Dairy Queen.

She's behind the counter, serving up soft-serve ice-cream cones, vanilla and chocolate laden with jimmies or a dip that hardens into a chocolate shell. This is her summer job; once she's back in class at the local community college, she'll quit. She notices that he's clean-cut among the young folks hanging around, his hair only a little long against his collar, not sporting the shoulder-length hair of his companions, and for a moment she wonders if he's a veteran, someone who's been to Vietnam. Before he even reaches her window, Alice decides that, no, he can't be in the service, or recently out. His face is open and cheerful, not like the faces of those older brothers of her friends who have chosen the service instead of college, or had it chosen for them. They've come back, most of them, looking thirty, not twenty. Not smiling.

Edward Parmalee, dark-haired and blue-eyed, topping six three, slender as the basketball player he was in high school, looks at Alice Thompson framed in the Dairy Queen window and smiles at her. For the first time she can ever remember, Alice full out blushes, the warmth in her cheeks migrating straight to the roots of her hair. She can even feel the heat prickle along the center part that separates her hair into two long sheets of honey blond.

Ed's smile opens a seam in her soul, a place that has been un-touched, unmined. She can barely stammer out the right words to take his order.

"Chocolate, rainbow sprinkles, and your telephone number." Ed has the good grace to blush himself, and she knows that he's never done that before, that this is a new boldness.

When he calls later that evening, they laugh, realizing that neither one has asked the other's name. "Is this you?"

"Yes. I'm Alice."

"I'm Ed Parmalee. I work at the plant."

Alice stands in the middle of her kitchen, a room she used to imagine remodeling, with a widened doorway to the dining room, an island counter, and a Mexican tile floor. Some time ago, she stopped thinking about changing anything in her house. Somehow it was better to leave things as they were, do nothing more than clean it and freshen up the paint now and then. A house that seemed too small for years now feels rambling, empty. The clutter and mess of a third inhabitant is relegated to a small bedroom that she dusts once a month. Nothing in that room moves out of place. The bed never needs changing.

Alice fills the teakettle, sets it on the stove, and lights the burner. She busies herself with choosing a cup, pulling a tea bag out of the box, refilling the sugar bowl. The dishwasher needs emptying. The trash is full. Homely tasks she'll take care of after a cuppa. Ed will come back with the dog, then take the bagged trash to the barrel. Ed said maybe no one will see it, the lost-and-found ad. Maybe Ed is also hoping that the dog will stay. But because he's already said no to having the dog, he will have to find an acceptable way to make it his idea. Alice pours the water into her cup, bounces the tea bag up and down a few times. She smiles a little. Edward will come around; she just knows it.

21

The dog sits alert and entertained in the front seat of the Cutlass, as if he were Miss Daisy and Ed the Morgan Freeman driver, the dog's pointy snout acting like a directional aid: Go this way, now that. Suddenly, the dog gets excited, standing in the front seat and staring out the passenger window as Ed drives by the cemetery gates where Alice found him. The dog's tail wags in a broad sweep, brushing Ed's arm. Ed doesn't slow down, doesn't look in the same direction as the dog, ignoring the dog's evident desire to stop. Ed won't stop. Not there.

First to Potter's to hang a poster. Tim Potter, fourth generation of the general store–owning Potters, is busy stocking shelves. Back when Tim's dad ran the place, it was filled with useful things like sewing notions and fishhooks. Ed doesn't fish anymore, so it doesn't matter so much that young Tim has gentrified the place and no longer carries six varieties of fishing line or bait. Now Potter's offers specialty foods like mangoes and guava paste, herbed vinegars and extra-extra-virgin olive oils, kalamata olives in fancy jars, costing what he used to spend on a tank of gas in the old days. Bushel baskets are filled with cute replicas of nineteenth-century objects like handmade candles and tin cookie cutters, and old-fashioned and essentially inedible candies like horehound drops. Frankly, Ed thinks, Tim would be better served, in this fairly touristless town, if he provided cell phone chargers and poster board so that people like him wouldn't have to trek to Wal-Mart. If the leaf peepers ever ventured off the Mohawk Trail this far, then maybe ciabatta bread would sell.

"Can I hang this somewhere?" Ed holds up his homemade poster for Tim to see.

With his hands busy restocking a display of Tom's of Maine toothpaste, Tim gestures with his chin toward a small bulletin board matted with colored sheets of paper advertising a myriad of activities, yard sales, horses for lease, fund-raising events for the local elementary school and the library. "You'll have to take something down."

Ed studies the array before he removes a vintage sheet advertising a concert that took place last year. Commandeering the pushpin, Ed pokes it through the card stock of his sign. His poster is bigger than any of the others and shoves its shoulders across the one for the library bake sale and the one announcing a lecture on recycling coming up at the town hall. Maybe his poster is too big for the few words on it. He never did get a photo to add to the poster. Seemed like too much effort.

Ed takes down his sign and folds it so it's smaller, then presses the pushpin, which has a broken top and is painful against his thumb. He sucks at the offended digit. Now no one will see his sign, obscured as it is by the clutter of other, more colorful messages. Ed takes his sign down again, scans the board for a better spot, and finally pins his found poster to the very edge, where it sticks out like a dull afterthought. He should have used colored markers.

Ed picks up a package of beef jerky. He doesn't really want it, and will have to hide the evidence from Alice, but he thinks he really should buy something at Potter's, given that he's using the message board. Not that Tim looks like he's concerned, but it's the right thing to do and it's right there, close at hand, and, face it, it's a guilty pleasure.

As Ed gets back in the Cutlass, the dog is instantly alert and curious about the dried meat. "Oh, you want some, eh?" Ed shoves a piece in his mouth, relishing the salty taste. "It can't be good for you. It's not good for me."

The dog sits in the passenger seat, ears forward, eyes fixed on Ed's hand as it holds the greasy plastic sleeve, his little pink tongue licking at his lips in anticipation.

"How bad you want this?"

The dog is eloquent in his request. He gracefully sits up, dainty forepaws dangling in the air, his back neat against the seat, as if to say, *How much more do I have to do to get you to give me a piece of that?*

"Okay. Guess you earned this." Ed breaks a piece off and holds it out to the dog. The dog takes the offering with a delicate gesture, no snapping up a treat for him.

"Now say thank you."

And to Ed's complete surprise, the dog does. A quick sharp bark and one paw held out to be shaken.

"You're not making this any easier. But if you've got so many tricks, there must be somebody out there who really misses you. It wouldn't be right not to try." Driving away from Potter's, Ed tries to remember where else he wants to hang a poster. There are two left in the backseat. But it's getting late, and he still wants to get the grass cut, hopefully the last mow of the season. Plus, there's all that hedge trimming he's been putting off. How bad would it be to put off hanging another poster until tomorrow?

The dog is back to sitting like Miss Daisy, eyes fixed on their direction, except that every few minutes, he tilts his head to look at Ed, eyes full of hope that another piece of jerky will appear. When none is forthcoming, he settles down.

"You want to head home?" When Ed says the word *home*, the dog cocks his head. "Guess that means yes."

Ed drives past the cemetery gates where they had first seen the dog. As he does every time they go by, the dog begins to whine. And every time he drives past it, Ed does not stop. He won't.

Alice and Ed sit at the little kitchen table, their plates pushed aside, waiting for the tea water to boil. Alice keeps her finger in the book she's reading while she waits. Ed stares off into space.

Squeak! The dog comes bounding into the kitchen, the soft orange hydrant clutched between his jaws, and he's making it sound like it's talking. *Squeak, squeakee, squawk.*

Ed makes a grab for the toy and the dog dashes madly around the room, his tail in the air, his eyes glinting with enjoyment. He drops the toy in front of Ed and stands with front legs spread wide in anticipation of the chase. Ed pitches the toy through the archway and into the living room. In a bound, the dog retrieves the toy and pushes it into Alice's hand. She joins in the game, and in a moment, all three are playing a game of the dog's invention.

22

E d is running the mower around the backyard when Alice goes into the garage to get another box of garbage bags from their Costco closet. She has to squeeze past the Cutlass, always a little too close to the wall—she wishes Ed would get his eyes checked— and sees the white poster board still in the backseat, along with the empty beef jerky package. It feels like he's brought her flowers.

For Ed to give up on an errand is unusual. Ed is more the forge ahead, fight the blizzard to get to the store, damn the torpedoes kind of guy. Always has been. It puzzles Alice that Ed came home with the task unfinished, not even saying a casual word about why. Did he run out of tape? Was he turned away from hanging one at Potter's?

The only answer she likes is one she interprets from the way the dog and man came bounding into the house, pals returning from an adventure. The dog greeted her with enthusiasm, prancing on his back legs as if he'd never expected to see her again. Ed hung the leash on a peg, then his hat, his back to her until she straightened up from petting the exuberant dog. He was smiling an old, familiar smile, the one he used to give her when they were young and every meeting was a gift. A smile that engaged his eyes, his dark blue smiling eyes now crease-framed by years of not wearing sunglasses. Ed had been smiling, but he hadn't said anything about not hanging the posters. What he did say was, "He's one smart dog. You should see what he can do."

The forgotten posters make her smile, and in the reflection of the car's back window, she sees a vestige of her old self, a ghost of the girl who smiled like that when her man came calling.

When they had given up on ever becoming parents, it was understandable to have found some other outlet for their unfulfilled nurturing urges. They adopted two mature cats, but neither one was affectionate and did nothing to fill the void. They sent money to Save the Children and got a letter every few months from the child in Peru who was supported by their donations. But they never heard her voice, or developed any real sense of her existence. Ed took the promotion to floor supervisor, putting in lots of hours, promising the extra money would ensure a comfortable retirement. And he nurtured her, encouraging Alice to sign up for classes at the community college, to seek out activities that would give her fulfillment. The years of frustrated trying had been irrevocably lost; now they would relax and accept their circumstances and enjoy the rest of their lives. The absence of child no longer felt like a hole; how could you miss something you'd never had?

And then they did.

On the eve of her thirty-ninth birthday, against all odds, Alice found herself pregnant.

And the second time they found themselves childless, there was simply no outlet. Alice pushed away Ed's devotion. She was too angry. For a long time, there was nothing she could do but wait for each day to pass and hope to sleep for a few hours at night. A few hours, at most two or three, when the circling thoughts simmered down enough to let her rest, when the *why* and the *what if* and the self-doubt and the desperate search for a reason might give way to the exhaustion and let her sleep unmolested until she'd wake before dawn and meet the incomprehensible truth wide-eyed.

23

The posters on the backseat mock Ed every time he gets into the Cutlass, nagging him with a task shirked. But he seems to forget about their existence the moment he pulls out of the garage. Especially if the dog is with him. Just goes out of his mind. Pfft. Gone. Oops, should remember to do that. Today, Ed remembers, and he takes the signs out, tears them into neat quarters, and stuffs them in the bag of trash he's jamming into the barrel for today's pickup.

Alice catches him in the act and he gets defensive. "Don't you think that it's odd that we haven't seen any lost posters? Wherever this little guy came from, it isn't from around here. He's either run away or been dumped, and there's no telling how far afield he's gone. We could be hanging posters and putting ads in all the wrong places. Let's give it a rest."

Ed doesn't miss the expression on her face, a look of relief with a suggestion of puzzled gratitude, and Ed walks out the door rather than look at her, because it has been too long since he's seen an expression like that on his wife's face.

It's not the same thing, but Ed remembers that smile the day that he offhandedly suggested that they stop birth control. It wasn't like she'd been pestering, or hinting, or sighing at the sight of babies, but somehow he knew that her thoughts, after a couple of years of marriage, were turning broody. "Let's let nature take its course." That was how he had inelegantly phrased it. But you would have thought that he'd given her diamonds, not so much that he had made the suggestion, but that he, Edward the oblivious, had recognized a need in his wife without having to be told outright. It was a big moment in their marriage. Of course, they had never expected that it would take so long to accomplish, that nature certainly took her course, but that pleased smile still lingers in his memory and whenever he thinks of the early days, the years before life got hard, he pictures Alice smiling like that.

Life is divided into uneven thirds: Before Stacy, Being Parents, and After It Happened. They are halfway to having lost her longer than having had her. And, after it happened, Ed stopped being able to read Alice. The clues and nuances became too hard to interpret, or maybe he just lost the knack for it. Maybe it just got too hard, or the telepathy they once had between them was like wires in an old electrical cord, frayed and dangerous. The connection cut in one disastrous moment.

Ed bends over his mower, a self-drive, electric start, mega sixteen-inch blade Toro. There's always a little regret in putting the Toro to bed in the fall. End to another summer. Not that anything particularly special happens in the summer. Now that he's enjoyed his first full unemployed summer, with no vacation to look forward to because, as his pals at Lil's say, every day's a vacation, Ed has had a hard time recognizing the season except for the sweltering heat of the dog days of August, when the heat lay thick in the air. That, and the endless tasks of watering and mowing. Mowing and watering, growing the grass to cut the grass. Ed wraps the tarp over the Toro, binds it with a length of clothesline, and tucks it into its corner of the garage. He'll have to get the snow blower serviced pretty soon. Don't want to wait until everyone else thinks of it and there's a rush at Stan's Tractor and Mower Repair.

A rush of despair rocks Ed with its suddenness. His whole life is calibrated by seasonal machinery. He thinks of that song: *Is that all there is?* Some singer with a sexy, husky voice. He can only recall that single line in the chorus, and it orbits through his mind: *Is that all there is? Is that all there is?*

Ed pulls himself upright. It's only from bending over that he's gotten these weird feelings. There's nothing wrong. It's fine. Mostly, day-to-day life is fine.

Suddenly, the dog is beside him, the silly squeaky toy gripped in his teeth, and he's shaking it furiously, as if it's a rodent. The thing squeaks like a mouse, so the pretense is pretty understandable.

"Hey, you wanna play? Gimma that thing!" Ed pries the toy out of the dog's mouth and plays a little hand-to-hand keep away. The dog actually looks like he's laughing and he rears up like a pony, catching the hydrant in midair as Ed tosses it.

The dog drops the toy at Ed's feet, looks up with expectation, and then sits. "You're such a good boy. Are you my good boy?" Ed swoops down and gives the dog a hug, burying his nose in the white fur of his ruff. "Who's a good boy?"

At the top of the stairs, Alice watches Ed play with the dog. She hears the baby talk and thinks that his friends would think that Ed had lost his mind. He doesn't look the baby talk type. But he is. When she couldn't soothe the baby, Ed always could. Stacy held close in big arms, against a wide chest, a whispered lullaby. "If that mocking bird don't sing, Daddy's gonna buy you a diamond ring."

Who's my little baby girl?

Even though the man has taken him on several go-for-a-rides, they haven't taken him to Justine. Mack loves go-for-a-ride. At least he did until go-for-a-ride ended up in the cab of that truck. But this man doesn't go far, or for long, and has only left him waiting for a little while, measured in whether Mack chooses to lie down and snooze or remain upright in the front seat, tail curled around his forepaws, eyes on the place where the man has gone. When the man comes back, he proffers a whole strip of bacon. Mack, being a well-trained dog, accepts this treat with gentleness, a tail wag, and a quick head bob. Bacon is Justine's training tool of choice. Little crumbles just big enough to hide in a hand, doled out at the correct completion of his movements: circle, reverse circle, side step. The man isn't making any of those hand signals that mean bacon; he's just handing it over, in a strip. Mack would be more than willing to do a few movements if asked, but this is okay, too. So go-for-a-ride is good. But it isn't getting him where he wants to be.

When Alice puts on her yoga pants and sneakers, Mack believes that it means they will dance. He accompanies her to the back door, prancing on his little white front feet, his pointy muzzle split into a grin. Maybe, just maybe, Justine will be where this woman takes him to dance. He will find Justine there.

When Justine first taught Mack to dance, he thought it was just more of the same sort of training that they had been doing for a long time. He enjoyed showing off to the others that he could sit-stay longer and more attentively than any of them. He loved the leaps over rails and the scurry through the fabric tunnel. He understood on some organic level that doing all these things, touching the right spots on the platform, leaping accurately and quickly over bars, weaving through the poles as fast as an otter, was the point of the exercise. When he did his best, there was always loud applause, and sometimes he got to stand by himself in the ring while the Important Person presented Justine with objects that Justine smiled to receive and always let him nose. No other dogs, just him.

Then Justine began to ask him to weave not through poles, but between her legs. Leap, not over a pole, but over a short cane. Rise up on his legs and wriggle his tail. Walk backward, forward, and place his paws against her back. Some hand signals were so subtle that he had to keep his eye on her at all times, sometimes having to decide what it was she wanted, because the movement was only a degree different from another one. A bow instead of a cocked head. Walk or army crawl.

So when Alice pulled on her yoga pants and tied her soft white shoes to her feet, Mack got excited. Those were practice clothes. When Justine wore those clothes, they'd head to the high school gym and meet up with Saundra and her pack. Juicy was always there, and Sambucca, the blue-eyed husky Mack has always had a crush on. And sometimes Griff, who was a slow learner but tried hard.

If Alice hadn't put on her go-to-dance clothes, Mack would have settled for another day of waiting. But she had and now he was excited. He even barked. One short piercing bark, just to let her know that he was pleased to be going back to work. Maybe Justine would be there.

But then Alice hadn't taken him where she was going. And when she came back, she smelled of sweat but not of other dogs. Not of Justine.

Go-for-a-ride is good. And walks are good. The kibble is different but good. The couch is okay, a little firmer than the soft cushions on the couch Mack uses at home with Justine. When Alice leaves the house or goes upstairs, he settles down on the right-hand cushion, balling himself up tight, nose tucked beneath tail. It's his default position, the one from which he takes the most comfort. Once asleep, he will unfurl like a flower, stretching to take up half the couch. But to start, he likes making himself small and compact, pretending he's a wolf on the tundra. At first, Alice made him get off the couch, but now she understands that snuggling on the couch is a good thing. Mack has taught her that it is nice to let him rest his head on her legs and stroke him. She's learned already about the nice soothing spot in his ear. They still haven't learned his name and he's not sure how to teach that to them.

Ed has learned about the ball. That's a good thing, especially since he throws it a lot farther than Justine does, so the game is much more challenging. Mack likes the long slope of the backyard and the way he has to dig in his feet to prevent himself from crashing into the bushes. Snapping up the ball, he runs pell-mell to the top of the hill, where Ed waits, slapping his knees to encourage speed. He's good with the squeaky toy, too. Knows the same game of keep away that Justine plays.

Mack doesn't know how long he's been here with Alice and Ed. He doesn't know how long it's been since Justine disappeared. Time is nothing to him, measured out in meals and walks but never adding up. Mack has adapted to the rhythms of this household, knowing that she rises first, that he goes to bed last. Breakfast is eaten in silence. The routine is more obvious to him now than it was at first. Like Justine, Alice has a set pattern that includes food, exercise, and baby talk. Ed has a less predictable pattern, but he seems to be the one with the car keys.

Alice takes him for walks. Although sometimes when they go, she talks to him in a serious, sad way. When she does that, Mack has learned that a joke is a good way to change that tone. So he'll grab her sleeve gently in his teeth, or fake nip at her heels as if to say, *This is about fun. Keep moving.* Sometimes he just barks until she breaks out of her mood with a laugh and half-hearted warning to stop it.

There has been a change in the air. Not only are the days a bit cooler, but the people in the house are treating him in a new way.

At first, being shy, they treated him with courtesy and a little distance, which was appropriate. He was a stranger in their home. But now, now they are more casual with him, easy. Ed keeps bringing him new toys. Today it was a stuffie. Mack loves stuffies, and, unlike his terrier brethren, he doesn't gut them to extract the squeaker, but gently bites the fuzzy bone-shaped toy to get it to emit the irresistible noise, then uses it as a pillow.

There's lots to like about being a guest here, but he still wants Justine to come and get him.

Every time they offer Mack go-for-a-ride, he thinks that Justine will be there. Every time they pass the cemetery gates, he asks them to let him out to see if there's a hint of her scent on the ground, to see if Justine has come to get him. But they never do.

24

He should have a name." Alice says this around a mouthful of spaghetti, as if slipping the concept of naming the dog around food disguises the larger concept of keeping him. The dog, for his part, sits at a distance, but his eagle eyes are alert to her right hand with the upraised fork. He isn't begging per se, but he is certainly interested in their mealtime.

Ed tears a hunk of Italian bread off the loaf on the table, butters it liberally with the fake spread that Alice buys because it's supposed to be healthier for them than the margarine she used to use. He doesn't respond, but she knows he's thinking. She waits patiently, familiar with the signs of Ed's thought process. He never voices his internal debates. Finally, just as she's taken another forkful of spaghetti, he sets his fork down. "What do you want to call him?"

"I don't know. Something different. I wish we knew what he was called."

"Then we'd know where he came from."

"How about Silver? Because of his color."

"Nah. What about Butch?"

"Never. Carlton?"

"Carlton? Why Carlton?"

"I like the name."

"Oh no. Not Carlton. I just can't see me owning a dog named Carlton."

"Then come up with something."

Ed just shovels another bite of spaghetti into his mouth. "Buddy. It's a good name. Watch." Ed swallows the spaghetti, scrapes his plate with the chunk of bread. "Here, Buddy."

The dog is by his side in an instant.

"See? Maybe that's really his name. He comes to it quick." Ed puts the plate on the kitchen floor. The dog happily licks the plate with a dainty tongue, scouring it for any hint of sauce.

"Ed. I'm shocked at you." Alice leaves a tiny bit more sauce and a scrap of sausage on her plate. "Okay. Buddy it is." She takes up Ed's sparkling plate and gives the dog hers.

"Well, I'm shocked at you. Letting a dog lick your plate. How uncharacteristic." Ed grabs both now virtually clean plates and sets them into the dishwasher. "I guess if we're going to keep him, we need to get a license. I'll do it tomorrow."

Alice is glad that her back is to him. She was expecting an argument. She was prepared for it, loaded, as they say, for bear. Ed has left her with her figurative powder dry and it is all she can do to stop from laughing out loud. "Sounds good." Alice bends over the dog to stroke his muzzle, to keep her surprised smile from belonging to Ed.

Nothing is ever cut-and-dried. That's what Ed thinks as he leaves the town clerk's office without a dog license. Buddy needs proof of a rabies shot before he can get a tag. Now he's got to find a vet, make an appointment, spend who knows how much, and then, only then, can he get the ten-dollar tag. No wonder people become scofflaws. "What do you say, pal, want to live outside the law?"

The dog is more interested in the scents surrounding the trash can outside the town hall.

They used to take those two ornery cats to the Moodyville Vet Clinic over on Route 101. It's been a long time since the last one moved on to mouse hunt on a higher plane, and Ed wonders if the place is still there. This time, he thinks to call Alice and tell her he's going to be late for lunch.

"Well, we probably should get him checked out anyway. See if you can get squeezed in today. If not, I can take him, as long as you can make an appointment that isn't on my day at the library."

"Do you want me to pick you up?" Ed holds the cell phone tight against his cheek. He still doesn't believe that you don't have to shout into them. "There's no way I'm going to remember your schedule."

There is no hesitation in Alice's reply. "Yes."

By the time Ed pulls into the driveway, Alice has called ahead to the clinic and gotten an appointment, which she knows will please Ed, who hates to wait for anything. Fortunately for them, there was a cancellation. Buddy is relegated to the backseat as Alice takes her place in front. He rests his chin on the seat back, suggesting that there is room for him between them. When neither of the people invite him to move up front, he settles into the left-hand seat to watch the scenery go by.

The Moodyville Veterinary Clinic is a much different place from the one where they used to take the cats. The boxy cedar-shingled building with the two chain-link runs outside has evolved into an architecturally designed animal hospital with tended gardens, and if there are runs, they are well hidden behind a flourishing boxwood hedge. The practice has clearly grown, and now there are four vets on staff instead of just old Doc Creighton, whose family has been so long in this town that there's a road named for them. Creighton's name is still on the masthead, along with those of his daughter and two others.

A staffer hands them a clipboard with a form on it. "Do you have insurance?"

Ed wonders if he's accidentally brought the dog to a people clinic. "Insurance?" His question is lost as the staffer grabs a ringing phone. Since when is there health insurance for animals? Is this in Obama's health-care package? Is that why people are so bent out of shape? Alice takes the clipboard and checks off "No" to that question.

They really don't know anything about him, and it shows. The form is mostly empty except for their names and contact info. Name: Buddy. Breed: Shetland sheepdog? Age: unknown. Last vaccination: unknown. Any health problems? unknown. Microchipped? Alice looks up from the form and points to that question. "What if he is?"

"Then we find out who he belongs to." Ed takes the clipboard from Alice.

There is no animal smell in the waiting room and barely any in the exam room where young Dr. Creighton meets them after a tech does all the routine things like weight (thirty-two pounds) and temperature (normal). Buddy takes it all like a champ. Like a dog quite used to being vetted. The clipboard with the microchip question is now in Dr. Creighton's hands and she is asking questions that Ed lets Alice answer because it isn't unlike being in the pediatrician's office with a child. A mother should answer those questions. Fathers should stay in the background.

Good appetite. Healthy bowels. No coughing. Playful. He sleeps on the couch; is that a bad idea? The whole time the vet is asking her general health questions, Alice is stroking Buddy, her fingers raking through the thick fur of his ruff. Little drifts of loosened hair float into the air.

Ed waits for the vet to ask where they got him. And if she does, will she insist on seeing if he is chipped? She opens Buddy's mouth and looks at his teeth, runs her hands down his sides and under his belly, where she spends a little longer palpating. She takes a look inside his ears and into his eyes. Ed watches as the vet's hands glide down the length of his back. She gives him an attaboy thump. "Good boy."

Buddy seems to agree. He nuzzles the vet's face.

"He has a little scar on his belly, which I think must have come from surgery. If he's been anaesthetized, he might have a chip. Do you want me to see?"

Alice doesn't answer. She wraps the leash around her hand, holding it tighter.

"He's not chipped." Ed puts a hand on Alice's shoulder. "The people we got him from didn't chip him."

Under his hand, Ed feels Alice's relief.

Ed gets the feeling the vet's not buying his story, but she isn't going to press the issue. She administers the rabies and distemper vaccines, draws blood for a heartworm test, and shoots a little medicine up Buddy's nose for kennel cough. "He's a lovely dog. You're very lucky. His former owners certainly took care of him."

"Yeah, they did. Till they couldn't do it anymore."

Two hundred and twenty-five dollars later, Ed, Alice, and Buddy head home. This time, Buddy sits in front.

Mack has never lived with two people at once. There have been visitors, even overnight guests, but never two people under the same roof, sharing a bed and bumping into each other in the hallway. He watches Ed and Alice as they go through their days. Her tongue language includes recognizable words like *dinner;* his, the word *no.* Ed says no to Alice a lot. Mostly when she asks him a question. "I don't know." "No thanks." "How should I know?" When they talk to each other, the sentences are short, and even a dog can tell that it isn't conversation as much as routine fact finding. The interesting thing is that when he is alone with either of them, their tongue language is smooth and flowing, filled with nuances and that chirpy sound that humans make when they are amused. Suddenly, they are using a word with him that he recognizes is what they want to call him. Buddy. That's okay. It's a familiar term and he'll respond to it if that's what they want.

What's hard is that they spend very little time in the same room. Buddy/Mack, still new to the double responsibility of two humans, goes between the television room and the kitchen, staring first at Ed, then at Alice. They should be in the same place; that's what his herd-dog requirements ask. Then Alice moves to the television room and Ed disappears into the bathroom. Buddy/Mack waits patiently, sitting just inside the archway so that he can monitor the television room and the bathroom. Ed comes out, and he wags his tail in relief. Okay, now he can move Ed into the same room as Alice. But Ed slips past him, giving him a pat on the head, going into the bedroom to watch the other television.

This is the first day that Alice hasn't been at home with him. Buddy/Mack recognized the word *work*, so he thinks that she may come back tonight smelling like food. That's what Justine always smelled like when she told him she was going to work. Food. Buddy/Mack licks his chops in anticipation that maybe tonight these new people will present him with a treat from work. After their daily ride, Ed has also left him alone in the house while he is outside. Buddy/Mack would like to tell Ed that he's perfectly dependable about staying in the yard, but he has no way of letting Ed know that. So he jumps onto the couch, circles, and buries his nose beneath his tail. He'll doze a little, one ear positioned to catch the sound of returning humans.

Since choosing to remain here to wait for Justine, Buddy/Mack has not slept. He has only dozed, and the lack of deep sleep is beginning to wear on him. Afraid that he'll miss hearing Justine's arrival, and a little nervous about being in the care of strangers, he hasn't allowed himself the healing sleep of the content. He has not dreamed running dreams. He hasn't dreamed chasing dreams. He sleeps the primordial sleep of his ancestors when hunting alone, always on the alert.

Today is the first day that he feels himself go into a deep sleep. Buddy/Mack isn't conscious that he's entered into REM sleep; he just knows that he is in a safe place and that he can finally slide into the relaxed sleep of a sheltered dog.

Buddy/Mack sighs, letting go of all the tension of the past few days. He tucks his nose deeper beneath his tail and falls asleep, his new stuffie tucked under him.

He is certain now that if Justine comes, she'll wake him up.

25

Alice walks through the kitchen door and Buddy greets her with a little dance of happiness. She barely has time to put down the green sack of groceries as he dashes around her in circles, making a little yipping noise of welcome, demanding her attention. "How's my boy? Did you miss me? I was gone a whole five hours. Did you think I wouldn't come back?" Alice says all this in a baby voice, the same voice she used to soothe her baby; the same voice she also used to mock her bad moods when Stacy was half-grown. "Who's a good boy?"

"Buddy's a good boy." Ed appears in the archway between the kitchen and the dining room. He's got a streak of something on his cheek, something automotive. Every now and again he decides to do his own servicing. "We visited Stan's today. I left the snow blower."

Alice shrugs off the light jacket she's wearing. "Looks like you might have thought about doing it yourself." She points to a spot on her cheek that corresponds to the streak on Ed's face.

"Huh? Oh." Ed wipes the streak with a finger, then wipes his finger against the leg of his old green work pants, which have been softened by years of abuse. "Did I get it?"

Alice wets a paper towel, beckons Ed close, and rubs hard

against the smudge. Buddy watches with herd-dog intensity as the two of them face each other. "That's it. Don't you dare sit down with those pants on."

"I won't."

"I thought I'd take Buddy for a walk to my mother's before I start dinner." After her shift in the library, it took Alice longer in the grocery store than she'd planned and all the time she was waiting in line behind some dimwit who didn't believe in the grammatically suspect 12 ITEMS OR LESS sign, she worried that Ed would have already taken Buddy out for his late-afternoon walk. She's never said how much she looks forward to it, as much for the casual saunter down the winding road to the conservation land, the scent of the forest and the quiet solitude after a busy day as for the obvious enjoyment the dog gets from the walk. She wants to be the one to give the dog this pleasure.

"He'd like that. We've mostly just done errands. He pooped in the backyard." Ed unbuckles his belt and lets his filthy pants drop to the kitchen floor. "Not much excitement for him today." He steps out of the pants, his heel catching the cuff, so that one leg is pulled inside out. He stands there with the tail of his denim shirt keeping him decent, long legs pale against the dark of the shirt. "Unless you count the pooping."

Alice takes the dirty pants from Ed's hands, rights the inverted leg. Despite the many years pounding the factory floors, his legs still look pretty good. Ed hasn't run to fat the way most men of his age have, but then she's a good cook, not a fancy one. Never got into lavish sauces or fancy desserts. Good nutrition, just like she was taught in home ec. Basic food groups, plus a treat now and then. Alice sniffs when she hears about the public outcry about obesity. Not in her family.

"I thought about taking him for a walk, but I knew that you'd want to do it when you got home."

Alice is surprised by that, by Ed's getting it.

Buddy flops down on the floor, his thumping tail the only thing to suggest he's not resting, but hopeful of some activity. Ed nudges him with his toe. "Hey Buddy, don't lose heart. Alice will give you what you want."

The dog jumps to his feet, yips a little.

"Guess I'll just go take a shower."

It's his using the word *just* that pricks Alice's conscience, making him sound something like a boy who's been left out of the game. Ed's had the dog all day, so why should he feel deprived? Alice wants her solitude, and this walk has become the only way she gets it now that Ed's been laid off. She wishes he wasn't so stubborn about finding another job, one that would at least get him out of the house with more purpose than coffee at Lil's. He is too present.

Ed bends over the dog, ruffling his fur all the way to the base of his tail. The dog swivels his head to look at Ed with those mismatched eyes, tongue lolling in doggy pleasure.

Alice woke up on the dawn of her wedding day and wondered if she'd been flattered into marrying a man she knew was kind, charming, and supremely confident of his decision-making abilities. A trait that, even then, in the full blush of romantic love, Alice knew would evolve into always thinking that he was right.

"Will you leash him for me?"

Buddy knows enough English to react to Alice's words, and he jumps up and dashes to the back door, ready to perform one of his tricks.

Alice did wake up on her wedding morning excited, nervous, maybe even a little nauseous, but she didn't wake up doubting her choice. That's a recent spin; that's three and a half decades of experience coloring in the outline of that young bride's expectations.

And in the last decade, Ed has learned the hard way that he isn't always right.

Ed takes the leash out of the dog's mouth and clips it to the collar. The fire hydrant–shaped license tinkles against the metal clip, a reassuring doggy sound. Alice wants to get a name tag as well, with their number and address printed on it. It's a good idea. No sense taking chances.

"Have fun."

Alice leaves the house quickly, just a little ashamed of herself.

Buddy/Mack stretches out on the sun-warmed deck, a long sigh of released energy shuddering through him. Alice has been grooming him, and his skin feels tingly in a pleasant way. Drifts of loosened hair float on the light breeze, up and away, too late for songbirds to use as nesting material.

Alice has on those clothes again, the ones just like those that Justine wears to dance with him. Buddy/Mack gets up from his idle sunbathing and prances, demonstrating to Alice that he can go with her to the dance place. In his dog's mind, it isn't unreasonable that Alice will take him to a place he knows and that Justine will be there waiting for him. He doesn't know why she's being so stubborn.

"Oh no, Buddy. You can't go to yoga. I'm sure that Ed will take you somewhere." Buddy/Mack understands only that she isn't taking him with her, not the tongue language. He doesn't understand the problem. Alice has on dance clothes. He always goes to dance when he sees those tight black pants and white shoes, the car keys, the water bottle almost like the one Justine shares with him. He can overlook one time when she might not take him, but not again. He stands on the alert, his blue eye and his brown eye fixed on Alice's face, waiting.

Then Alice makes a gesture. Even a dog knows that she doesn't mean to get him to react to it, but he does, happy to show off his talent. Alice flips her right hand, palm up, and Buddy/Mack rises to his back legs and spins. He can tell by her expression that she is surprised. Humans reveal so much with their mouths. Buddy/Mack watches to see if she'll try any other familiar gesture, and he isn't disappointed. A quick hand to her brow, and Buddy/Mack, still on his back legs, maneuvers himself behind her, the back of his skull fitting neatly against her backside. She moves forward and he moves with her. She moves to the side and he keeps with her. He waits for another signal, then decides on his own that back-to-back is over and, still balanced on his hind legs, chooses to hip-hop back in front of Alice. She reaches for his front paws and he extends them to her. His muzzle is split in a wide grin. She's dancing with him.

Now can we go?

26

I've worked in a nursing home. I once thought about getting my certification as a nurse's aide, but I never got around to it. I did learn how to change a bed with a patient in it. I learned about bedsores. I watched the CNAs as they fed, bathed, changed, and spoke in humiliating baby talk to the old people, treating them like unthinking imbeciles simply because age or disease had taken away their speech or their mobility. I'm not squeamish. A woman who has had to support herself and a child alone can't afford the vapors when a good job pays up to seventeen dollars an hour.

I stand over my father and wait until he signals that he'll take another spoonful of soup. He can feed himself, but he prefers being helped to having tomato stains on his pajamas.

"Ready for another spoonful?"

"No. I'm done. Take it away."

I look down on his blanket-covered knees and try not to think how emaciated this disease has left him. Adele can stuff him with all the soup and protein drinks he can tolerate, but there is no reversing this decline. I take back my earlier assessment; this wait will not be long.

"Just one more." I sound like I did when I was coaxing Tony to eat peas.

"I said no. I'm not hungry." My father sounds like Tony when he wouldn't eat those peas. Petulant. When did this grown man become petulant? I remember him as silent, accepting, probably cowed by the woman he replaced my mother with, but never petulant.

"Okay." I pull the tea towel out from under his chin.

"Give me the remote."

Fighting the temptation to make him say *please*, I hand him the clicker and leave the room.

Adele has gone to lie down, so I am alone in the kitchen to clean up the minimal debris left from heating a can of Campbell's soup. It may only be a saucepan and a ladle, but cleaning up without making a sound that might disturb the resting and the dying is hard work, and at the end of it, I am exhausted. I sink onto a kitchen chair, which I instinctively choose, the one that was mine for all those years, my back against the wall. There is a notepad tucked into the napkin holder on the table and I take it and find a pencil. I need to figure out what to do next. I hunt down the New Bedford phone book, right where it has always been, in the top drawer, and try to think of whom to call. Maybe the local rescue can get me started with a search. What I really need is a computer and Internet access. I need to get online and map out a nationwide strategy. I open the phone book, searching for "Animal Rescue" in the Yellow Pages, and there it is under "Automotive": Markham Motors.

For forty years, my father worked for Markham Motors. He sold Chevrolets until Markham Motors expanded into the foreign car market, and then he sold Toyotas, although he always drove Chevys. Every year, Markham awarded sales prizes and almost every year my father came away with another bronze plaque to hang on his wall at work. The name Markham was sacrosanct in this house. It wasn't like it is now, people changing jobs and moving from one career "path" to another. In those days, and especially with a man like my father, loyalty to an employer was admirable. As long as he identified himself as a Markham man, my father was happy. He never anticipated anything other than retiring from Markham Motors.

I pull my finger away from the listing and flip the Yellow Pages back to the animal listings. Before I can find what I'm looking for, my phone rings. I don't recognize the phone number on the display. Then I do. "Mitch?"

"Hi. Just thought I'd check in and see how you're doing. Where are you?"

"I made it to New Bedford."

"And the dog?"

"Nothing yet."

"I'm sorry."

"Thanks." I am touched by the fact that this stranger whose body I clung to for a hundred miles is thinking of me. "I have a couple of leads. The truckers are using their CBs to try to locate Artie." It's a bit of an exaggeration, but I comfort myself by just saying it.

"I've posted your lost dog story on my Facebook page. I've gotten lots of comments."

"That's sweet of you."

"So many people out there can relate to losing a pet. Makes you want to cry."

The image of this tough-looking, one-legged, Harley-riding violinist crying makes me smile.

"And how are things in New Bedford?"

"All right." And that makes me feel a little better, too. "How did your concert go?"

"Same old, same old. A little Vivaldi paired with a modern piece that has no discernible melody."

I laugh. "Maybe someday I'll go to one of your concerts. I'd like to hear the Vivaldi." This is true; I'm not just making conversation. Over the years, I've developed a taste for good music. Candy doesn't object too much when I pop a classical CD into the player as we close up the bar for the night, although she won't let me do that until the last customer is gone.

"Look, Justine. I have a little break coming up. We've just finished the last of the summer season and rehearsals for the winter series don't start for a couple of weeks."

It's the "Look" that alerts me, a verbal hint that something more than a change of topic is coming. "A little vacation, then. What will you do?"

"Thought I might jump on the bike and go see the Whaling Museum in New Bedford."

"It's a nice museum."

"I can be there tomorrow, day after if I take my time."

"That would be nice. But I don't think you should."

"Because it would be inconvenient?"

"Sort of. I'm staying at my father's house. I don't know for how long."

"Not because you are being too polite to tell me to back off?"

"No. No. It would be nice to have a friendly face here." I can conjure up the feel of Mitch's leather coat on my cheek, the scent of him, but not the eyes that were behind sunglasses the whole time we rode together. "It would be nice to have a friend, but I don't think that this is the time."

"I understand."

"It's just . . ." Just what? Another guy hitting on me? Something that has happened to me all my life and I'm no longer flattered? It doesn't feel like that. It feels like something I would encourage. But not now. I have too many emotional irons in the fire to think about encouraging a man to drive from Cleveland to New Bedford on a whim. "After this. When I leave, maybe I can . . ."

"No problem. Really. It was just an idea. Stupid. Of course you're all tied up. I was being impulsive."

"Mitch. It's fine. A really sweet idea. Maybe on my way back to Washington I can stop."

There is a quiet moment while we both adjust our thinking. He wants to come; I won't let him. He was a ride when I needed it; now he thinks of me.

I hear Adele talking to my father. I need to get off the phone and see what else she has in mind for me.

"If I had a picture of your dog, it would help. On the Facebook thing."

For the first time, I wish that I'd invested in one of those fancy camera, e-mail, text, do-your-laundry phones. But all I have is an ancient Nokia that simply acts like a phone. "I don't have one with me. But my friend Saundra does. I can have her send you something." Saundra is the unofficial photographer at our freestyle competitions. She has dozens of photos of dogs performing, and surely one of Mack can be e-mailed to Mitch.

I get his e-mail address. "Thanks for helping, Mitch. And thanks for calling me. I really appreciate it." I just can't appreciate his showing up. That's the thought dangling out there. For once, I have to keep my eye on the ball.

"Don't hesitate to call me if you need to." He sounds sincere, but I doubt that Mitch will repeat this act of kindness. In the old days, I would have told him to come. But I'm older and wiser now; I know how tempting a distraction is, and how destructive.

After I left Anthony, I headed south, attracted by the warmth and the purported lower cost of living. I waitressed in Orlando, worked in a nursing home in New Orleans, got a receptionist's job in Dallas. By the time Tony was five, I was hollowed out. I was exhausted from the responsibility of being the sole source of emotional strength, of decision making, of punishment and reward.

The girls I met at my various jobs were still playing. They made plans to meet at nine at night; I was in bed, my son safe in his own bed, the night-light illuminating the dinosaurs on his sleeper. They invited me out of politeness; I declined because I couldn't do it, leave Tony with a baby-sitter I couldn't afford to drink margaritas I also couldn't afford. To be reckless when I was the only support for a little child. I had taken on single motherhood by my own choice, and I was dedicated to it. But even a dedicated mother gets tired and resentful and frustrated.

The first time Dan asked me out and said he'd pay for the baby-sitter, I told myself that it would be fine. And it was. Then it was Carl, then Bruce, then a host of other men willing to see me as more than just a mommy. Their attention, however brief, reminded me that I was still young, still in my twenties, and maybe I didn't have to be alone. Didn't I deserve a little adult time? A few hours more with a sitter at the end of the workday wasn't going to warp my kid. Even a two-parent child got left with a sitter.

I loved having a little grown-up time, and it became a habit. Dressing up and going out told me that I could have a life outside my role as a mother and provider. Talking about something other than homework and play dates, being kissed—both reminded me that I still had a Life.

And then they each moved on. Leaving me lonelier than ever. Although they never exactly said it, I knew that having a kid was a drawback, especially as Tony grew up and was no longer easily charmed by presents and being tossed into the air; when he no longer went off and played by himself as my guest and I waited for the sitter to arrive, but wanted to be a part of the conversation.

When push came to shove, they all wanted an unencumbered woman. Each time, each disappointment, and I'd swear to myself that I'd stick with my little boy and forget men. I just didn't realize that Tony wasn't an oblivious little child; he was growing up and was all too aware of my failures.

No, I don't need a distraction now. I need to stay focused and leave comfort aside for now.

"Justine." Adele is beckoning from the sickroom.

I snap my phone shut and head in to get my next set of orders.

27

The chief help I seem to be able to give is to run errands. Adele sends me to the grocery store, to the pharmacy, to the jewelry store, where she's left her watch to be repaired. She thinks of these tasks individually, so that I am out of the house more than I am in it. As if by summoning me, she surprised herself and now needs to remove me. I go, happier to be driving around on fool's errands than sitting in that house, waiting to feed my father his next bowl of soup, or sit on the surprisingly comfortable couch, waiting for my next order. This is when I miss Mack the most; the reason I wanted him with me. To give me an ally. A reason to leave the house, a reminder that I am important in the life of at least one creature.

So far, Adele has done the more intimate nursing tasks. My "help" is mostly kept outside the bedroom door. I think that she's a little afraid to leave me alone with my father. Afraid of what I might say, or of what he might admit. So I run to Stop & Shop and to CVS and linger a little while at the North Dartmouth Mall before claiming her watch from Zales Jewelers. I use the time to check in with Candy, joining the club of women wandering the mall avenues, cell phone pressed against an ear, isolated in a crowd by the voice of a distant friend. When I hear Candy's "Candy's Place," I so want to be home, home with Mack.

"Any trucker who comes in, I ask if they've seen Artie, but no one has, and most don't know him at all. It's like he disappeared off the edge of the world."

"Or he's hiding from me."

"One guy did say that he thought he knew who Artie's agent is. But he couldn't remember the name. Says he'll find out and get back to me. I didn't want to bother you with that bit of non-information."

"Artie is like the invisible man. No one sees him. No one knows him."

"What if he was in an accident or something? Maybe that's why he's invisible."

It's a good idea, and I wonder if I can get the state police to tell me if an Arthur Schmidt was involved in any accidents, is maybe dead. As long as he didn't have my dog with him at the time, it wouldn't break my heart. But the idea doesn't take hold. "He's a gypsy driver. Accountable to no one that we know of. Rockin' Roadie. That's all anyone on the road knows him by. He could have gotten a load and headed to Canada, or gone down south, or driven anywhere but back to Washington."

"Justine, he's got to be somewhere, and so does Mack." I can tell by the tone of her voice that Candy is distracted, customers coming in for an early-morning pop. It's only nine there.

A beep beckons me away from Candy to another call. I wouldn't jump from Candy's call except that it might be the one that I'm waiting for, the next call to move me closer to finding Mack. Every time the phone rings, my heart does a little dance of useless hope.

It's Adele, wondering where I am and why am I not there. Could it be because she sent me away? There have been a couple of moments when I've wondered if she is all right mentally. She's made little slips that have puzzled me, like when she lost the word for toilet paper, or when she told me something that just didn't add up about Paul's kids, as if she was talking about much younger children. I've worked in a nursing home. I've been assigned to the Alzheimer's wing. I know the difference between forgetfulness and senility. But I have never been there at the beginning, when the mind begins to retract. I'm not sure if incipient senility is what I'm seeing, or if my opinion of Adele is so harsh, I'm wishing.

"Are you on your way back?"

"In a minute, I'm waiting for them to find your watch."

"Don't wait for it. Come now."

Normally, that demand would have been spoken in Adele's naturally imperious tone. Not this time. She sounds panicked.

"I'm fifteen minutes away. I'm on my way."

Adele ends the call, as she always does, without saying good-bye.

I bang through the back door and drop everything on the kitchen table. Adele is in my father's room and I hear her voice and the sound of the television tuned into some chat show where the audience is compelled to applaud at every line the host utters. I snap it off. In the sudden quiet, Adele's voice also shuts off. My father is lying flat on his back, his mouth gaping open, and the odor of urine is pungent. Adele is standing over him, a wet washcloth bunched in her hands.

"He won't wake up."

"How long has he been like this?" I reach for the bedside phone.

"A few minutes."

"But he was he like this when you called me?"

"Yes."

"Why didn't you call the ambulance?"

"I don't want him to go."

I dial 911.

"Where's Paul?" I assume she tried him first.

"I didn't call him."

"Okay. I'll call him." I don't want to be alone with his mother in this.

Adele keeps wiping my father's face with the cold washcloth. "I don't want him to go to the hospital. He should be here."

"He'll need to go for a little while. We'll bring him back." I don't know why I promise this, except that I'm pretty certain the outcome isn't going to be one that gives us a choice in the matter. These are cheap words to offer. In the same moment, I realize that this means I will never get from my father what I've wanted since I was seventeen years old—an apology. No cheap words for me now.

Done with his first year at college, Paul came home that summer and fell back in with his friends from high school. They were jocks, three-season athletes. One or two had gone to good schools on athletic scholarships. More of them had stayed in New Bedford and gone into their fathers' businesses, or gone to technical school for the nine months between graduation and an apprentice license as electricians or plumbers. Those were some of the kids Paul hung out with. They met together every night to act out Bruce Springsteen's "Glory Days." They were still under-age, so their preferred hangout was the outdoor basketball court at the high school, where they could sit in a car, between games of skins versus shirts, and knock back Bud Lights without too much scrutiny from slow-rolling police cars. In their minds, anyone who might see the former heroes of the basketball court, or the baseball diamond, or, best of all, the football field, playing a pickup game would think back to those golden hours and be charmed by the scene of these gods on earth still flaunting the jump shots of their high school years. The drunker they got, the more those glory days revealed the flaws in their postgraduation lives. Some were doing grunt jobs, ordered around by bosses who had once themselves been glory boys. Or, they were like Paul, an average student but a moderately talented athlete, which got him a scholarship to play on an average state basketball team that never even made it into the play-offs.

Ronnie Markham was one of the boys who made it to a big school on an athletic scholarship. They always talked about how someday there would be a trophy named after him; his athletic prowess had put the school on the map time and again. It helped that his father had the largest, most successful car dealership in the area. Markham Motors, three generations old, enjoyed a fair amount of signage on the playing fields of our high school.

It had been a while since Ronnie had hung out with Paul. A year older than Paul, he had finished his sophomore year at BU. They'd reconnected on the basketball court and now Ronnie showed up at our house three days out of four. He and Paul would go out, shoot those baskets at the high school, and then do whatever it was that they did until the early hours of the next day. Sometimes I'd open the door and there he'd be on our front step, still the Greek god of New Bedford. "Hey, kid. Where's Paul?" That was the sum total of his interest in me.

And then it wasn't.

That summer, Markham Motors did a little trimming. Cost cutting. Belt tightening. My father's job was on the line; it had been a few years since the last bronze plaque.

I can hear them talking about it through the thin walls of my converted closet, Adele's badgering tone, imploring my father to call a meeting with Markham and point out all his years of success and experience. "Tell him that if he's smart, he'll make you the manager. Put the experience at the top of the heap." I'm a smart kid, and I know that experience isn't always the best card in the hand. Youth is. After all, youth rules, no old folks in the commercials.

My father's reply is muted, his words mostly inaudible through the
wall. Just one coming through: "Can't."

"Won't is more like it."

My father must be moving around the room, because suddenly I
can hear his voice clearly. "We have the rents. It'll be all right."

Adele's reaction to that is plain: "Not enough."

"We don't know that Markham will let me go. Let's not worry."

"That's all right for you to say, but I have to run this house on your
salary. It's not easy. It's never been enough. Don't you think I want a
little luxury now? A little improvement? Some of the things that I've
been putting off for years? If he lays you off, how far do you think those
rents will take us? They barely pay for the upkeep on that house. We'll
have to raise them. Bottom line. We raise the rents."

This isn't the first time I've overheard that conversation. Adele is
obsessing on what she thinks is inevitable, while my father keeps his
head buried in the sand. The discussions have moved out of their bed-
room and into the kitchen, where the staple diet of conversation is the
relentless conjecture: If Markham fires my father, how will we survive?

When Ronnie Markham began to show up at our house, my father did everything to encourage the friendship. Everything. In
the end, Markham didn't fire my father. I've never been able to
decide if it was because of Paul's friendship or my spectacularly bad
date with Ronnie that kept my father employed until retirement.

The ambulance has arrived; the flashing lights bounce off the
bedroom walls. I take Adele by the hand and drag her out of the
room so that the EMTs can transfer my father's inert body to a
stretcher. Someone is trying to extract information from Adele,
but, for once, she is silent.

28

If he's so smart, why don't you check out doing obedience with him?" Sally Perkins, Alice's coworker at the library, pushes the cartload of books to be reshelved. It's midafternoon, a slow time on a weekday, too early for the kids who come in to play computer games instead of doing their homework, too late for the senior citizens who come by the little bus; the nonworking mothers are about the only people drifting through the stacks, killing time before the little kids get off the bus, poking through the romance novels and the self-improvement books.

Alice has been telling Sally all about Buddy's spontaneous trick of standing on his hind legs and spinning. She is ahead of Sally in the stacks, straightening out the disorder of improperly shelved books. How come patrons can't put them back where they found them? The one marked 941.45 HE belongs left of 941.45 HI. Alice reverses the order of the nonfiction on the shelf. "He already knows the basics. Sit, stay, down." Buddy even heels, although she's never asked him to. Every time he performs a trick or obeys a command, Alice tries not to make too much of it. If he's this clever, someone spent a lot of time with him. And that line of thinking makes her nervous. It isn't hard to put herself in the place of whoever has lost this dog.

"Then you could go into an advanced class. It'd be fun." Sally has been a dog person all her life. Alice is discovering that a lot of her friends like to label themselves "dog person." Like Mary Jackson. Alice has known Mary all her life and knows that she's never been without a dog, but it wasn't until Alice began to talk about Buddy that Mary opened up about her beloved shih tzu, as if she was talking about her kids. Sally, too, was going on about Ralphie, her rescued pit bull. Suddenly, this common ground has added a dimension to their friendship. Or maybe filled a gap.

After it happened, Alice's friends stopped talking about their children. Alice knew that it was their way of being sensitive to her loss, and their way of keeping Alice's bad fortune away from themselves. It was something beyond trying not to remind her of what happened, as if silence would prevent her from thinking about it every minute of every day. It was also their being afraid of her, of what had happened to her, afraid that it proved that their children were vulnerable. That the worst thing *could* happen. It hadn't helped that Alice had withdrawn into herself, finding any conversation at all abrasive to her tender nerves. She did not care about the price of peas at Potter's. She couldn't raise the least bit of interest in the latest small-town scandal, when the church secretary was discovered embezzling funds to support her scratch-ticket habit. Alice found herself angry at everyone, thinking, Do they not know what has happened? How can they care about a television show or the outcome of some baseball game? For a long time, Alice resented everyone for having a life without a lost child.

"I don't know. Is anybody doing dog training around here?" Alice switches a couple of out-of-order books. "Besides, he's trained enough for us. What would be the reason?"

"Just to have fun. You could enter him in obedience shows. They earn letters, like college students earning a BA or a BS.

Dogs get a CD—companion dog—or something. Or maybe he'd be a good therapy dog. You could take him to the nursing home."

Alice imagines her silver-and-white dog resting his head on the knee of some wheelchair-bound elder, the expressive little black eyebrows making him look interested in whatever the old-ster might say. It seems like something the dog would do well. He sits with his chin on her legs all the time, those mismatched eyes studying her face, as if he expects her to do something. Alice thinks of the feel of the dog's soft fur under her hand, how easy it is to get lost in stroking him.

Sally reshelves a book from her rolling cart. "I'm thinking that I might get another dog. There are so many out there need-ing homes. What if I got another and we could go together?"

Alice pokes David McCullough into his correct space on the biographies shelf. "What would you get?"

"Probably another pit bull. Maybe a puppy rescued from that New Bedford raid."

"So you've been thinking about this?"

"No. Well, maybe. Hearing about those puppies just got me thinking. And when you got Buddy, my dog-parent juices started flowing again."

Alice takes the last book off the cart and studies it. *Merle's Door*. She tucks it under her arm; she'll take this one about an author's observations of life with his free-ranging dog home to read. She's already zipped through *Marley & Me* and is grateful that the dog she found isn't a giant slobbery Lab, but a well-mannered, dignified Shetland sheepdog. She's pored through the one book in the library about the breed and now she knows that Buddy is a blue merle and that blue eyes are common. She has confirma-tion of what she already knows: This is one smart breed of dog. One that likes to have a job.

She thinks that Sally is right: It might be fun to do something with him like obedience or therapy training. "I'll think about it. Might be fun."

When she couldn't get pregnant, Alice read every book on the topic. When she found herself a late-in-life expectant mother, she scoured every book on pregnancy. By the time Stacy was six months old, Alice didn't have the time or energy to read. After it happened, well-meaning friends foisted memoirs and essay books on her, books meant to explain the inexplicable, to make it comprehensible and maybe even acceptable. They sat piled like unused bricks on the coffee table, where she would occasionally run a dust cloth over their covers. She returned them, one by one, never saying that she hadn't read them.

29

Ed drives past the cemetery gates; from their road, it's not possible to get to the main route in Moodyville without passing this way. As he does every single time they do this, Buddy arches his neck, swivels his ears, and points his nose at the place where Alice first saw him. His mouth opens and his tongue lolls out; he pants, short intakes of breath, not like he's hot or has been running, more like a vocalization. A question: *Huh? Huh?*

Usually, Ed speeds up at this point, pressing the accelerator to kick the old Cutlass awake, but today he pulls to a stop across from the cemetery driveway. Buddy jumps from front seat to back, a blur of silver and white. He climbs over Ed and presses his front feet against the driver's side window. His excitement is obvious, and Ed can't fathom what is causing it. He opens his door and the dog leaps out, the leash whipping after him and out of Ed's reach. Thank God there are no oncoming cars. If anything happened to this dog . . . Ed cannot finish that thought. This is a bad idea and he regrets whatever impulse made him stop.

The dog is in the cemetery, coursing up and down the cracked and weedy drive. Must be squirrels, Ed thinks. The dog is mad for squirrels. But the dog doesn't run toward the tree line. He stands there, sniffing the air with an upturned snout. He tracks along the drive, going farther than Ed should let him go. For an instant, Ed is afraid that the dog will desecrate a grave, but he doesn't.

Ed leans against one of the pair of painted brick columns that flank the cemetery drive. The white paint has flaked away, leaving the bricks exposed. This old cemetery is fairly neglected; the grass gets cut, but little else is done to it. Only the more recent graves look visited. Some folks still have room in family plots owned since the eighteenth century. So many of the ancient stones are wafer-thin, like graham crackers left out in the humidity, their legends obscured by time and climate. Every Halloween, there is another one toppled. Old-fashioned angels sit in faceless guard over family plots, the history of the town in brownstone and granite. Founders and scoundrels.

A few yards further and he would come to the place he hasn't been able to bring himself to visit, the place that Alice spends too much time tending. He gets mad at her sometimes, devoting all that attention to it, as if it's a flower bed; it wasn't good for her then and it still worries him when she gets into one of those moods. It can't be healthy. He doesn't have to read a headstone to remind himself of what happened. It doesn't make him more accepting, or content, or reconciled. It just pisses him off. And Alice doesn't get that. Goddamn chrysanthemums aren't going to change things.

The dog returns to Ed, leash trailing behind, no longer excited. He sits, but his nose keeps working and his ears twist like little radar dishes. Ed needs to talk himself out of thinking that the dog is waiting for someone. Still, the dog looks disappointed. That is as clear as day.

"Time to go." Ed picks up the end of the leash.

"Watch me, Daddy!" A little girl in a polka-dot bikini, her hair long hanks of dark seaweed against her shoulders. "Watch me!" For the hun-

dredth time, Stacy launches herself off the side of the pool into the churned-up water, bobbing to the surface, laughing and grinning, proud of herself for conquering a seven-year-old's fear of submersion. She paddles to the ladder and hauls herself out, water streaming, a human naiad. She shivers and looks pale and blue-tinged in the pool lights. The vaulted ceiling of the indoor pool room at the Holiday Inn echoes with her glee. Ed knows that he should make her come out, but he doesn't.

Buddy/Mack just doesn't understand why Justine wasn't there. Ed took him there, as if he also expected that Justine would be waiting in that place to pick up the end of the leash and take him home. So why wasn't she there? Buddy/Mack doesn't have the capacity to think, Maybe next time. For him, there is no hope beyond a few minutes, a hope contrived by human action. He cannot hope that Ed will go back to the cemetery, to "there," because it's not in his power to hope. He can only expect. He has begun to expect the ride in the car to Lil's. He expects two meals a day. He expects a walk, because Alice is a creature of habit.

When Alice accidentally signals a movement—a spin or a stand, a bow or a rump wiggle—Buddy/Mack doesn't hope that she will dance with him; he expects that she will. And when she doesn't, he has to be satisfied with her laugh. Sometimes he thinks that these new people are hard of hearing. They don't understand his very simple requests, suggestions, and comments.

The good news is that lately, at night, after Alice finishes banging around in the kitchen and Ed has taken the trash out, they sit side by side on the couch so that he can lie between them. He takes turns resting his chin on their legs. First, Ed strokes him, and then, when Ed gets up to get a drink or use the bathroom, Buddy/Mack shifts over to Alice. She twiddles his ears in just the same way that Justine does, so he stays longest on her lap. They have begun talking over him. Talking about him. He hears the Buddy word over and over, sometimes with that little sound in the throat that means people are in a good mood. Once in a while, he lets them know that he's listening by thumping his tail. Ed plays with the thing that Justine calls a "clicker." Buddy/Mack doesn't know what Ed calls it, because he hasn't asked him to fetch it. If Ed had the word, the command, then he'd get a big surprise when Buddy/Mack dropped it in his hands. But Ed doesn't ask, so Buddy/Mack doesn't fetch.

Buddy/Mack stretches out between Ed and Alice; the distance between them is exactly wide enough for him to have his head on her lap and his back legs on Ed's. They've stopped talking now, but Alice's fingers still tickle the inside of his ear and Ed's hand still strokes Buddy/Mack's rump.

30

It is Stacy's birthday. It's hard to fathom, but she would have turned twenty-two today. If it hadn't happened, she would have been out of college. By now, Stacy would have had a fantastic career. She talked about becoming an archaeologist or a doctor. At ten, anything seemed possible; at thirteen, the choices were unlimited. Maybe she would have been engaged, or traveling through Europe with friends. Maybe all the things that everyone else's child accomplishes by twenty-two would have been celebrated today. Maybe fifteen wouldn't have marked the end of all dreams.

Buddy sits in what has become his place of choice, a corner of the kitchen where he's out of the way and yet able to keep his eyes on her. It's only when she's done in the kitchen, heading off to make the bed or get the laundry together, that he settles on the couch to wait for the next event. Today, he follows her to the bedroom, sits in the doorway. Alice stuffs a tissue in the pocket of her jeans. Good dog. He's watching her, little tipped ears cocked and listening as she breathes in one sigh after another. She sits on her bed and fights the urge to crawl back in, to draw the covers over her head and stare at the filtered light. Ed is out doing who knows what. Anything so as to not be in their house today. Anything to avoid her.

Maybe she should have arranged to work today, so that for a few hours she would have been forced to talk with people, hear the sound of voices other than those occupying her mind, reminding her of all that is lost. That's what she should have done, but she looked at the schedule and never thought to ask for a different one. It's hard enough on Sally to arrange the cobbled-together schedule so that everyone, part-timers and volunteers, gets what they want.

Buddy woofs softly from his place in the doorway. It's an interrogatory woof, as if to ask her, *Are we going to do anything today?* He cocks his head, clearly wondering why she is sitting there. Even the dog knows that she never sits down until the last task is done. He woofs again, this time a little more insistently, a little more *I need.*

"Do you need to go out?"

The dog responds by standing up, shaking himself from the tip of his nose to the tip of his tail. Excited by her words, he does his little two-step prance.

"Okay." Alice lets go of the blanket she's balled up into her fists. "Let's go."

You can't drive around to get away from your thoughts. They just sink in deeper, unperturbed by the need to pay attention to the road or the scenery passing by. The radio does nothing to mask the insistent thoughts, only exacerbates them with evocative music like Fauré's Requiem, and talk radio fades into background noise. But having Buddy sitting beside her in the minivan seems to help. He points the way with his nose. They pass the cemetery gates and he whimpers, but she doesn't slow down. She'll go later, deadhead the mums. It hasn't rained, so she'll give them a drink. Whisper "Happy birthday" under her breath. As usual, Ed won't go with her. He thinks she is obsessed. He's deluding himself if he thinks not seeing the grave makes one iota of difference; he can't pretend it didn't happen just because he doesn't help her plant flowers.

It's not that she even offers prayers. She just needs to have one task still connecting her to Stacy. She's not one of those parents who talk to a gravestone, pretending their child is attending their every thought, or blame minor coincidences on an angel that was once their daughter. Alice is grounded in reality. Her child is dead.

The dog trainer Sally recommended is in Amherst. It's a pretty day, and the ride up route 181 is pleasant and will take long enough that if she includes lunch at Panera, plus an hour or so poking around the JC Penney at the Hampshire Mall, this little jaunt will take up the hard part of this day. Alice has called ahead and the trainer has agreed to meet for an assessment. Kids have assessments; so, apparently, do dogs. Buddy will certainly assess at the top of the chart.

Alice finds the place after a couple of missed turns. Expecting a kennel, she is surprised to find a modest Cape-style house on a side street not far from the University of Massachusetts. No dogs bark as she and Buddy stand on the stoop, but there are the telltale flags arrayed around the tiny lot, signifying underground electric fencing to keep an animal in. She rings the doorbell twice. Finally, a woman comes to the door, a bundle of fluff cradled in the crook of her elbow.

"Come in. Don't mind the mess."

The mess seems to consist of several unoccupied dog beds and two dog crates with artistically draped scarves over the tops, as if to convert the cages into furniture. The house definitely has a thin suggestion of animal, but otherwise it is quite clean.

"Arabella. And you're Alice?" Arabella plops the ball of fluff into one of the crates. Its secret identity revealed as a tiny dog, it curls its lip at Buddy, growls once, and then curls up for a nap, exhausted by the effort.

"Yes, Alice Parmalee, and this is Buddy."

Arabella doesn't bend over to acknowledge Buddy's existence like everyone else who meets him has done. In fact, she stands quite deliberately away from him, but Alice sees that her eyes are glancing at him, assessing him.

"He's pretty. How old?"

Alice has prepared a story. "He's a rescue, an abandoned dog. We just adopted him, and the vet thinks he's no more than four. He's very smart."

"Any behavioral problems? Biting, chewing, peeing in the house?"

"No. He's very well behaved. Not one mistake."

"Then what do you want from me?"

"My friend Sally thought he should become a therapy dog."

"What do you think?"

When Buddy so clearly asked her to do something today, he was being a therapy dog, but she doesn't say that. "I think he's perfect for that. He's also got a lot of tricks."

"Maybe he could become a circus dog."

"He's certainly that. Watch." Alice flips her hand over, but the dog sits looking at her as if he's never seen that hand signal before. "Buddy, you know that that means." Alice tries again, adjusting the plane of her hand. Buddy doesn't rise to his back legs. He just shakes his head and sneezes. "Really, he does this little spin on his back legs." Alice tries again, and again the dog just sits there.

"Maybe he's being shy."

"Maybe." If he'd been a child, she would have given him the evil eye to let him know they'd be having a little discussion in the car. But he's a dog. There's nothing to discuss.

"Well, here's what I can do for you." Arabella outlines her program for developing therapy dogs, ending her spiel with her substantial fee, the amount of which drives Alice into a non-committal "We'll see." That's a lot of money for a hobby; Ed will blow a gasket. She gets into the minivan, snaps her seat belt into place. Forget Ed; if she wants to do this, she will. Ed has no right to an opinion.

Ed has spent the day making up errands. He stopped by Toolie's to see about a tune-up for the minivan. He never drives Alice's car and it's always last on his list of things with motors to tend to, but he thought of it this morning and pulled in to get an appointment. Afterward, he and Toolie, who has been his auto mechanic almost since the day Ed moved to Moodyville, shot the shit for a while. Then Ed lingered at Lil's long enough that she asked him if he wanted a lunch menu. He did.

After a BLT, Ed knows that he's out of stuff to do to keep him away from the house. The fact of his leaving Alice alone on this day doesn't escape him, and he takes the long way home with a guilty procrastination. It's just that this particular day, even more than the other anniversary, is the hardest on her, and his inability to make it better feels like a failing. Every time he's tried to distract her, or reason with her, or change Alice's focus on this day, his efforts have been met with anger and accusation and no relief for either of them. There have been years, especially the first two or three, when neither of them spoke to the other because there were only terrible words to say.

Ed knows he is avoiding the inevitable, but he takes the long way home.

The second bay of the two-car garage is empty. Ed pulls the Cutlass into its berth, shuts it off, and triggers the garage door to shut. The slow-rolling thunder of the automatic door closing behind him masks Ed's sudden weeping.

It's a brief jag, and Ed backhands the tears away, draws a long breath, and pushes open the car door, banging it, as he so often does, into the plastic Costco closet.

Seven years and uncounted sessions with grief counselors and well-meaning clergymen haven't erased the questions. Nor have they provided a good answer to the big one: Why?

Alice has left him a note and a sandwich, which Ed eats, even though he's just had a BLT at Lil's. Their bed is unmade and strangely welcoming. Ed lies down, stretching out full length on his back, staring at the ceiling with its faded water mark from the roof leak that no one can seem to fix. Alice doesn't know when she'll be back. She's got the dog and she's going to see a trainer. Ed would scoff at the idea of turning Buddy into some kind of performing bear, but the idea has gotten Alice out of the house today, and for that he's grateful. This dog has been good for her. After it happened, Alice became this shadow woman. Most days, he can only see her outline as she goes through the motions of day-to-day living. Somehow, having this dog in the house, with his needs and his antics, has begun to put color in the old Alice.

Now he's the one alone in the house. Even the sad presence of his wife is preferable to the loneliness of being in the house with only his thoughts to keep him company. As pleased as he is that the dog is with Alice on this critical day, Ed wishes the dog were here, keeping him company instead.

Ed rolls off the bed and goes into Stacy's room, which is opposite theirs. The room is filled with Stacy's things and completely devoid of life—a stage waiting for the play to begin. No, a stage after the play has ended. They have left everything as it was, just as if Stacy has walked out of the room. It is a room clearly once the domain of an adolescent girl. The Barbies have long since been packed away in the closet, instead of scattered all over the room, to be expected when a girl enters high school. Novels and poetry line the bookshelf instead of The Baby-sitter's Club. Plath, Woolf, and Shakespeare—typical reading for a girl in honors English. On the wall, a famous print depicting Ophelia floating down the stream, looking peaceful and untouched, her arms open and her gaze upward, singing. Stacy had brought that back from some school field trip to a museum.

Ed touches the trophy Stacy earned in the eighth grade for

soccer. He turns it a little, just enough to dispel the museum-quality stasis of Alice's rule over this room.

As he leaves the room, his foot hits something. Ed bends down to retrieve the dog's latest stuffed toy, a faceless teddy bear. Ed can't imagine how the dog's toy got here.

Today's go-for-a-ride took him too far from where Buddy/Mack thinks that Justine will find him. At first, he thought Alice was going to take him all the way home. They were in the car for far longer, even by a dog's reckoning, than ever before. Which might have meant it was time to go home. When they ended up at that house with the dog smells, Buddy/Mack expected that something was going to happen. Nothing did, except Alice's clumsy attempt to get him to perform. All he could think was that Alice had come to the wrong place to find Justine. It was a little like Saundra's house with her pack, but the silence was unnerving. Who had dogs that didn't welcome visitors? Finally, Alice put him back in the car and they drove home, Alice talking the whole way home, as if she was trying to convince him of something.

When they came in through the back door, Ed was there and greeted him with a long back scratch and lots of soft words spoken into his ruff. Then Ed straightened up and went to where Alice remained in the doorway. They stared at each other for a moment, long enough that Buddy/Mack got worried. They were like two stranger dogs meeting for the first time, studying each other for signs of fear or friendliness, aggression or attraction. Finally, they did something that Buddy/Mack hadn't seen them do before: They touched.

Buddy/Mack watched with careful shepherd eyes as Alice and Ed touched and stayed close for such a long time that he felt he had to interrupt. A dog needs dinner, after all.

31

If you had music, that would look a lot like dancing." Jen puts her hand out and takes the beer from her boyfriend, Derek. Jen Coulter has lived next door to the Parmalees since she was in sixth grade, and when they had Stacy, she had been their baby-sitter, practically living with them. When her parents moved to Florida, Jen, a nurse practitioner, bought their house, and she now lives there with Derek, who is beginning to look like a keeper. Stacy had outgrown needing a baby-sitter, but Jen had remained a good friend, the teenage baby-sitter growing up into a good neighbor, and she is the only friend who always remembers this difficult day. It has become a tradition, this spontaneous gathering on this particular September day. No one plans it, at least not officially. And maybe someday Jen won't come; she may forget the significance of this date and go on with her life. But it is nice when Jen calls and says, "You up for company?" And then Ed brings home a six-pack, even before he knows they will come. And Alice just happened to thaw out the roast beef she's had in the freezer for a few weeks. All the seemingly accidental decisions converge for a midweek dinner at which no one speaks of the real reason they are together. Alice is glad that she spent the day away, and just as glad she got home in time to throw the roast in.

"That's not all; watch this." Alice turns to face the dog, who is still up on his back legs. She twiddles her fingers in a rough circle and the dog spins. Then he drops to all fours, his eyes fixed on Alice, waiting for the next thing. "Now why he wouldn't do this for that dog trainer is beyond me. He was like a kid refusing to perform in front of company."

"Ed, do you have a CD player or a radio?" Jen hands the beer back to Derek.

Ed does, and he brings out the little player that he keeps in his workshop. He's pulled out a few CDs from his collection, which tends toward classic rock.

Jen flips through the selection, choosing the Beatles' "White Album." "Pop this in and find 'Ob-La-Di, Ob-La-Da.'"

Ed does, then stands back to give Alice and the dog more room on the deck. Derek holds his new iPhone in position and Ed fires up the tune.

With the catchy tune playing, the dog's motions suddenly take on a meaning. Jen is right: This dog is dancing. Alice takes him through certain moves that she has inadvertently discovered, then tries a couple more purely invented signals to see if something else will happen. At first, nothing does; the dog stops. She tries again, and suddenly he's backing up, then pivoting on his rear legs in a perfect circle. He stops, waits for more from Alice. She waves at him. He comes forward, but on his forearms, his rear end up in the air, his tail waving like a pennant in the breeze. When everyone applauds, the dog tucks one forepaw under his chest, dipping his head in a perfect courtly bow.

"Do it again, Alice. See if you can get it smoother. Derek, are you getting the video?" Jen starts shoving the deck furniture out of the shot. Someone flips on the floodlights against the growing dark.

Alice waits for the music to start. "Ready, Buddy?" She flips her hand over and Buddy repeats his first moves. For half a minute,

they perform a dance routine, the dog contributing several movements ad lib. At the end, the people all laugh and clap and the
dog barks and barks, clearly pleased with himself. Derek has
caught it on his new iPhone with its multitude of apps.

Jen and Derek leave around nine, the good-bye hugs maybe
just a little tighter, a little longer than a casual dinner among
friends might suggest. Ed and Alice stand on the front steps,
waving them off. Ed drapes an arm around Alice, squeezes her
shoulder gently. She doesn't pull away but releases a soft sigh.
Buddy/Mack pushes his way between them, fitting himself
against their legs. They stand that way, the three of them, long
after the porch light next door shuts off.

*The three of them sit at the kitchen table, a small cake laden with
sixteen candles glowing in the dimmed dining room light. Stacy stares
at those candles as if hypnotized. "Make a wish, honey." Ed has the
video camera pointed at her and they wait for the moment when
Stacy will make a wish and blow out the fifteen candles, plus one for
good luck.*

*Stacy looks up from her trance and points at Ed, who's holding the
camera. "Don't."*

Ed reluctantly lowers the video camera.

*Stacy sweeps her hair into her fist and leans toward the candles.
When she is done blowing, one candle remains lighted. She reaches
over and snuffs it out between pinched fingers.*

Buddy/Mack lies on the deck, his position sphinxlike, his attention on the distant sound of a woodpecker hammering a tree.
He'd like to see a squirrel to chase. He'd be off the deck in a split
second, in full voice, and catch it. He always expects to catch the
squirrels he chases. That's his dream.

Alice is in the house, pushing the vacuum. Ed is in the garage, doing something with the car. Buddy/Mack is enjoying a few minutes by himself. Unlike Justine, who left Buddy/Mack alone for good chunks of time, these people seem intent on keeping him company. It's not that companionship isn't nice; it's just that he can't get a full nap in. There is always someone there to stroke him, or speak to him, or make him move over; some adventure being cooked up, like go-for-a-ride or go-for-a-walk. The day-to-day activity of these humans, who continually wander around their house, needing to have an eye kept on their movements, keeps him busy. Following them as they go from bedroom to cellar to kitchen to living room is an exhausting business. He's glad Alice suggested that he wait on the deck while she uses that infernal machine, has let him go out on the deck to watch the wildlife, catch a few minutes of a nap, and expect that there might be a squirrel to chase.

Then, miraculously, there is a squirrel. It's brazenly creeping across the expanse of backyard, stopping here and there to root around for whatever it is squirrels like to find. It sits up, something in its little useful hands, then drops to the ground and continues to hunt. Buddy/Mack is on his feet, the growl rumbling in his throat, the pulse of defender of the territory pounding through the length of him; he beats a quickstep before launching himself after his nemesis. His toenails scramble against the decking, unable to gain a purchase. He flings himself toward the steps and comes to a complete choking halt. He is tied.

This has never happened to him before. No one has ever tied him up. A simple "Stay" is enough to keep even Buddy/Mack from hurtling after squirrels, even though the command is frustrating. But this, this restraint, is shameful. Buddy/Mack shakes, whines a little as the squirrel continues on its unthreatened path, then resumes his sphinx pose. But the fun has gone out of it. How do these people expect him to defend their property if he's tied, like some cur, to their deck rail? Why have they figured out the dance part of his repertory but not the simple obedience words he lives by? It's the same as when Alice takes him on a walk. He wants to tell her that he can be trusted to return to her at a call, but she won't ever let him off the leash. Off-leash work is puppy work. He's been doing it for years.

Buddy/Mack remembers that he's waiting for Justine. This is just what's happening today, this being tied business. He is waiting for Justine, but these people don't seem to understand that. Justine will tell them in their tongue language that he is not the kind of dog that is tied. He needs to get back to the cemetery gates, where he thinks that Justine will come to get him.

He is still nursing his frustration when Ed comes to the sliding door and offers to take him on go-for-a-ride. And, as he thinks every time Ed suggests a ride, Buddy/Mack hopes that the cemetery will be the destination and that Justine will be waiting for him.

32

E d sits in the Cutlass but doesn't start the car. Buddy is sitting beside him, waiting patiently for the ride to begin. Alice is doing her usual morning routine of vacuuming, something she's doing more often now that they have this furry dog living with them. He's on his way to Lil's. Again. Ed sighs. What would be the harm in changing routine today? He's already had two cups of coffee. He doesn't need a third or fourth. But what would he do? He's run out of household tasks. In the year of his unemployment, aka retirement, he's painted the trim and edged the walk, taken care of all those little jobs that had been waiting for him to have the time to attend to. Turns out, there weren't so many after all. Now he's left with puttering—cleaning out the workshop, sorting through nails and screws. He's not the kind of guy to sit around watching daytime television; he's a doer, not a sitter.

It is a crisp, clear September weekday morning and the best he has to do is sit in a coffee shop with guys he has little more in common with than their early retirement, or their living in this little town. Their allegiance to the Sox. Okay, so a few things in common, but is it enough? Ed gets out of the car. Buddy looks at him anxiously, as if to say, *What? No ride?*

"Be right back."

The dog seems to nod, but Ed knows that's just his imagination.

Ed lets himself into his workshop. The garage of the raised ranch leads directly into his work space and Alice's laundry room. The washer is beating out a rhythm as he opens the cabinet filled with his paint supplies. Ed grabs his wire brush, a whisk broom, and a dustpan and dumps them in the trunk. He has a purpose.

Buddy is furiously excited to stop at the cemetery. He's behaving like a little kid being taken to the circus, jumping from front seat to back, making this little yipping noise that almost sounds like hiccups. This time, Ed parks the car just inside the flaking pillars and lets the dog out. As he has done before, Buddy courses up and down the driveway until he collapses in the shade of the car. Overprotective Alice would be royally pissed that the dog isn't on a leash, but that's their little secret. Buddy isn't going anywhere.

Ed gets to work scraping the flaking paint from the left-hand column. He'll give Buck Franklin a call tonight and let him know that if the cemetery commissioner won't take care of this part of the cemetery, he'll be losing Ed's vote in November. The paint drifts down like lead-based snow, covering Ed's shoes and his face. His bare forearms begin to speckle. He probably should have brought a mask.

The wire brush sings its own song against the rough brick. Stacystacystacy, it whispers.

When Stacy was born, a seven-pound-four-ounce beautiful baby girl, he dreamed of those iconic father-of-a-daughter moments, teaching her to drive and walking her down the aisle. But as she grew up, he found that he got to do those things he might have expected with a son. He taught her to throw a knuckle ball, dribble a basketball, understand football strategies; how to kick a soccer ball.

"Did you have tryouts today?" Ed has seen the high school athletic department's announcement on the marquee, donated by the class of 1975, for fall sports tryouts. Stacy had been the high-point earner on her middle school soccer team, playing forward, and everyone assumes she'll be a shoo-in for the JV team now that she's in high school.

Stacy is dressed in jeans and a T-shirt, no sign of the soccer clothes that she lived in for most of middle school.

"I forgot." Stacy ladles a spoonful of chili out of the simmering pot on the stove. Alice is in the laundry room, and Ed can hear the bang, bang, bang of a sneaker in the dryer.

"How could you forget?"

"I just did. No big deal."

"Can you try out later?"

"I don't know. Maybe."

"You don't sound like this is important to you? Don't you care?"

Stacy licks the back of the spoon, focusing on anything but looking him in the eye. "I guess so."

"You guess you care? If you don't want to play, that's fine; just don't 'forget' to try out."

"I just did. People forget things. It's, like, not the end of the world."

Ed knows that he needs to back off. In a moment of sharp parental self-awareness, he wonders if it is he who wants her to be on the soccer field. He'd been a decent basketball player, and he understands the benefits of being part of a team, of being active, of being a little bit celebrated while in high school.

Ed thinks that maybe Stacy is just coming into her antijock phase, and he is mindful to let her make her own decisions. But he can't help asking the question: "Are you afraid you won't make the team?"

Stacy takes another mouthful of chili. "More like I'm afraid I will."

Ed rasps the wire brush across three courses of brick, over and over, until his right arm aches and a thin line of sweat darkens the back of his shirt. This is going to be more than a one-morning job, but Ed has plenty of time.

Finally! Finally, Ed has realized that they should wait here for Justine. Such a relief. Ed has found something to do, which seems like what this human requires for happiness—activity. But there is something about the manic way he's going about this task that keeps Buddy/Mack alert and concerned. Ed is going at the task like he's in a battle.

They are there from when the shadows cover him entirely until the shadows disappear and, even in the cool air, Buddy/Mack gets warm. He stands and shakes. Sits, watches Ed. Walks around, sniffs. He hears a squirrel and ponders the chase.

Ed finally tires of his activity and sinks down to sit with his back against the pillar he's been scrubbing so vigorously. Buddy/Mack comes over to him and sits down, happy that they both will sit here waiting for Justine.

After a few minutes, Ed gets up, complaining in tongue language as he climbs to his feet. He opens the car door. "Let's go."

Buddy/Mack's ears droop in disappointment.

Justine has still not come.

33

He's doing the same damn thing with the dog that he did with Stacy—being the fun parent, being the entertainment, monopolizing him. Arms crossed, Alice stares out the living room window, waiting for Ed to return with the dog so that she can get to his first training class on time. Ed knows she's doing this today, so why ever did he take Buddy with him?

When Stacy was born, it was a no-brainer, as they say, for Alice to quit her job as a medical secretary outright and become, at age forty, a true stay-at-home mom. Eight hours or more a day were spend being in charge, caring for their daughter, planning meals, and watching out the back window as Stacy and her pals played in the backyard; being the taxi driver and the negotiator; being disappointed when Stacy refused to go back to dancing school, and signing up for booster club when she took up soccer. And yet, when he was around, it was Ed who dazzled their daughter's eyes.

And now it's Buddy who dances and prances when Ed comes in the door.

Even before Ed shuts the car off, Alice is out the door. "I'm going to be late."

"For what?"

"His first class."

"I forgot."

Alice gets a good look at Ed as he climbs out of his car. Head to toe, he's covered in white flakes. "Is the dog as much of a mess as you are?"

Buddy jumps out of the Cutlass and stands beside Alice. His pink tongue lolls out of his mouth; it's not because he's panting, but from that happy look that he gets when both of them are there.

"Where is his leash?"

Ed doesn't answer.

Alice checks the dog over, clearly annoyed. She brushes a hand over the dog's back, clips on the requisite six-foot training leash, and points him into the open door of the minivan.

Buddy looks inordinately pleased to be asked to go for another ride.

"He might need some water before you go."

"Take him in, but hurry up. I have to get to Amherst."

Once, Ed had taken Stacy to the shoe store three-quarters of an hour before she was supposed to be at a game. Neither one of them remembered the game, and Alice was left on the sidelines, furious, apologetic when the coach came looking for his player, and, finally, worried. Eventually, they showed up, sheepish but not nearly contrite enough. That might have been when Alice insisted they invest in cell phones.

Buddy takes no time at all to lap up some water and races back to the garage to take up his place in the minivan.

"Have fun." Ed presses the button to raise the garage door for Alice.

It is suddenly too much like being a mother. Alice gets to the end of their street and has to pull off the road. It is too familiar, this going to a lesson, not quite déjà vu, but something so close to old habit that she tastes the past on her tongue. The smell of a

September Saturday afternoon, something in the way the light hits the road, and Alice is transported back to the years when she spent more time in her van, this minivan, than she did in her kitchen. The dog sneezes, and the ghost of another passenger sits behind her.

Alice reaches back and strokes the dog's head. It's a dog, a silent companion, not a child back there. They are going to a dog class, to learn how to make sick people feel better and old people happy. "Come on up." Alice pats the passenger seat. Buddy hops into it. Maybe they should invest in a dog seat belt. She puts the car in gear and pulls away from the stop sign.

Alice tries not to blame Ed anymore. She's been advised by grief counselors that blame is destructive and no one can be blamed for what happened. Still, once in a while, when memory and the scent of September air remind her of the abrupt cessation of being a mom, the mother of a living child, Alice blames Ed.

Alice emanates unhappiness and Buddy/Mack whines softly in response. In the minivan, they are divided by the center console, so he is unable to rest his head in her lap, which was a technique that always proved successful with Justine when the low scent of unhappiness radiated from her. Sometimes this would happen after she tossed her cell down hard; sometimes it would happen in the middle of the night, when he would work his way up from the end of the bed to press himself against her until her arm would go over his body and she would draw him close to her.

Alice, because she still forbids him to climb on the bed she shares with Ed, has not yet snuggled him close, but Buddy/Mack knows that if she would, she'd feel better. He's watched them as they sleep, two people with the space of a foot between them. Whenever one of them touches the other, there is a grunt or a snort and they move apart. Buddy/Mack thinks that that space between them in the bed would be just about perfect, exactly the right dimension for him to slip his body in and become the final link in the chain.

Squirrel!

Buddy/Mack sees the little rodent dash across the road in front of them. Alice slows, avoids contact. *Let me get him for you!* But Alice keeps driving, oblivious to the skilled hunter in the seat beside her. He vocalizes, not a bark, but a complaint that Alice is a lousy partner.

Alice comes to the cemetery and, lo and behold, she, too, pulls between the gates, going all the way up the drive before stopping. But she doesn't let him out of the car, even as she gets out and stands in front of one of the stones.

Buddy/Mack does bark, his place short and demanding. *Please let me out; please let me wait with you.*

Alice pauses only a moment, brushes something from the top of the stone, plucks a dead bloom from the chrysanthemums, shudders, and then gets back into the car. "What's all your noise about?" She strokes his head, nose to ears, over and over, until Buddy/Mack senses that the unhappiness has ebbed and Alice is ready to move on.

Part 3

34

I never would have pegged Adele as the stay-by-the-bedside type. They've assigned my father a bed on a quiet floor, where the only other inhabitants are several doors away from him and one another, as if making it easy on nurses isn't the plan. At this point, the doctors all seem to agree that he isn't dead, but comatose, and that he most likely won't wake up from that, but sink deeper. My stepmother can't seem to wrap her mind around the ultimate eventuality and acts like this is some sort of television drama where keeping up a constant patter of chat saves the patient. Then again, Adele, as long as I have known her, has kept up a constant patter of chat. I guess it doesn't matter if the person she's talking to is unconscious or not. I am uncharitable enough to imagine that my father is sinking faster and deeper just to get away from the persistent sound of her voice.

Any idea that this vigil is based on true affection is ludicrous. Adele is auditioning for the role of martyr. I can hear the ladies at bingo singing her praises: *She stayed by his side, la da la da, by his side, by his side, la da, la da.* I image it sung as a Strauss waltz.

Adele is so relentless in her vigil that I am stunned when she finally goes out of the room, leaving me alone with my father.

We're both a little squeamish about using the lavatory in the room, so I realize that she's gone to the public ladies' room down the end of the hall.

My father is tilted up at a slight incline, as if he might want to relax in bed and watch the news on the suspended television. I reach out and touch the undisturbed thermal blanket, which is just a little off center, gently teasing it into plumb. As I do, I feel the warmth that still radiates from his yet-living body. There is a tiny flutter of breath. I stare at him, trying hard to find something to anchor me to the moment, to the right emotion, to the *feelings* I should have. What good memory should I cast back for? What bad memory should I cast off?

I remember wandering into Adele's kitchen, to find my father staring out the window, looking across the fence to our house. It was before they got married, it must have been, because I was wearing a pair of sneakers that were too short for me; I got new ones just before the wedding day. Why this image sticks with me is because I had never seen such an expression on his face before. It was not grief, not even lingering sadness, but almost that of panicked regret.

"What's the matter, Daddy?"

"Nothing."

"What are you doing?"

"Thinking."

"About Mom?"

"I guess. Yes."

"I miss Mommy." I am still talking to his back. He rubs his face with both hands but says nothing.

"Is Adele going to be my mother?"

"Yes." His voice is raspy, as if he has a sore throat.

"Daddy, I want to go home."
"This is home now."

Another man might have reached out and hugged his daughter, but the great withdrawal had already begun. Adele walked into the room and he quickly turned around and reached for her.

I give the thermal blanket another adjustment, just to feel that he's still warm.

Adele is back, and I move away from him.

I am not staying by his bedside. I am at Paul's office, checking my e-mails. There are the usual junk e-mails, a couple of notifications that my online bill pay is about to take money out of my account, a thought that chills me to the bone until I check my bank account and see that my dear friend and boss, Candy Kane, has direct-deposited an unearned paycheck into my account. I don't normally get weepy, but that brings tears to my eyes. I fire off a thank-you e-mail with a promise to work it off. There are e-mails from Candy and Saundra with messages of hope and "Hang in there."

But there is no e-mail to say "Found your dog." I scroll down, check the junk-mail folder. I don't know why I think an e-mail will save my life, but I do, and the lack of an e-mail with that subject line is monstrously disappointing. Alerts have been posted across the country on a million Web sites devoted to lost pets, Shetland sheepdog rescues, animal rights and the like. I follow the list of links Saundra has given me, but not one has a clue as to Mack's whereabouts, only gentle, supportive comments.

Back at the hospital, Adele is still talking to my comatose father. The relentless beep of the monitor is the only thing telling me that he still lives. I watch it as if it's live television, rapt with the spikes and valleys of the constantly streaming green line. I really don't know what it means, just that as long as it maintains its steady beat, we remain here.

I've brought back lunch. Adele slides the bedside tray table away from my father, who for some reason has been given lunch, although he is clearly nonfunctioning. She looks at the ham and Swiss on rye with a little twist to her mouth. "No mayonnaise?"

"In the packets, in the bag."

"These are always so hard to open."

I take the mayonnaise and the mustard and bite into the tough plastic, ripping both open with my teeth. "Here. Squeeze."

Adele takes the packets from me like they might be contaminated, but she squeezes both condiments liberally on the bread.

We are on death watch and we eat every bite of our sandwiches.

"I've been telling your father that once he's out of here, we should be thinking about selling the house. We could move into one of those residences they built in that warehouse complex. You actually have a view of the water. The house is too much for him to keep up."

I look away from staring at the monitor. Adele is fiddling with the arrangement of covers over my father. She is telling my dying father that she has plans; that they'll take up housekeeping in an expensive retirement community when he dodges death. And then I get it. Adele knows perfectly well that she will be making that move by herself, but she doesn't want my father, if by some miracle he's still cogent beneath the surface, to think she's leaving him behind.

"If you sell your house, you'll be able to live pretty well. Or maybe sell both houses. That should keep you going for a long time." I'm just making conversation here, nothing more.

Adele purses her lips in that familiar way I remember so well from my childhood, a sour "I do this for your own good" look she'd get when she was about to impart her peculiar justice. Controlled anger. "What do you know about it?"

"What do you mean?"

"You have no idea how hard it was."

"I think I do. I fed my son oatmeal for dinner often enough."

"That was your own fault. You left home; you got pregnant and left your husband. Now you think you can swan back here and take over."

This leap from simple conversation to attack makes me think my earlier impression—that Adele was showing signs of dementia—was more accurate than mean-spirited.

"I'm not taking anything over."

"We needed those rents, Justine. We still do."

The tiny hospital room is filled with the mechanics of keeping my father alive. Adele sits at his side in the only comfortable chair. I am perched on a closed commode. The air is tainted with the scent of disinfectant and bodily functions. The single window, a solid pane of immovable glass fretted with wire, throws a glare into the room, so that the white of the thermal blanket and the white of Adele's hair appear haloed. I throw back the rolling commode and leave the room. I'm done here.

Once again, I wish that I smoked. I could join the small band of hospital employees huddled across the street, puffing on cigarettes, flicking ash into the gutter. A couple of them sip from paper cups. There's a small coffee shop halfway down the block from the hospital entrance, and I find myself jerking the door open to the sound of clanging bells. I order a large coffee to go and then wonder where I'm going. As I pay, my cell phone rings.

I wonder if my heart is going to keep leaping like this every time it does. It's Troy.

"I found him."

"Mack?" I have to lean against the faux-marble counter in order to keep on my feet. My heart bangs against my chest with an audible thump. Mack!

"No. Sorry. Rockin' Roadie. His rig blew a rod and he's been cooling his heels in Worcester for the past few days. One of my regulars was on the horn with him just this morning. Got a location, if you want it."

I will not let my optimistic mistake show. I shove too much money into the hand of the barista. I grab a small table and a napkin. "Shoot."

Troy gives me an address and simple directions to the A-1 Truck Service Center.

"Troy, did your guy mention if Artie still has my dog?"

"I would have said that first. No. Course, he didn't ask him, either, so maybe he does."

I hold back the disappointment. "I owe you, my friend."

"No biggie. Just go find him. Let me know what happens, okay?"

I know where Artie is. I'm a couple of hours away from tagging him. My only problem is, how am I going to get there?

When we took up canine freestyle, no one knew what I was talking about. Dog dancing? What, like waltzing? Like circus dogs? Then the British version of that television talent show featured a young woman with her dog, a Border collie, dancing to a James Bond theme. Even the professionally dour Simon Cowell was impressed. The video went viral and dog dancing entered the world of YouTube. Even Mack and I have made it onto the Internet. Saundra records all our competitions and demonstrations and posts the best of them. What Mack and I like to do best are the demonstrations. These usually take place during lulls in big dog shows, sort of like half-time performances. The crowd can really get into the act, clapping in time with the music, laughing, cheering us on. Mack is a real ham and loves it—the louder the crowd, the better. I'm always mindful of his dignity and will never subject him to some of the weirder costumes my peers often inflict on their dogs, especially the small dogs. Not for Mack some gold lamé outfit. With his natural silver-and-black coat, he needs only a "formal" collar that looks like a black tie. The black tie looks so snappy against his white ruff. Oh how happy he is when he sees me pull out his "tie." He wriggles and makes this little chuffing noise in his throat, telling me in no uncertain terms that he's ready to party.

Everything that has been going on around me fades into the background. I have my first real chance at recovering my dog. My dancing dog.

My mind is racing. How am I going to get to where Artie, miraculously, is held up? I have to get there now; if his truck is fixed even by this afternoon, it will be too late. I have to go now. I can make it from New Bedford to Worcester in two hours, two and a half at the worst if the Pike is backed up. It's already 1:30. He could be on the road by four o'clock. I need a car. I need to get the car keys from Adele. My heart races and my forgotten container of coffee sloshes in my hand as I race back to the hospital, where I dump it in the nearest trash can.

The visitor elevator tortures me with its slowness in arriving and with its painful floor-by-floor ascent. I should have taken the stairs. When I get to the room, Paul is there, occupying most of the rest of the available space in the room. "Paul, can you take Adele home? I need to borrow the car."

Paul turns to look at me with a crumpled face. "Justine, he's gone."

I wonder for a split second how Paul knows that Artie is gone. And then I understand what he means.

My father is dead.

I am not prepared for this. Ridiculous, I know, since it's why I'm here. But still, the fact, the hard, cold fact of his death, has stunned me. It's like being on a roller coaster. You know it's going down, and you're going to have that swooping feeling of lost gravity and maybe your breakfast rising, but you're surprised anyway. You scream. I don't scream, but I do reach for the wall to support myself as the room spins just a little. Adele and Paul step apart and I see him there: pale, waxy. The hands that once wrote sales contracts by the dozens are now stilled. Even when he was comatose, they had not seemed inert, devoid of life.

I wish, vainly, that I could be properly grief-stricken. And then I find myself weeping, and the grief is real.

Adele sits on the bed, her back to me, one hand on my father's left hand, which is free now of the web of plastic tubes. The monitor with its incessant beeping is quiet, shoved off to one side. I should have realized the minute I walked into the room that it was quiet and in that silence heard the news that Paul, with his large weeping face, has given me. But I was so noisy with my own news that I couldn't hear the silence.

Someone, a nurse maybe, or an aide, has tidied him up. Someone else, a doctor maybe, has granted "the family" permission to sit as long as we want to with the deceased. So we sit, as expected, with the fragments. Who will be the first to blink? What next? We don't speak, pretending to be contemplating the meaning of life. Praying. I should be praying for my father's soul, but I am praying that Artie stays put.

"They'll steal his clothes. Make sure that you get everything of his out of the cupboard." Adele's first concern is equally practical and offensive. Who is going to want the old man's underwear? He arrived without shoes. I want to scream at Adele, tell her to leave it all here. It's useless. Better for to it disappear than have someone take it to Goodwill. But I don't. I get up and squeeze around Paul to open the cupboard, where a blue bag hangs, containing the pitiful pajama bottoms and socks in which my father left his house for the last time. It smells.

"Can you take Adele home?" An hour has slipped by, a precious hour. If I can get on the road now, I can be back by early evening. There is nothing to be done now. The undertaker will be in soon to take the remains once we vacate the room. Adele is Paul's mother; let him deal with her. Tomorrow, we will make the arrangements. Today, I can find Mack. They won't miss me.

"Where are you going?" He is incredulous that I'd bolt now. I'm a little incredulous myself, but there's nothing I can do here, and I'm mere hours away from reclaiming my dog. If I miss this chance, I may never have another one. It's colossally bad timing, I know, but I can't help it. There's no way I'm not going to try to catch Artie.

I don't answer Paul's understandable question; it would be too hard to explain. "Please, it's important."

Finally, he nods, and I run out the door. As soon as I get to the car, I feel like the weight of darkness in my life is beginning to lighten. I am suddenly free, and if this wasn't Adele's car, I am not certain that I would turn around and come back once I find Artie and, God willing, Mack.

35

Is Andy going to be my father?" Tony is leaning into the doorway of my bedroom. He's ten years old but has the world-weary look of a thirty-year-old whose plans haven't panned out. Andy has left, dragging himself out of bed to get to work on time. He's a framer, and his day on the job starts early. We've been together for a few months, maybe half a year, and Tony likes him. He likes it when Andy pays attention to him. Maybe because Andy is still a boy himself. He's younger than I am, by a couple of years, and his sense of play hasn't been squashed entirely. Andy hooked up a PlayStation to my TV and he and Tony play for at least an hour every time Andy comes, which is getting to be more and more often. The sleeping-over part has commenced and the next step will be to move some of his stuff into my house.

I don't know how to answer Tony. This isn't the first time that he's asked that question. He asked it about Mark, and about Teddy, two guys I dated fairly seriously when Tony was much younger. Since then, he hasn't paid much attention to my boyfriends, so asking about Andy is a big deal to me. I like Andy and have a good feeling about this one. Still, Andy hasn't been making any sounds of commitment.

"I don't know, honey."

You are never truly separate from an ex; despite distance and years, you are still connected if you have a child. Even though Anthony willingly let us go, over the past few years he's taken to calling us and adding more money to the child support, even though I've never asked. He's even visited Tony twice, taking him out to dinner and letting him pick out some desirable new toy. I'm ambivalent about this contact; he's not exactly a presence in the boy's life, just an interruption. Tony doesn't call him "Dad." He doesn't call Anthony anything anymore. Long ago, he stopped asking when Daddy was going to come. Now he takes Anthony's phone calls and mumbles replies. I can't tell if there's some resentment Tony has toward his father, which would be understandable, or if it's simply that the man is more of a stranger to him than, say, Andy is at the moment. Which makes me smile. "Would you like him to be?"

Tony pushes himself away from the door frame. "No. I'm just wondering when he's going to leave."

"Why would you wonder that?"

"Because they all do."

I get a call from the school. Tony has been in a fight. I leave work to get my bruised son, mother bear furious at the other kid.

"Ms. Meade, Tony admits to starting it." The teacher, Miss Fletcher, folds her arms across her chest and turns a teacherly scowl at me and my son. "Tony can be very provoking. It's not the first time he's done this."

"Is this true?" I squat to face Tony. "That you started the fight?"

"Maybe."

"Why?"

"Dunno."

He is awfully young to be so sullen. "Tony, why did you fight with him?"

"'Cause I didn't like the way he looked at me."

The big-haired Dallas debutante teacher pipes in, as if she knows my son better than I do. "That's not a reason, and you know that, young man. Actions have consequences."

"I'll handle my own son, if you don't mind. I'm sure there was a reason he got mad. People get mad."

"People get angry, but even a child knows better than to throw punches. We use our words. We discuss our issues."

I take Tony by the hand and walk out of that classroom and out of that school.

We left Dallas and headed for Los Angeles. I had a friend we could stay with till I found a new job. Tony would start at a new school and get a fresh start, make some new friends, have another chance. Andy was gone anyway, the romance evaporating in direct contrast to my desire to move on to the next phase of the relationship. Apparently, Andy got cold feet at the thought of living with me and a ten-year-old.

I shoot up Route 24. After a clot of traffic breaks up around the Silver City Galleria, it's clear sailing to the 495 West exit. Four ninety-five opens like a smooth pathway for me; even the inevitable road construction doesn't slow me down appreciably. I feel like I'm flying. A look at the speedometer and I realize that, actually, I am. I slow it down from eighty to a more reasonable seventy-five and hope that no cop in the area will believe that a dull brown Chevy is doing ten over the speed limit. I am prepared to cry if stopped. I'm prepared to convince any trooper who might stop me that he should give me an escort all the way to Worcester—sirens blaring and lights flashing, letting everyone know they need to make way for an outraged woman.

I fluctuate between believing that Artie has kept Mack with him all this time and dread that he has no idea where the dog might be.

In what feels like a lifetime, I haven't allowed myself to think about not recovering Mack. I won't think about life without him. I will go to the ends of the earth to find him. Too many others in my life have chosen to live without me; I will not choose to live without Mack. Not when there's the slightest hope.

Mack and I are performing during the lull before best in show is judged at a benched show in Portland, Oregon. It is by far the biggest event we've been to. Saundra and some of the other members of our freestyle club are here and have already performed. Mack and I are going to premier our newest dance, choreographed to the Beatles' "Help." It is a change from "Puttin' on the Ritz" and has lots of new moves.

I come out by myself, pretending to be a lonely woman. Once the lyrics reach the words "but now I'm not so self-assured," Mack comes dashing out of the wings, prancing around me, pulling playfully at my pant legs, and leaping into the air to bounce over my bent back, portraying someone trying to cheer a friend out of a funk. It is a showy piece, featuring his high-jumping abilities and comedic skill.

The crowd loves it. Suddenly, Mack comes down a little hard on one leap. For one brief, horrible moment, I think he's injured. But within a second, Mack shakes off the pain and is watching my every signal. For first time, I wonder how long we'll be able to continue these performances. There will come a day when he'll be too old to do it. We'll have to retire. At my subtle command, my dog—my partner—rises on his hind legs and pirouettes around me in perfect clockwise rotation, a little furry ballerina. I relax. It will be a long time before we stop dancing, and only when Mack tells me he wants to.

I touch my mouth with the memory of Mack's happy jumps. I miss him so much. In my life, he is the only one who hasn't let me down.

Los Angeles was pretty good for a while. I had a nice job at a health-care center, where I did patient intake. I liked it, a first for me. Tony entered junior high there. He seemed to like school, had a few friends he hung around with, boys from around the neighborhood where I had found us a small place to rent, a neighborhood that edged up close to South L.A.

"Mrs. Meade, we found your son with three other boys and a bottle of vodka." The principal is a burly guy, Hispanic, and fighting hard to keep an unruly school population in check. He uses the words "zero tolerance" like a cudgel. My pubescent boy is being suspended.

"It's Ms., not Mrs. What am I supposed to do?"

"He'll have to keep up with his schoolwork. His teachers will give you what you need."

"I mean, what do I do to prevent this from happening again?"

Mr. Chavez just looks at me, a flicker of something that might be sympathy in his eyes. "Keep him away from those boys, first. Second, keep him busy. Third, you might want to see about counseling. I wish I could say that this is a boyish experiment, but there have been other incidents, as you know."

I do know. The fights, the inappropriate language, getting caught smoking in the boys' lav; the bad grades, which weren't a result of not understanding the material, but of failing to do the homework. It's overwhelming. I have to work; I can't be on him every second. Besides, that never worked for me, so why would it work for Tony? He's my baby, my only family, and lately he's become a stranger to me. Secretive, rude. I feel the tears working their way into my eyes, but I won't let them come. "I'll take care of it."

I've reached the MassPike and I am impatient as the tollbooth attendant languidly passes out tickets to the five cars ahead of me.

I wish that the car had a FastLane transponder so that I wouldn't have to stop again, just glide through the exit at Worcester and catch up to Artie. Immediately after getting on the Pike, I pull off at the Westboro service center to pee and to call the truck-repair place. I'll ask them to keep Artie there. Bladder empty, phone in hand, I am ready to confront Artie Schmidt.

As soon as I punch in the telephone number that Troy has given me, I suddenly wonder if this is a good idea. I'd like to know if Artie's still there, but what if they tip him off that I'm coming and he bolts? In the end, I snap my phone shut. A quick study of the napkin with the scrawled directions and I'm fairly confident that I can find A-1 Truck Service. It's just off Exit 11. Bang a right, a left, and then take the next right. It's bound to be easy, so that all these big rigs can locate it without any trouble; there's probably one of those huge signs visible from the highway. On the road, I dig out the money needed for the toll and drive with it gripped in one hand. I can't waste any more time.

We left California when Tony was thirteen, ending up in Kanab, Utah, on the promise of a hotel manager's job in what turned out to be a seedy, run-down motel on the main drag. The first thing I did was to move us out of the manager's pitiful accommodations and into an apartment. In all our moving around, this was by far the nicest place we'd ever lived. Instead of renting a furnished place, I found an empty two-bedroom apartment on the third floor of a Victorian house complete with gingerbread and a circular turret. The bulge of that turret was our living room and we looked out toward the mountains that rose like protection around us. I slowly filled the place with secondhand but decent furniture, some of it donated by our landlords.

Marta and Henry Sanchez were the grandparents Tony had never had. He spent more time in their kitchen than in ours, sampling Marta's cooking—tamales, chimichangas, homemade red and green sauces. We spent Thanksgiving with them, and popped in for Christmas Eve eggnog. Henry taught Tony how to drive a nail and change the oil in a car. Marta simply loved him.

It wasn't the job of my dreams, but moving to Kanab put the brakes on Tony's bad behavior. Maybe time would have done that, but Kanab and the Sanchez couple were good for him.

Things went much better in Kanab, until I had an offer I couldn't turn down.

36

"You should have seen him. Arabella thinks that he can get his therapy dog certification in four weeks. He's a natural." Alice is gushing and she knows it, but this half hour of dog training has pumped her up. She drapes the leash over the peg beside the back door.

"Well, we know he's a smart boy." Ed is scrambling Buddy's fur with both hands, all the way up and down the dog's body. Loose hair floats into the air, but Alice doesn't mind.

"Once he has that, we can take him to the nursing home a couple of times a week. The residents love having animals come because it makes them feel at home and not so alone."

"You can practice on your mother." Ed has finished mussing up the dog's coat. Buddy has flopped onto the floor beside Ed's chair. "She'll love that." He suddenly realizes that Alice has said "we."

"Not a bad idea." Alice drops into a kitchen chair, runs a hand along a spray of loose hair, and tucks it into her twist. "How about a cup of tea?"

"Sounds good." He's still pondering her use of the plural pronoun. Alice hasn't included him in anything more than obligatory family gatherings in years. Slip or significant?

Alice leans across the table. "I think that this is going to be a good thing. Having Buddy is a good thing."

Ed reaches across the table and extracts one of Alice's hands. "I'm glad we decided to keep him."

Alice keeps her hand in Ed's, squeezing his fingers a little. Significant.

Buddy slowly rolls over onto his back, stretching his forelegs and hind legs in opposite directions, so that he looks elongated. He doesn't wriggle, but lies still, flat on his back. He lifts his head, looks at them, as if to make sure they notice, and then flops back, all crocodile sunbathing in the Nile.

"I think he wants a belly rub." Alice takes her hand away from Ed.

Ed slides off his worn slipper and starts rubbing the dog's exposed belly with his toes. The dog wriggles with pleasure. "So, do you want to walk him over to your mother's in a bit, let him practice his therapy?" He is warm from the experience of holding Alice's hand, an action so out of character that he is nearly embarrassed. His wanting to take it, and the equally surprising fact that she let him, has infused Ed like a tea bag in hot water. Not a sexual response, but a thawing. Ed keeps rubbing Buddy's belly, keeps his eyes on the dog, but he is acutely aware of Alice in the room, the soft squeak of her sneakers on the kitchen floor, the opening of the refrigerator door. It's almost like someone from his past is visiting. Ed shakes off the notion. It's just Alice.

Alice leans over Ed to place a mug of tea in front of him. As she does, Ed recognizes the visitor. It is cheer. Alice is relaxed and cheerful. Her dark shadow is, for a little while, gone. Buddy stands up and shakes, tap-dances a little. Ed contemplates the tea bag in his mug. Alice sits down, pushes a plate of Pepperidge Farm cookies toward him. She's still talking about the dog class. She's repeating herself, going on about Buddy's cleverness, aptitude.

Ed looks up from his mug and smiles at his wife. She is beautiful.

The dog sits; then, having realized that the people are going to stay put in the same room for a little while, he gets up and goes into the living room to jump up on the couch. Ed dunks his tea bag and then drops it back into the mug. "Buddy, come here."

The dog bounds into the kitchen, fully ready to take on whatever challenge or treat Ed is thinking of.

"Sit."

Buddy does.

"What's the command?"

"Arabella asks for 'greet.'"

Ed taps Alice's knee. "Buddy, greet."

Buddy rests his head on Alice's knee, raises his eyes to her face. Ed watches—not the dog, but the woman. There it is. The look that has eluded him for seven years. The look on Alice's face that means she's moving ahead. Not happiness—neither one of them is allowed that again—but some measure of contentment.

"Good boy." Ed lifts the dog into his arms and buries his face in his ruff. "Good boy."

This new work is fun, but certainly not demanding. The woman Alice calls Arabella clearly understands about command and patience. But all of the commands are puppy commands: sit, stay, down. Buddy/Mack executes them in an offhand manner and then looks at Alice for a more challenging set of commands. Then there is something new—well, not new, but a variation on a puppy task. Sit quietly with chin on knee. No sniffing, no licking, no wriggling. The old person they are asking him to do this with gently strokes him on the head. So, big deal. When are they going to let him leap or spin, even climb up the ramp he sees in the corner of the small yard? Buddy/Mack feels like a professional being asked to begin over at the elementary level. He sighs, adds a little variation of his own. One little white paw extends and joins his chin on the old person's knee. The people around him seemed pleased with that. He lifts his eyes to the face of the old person, sets his ears back in passive greeting. Everyone pets him. "Good boy!" they say.

Alice is clearly pleased with him and praises him for ordinary behavior all the way home. The unhappiness that she had emanated earlier is gone and she is singing along with the radio. In the dog's eyes, Alice is lighter.

It's nice to be in partnership again with someone. But if this primary training is the limit of what Alice wants to do with him, he's disappointed. He's already shown her how to dance; why doesn't she want to do that? For such a simple act, which he would do without command, Buddy/Mack is given the kind of praise that only Justine has ever given him. Not the praise of food, or "Attaboy," but the praise of connection.

Ed has signaled that he is ready to partner up. Hanging out with him isn't the same thing as partnering. Ed has been a good host, but now it feels like he's ready to connect. Alice has long since done that, so it is nice to think that if Ed is equally on board, Buddy/Mack may find it easier to get the two of them into the same room. Already they're in the kitchen together for a longer period of time than to eat, and together they took him to an older person's home to work on his "greet" skills. Sweet. They are doing more tongue language that isn't directed at him, although he hears this word *Buddy* frequently enough that he knows they are talking about him. He likes the sound of Ed's soft, rumbly voice, which he has been using at night when they climb into the bed. Alice doesn't always talk then, but sometimes she sighs or laughs in response to something Ed has said. Last night, they invited him into the bed. He burrowed into the space between them, feeling the double weight of their arms over him. It was nice to be invited, but he only stayed till they slept. He heads back into the living room to stretch out on the couch—the better to keep an ear out for trespassers.

Buddy/Mack knows that he is no longer a guest. He is now responsible for the safety of this place.

He is their Buddy.

37

J en Coulter is at the door, a basket of late-season vegetables
over one arm, a bottle of wine in the other. "I can't stand any
more squash. You have to eat these or throw them out when I'm
not looking." She puts the basket on the counter beside the sink
and hands Alice the bottle of wine. "Somebody at work gave
Derek a ticket to the Sox, so he's in Boston and won't be home
till midnight. Thought we could both use a little company."

Jen knows that Ed's out tonight at the semimonthly zoning
board meeting, vainly attempting to preserve the rules without
giving into the variances that are beginning to change the face
of their town. Jen is young enough to think that Alice would
prefer company over a solitary evening at home watching her favorite shows without argument. The new television season is
about to begin and she was really looking forward to it. Alice
smiles at Jen and takes the bottle of wine, wishing that she had
one of those DVR things that would allow her to stop time.

"Have you looked at the YouTube clip yet?"

Alice is hunting down the corkscrew. "What YouTube clip?"

"Of you and the dog dancing. Derek posted it on the Internet. All of our friends are raving about it and it's gone viral."

Alice finds the corkscrew and brings down two wineglasses.

"So you're saying that the whole world can watch me being foolish."

Jen takes the opener, digs the tip of the screw into the soft cork of the bottle, drawing it out with a soft pop. "It's not foolish; it's great. Pour us some wine and then we can go look at it on your computer."

"I'm not sure I like the idea of being on the Web."

Jen just laughs, as if Alice is hopelessly naïve. Sometimes Jen feels like a peer, and at other times, like right now, Alice feels the generation gap and remembers that she's old enough to be Jen's mother. More than old enough. Jen's mom and she are exactly the same age. If she'd had Stacy earlier, Stacy would have been Jen's friend, not her charge. One of the maybes that tortured Alice was the fact that she was forty when Stacy was born. Just as Stacy entered a very difficult adolescence, she'd reached menopause. Ed called it "menopause meets puberty—clash of the hormones," but the strength, patience, and flexibility Stacy had needed was subsumed by hot flashes and irritation. Maybe if she hadn't felt so edgy and overwhelmed by her own physical changes, she would have been more aware of Stacy's own difficulties. Difficulties that weren't obvious to the naked eye, beyond her physical changes. Taller, but not tall; built like a soccer player, then suddenly thin as a reed. Silent, not quiet. A new tendency to insomnia.

"Jen's a nurse, Alice. She knows what she's talking about." Ed paces in front of her. It is a beautiful Saturday afternoon and Stacy is in her bedroom, the door shut, not even the sound of music leaking out from under the locked door. Sleeping, or crying—they can't tell which. "She thinks that we should take her to someone who can help figure out why she's so unhappy."

"She's a kid, Ed. An adolescent. They invented angst." Another hot

flash is beginning to rise up out of her core, flushing her cheeks and making her want to throw off her clothes and run out into the chill March air.

"This is different and you know it." This is classic Ed, the authority, the knower of all things. The insister.

"See, here it is." Jen has booted up their PC and signed into her YouTube account.

Alice watches herself and Buddy dance right there on the little screen. He looks so happy, and his soft grey-and-white coat with its wash of black sparkles in the floodlights of their deck. Derek had even gotten a good shot of Buddy's odd blue and brown eyes. The dog pirouettes, dips, and bows. Alice is charmed, and pleased that she doesn't look entirely foolish. She actually looks fairly good. The clip lasts little more than a minute, so they play it again.

"Let's get you set up with your own account and then you can look at this anytime. We posted it so anyone can see it. Just search for 'dancing dog.' There are a lot of them—you wouldn't believe it—but his is popping up almost at the top. You can save it to your account."

"Ed will love this." Alice sips at her glass of wine and replays the video one more time. The Beatles music is going to be stuck in her head for hours, but it's such fun watching the dog's antics. Jen is right; there is a whole strip of thumbnails offering dog-dancing videos. The still photo in one of them even looks like Buddy, except that he's wearing a little black bow tie.

Alice lets Jen set up the account. Maybe tonight, if Ed doesn't get home too late, she'll play it for him.

38

It's almost like a noir movie. There's been an accident, and two miles from the Westboro plaza the cars are stopped dead in the water. Or maybe it's road construction. Whatever it is, I crawl along the center lane like a wounded ant. My heart is pumping as if I'm running a half marathon, but the speedometer reads fifteen miles per hour/ten miles/five miles/fifteen miles per hour. I begin to worry that Adele's car might overheat. God only knows the last time it was serviced.

I feel the panic rise in my throat in the same way a nightmare about being late or not finding a door or running away from something bad will choke you until you wake up and realize it's only a dream. Except that this isn't only a dream. Every inch I crawl along the MassPike is one inch closer to Artie. But it's only an inch and time is going by. I'm already at least a half hour later than I hoped to be. I had hoped to be standing in front of Artie this very minute. How long before his truck is fixed and he's back on the road? How late is A-1 Truck Service open? It's already past four. I should be there. I could be mere miles away from getting Mack back and still miss him because of this mess.

This is torture. I am running in molasses; every step of the way is barricaded or delayed, thwarted. I feel like God is laughing at me. Or maybe mad at me. Is this some kind of divine retribution for loving a dog more than almost any human? For running out on Adele and Paul; for leaving an hour after my father has died?

I'm going slowly enough that I consider hitting that call button. The number for A-1 is still on the screen. One push and I can reach them and ask if Artie is still there, beg them not to tell him I'm coming. Appeal to the stranger on the other end of the line, saying that they need to keep Artie where he is. Strangers have been helping me all along—Mitch, Tyler the car-rental kid, Troy. I just need one more savior. Then, for no apparent reason, the traffic picks up and I'm back up to seventy-five.

The one blessing is that the A-1 Truck Service center is easy to find. Detached rigs fill the parking lot, and the noise coming from the three monumental bays is deafening with the roar of diesel engines being gunned. I squeeze Adele's car between two trucks like a slice of ham between bulky rolls. I leave everything in the car except the keys, which I pocket. I want my hands free. I take a quick look around the parking lot of waiting behemoths and don't spot Artie's truck. I don't know whether this is good or bad, but it leaves me with one last hope that one of the rigs currently occupying the garage has to be his.

I walk slowly past the open doors. A sleek black truck is in the first bay. A dented red dump truck is in the second. The third bay contains a green rig with its hood yawning open. I have only to walk in to be able to read the lettering on the door. I can see the Washington State tag on the front. I walk in, ignoring the sign forbidding anyone but personnel to enter. Arthur B. Schmidt Trucking. I quickly jump up on the running board and haul the door open, squeezing my eyes shut in a frantic prayer.

The cab is empty. No Mack. I even call his name, but I know

even before opening the door that he's not in there. If he was anywhere around, I'd hear his joyful bark. He'd know instantly that I was here. That I'd finally found him.

I am suddenly very thirsty, parched. My tongue sticks to the roof of my mouth. Confrontation does this to me. I am going to kill Artie Schmidt.

"Can I help you?" The voice is clearly annoyed at finding an interloper in his secure manly space. I turn to face a barrel-chested guy in a smoke-gray uniform with the name Al stitched over the A-1 emblem. There is a line of grease on his face that makes me think of war paint.

"I'm looking for the owner of this truck." I shut the door and place a hand on the fender, as if I think this guy won't understand which truck I'm talking about.

"He's in the lounge. Over there." The mechanic jabs a finger toward a glass wall. I can see the backs of heads as the room's three occupants sit in a line of chairs facing a big-screen TV that's tuned to ESPN. There's a baseball game on. I think it's clever that A-1 faces its customers away from watching what's happening with their trucks, mesmerizing them with the lure of big heads on bigger screens. Each one of the lounge sitters wears a cap. They sit apart, like strangers in an airport, one or two chairs between them. From behind, I can't tell which one is Artie.

"Thank you." I start toward the glass wall.

"You get in through the office." Al nods at a metal door at the far end of the garage.

I feel his eyes on me as I walk to the door. I throw a little sashay into my walk. I might need this guy if Artie gets nasty.

I have imagined this moment for a week. I have pictured myself grabbing Artie by his filthy shirt and shaking him like Mack shakes a rag doll. I've pictured myself screaming at him, calling him foul names, even slugging him. I've imagined him defiant, aggressive. What I haven't pictured is the sheer surprise on his pug face when I suddenly reappear in his life. The entrance to the lounge puts me exactly in his sight line. At first, he looks at me as men often do, with that "Well, well, what have we here?" look of a man who has no idea how unattractive he is. Then he recognizes me. Then his expression drains from recognition to realization. Here in the flesh is the woman he abandoned on an Ohio highway, the woman whose dog he stole. Artie looks right and left at the two guys in the room with him, as if looking for back up in a shoot-out at the O.K. Corral. They are also looking at me, but their interest fades as something important happens on the muted television. They cheer, throwing themselves out of the plastic chairs. Artie and I face each other.

"Hello, Artie."

"Justine. Hi. How are you?" Artie sweeps off his gimme cap and squeezes it between his hands. I feel like I'm looking at an actor portraying an embarrassed man. But Artie's color deepens, going from his normal gray pallor to the color of meat that's gone bad.

"Where is my dog?" I have gone from sweating with anxiety to feeling ice-cold. The room, even on this September day, is air-conditioned. But it's more than that; I am solid with the ice of fear, fear that he's about to say something that will wreck me.

Behind me, the silent television no longer holds the interest of the other two men. Suddenly, Artie and I are of interest.

"How'd you find me?"

"Where is Mack? Just tell me."

"Tell her, man. What'd you do?" These two strangers get off their chairs and flank Artie. I manage a grateful smile at both of them, a nod to their chivalry.

"I don't know. I don't know where he is. He, uh, ran away." Artie keeps looking behind me, as if I might have a Hell's Angel tagging along.

These two strangers, one a little older than a boy, the other a man old enough to be my father, step closer to Artie.

"That's crap, Artie, and you know it. What have you done with my dog?"

"You're the guy, the guy who ditched a woman and stole her dog." The younger guy points a finger at Artie. He looks back at me, looking for confirmation. "Is he?"

I'm surprised beyond words to hear my story come out of the mouth of a stranger. Then I get it. "Yes, this is Rockin' Roadie." My story has been traveling from CB to CB all around the state.

"What'd you do with her dog?" The older trucker drops a meaty hand on Artie's shoulder, clenches his fist, and Artie winces like the victim of a Vulcan pinch.

"Get off me; I'll have you arrested for assault." Artie squirms, but the big guy doesn't let go.

"Where's the dog?"

It seems like such a simple question. But Artie is clearly unwilling or incapable of answering it. If I wasn't so angry, I could almost feel sorry for him as the guy continues to trap him between his fingers. When tears actually come to Artie's eyes, I call him off. "Enough, please. It's okay. Let him go."

The older man drops his hand reluctantly, clearly not pleased to be stopped. He has the look of a dad whose daughter's boyfriend has broken her heart. A man bent on exacting payment.

Artie grabs his shoulder and rubs it. "Look, I don't know where he ended up, but I left him near Exit Eight—eastbound."

"Oh my God, you left him on the side of the MassPike?" The ice unblocks from my veins and the heat of despair causes me to break out in a sweat. How would my dog survive that? A loose animal on that major highway is doomed. Driving here today, I have seen the carcasses littering the shoulder—raccoons, a fox, lost pets. I can't breathe.

"You shit for brains. Why'd you do something like that?" The younger guy raises his fists but doesn't step any closer to Artie.

Artie fixes his eyes on me, all indignant. "Your goon

threatened me. If the dog wasn't with me, they couldn't prove anything."

"They who?"

"You know." Artie drops his voice to a whisper. "The Hell's Angels."

"If you'd answered your phone even once when I was trying to reach you, he wouldn't have had to threaten you." Clearly Mitch's voice-mail message had an effect.

"I didn't know I had the dog. Honest. When I finally saw him, we were already into Massachusetts. What was I going to do? Turn around? I had a delivery." Artie slaps his cap back on his head. He looks at the other two truckers for understanding, for sympathy, or empathy, or whichever one it is that will make him feel like he didn't do a stupid, cruel thing. He gets nothing.

"You fuckin' left a woman alone at a rest stop and then think it's okay to toss a dog out onto a highway?" Young Trucker is up in Artie's face now and Old Trucker does nothing to back him off. I am so weak at the knees, I sink onto one of the orange plastic chairs. I put my head between my legs. I am either going to pass out or throw up.

"What are you going to say to this lady? Huh? What have you got to say, mister?" Young Trucker takes on the school bully persona that is at odds with a rather baby face. He's probably had to kick ass more than once to prove his masculinity. He jabs Artie in the chest with a slim, clean finger. Old Trucker stands behind Artie so that he can't back away.

I need to stop this. "Thanks, both of you. He's told me enough. There's nothing else he can say." I really don't care if this kid beats the crap out of Artie; I just need to think for a few minutes. Neither one of them backs down. I can nearly smell the testosterone emanating from two guys who see a chance to blow off some steam.

"What kind of asshole are you to ditch this woman and

dump her dog?" Clearly, Artie hasn't answered this question to the satisfaction of Young Trucker.

"She was making me late. You know what that's like, keeping to schedule. And I didn't know her goddamned dog was in the backseat—where he didn't belong." Artie raises his own finger now, waving it in the kid's face.

"Arthur Schmidt? Your truck's ready." Al's sudden appearance at the doorway to the lounge snaps all of us out of the drama.

Both of my knights step away from Artie, letting him take the invoice out of Al's hand. Al looks at all of us, shrugs, and leaves the lounge. As long as Artie pays his bill, it's nothing to Al if three strangers gang up on him.

Old Trucker is still behind Artie and now he leans in so that his mouth is next to Artie's right ear. "What are you going to do to make this right?"

"What can I do? I don't know where her frickin' dog is. What am I supposed to do?"

Old Trucker smacks Artie against the back of his head, tipping his dirty cap forward. "Apologize, you shitwad."

I could almost laugh. Almost. The look on Artie's face is priceless, but it isn't the price I want him to pay. For what he's done to me, there is no price. Apologizing can't bring Mack back to me. And I highly doubt that Artie has the capability of apologizing with any sincerity, or any true sense of being in the wrong.

Nonetheless, Artie pulls his cap off his head and nods. "Justine, I am truly sorry for leaving you behind. But you—" Another smack from Old Trucker stops his feeble attempt to pin the blame on me. "I'm sorry."

"I don't care that you left me behind. I do care that you were so cruel to my dog. An innocent animal. Why didn't you—" This time I'm cut off.

"There weren't a lot of choices out there. If I'd missed my

deadline again, that would be the last time my agent was gonna get me work. It was my last chance."

"Then why not just hang on to him? Take him to Boston with you. Make your deadline. Then call me to come get him." I am suddenly gasping for breath, as if I have asthma. "Why didn't you just answer the phone and we could have straightened this all out?"

Artie squeezes the bill of his cap and then replaces it on his head. "Didn't think of it. I have to go. See you around."

He almost gets away, but one look from me and my two new friends block his way. "Is there something you'd like us to do, ma'am?" The older guy meets my eye; then the pair of them take Artie by either arm. We all look through the glass to the garage to make sure we're unobserved.

"I can do it myself." I punch Artie in the gut with all the force of my anger and grief for my dog. The two let go and he drops to his knees.

"One thing's for certain, Artie Schmidt. Don't you ever show your face in Candy's Place ever again."

Artie leans on one of the plastic chairs to get to his feet. This time, Old Trucker and Young Trucker let Artie leave the room. They drift back to watching the ball game and I stand at the glass wall, watching as Artie makes it back to his truck. Then I remember something. I race back to the bay.

"Wait." I run to the right side of the truck and swing open the door, climbing up on the running board to get inside. I find what I'm looking for easily. Mack's collar is caught in my sleeping bag. I retrieve my last connection to Mack. The feel of his leather collar in my hand pushes a new surge of anger and despair through me. My dog was abandoned on the highway.

Artie has climbed into his seat and is staring at me, as if he half-expects I'm going to stay in the cab.

"You never fulfilled your promise. You took my money and

dropped me. The way I see it, you got me only halfway to where I was going, so you should give me back half the money."

"You know I don't have it, or didn't you just see me pay Al?"

I don't have my knights with me, so I end negotiations. "You are a piece of work. Get out of my sight."

I stand aside as Artie guns the big engine and laboriously emerges from the open bay. Cranking through the gears, he makes his way to the exit and pulls away.

I need to get back on the road. Paul and Adele will be gnashing their teeth at my absence. I'm sure they'll want her car back sooner rather than later. But there is something else I need to do. Before I pull out from between the rigs, I call Tony. He's never met this grandfather, but he needs to know that he's lost one.

Typically, his phone goes to voice mail. Is this the kind of message you leave on voice mail? In this case, it is. "Tony, your grandfather died today. Peacefully, I think. I don't know the plans yet, but I guess I'll be heading home soon."

I should point this car west. But I don't have my duffel, and I don't relish being accused of being a car thief. I find the eastbound Pike entrance and collect my ticket. Even before I reach sixty-five miles per hour, I have to pull over onto the shoulder. Cars whiz by me and Adele's car is shaken by the backwash of a semi like a mini earthquake. How in God's name could Mack have survived this?

I am awash in tears, snot runs down my nose, and I bury my head in my arms, hoping that no well-meaning Samaritan knocks on my window. What would I say? As a human being, I should say that I'm crying for my father, for his merciful death. But I'm not weeping for that. I am weeping for Mack, for his loss, for imaging the worst death right here on this road.

The car rocks violently with the rush of traffic. I have no tissue and I'm reduced to using my sleeve to wipe up the mess. I fumble in Adele's glove compartment and find some Kleenex. I am choking on the fear that my dancing dog is dancing in heaven.

39

Alice paces past the breakfront cupboard with the old video-tapes, waiting for Ed to get home, impatient. She can't wait to show Ed the YouTube video of Buddy and her dancing. His meeting seems to be taking a long time, or maybe it's always this late and she's never been awake to notice. She knows that sometimes he goes out with one of the other board members for a quick beer. He never used to do that, back when he was working, but now, without an early get-up, he can. He creeps in as if he won't disturb her if he's tiptoeing, which, of course, only disturbs her more. He tries so hard not disturb her, awake or asleep.

In the little video, Derek has caught Ed watching her dance with the dog. His expression is so unguarded, so full of the laughter that they never seem to enjoy with each other anymore. This dog has made them both laugh.

Jen has gone home, leaving the squash on Alice's counter. Buddy, after having escorted Jen to the door like a polite host, curled up on the couch, looking at her with one eye, as if to say, *Come sit with me.* Alice did and flipped on the television just in time to catch the end of her program. Now the news is on and she watches the murder and mayhem channel with scant attention.

Suddenly, Buddy's head goes up, moments before Alice hears the garage door rumble open. He jumps down and stretches, bowing deeply, his tail swishing over his back. He goes to the stairs leading to the basement level and sits, waiting for Ed to appear. Alice stands behind him, one hand tucking loose strands of hair up into her knot.

Ed comes up the stairs quietly, head down, shoes off. He looks tired, Alice thinks. It must have been a tough meeting. Buddy runs down the stairs to meet him, and Ed, not seeing her there, bends to accept the dog's greeting, muttering soft words into Buddy's ears. The weariness lifts. Is there no greeting more perfect than that of man and dog?

Then he looks up and sees her standing there. "Oh, I didn't expect you to still be up." Maybe there is a more perfect greeting— that of man to wife after a hard meeting. Ed swoops the dog into his arms and comes up the short flight of steps, then second-guesses his pleasure in seeing her waiting up for him. "Is there something wrong?"

"No. No. I have something to show you." Alice feels like a kid, wanting to show a parent a new trick. *Look what I can do.* Like Stacy learning to ride her bike, or maybe more like when she learned to whistle.

They sit side by side in front of the computer. Alice logs on to her brand-new account and asks for "dancing dog" in the search bar. "Watch this." They wait while the array of dog-dancing clips load. There's Buddy, a little triangle placed over his body for her to click on. "Jen's so smart with these things. But, really, it isn't hard. Now watch."

The tiny square opens up to reveal their dog bowing and crawling, leaping and pirouetting. Dancing for all he's worth, his open mouth so much like he's smiling, keeping uncanny time to the Beatles' music.

Ed and Alice sit still. He's dancing to "Help"; he's dancing with someone else.

"That's not Buddy." Ed pushes away from the computer. "Obviously similar, but not our dog. Where's the clip with our dog?"

"I'm sorry, I thought it would be the first one." Alice slides the cursor down the array and finds the one she knows is theirs. "I guess he's not the only Sheltie who likes to dance."

"Some coincidence." Ed has his hand on Buddy's head, cupping the narrow skull with his whole hand. "Just find the right one. I'm beat."

This time Alice has the right clip. She plays it twice for them and they both laugh where they should at the sight of Alice and Buddy performing their impromptu pas de deux, but underneath the enjoyment is the thought of another dog, so similar, doing the same thing.

"That's wonderful. Really neat." He logs out of the program and shuts down the computer. "Well, time for this one to go out."

Alone in the third bedroom, still in front of the computer, Alice hears the slider open as they go outside. She worries that Ed won't have leashed Buddy. She worries that he'll dash off after some night creature and disappear. In a moment, she hears the slider open, listens to Ed talking to Buddy and the distinct sound of the clip end of the leash banging against the wall as Ed hangs it up. She lets out the breath she's been holding.

40

Alice is at the library and Ed is left at home. It's raining, which is a good thing, as it's been a very dry month so far. Still, it keeps him inside, bumbling around the house, looking for a task that will occupy him. He wants to get back to wire-brushing the cemetery gates, but that will have to wait. Buddy patiently follows Ed around the house: down into the basement to get a screwdriver, back upstairs to fiddle with the loose door-knob, back down into the garage to pull a fresh box of crackers out of the Costco closet, upstairs to make lunch, then into the third bedroom, where the computer lives.

Ed boots it up and finds YouTube on the Web. He doesn't even log on to Alice's new account, just types in "dog dancing," and public videos crop up, a long line of "dancing" titles, including theirs: "Dog Dancing with Buddy." Ed is annoyed at Jen for not safeguarding their privacy and keeping this one-and-a-half-minute clip inaccessible. The nerve. These kids nowadays think that everything should be out there, available to all. The fact that it pops up almost at the top just means that more people will see it. But Ed isn't looking for Buddy's clip. He scrolls down slowly until he comes to the image of the other Sheltie.

The light from the monitor glows like a lamp in the rain-gloomy room. This is a neutral space. A bed is set up for the rare overnight visitor, but otherwise it serves, as it always has done, as a sewing room, a computer room, a room where they keep off-season clothing in the good-size closet. North-facing, it is never as bright as the other bedrooms. Because they have this room, they never had to change a thing in Stacy's room. All the bits and pieces that belonged to her that had drifted into other parts of the house have long since been moved back to her room. The torn athletic shorts, now mended, are in the bureau drawer. All the tiny patterns Alice used to make toddler clothes and the remnants of homemade Halloween costumes are all packed away. There is nothing of their daughter in any room except her own.

They called it "depression." A common-enough word. A meteorological word, a financial word. An emotional word. Apparently, a treatable word with the right drugs. Drugs for a child.

Drugs that came with a booklet of contraindications.

Ed clicks on the image of the dog that looks like Buddy. A showy announcer's voice booms, "Introducing Justine Meade and her wonder dog, Maksim." At first, there's only the woman, a tall, lithe-looking woman dressed in a stretchy white suit with sequins sparkling in the lights. The Beatles' familiar song "Help" begins and she mimics loneliness. Suddenly, the dog, her dog, races into the spotlight and teases her into action. He leaps and spins and literally sails up and over her back. At the end, the announcer repeats their names: "Justine Meade of Seattle, Washington, and her Sheltie, Maksim. Good job, Justine and Mack!"

Buddy is sitting behind Ed, looking every bit like he wants to watch this video, too. His ears are on the alert and he keeps his eye on Ed, waiting for some signal, waiting for some action. Ed looks at the still image of the dancing Sheltie. Both of the dog's eyes are visible. Unmistakable.

"Mack?"

Mack hears his name and cocks his head. He knows this word. This is so exciting. Finally, this guy remembers what to call him. Mack jumps to his feet and barks a short, sharp yap, just to say, *Yessss!* Spontaneously, he spins around, pivoting on his back legs. He barks again. *Woohoo!*

Then Ed says something else, using the *Buddy* word this time. Mack doesn't understand what he says, but he hears the grief in the saying of it, which stops his barking and spinning. He flops onto the carpet, down but keeping his eyes on Ed. He's not sure what Ed wants. A good dog, he focuses on the man's face and waits for clarity. For a long moment, nothing happens except that Ed's head is down and his hands are clasped together between his knees.

Suddenly, Ed rolls the desk chair away from the computer table and calls the dog over. Buddy jumps up from his self-imposed down-stay and snuggles up between Ed's knees, happy to have the back scratch, hoping that maybe they'll go someplace. But Ed's touch feels unhappy. Buddy presses himself closer.

When Ed gets up, Buddy follows him out of the spare room and down the stairs to the garage. Excited, anticipating a ride in the car, Buddy makes a little chortling sound, encouraging Ed to get a move on. Maybe just a quick run to Potter's for jerky, or another ride to Lil's. It doesn't really matter; a ride is just fun. Ed lets Buddy into the Cutlass and the dog assumes his shotgun position, ready to navigate. Ready to do this job that Ed has given him, to be a good passenger and point out squirrels. He swings a look in Ed's direction. *Ready? Let's go!* Finally the rumble of the garage door signals departure. Ed starts the car and backs out of the garage. He hasn't said a word, not the *Buddy* word or the *Mack* one since leaving the spare room, but now Ed begins to talk. Ed uses another word; his monologue is laced with it until Buddy gives up trying to figure out if it's meant as a command or a praise word; a random vocalization or a human word not meant for canine comprehension. *Stacy.* Buddy doesn't know what Ed is saying, but he grasps what he needs to do.

Buddy moves from his shotgun position to the middle of the front seat, scooting his rump over so that it touches Ed's hip. Ed wraps his right arm around the dog. He keeps talking, his voice streaming out a story that even a dog can understand, because he's felt the same way.

Lost.

41

The rain is slackening off, and Ed kicks the wipers back to
intermittent. He has no idea where he's going, a fact that
bothers him. He wasn't brought up to do meaningless things.
Every car trip must have a purpose; every man feeds his family.
The weight of his unemployment, call it that, a more accurate
name for early retirement, feels like shame. Even in the darkest
days after Stacy's death, he had his job, his work to retreat into.
Retreating from Alice, from her unassailable grief. He grieved,
too, but Alice's grief was like a mushroom cloud, obscuring and
consuming. He might have believed that she loved her grief. So
he worked. He kept his distance. He allowed his own sorrow to
form a thick scar of manliness. No one ever asked him how he
was doing, patted his hand or his back. The workers in his plant
did treat him with a softer deference for a few months, but then
they allowed him to master his tragedy.

"So, where're we going, Buddy?" Ed pulls gently on the dog's
ear.

The dog sighs, a rattling exhalation. He seems to sense Ed's
distress and leans against him as if to help shoulder the burden
of his thoughts.

"I know where."

The rain has stopped completely as Ed reaches the old pistol factory ruins. A rude parking lot has developed alongside the road, where fishermen and hikers leave their cars. Shattered glass, cigarette butts, and soggy beech leaves litter the stony turnout. The place is empty right now, midday, a school day, a workday. He and Buddy are the only souls there. Ed realizes that he has no leash; he's left the house in such a hurry, he's forgotten it. Rather than chance the dog's getting hit by an oncoming car, Ed takes him into his arms and carries him across the road to the ruins. The dog doesn't even squirm, but he does lick Ed's nose, as if to say, *This is cool.*

The brick facade of the pistol factory is intact, although all the windows are gone and the interior has been gutted over the past hundred years. Rumors at the zoning meeting last night suggest that some developer has a plan to buy the place and turn it into something. Someone said condominiums; someone else had heard shops. Locals chuckled at the notion that anyone would buy a condo in Moodyville, much less draw the traffic that would support a bunch of chichi shops. Ed would love to see it purchased by a small manufacturer and have it restored back to its original purpose. Maybe not pistols, but certainly something could be produced here. The place still has good bones.

Ed sets Buddy down and he and the dog climb down the steep stairs to the apron that runs around the building to the millpond and the steps that lead to the old path. Immediately, the dog sets about squirrel hunting. "You already scared them off." He pats his thigh and the dog comes bounding back. "Stick close. It can be dangerous here."

The millpond is low, a good foot beneath the lip of the dam, as the dry summer has depleted the dammed river of its volume. It halfheartedly escapes through one open sluice gate. Today's rain has given the usually placid surface a little motion, and leaves float like little empty boats, ganging up where the unseen force of the thwarted river pushes them against the stones.

Ed hasn't been here for seven years.

Ed stares down into the bronze-colored water of the mill-pond. The power of the moving water to make the shaft work is in the flowing of it into the waterwheel, long since gone. Only the real old-timers remember when it was there, and even then just a broken vestige of industry.

Five feet deep. A mere five feet of accumulated river water, and all the power of strategically released water moves the wheel. Five feet. Deep enough to swim in. Deep enough to keep the trout alive. Deep enough if your pockets are full of rocks.

Moodyville doesn't have a police force. When emergencies happen, car crashes and the like, the resident state trooper does what is necessary. A 911 call will get the volunteer fire department out, and the EMTs. Neighbors. Colleagues. When a fisherman who was hoping only to catch a fish on opening day snagged his line and discovered the drowned body of a young girl, it was left to the resident trooper, arriving after the fire department and the EMTs, to make the unhappy connection between the girl in the pond and the parents who had made the missing-person call two days earlier. The fire department lieutenant and the driver of the town ambulance looked each other in the eye and were glad that they, who know the Parmalees well, wouldn't have to make that visit. No one wants to bring that kind of news into a neighbor's house.

They think that she's run away. Unlike many parents who would default to a belief that their daughter has been abducted, Ed and Alice both know that this is Stacy's doing. Although there is no note, no missing items—not even her stuffed rabbit, which, even at her age, she still clings to—they know that there is no outside force. When she was a little girl, maybe five, she decided to run away and got as far as the end of the road before turning back, informing her parents that she had decided not to run away that day after all. Alice, who had watched her march down the road, her stuffed rabbit tucked under one arm and her Barbie backpack bouncing against her little bum, thought that the few minutes it took for Stacy to "run away" felt as long as the time it had taken for her to take her first breath; it felt similar, the wait for the breath of life, or for the childish threat to resolve. Would she take that first gasp of air? How long to wait before running after her?

Stacy has seemed so much brighter in the past month. She has smiled more, listened to more cheerful music, spent more time with them at the dinner table. She even went to a sleepover. Ed has begun to relax, thinking that if things continue to improve, it will just prove that he was right to insist on her taking this course of medication. He has been collecting the evidence of Stacy's being more like herself, like the self they understand, to show for his bold defiance of his wife. This running away is a mistake, a misunderstanding. They know that the antidepressants can cause odd behavior as a side effect. They call her cell phone and it rings in her empty bedroom. They call all her friends, but no one has seen her. Her bike is in the garage. Her purse is on the counter.

And then the resident trooper, Trooper Rossman, is at their front door. He is the same trooper who took their missing-person report, asking questions about Stacy's friends and whether they thought she took drugs.

"Antidepressants." Alice spit the word out, and Ed knew that however this ended, he might never be forgiven.

Ed had insisted that they follow doctor's recommendations and put Stacy on the antidepressants. The side effects were simple legal jargon to cover the pharmaceutical company's liability. "We have to try. She needs a little help so that the counseling can help."

"No." Being her mother, Alice had known that this was a bad idea. Stacy didn't want to take them, and Alice stood by her right to defend

her daughter's decision. She wasn't a little child; she was a young woman who knew her own mind.

Overruled.

Trooper Rossman holds his hat is in his hands now. Uncovered, he looks younger, more human. Regretful.

It is an April afternoon, the sun just sliding behind the hills to the west. The air is fresh but damp; rain is imminent—the first of the April showers. Alice is standing behind Ed as he lets the trooper into the house. Ed knows he is letting death in. By opening the door, death is invited in. He should have shut the door and barricaded it with his shoulder.

They don't go into the living room this time; for some reason, Ed leads them into the kitchen, where he gestures for the trooper to sit at the table. He then holds a chair for Alice. She doesn't look at him as she sits. She has barely spoken. The prescription bottle is on the counter, its label facing the wall.

Alice says nothing as Rossman gently breaks the news of finding Stacy in the pond.

"But I went to the pond. She wasn't there." Ed isn't calling the man a liar, just mistaken. "How could I not have seen her?"

"She was under the water."

Ed has to ask if it was an accident, and the need to ask that question reveals his deepest fear. "She fell in? How?"

"There will be an investigation."

"But you think that it was"—Ed hits upon a word he can't utter—"not an accident?"

"As I said, there will be an investigation." Rossman has set his trooper's hat on the empty chair at the table and he touches it gently on the crown. "I have to ask. Is there a note?" He asked this before, when Stacy was simply a missing person. This time, it is less of a question and more of a demand for a piece of evidence.

Ed remembers the warning on the bottle: Thoughts of suicide may increase when first taking this medication.

Alice stares at the trooper, great tears running unchecked down her cheeks, into the grooves that have appeared at the corners of her mouth; she makes no noise, makes no attempt to wipe them away. It is as if she has no idea that she is crying.

Trooper Rossman stands up and gathers his hat to his chest. "Mr. and Mrs. Parmalee, I am sorry for your loss."

Ed sees the trooper out. He turns to take Alice in his arms and is met with a flat-handed slap.

"I never want you to touch me again."

Buddy whizzes past Ed at a dead run, the lure of low-hanging squirrels too much for him. Suddenly, the dog finds himself perched on the lip of the dam. Daintily, he travels the edge like a gymnast on a balance beam, moving skillfully away from Ed, toward the opposite bank of the pond.

"Buddy!" Ed watches the dog disappear into the woods. "Goddamn it! Buddy!" He's going to have a heart attack right here and now. "Buddy! Come!" He tries to whistle, but his mouth is too dry. He claps and calls, shouting the dog's name. He's never not come before. Every time Ed has let him off the leash, in defiance of Alice's overprotectiveness, the dog has come like a shot at his call. Now the only sound is the brush beneath the trees rustling as the dog moves away from him. Ed braces himself against his knees and fights a surge of panic. He's been their dog for only a little while. What if he's running away from them? "Buddy!"

Then the dog is back on the dam, trotting along the six-inch-wide coaming as unconcernedly as a high-wire walker on pavement. He sees Ed and picks up the pace.

"Easy, slow down." Just as the dog reaches Ed, who is kneeling on the rain-slick cement of the abutment, his hind foot slips on a scattering of wet leaves and suddenly he is scrambling. Ed reaches out and grabs the dog by the ruff.

"Sweet Jesus, I thought I'd lost you."

42

I make it back to Adele's house, only to find it empty. She's probably at Paul's. That makes sense. Why would she come back to this empty place, be here alone with me? There's a newspaper on the front walk, and I pause for a moment after retrieving it to contemplate the triple-decker next door, the house that I once lived in. If Adele meant what she said about going into that retirement community, it could be sold fairly soon if she wants to convert it into liquid assets. Or maybe the rents will offset the expense of senior housing and she'll hang on to it.

Lights are on in all three flats, diffused through drawn curtains or lowered blinds. Even in the murky half-light of dusk, the place looks in need of paint and a little TLC. It occurs to me that I lived in that house almost exactly as long as I lived in Adele's—nine years. I haven't been inside since the day we moved out, so I still picture the living room walls as mint green and cream, the shag rug a blend of olive and russet fibers. Hideous by today's standards, but what I remember fondly.

A welcome thought rattles through me: I am free. With my father's passing, I no longer have any connection to Adele Rose. As cut off as I have been, there has always been this lingering attachment I could never quite break free from. As long as my father was alive, there was communication, however sparse. Like being called here to attend him like some unpaid nurse. A Christmas card with a twenty-five-dollar check in it, signed by Adele. That will stop now.

The door of the first-floor flat opens and a woman comes out. She's carrying a casserole dish and she heads right for me. I don't know her, but she's dressed in a tracksuit that emphasizes her ampleness, big hair caught up in a topknot, Crocs on her feet. She is comfortingly like the women I knew growing up, big and generous, a little loud but kind. I can smell the cigarette smoke on her.

"Are you Justine?"

"Yes."

"I heard about your dad. I'm so sorry. I made you this." My new friend hands me the still-warm casserole. I can smell tuna and cheese, and suddenly I'm so hungry, I could sit down and eat all of it.

"Thank you so much. I think Adele is at Paul's. Do you mind if I take your dish there?"

"Not at all. Just leave the dish on the porch when you're through with it. Don't even wash it."

"What's your name?"

"I'm Diane Santos. We've lived in that house for ten years. Your dad was so good to us. I'm going to miss him." Unbelievably, she actually tears up, adding to my impression that she, like so many of the women I knew around here, keeps her emotions handy.

"I don't know what the arrangements are yet, but please come if you can."

She presses a hand to my hand. "I will. And if there's anything . . ."

"I'll let you know."

Diane leaves me standing on the walk with the warm casserole in my hands. She turns and waves as she goes back into her house, into the very apartment I once lived in with two parents. I'm almost tempted to ask if I can go inside, see if there is anything there that will give me one more memory of my early life.

I walk inside and put the casserole on the counter. The delicious and familiar odor of my favorite comfort food wafts up, and I yank open the silverware drawer and pull out a fork. I'll just have a little. I'm still buzzed from the long drive and from my encounter with Artie. I can't keep the image of my dog dead on the side of the road out of my mind. I need a moment to regroup before heading over to Paul's and the fresh drama that awaits me. I have no doubt that they will be royally pissed that I disappeared for half the day on the day that my father died.

I take a bite of the tuna noodle casserole. It's every bit as good as it smells and brings me back to Tony as a little boy, when I made it for him. He would never let me use egg noodles, like Diane has, always ziti. He had his little-boy rigidness about certain things—what kind of pasta constituted macaroni and cheese, and what kind was meant for tuna casserole. Wheat bread was verboten; only squishy white bread would suffice for PB&J. I wonder if he's listened to my message about my father. Does he ever listen to my messages?

Tony was almost sixteen when I announced that I was moving us to Washington State. It wasn't an arbitrary decision; it was a fantastic opportunity. I'd been seeing a guy who was opening a new high-end restaurant. When he offered me the chance to be his manager, with a salary and benefits, I thought that it sounded wonderful. Greg was offering stability, even a career. I was still young enough to believe that there were good opportunities left in the world and that taking them was the important part. Better to try and fail than never to try at all. That's what I said to Tony.

"Fail at what? Another 'relationship'?" This from my teenager, sarcasm complete with air quotes.

"It's not about a 'relationship,' it's about being in at the ground floor on a successful business." I imitate his flippant gesture and use air quotes. "Greg's a nice guy, but this isn't romantic . Greg is a good businessman and this is a good opportunity for us."

"No. I won't go. Enough is enough. This is the longest we've ever lived anywhere and I like it here."

"I understand, honey; moving isn't easy. But this is a fantastic opportunity."

"It's always a fantastic opportunity. Or a fantastic new guy. When are you ever going to be satisfied?"

I am speechless, then angry. "You don't get to decide what's best for this family. I do."

"And you think pursuing this newest crazy idea of yours is the best thing? You'll keep moving because you can't just accept that this is the best it ever gets. A place, a job, nice neighbors. That's all life is really made up of."

"I'm your sole support, and I need to have the best job I can get."

"With the newest best guy?"

"This is not about Greg."

"Then who is it about?"

"You."

"It's never been about me, Mom. Even moving here was about that great job you were going to have."

I pace the arc of the turret six times, my fists clenched so tight that I leave nail marks in my palms. "You're grounded." A mother's weakest weapon. He is way out of bounds here. Every move we've made has been to better his life.

"Can't you at least wait until I graduate? Then we can move. You can move." His voice is still unreliable and he croaks on those words.

"Discussion over."

Tony draws himself up to full height, shocking me with the fact *that he is close to six feet tall. He runs a hand through his thick, dark hair in a gesture so like his father's that I have to blink hard to dispel the notion that Anthony is standing there. "I'm not going."*

"Of course you are. You're my son."

"Mr. and Mrs. Sanchez will let me stay with them until I graduate."

"I don't think that Marta and Henry are willing or able to take on a teenage boy." I take another lap of the turret. "It's a ridiculous notion."

"No, it's not. Ask Mrs. S. She'll tell you."

"Why do you think they'd be willing to do this for you?"

Tony actually blushes, the roses against his olive skin making him look equally child and grown man. Petulance and desire. "They know about all our constant moving. Ten places since I was three years old. They know that's not good. That you'll just keep moving me until I . . ."

"What? Until you what?" I should remind him that the last two moves were a partially a result of his own behavior, but some things are unfair when wielded by a parent.

"Leave home."

I take a deep breath. This is nothing more than a half-grown child's fantasy of "I'll run away and show you." I know about that fantasy. Oh yes, I do.

Tony stands before me, a perfect model of anguished youth. He isn't crying, but his mouth forms a thin line of holding back—holding back tears, or holding back very angry words; I'm not sure which. It's like watching two entities struggling to form a single unit, the blur of the child he has been, the one I know so well, and the overlay of this almost adult, this man-child who is a stranger to me. We face each other, a gap of five feet between us. My maternal instincts are to go hug him, tell him everything will be all right, that he just has to trust me. Then the shadow of the child is gone and I see the future man standing in front of me. Not quite fully formed, but no longer a boy.

"Mom, I just can't keep living like this." Tears slide out from under his lashes. He makes no move to acknowledge them, just lets them drift

down until they meet the scruff of beard on his adolescent cheeks and vanish.

It is a crystal moment. I have exactly two choices: move to Seattle and take a great job, or stay put for another three years and wait for another golden opportunity to break out of the shit-job rail that I am riding. I'm thirty-six, and I feel as if life is beginning to run dry on good opportunities for me. Greg offers the best yet. Besides, Seattle is a great place, filled with opportunities for a young man—good schools, new friends, the music scene.

I know that Tony has good friends here, a world of difference from his L.A. friends; he's even joined the baseball team. He hasn't been in one fight, has even made the honor roll. But I need something, too. I need a better job than managing a flophouse of a motel.

Tony will just have to suck it up.

"We're moving."

"How can you not understand what I'm saying?"

"I do. You don't want to move again. I understand that. But we have to take chances."

"Three more years, Mom, that's all I'm asking."

"I don't have three more years."

"Then you don't have me."

I finish off another big bite of the casserole and cover it up. Time to go.

Paul lives in Fairhaven, over the Acushnet River from New Bedford and off of route 240. He's managed, on an accountant's salary, to buy a house with a water view. It's a tiny house, to be sure, someone's summer cottage tarted up, but from his back deck, you catch a glimpse of the Acushnet and the New Bedford waterfront on the opposite shore. Once inside, I can't imagine how he raised his two huge children in this space. His wife, Melanie, greets me with great sympathy, assuming that I am devastated. She, too, has grown large since the last time I saw her—at their wedding. But her largeness suits her, and she wears it with pride. She keeps hold of my hand as she pilots me through the living room and into the dining room, where she finds space for the deflowered casserole among the massive collection of platters and dishes, remnants of pies, and salads.

"Adele's resting now. If you want to go look in on her . . ." Melanie says this without irony.

"That's okay. Let her rest. Where's Paul?"

"Outside. Eat something!"

I don't, but I do grab a chilled bottle of Sam Adams and head out to the deck, where Paul and a host of other men have congregated, much like this is Super Bowl Sunday and not a sad occasion. They're laughing, until they realize who I am. I have no idea who these people are, but they murmur appropriate sentiments: "Sorry for your loss." I keep thinking that they mean Mack. I'm sure that they think that the very real grief on my face is attributable to the human loss and natural filial feelings.

If only they knew that I lost my father years ago. That loss is hardened into my bones. I murmur my appropriate responses. Paul plays host and starts introducing them to me. I shake hands and smile and keep the urge to howl at bay. I take a quick sip of the beer, tell myself I need to behave like a grown-up, thank them for their kindness in being on Paul's deck on a weeknight.

"You remember Ron Markham?"

Nearly thirty years changes a man. Changes a boy into a man. Changes sleek and Greek into a schlub. This Ronnie Markham is soft-faced; a ring of untidy brown hair frames a bald head, and his eyebrows are trying to make up for the loss. He sports a bristly mustache and looks the part of a used-car salesman to a T. His hands are feminine, small and soft as he takes my unoffered hand in his. He freaking pats it. "Justine, I'm so sorry about your dad. He was always one of our best people."

"Right." I extract my hand from his. Markham's best.

I am so excited, as only a girl can be whose dream guy has suddenly woken up from his obliviousness and seen her for a desirable woman. Golden boy, king of the football field, legendary Ronnie Markham is taking me out. It is one of the few times I can remember Adele smiling at me with genuine pleasure, as if I have turned from straw into gold. My dating Ronnie Markham is clearly a feather in her social cap.

I dress with such excited panic. Is the floral dress with the outsize shoulder pads the best thing? I decide that I shouldn't be too dressy. I pull on my black leggings and fashionably droopy boat-neck top. Using electric rollers, I curl my hair, and tease my bangs into a lofty height. Ron, a little early, is in the kitchen, drinking Coke with Paul. I walk into the room and, oh Lord, he stands up, like a gentleman caller, and helps me into my fake-leather bomber jacket. I hope that my deodorant does its job and I'm not going to embarrass myself with wet circles under my perspiring armpits. I am so nervous.

When Ronnie asked me out, it was an afterthought. "Hey, Justine, want to go out sometime?"

I looked at Paul, standing beside Ronnie, absolutely sure this was a joke. When Paul didn't burst into laughter, I nodded. "Yeah. Sure."

"You look beautiful." Ronnie sounds sincere, although I catch a half smile on Paul's face, just like he's in on a joke. I wait half a beat, fully expecting that Ronnie and Paul will pull the plug on this charade.

"You two kids have a nice time." Paul slaps Ron on the back and waves as we walk to Ron's car, which is parked at the curb. Predictably, his car is a brand-new Chevy Camaro with all the bells and whistles, a throaty muscle car. Ronnie pulls away from the curb like he's launching a rocket.

"I thought we'd go to the Pizza Palace and then maybe take a drive."

My hands are clasped between my knees so that Ron can't see how nervous I am. "That's sounds nice." Anything sounds nice. I've never been out with a college boy before, and I suppose that Ron won't be interested in the usual stuff of high school dates, McDonald's and the Game Room. The very fact that this isn't a double date seems so sophisticated to me, but on the other hand, I wish that I had a friend with me, someone who would be a witness to my success, or failure. Someone I could go home with at the end of the date and analyze every word and gesture for deeper meaning.

Ron has a lot of his father's car salesman charm and keeps the conversation in the restaurant going single-handedly against my tongue-tied hero worship. He talks about his athletic achievements at college. That topic moves easily into his academic stardom. In the end, he isn't a whole lot different from the other boys I date. As long as I keep nodding and smiling, he keeps talking.

I begin to relax a little, the glow of his aura dimming enough that I can actually look across the table at him. I sit up a little straighter, hoping that someone, anyone, will come in and see me, Justine Meade, sitting here alone with Ronnie Markham. For once in my life, I'm glad to be popular Paul Rose's stepsister.

Later, we drive around a bit aimlessly until we get to the beach, stopping at a point that is a popular make-out spot, especially in the warm weather, when a blanket and the sand behind the dunes make a perfect nest. The engine pings softly as we sit there looking out over the water through the broad windshield of the car.

"Your brother's a great guy."

This seems like a strange statement to make, sitting, as we are, in the most popular make-out spot in New Bedford.

"He's all right." I'm hardly going to complain about Paul tonight.

"He convinced me to take you out."

I felt like I'd been kicked. "Figures. What did he promise you?"

"Doesn't matter. The point is, I like you. I'm glad I did."

"I don't need Paul to get me dates."

"No, you don't. I was blind. Paul opened my eyes."

It is just warm enough to be outside, so Ron pops the trunk, extracting a blanket and a six-pack. We lie back on our elbows, drinking the beer, pretending to be fascinated with the stars. The beer isn't cold and tastes like metallic water, but I sip from the can as if I enjoy it. A shooting star streaks across the sky.

"Oh! Look at that. Make a wish!" I point skyward, wishing my own wish.

Ronnie pats my knee, then rubs my back.

My star wish was that he'd kiss me. When he doesn't, I kiss him.

I will always admit that I made the first move. But Ronnie Markham took things too far.

Ron Markham, not Ronnie, leans close to my ear now. The impression of softness disappears. "Did you know that your father came to me? Privately."

"No."

"Your father was a pretty big guy back then. I was taller, but he got me by the shirt and slammed me into a wall and told me in no uncertain terms that I'd better stay away from you. I told him the truth, that nothing had happened."

"What do you mean, nothing happened? Something did happen. You wouldn't stop when I asked you to."

"I did stop before anything happened. But I was turned on and didn't behave like a gentleman. I took advantage of your age, but your brother said . . ."

"What?"

"That you would. You know. Once I realized you wouldn't, I stopped. Don't you remember?"

I remember the feel of his mouth all over me, the weight of his hands on my skin after he'd managed to pull my shirt off. I remember tugging at my clothes, desperate to cover myself, the damp night air chilling me, and then walking to his car with his arm around my shoulder as if I needed help. I have zeroed out the rest.

I sat that night in the kitchen. I was sobbing. "Paul set me up." Paul had slunk off as soon as I walked in the door, my artfully arranged hair tangled and my *Flashdance* top stretched askew, my mascara streaked. He'd taken one look at what he'd done and fled.

"He told Ronnie he could have me."

"Shut up." Adele stalks over to me. "He did nothing of the sort. You dress like a tramp, you get treated like a tramp."

"I'll have a talk with the boy." My father stands in the archway of the dining room. "With Ronnie."

"You will not." Adele grabs the back of my head, twisting my face toward my father. "Are you willing to sacrifice your job for her?"

It was his silence that I took for betrayal. He wouldn't stand up to her, not then, not ever.

In all this, I have never thought about Ron Markham. It's always been my father's sin of failure to stand up for me that I've remembered with such pain. Now here is the man, the grown-up version of the boy who almost got my virginity. Never did I imagine that he, of all people, would be the one to tell me my father had stood up for me after all.

At this point, Paul has literally shouldered us off the deck and into the empty yard. I know that the people on the deck, and by now there are several wives out there, can hear every word. I'm not raising my voice, but the evening has become foggy and the fog acts like a band shell.

Out of the fog I hear her voice.

Marriage, motherhood, divorce; reinventing myself every few years, living through 9/11 and two Iraq wars, even at that, the sight of Adele Rose Meade standing on that deck, looking down on me, scares the shit out of me. In a curious way, the deck floodlights illumine her and her only; the rest of the audience, Greek chorus now, have faded into the shadows. I feel myself shrinking.

"Justine. You need to come in." The transformation is complete. I am ten.

"Mrs. Meade, give us a minute." Ron doesn't touch me, but I follow him a few steps away from the deck, deeper into the wet grass and the fog, mostly out of earshot. I wonder if this is a good idea. Not that I imagine he'll touch me. It just looks compromising, and I have an idea that his wife—surely there is one—is not going to understand this.

"Whatever happened that night, I want you to know that I am truly sorry. A boy looks at these things differently. Not that I'm saying it was right, or acceptable, but I'm sorry."

This is so unexpected. An apology. From Ron. But it's not the one I wanted.

Suddenly, it hits me: The reason my father never apologized is because he had nothing to apologize for. Tears build in the corner of my eyes.

"Thank you."

I have this strange sense of being like a creature that molts its skin; what has held me together cracks open and I feel my life slide out, fresh. Ron Markham, in clumsy fashion, has offered me closure.

"Justine?" Adele's voice fades into the mist. A ghostly sound, meaningless.

"Puttin' on the Ritz" jangles on my cell phone, startling us both. It gives Ron an exit and he disappears into the fog, leaving me alone at the edge of the yard. Crickets are all wound up, droning their September song as I look at the display. It's Mitch, my one-legged violinist. I take three rings to collect myself, to find the voice that won't sound cloudy with emotion.

"Hey, Mitch."

"How's it going?"

We sound like two adolescents with nothing much to say.

"My father passed today, so we're at my stepbrother's, eating."

"My condolences."

"It's fine."

If only my father had said something to me, just let me know that he had taken take my side, even if I was the only one to know it. It's too late. It's like trying to turn the *Titanic* to give up my hardened sense of injustice. "The funeral's on Saturday. Then I guess I'll head home."

Just saying that pains me. I tell Mitch about finding Artie, about how Artie's scared to death that the Hell's Angels are on his trail. For a split second, I wonder if Mitch will think I blame him for what Artie's done. I don't, not really. I don't mention socking Artie in the gut, but I do tell him about the truckers. And then the threatened tears win the battle and I sob into the phone that my dog is most likely dead on the MassPike.

"Justine, maybe not. This may sound weird, but I think I saw your dog on Facebook."

"It's probably one that Saundra put up. We're in a lot of her YouTube clips." I don't want an image of Mack; I want Mack.

"Except that the woman with the dog isn't you."

This stops me. I knuckle away the tears. "What?"

"I've sent you the link. You just look at it and see for yourself."

"Mack isn't the only dancing Sheltie." I can't allow myself false hope.

"I'm not asking you to get your hopes up, but don't you want to see this?"

There is a moment of silence between Cleveland and here and I hear the Vineyard ferry horn blasting. Mitch doesn't want me to get my hopes up, but he offers me hope by telling me that someone is dancing with my dog?

If Mitch is right, that this online Sheltie is Mack, somehow safe, it means that I can't leave until I exhaust every avenue in finding him. I don't know how long Candy will keep my job open, but I've quit plenty of jobs for far less compelling reasons.

"A silver-and-black Sheltie, big white ruff, one blue eye, one brown?"

"Justine, go look at the video."

The consoling crowd has thinned out. Two of the men who were on the deck with Paul turn out to be my nephews. They call me "Aunt Justine," as if we have blood in common. They call my father "Grandpa."

"Do you guys have a computer I can use? I need to check my e-mail."

Ryan, the elder one, shows me to his bedroom, where he has a laptop. He opens it up for me and kindly leaves me to it. The room looks tidied for company, but the odor is pure man-boy, and I inhale it with a certain nostalgia. A sock pokes out from under the bed, a grayish white tongue licking the floor. I picture Melanie racing around, trying to get the place in order, never having planned on entertaining on a weeknight. Even an expected death comes unexpectedly.

I open the e-mail from firstchairharleyplayer. "I hope this is your dog."

I click on the link, hoping, too, that it is my dog.

I watch the short clip, my hand over my mouth, trying not to cry out. The sound quality is poor, the image a little jiggly, but "Ob-La-Di, Ob-La-Da" distinct as Mack does his routine. I can tell he's improvising; the woman with him isn't giving him any good hand signals, but he has figured out enough of them to know what she wants. He is that smart. Then I hear a name, Alice. "Keep going, Alice." Is that enough to be able to find my dog? A woman named Alice is dancing with him? Then I hear a second name, Buddy. That's what she's calling him. It is Mack. Even though there are plenty of blue merle Shelties in the world, only this one is mine. Unmistakable.

The relief acts like a drug, and I start shaking, my hands trembling so much that I have a hard time texting Mitch to let him know he's right. I can't talk now; I have to process this flicker of hope.

"You okay, Aunt Justine?" Ryan is standing in the doorway.

"I am." Or very nearly.

43

Officer Rossman sits in their kitchen like some malevolent spirit, a tight frown on his face, as if he's practiced giving bad news and knows the right facial expression. There is something wrong with her hearing; Alice can only hear phrases coming out of his mouth, not full sentences, not complete thoughts. "There will be an investigation." "The medical examiner. . . ."

She is aware of a sound like the susurration of the ocean. It's been a long time since they went to the shore; maybe this summer they'll rent a place on Cape Cod. The susurration begins to hiss and build, until what's in her ears is a roar. Her own heartbeat, her own blood pounding up and through her brain, clouding the words coming out of Rossman's mouth, obscuring the meaning until it breaks free of his mouth and penetrates her soul.

Stacy is dead.

This is Ed's fault.

"Hey, Alice."

Alice is furiously vacuuming again.

"Alice, put that thing away and come with me." Ed was on

his way to Lil's when he changed his mind. Buddy is in the Cutlass, waiting for his daily ride.

Alice can't hear him. Ed steps on the off button of the canister vac. "I said, forget this and come with me."

"I've got to finish this." She steps on the button.

Ed pushes it off. "Let's do something, go somewhere. You'll never finish vacuuming."

"Where?" She doesn't move to restart the vac. She shoves a strand of hair behind her ear in a girlish motion.

"I don't know, but it's too fine a Saturday to be wasted on vacuuming. Grab your jacket; let's go do something."

Alice stands there with the vacuum nozzle in her hands. Her hair isn't yet in its twist, just pulled back in a workaday ponytail. The morning sun filters through the window, backlighting her, so that the uncaught strands look like a halo around her head. "Like what?"

"Time for a little adventure. Want to go look at cars?"

"That's an adventure?"

"Have you looked at cars lately? They're all about the adventure."

Ed can see her debating his offer. In the old days, the really old days, there would have been no hesitation. Now everything is a debate.

"What about Buddy?"

"He's waiting in the car. We need to find something that he likes, too."

"When did we decide to get a new car?"

"We haven't. I just thought it might be nice to see what's out there."

"I'll get my jacket."

Why does it feel like he's won a major victory?

Alice pulls off the thin T-shirt she's wearing and puts on a blue oxford shirt, puts her feet into her Dansko clogs, and runs a brush through her hair, sweeping it up and securing it with a clip. She's done this so often that she doesn't think about the action, just checks the result in the mirror hanging over her bureau. She should put on lipstick.

Ed is standing in the doorway, his reflection behind hers, his eyes admiring what her reflection doesn't reveal to her. Alice watches as Ed's reflection bends to kiss the back of her neck. It's like watching strangers through a window—avatars of Ed and Alice Parmalee.

The softness of Ed's lips against her skin is not a reflection, but real, and sends a frisson of energy through her body, a quickening of something she's forgotten existed. For once, she doesn't say "Oh Ed." For the first time in a very long time, it feels like her idea.

"I forgot about Buddy."

"It's cool in the garage. He's fine." Alice sits on the edge of the scrambled bed and pulls on her jeans. "But let's go. He's probably wondering what happened to you."

Ed reaches for Alice's shoulder and pulls her down against his bare chest. "Let's not tell him."

Alice swings her feet back onto the bed and sighs. "I think he may figure it out." She doesn't struggle to break free of his embrace, but settles herself into it. "He's such a smart dog. It's like he understands everything."

"He's really great, isn't he?" Ed shifts a little, begins to stroke a lock of her hair as if he's stroking the soft ears of the dog. "I went there yesterday. To the millpond."

Alice lies very still. Her heart is beating. She is breathing. She feels the weight of each individual rock pressing against her own ribs. The water rises but does not crest the dam of her grief. "Was it all right?"

"After a while. Buddy was there and he went a little nuts on a squirrel that literally dashed right under his nose. He nearly fell in, but didn't. He did look a little embarrassed, though. Alice, he made me laugh. There. That place. I laughed."

And then Ed holds her so close that the weight of the rocks is nothing compared to the pressure of his arms and his need. The grief does not subside, but the waters do, and Alice pats Ed's arm. "It's okay, Ed. It was good for you to go. It's the same for me when I go to the cemetery. There's some comfort in the tangible."

"I thought maybe I'd figure it out, if I finally looked at it. But all I figured out is that people still fish there and it's still a pretty spot. The leaves are already changing and the big trees are re-flected in the millpond, like you're seeing everything double. Peaceful. Except for that squirrel, completely still. Nothing about it explained anything. She wasn't there, Alice."

"She wouldn't be there, Ed. Any more than I find her in the cemetery. She's here. And not. We lost her. We had her for a little while and we lost her. End of story." Alice pulls herself away from Ed and they both sit on the edge of the bed. "Some-times I think that I need to gut her room and turn it into a den or an office or something useful. Put all of it away. And then I realize that once I do, I will have accepted her death."

"I think that maybe we have accepted her death, but not the reason for it. It wasn't like a car accident, where you'd put a cross and a teddy bear at the scene; it was an illness. It was something so out of our experience, we will never be able to understand how she felt."

They are silent again. But this time, the silence isn't a wall, but a cocoon.

"What do we do, Ed?"

Buddy barks suddenly, an impatient complaint of abandonment.

Ed kisses Alice. "Let's go look at cars."

"Maybe we should turn in the van. Get a Prius. Something economical. I don't need all that space."

"The Cutlass is older. Maybe we should see what they'd give us for that."

Ed is dressed first and goes out to the garage to soothe Buddy. Alice is back in front of the mirror, repairing her hair, putting on a little lipstick. She sees herself smiling, which is a surprise. Maybe it's the diffused light through the ivory-colored shades in this bedroom, or maybe it's something else, but the reflection coming back at her isn't as pinched as it's been. She's got good color in her cheeks, probably from all the walks she's been taking with Buddy. If she turns her head in a certain way, she even looks a little pretty, a little girlish. Alice looks at herself in the mirror and sees a hint of roses in her cheeks, something besides sadness in her eyes. What they've said was hard but, in a strange way, comforting. As if they've faced a common enemy and not fled.

At first, it was nice to have the front seat all to himself. Buddy doesn't know how long Ed will be. But after a couple of minutes, he settles down, nose under tail, eyes closed, but ears alert for Ed's return. Eventually, he dozes. Then he wakes and is puzzled. He hasn't been left alone in a car for this long, and never without being someplace other than where they started. He barks. This is a little naughty for a dog who can down-stay for hours, but there was no command. He barks again: *Hey, where are you?*

Ed comes back, all treats and apologies, which is good. But still they don't move. "Backseat, boy." Ed waves Buddy over the seat back. Now Buddy is intrigued. A passenger? This is unprecedented except when they both took him to the vet. Vet? Buddy makes a little interrogative noise in his throat. *What's up?*

Alice appears and climbs into the Cutlass. They talk and suddenly everyone climbs out and gets into the minivan. This is better. The middle seat offers a great view, which he can change by going from side to side. Buddy is excited; the routine is different. Something new is happening. Like yesterday, when he and Ed went to that pond where the squirrels were lush on the ground and plenteous in the trees. That was fun. An adventure. Except that Ed slowed down and stopped. Stood at the edge of the water without moving for a long time; stuck like humans sometimes get when their activity is invisible and is often accompanied by sighing. Not the sighing of comfort like a dog when he settles for the night, but that sighing that broadcasts human distress. This clearly wasn't meant to be a walk, just a visit. Maybe Ed thought that Buddy would rid the place of its squirrel vermin. He tried, very nearly ending up in water, something that he has no interest in doing. Water is for Labradors. That flushed Ed out of his immobility. That stopped his sighing.

This is bound to be an adventure, both humans in one place. No need to herd them; they are willingly together. Buddy sniffs the air behind the humans. He cocks his head. Notices that their hands touch now that Ed has the minivan on the road. Buddy loses interest in the scenery going by, doesn't think to look for squirrels, or cats or bikes. He keeps his herd-dog eyes on the touching hands visible in the space between the front seats.

He fails to notice the cemetery gates as they drive by, the left-hand pillar nearly scraped clean of its flaking paint; he is intent on the humans here with him now.

44

I should have known that Adele would want to pull out all the stops. Rather than a simple funeral home service, she has opted for the grand send-off at the largest Episcopal church in New Bedford. My father was a Catholic when he married my mother. Somewhere along the line, Adele had converted him to what I'm sure she thinks of as her classier denomination. She doesn't actually attend the church, but she swears that we need to use the huge space for the hundreds of friends who will show up. I'm sure that the nave will look like an empty boat.

We climb into our limousine in our suitable new clothes— Adele in Lord & Taylor widow's weeds, me in Kohl's basic black pantsuit, also useful for job interviews and visiting New York— and drive in luxury to the church.

I hadn't counted on Paul's clients and Melanie's circle of friends. It's not a bad crowd, for a perfect September Saturday morning, more suitable for a round of golf than a funeral. The four of us emerge from our limo, are met by Ryan and Peter, the younger boy, who have come in the family Lexus. Hugs shared all around. Paul supports Adele, but the sight of his bulk and her bent-over figure make me think irreverently of Shrek and a

Hobbit. Then my nephew, my stepnephew, young Ryan, offers his arm to me, and I am touched to tears.

I have spent the previous evening looking at the face of my dead father. In death, in this waxy repose, he was diminished, as I guess death diminishes us all. Strangers filed in, in twos and threes; some people I sort of recognized, old friends, most of them tottering about, pushing walkers, aged way past how I remember them; old customers coming in to pay their respects. They all offered such lovely platitudes: ". . . a better place." "He will be missed." ". . . hell of a guy." Some even cried. Who were these people to weep over my father's death? Adele greeted each and every one of them with what I can only describe as queenly calm. Paul knew them all. Teammates of Peter's showed up, stringy boys dressed in rumpled jackets and poorly tied ties. "Sorry man," they said, giving awkward boy hugs. Grandpa, it seemed, had attended all the games. Had a jersey with NUMBER ONE FAN printed on it and all the kids' signatures on the back.

I was the mystery daughter, tacked onto the end of the receiving line. "You must be Justine!" people would say. One person with a familiar face finally showed up, my parents' tenant, Diane Santos. She and her husband waited at the end of the line parading past the coffin, made their prayer with a nice big Catholic sign of the cross, and worked the line down to me. Diane, like so many of these other strangers, didn't feel odd about giving me a sympathetic hug. But with Diane, at least we'd been introduced. I'd eaten her food. I thanked her for it with the first genuine sentence I'd spoken since this tortured evening began.

During a lull, I wandered away from the family and took a look at the flowers that had been artfully arranged around the coffin like floral soldiers at attention on pedestals. One was from Markham Motors; another came from my father's Masonic chapter. A couple were from distant relatives. A late-arriving spray didn't get a pedestal, but sat on the floor, so I bent over to read the card. "In deepest sympathy." It was from Anthony Marcone.

That spray, pink gladioli and ivory lilies, sits on the chancel steps, its stems crushed together with those of all the other arrangements. When we go to the cemetery, they'll all be arrayed around the grave, left there until the coffin is lowered, a sight Americans don't usually watch, despite how it's portrayed on television. Soon enough, they'll be trashed, tossed out with the rest of the debris.

At the end of the service, before the funeral home guy collects the flowers, I pluck that telling card from the holder and pocket it.

Despite Tony's protestations, I moved us to Seattle, swearing that this really would be the better life. Six months later, I was collecting unemployment again. When Tony didn't come home from school on a Thursday afternoon, I went into his bedroom in the sublet we were renting and found a note on his desk. "Mom, I'll be okay, and I'll call you when I can. Love, Tony."

My son was gone.

The family files out of the church to the waiting limo and I follow slowly, the little card from Flora.com in my pocket. I pause on the church steps, wishing I could just pile into the Lexus with the boys, but the rear door to the limo gapes open, waiting for me.

"Justine?"

A man in a black suit stands on the steps beside me. Moderately tall, he is clean-shaven and has the deepest blue eyes beneath a wide forehead. His hair is short, and in the sunlight it is tipped with silver. I know him but can't place him.

"It's Mitch." He's seen my confusion. "I'm out of context. Besides, you only really ever knew the back of me."

"My Harley rider?"

Mitch, on two feet, comes closer. "I'm here. At your service again."

Going down the steps, I figure out that he's wearing a prosthesis. He's pretty facile, but there is a little hop in his gait that isn't quite normal. "You don't look like you came here on a bike."

"Left it home. That's my ride." He points to a Camry parked across the street. "Not very glamorous, but I figured that we may have a lot of driving to do.

"I don't know where I'm going next."

Mitch touches my elbow. "Wherever the search takes us."

On Saturday, Mr. Sanchez calls me to let me know that Tony had arrived at their house in Kanab. The boy had tried to swear the old man to secrecy, but Mr. Sanchez is having none of that. "I told him a man doesn't ask another man to lie. Secrecy is a lie."

"Thank you. I'm going to see if I can fly down and get him. I just have to . . ."

"No hurry. He's safe here. But, Justine, this is serious. A kid shouldn't run away."

"He's still mad that I moved him."

"How's that worked out for you?"

"I'm sure he's told you; the restaurant never even opened. I'm temping for now."

"I'm sorry to hear it."

For one second, I wonder if he's going to offer me our apartment back. Would I take that awful motel job again? No. That ship has sailed. "I thought that he was okay here."

"He's a boy without a good male influence, a kid who has never had any stability in his life beyond a loving mother. Justine, sometimes you just need more than good intentions."

Mr. Sanchez is breaking my heart with something I already know. I used to tell Tony that we were on a voyage of adventure, who knew what new and exciting things lay ahead of us. In the end, our voyage has hit the shoals and I have only one choice to make.

45

"You missed your pals this morning." Lil swipes the countertop with a rag. "They got worried."

"That's dumb. Now I have to call in sick if I miss a morning?" Ed goes past his usual stool and slides into a booth. Alice is across the street at the tiny town green with Buddy and a plastic bag. "I can't spend Saturday with my wife?"

"Hey, I'm just saying they were looking for you." Lil hefts the Bunn coffeepot. "Can I start you?"

"Thanks." Ed sees Alice come back across the street and pop Buddy back into the minivan. She rolls the windows down just enough. She sees Ed watching her and waves.

Ed isn't sure what's happened, only that he feels pretty good today.

Alice slips into the booth opposite him. "He'll be fine out there. We won't be long."

"He sits out there every morning waiting for me. He likes to keep tabs on all the comings and goings, the little mayor of Moodyville."

"You won't be able to do this in the summer, though. You can't leave a dog in a hot car."

"I know. Maybe I'll do something else in the summer."

Alice studies the plastic menu. Ed has it memorized. They both order grilled cheese—his with tomato, hers without.

When Lil comes with their order, she slips a little bag of bacon onto the table. "For my pal out there."

"You give him bacon?" Alice hisses as Lil drifts to another table.

"Just a strip."

Alice adds a little sugar to her cup, stirs it with a back-and-forth motion. "What else would you do in the summer?"

"I don't know. Maybe it's time we took one of those vacations we always talked about. Drive to the Cape or up to the mountains."

"We don't have to wait till summer to do that. There's nothing says we can't go somewhere now."

Another reminder of his unemployed status. All the time in the world.

Ed aligns his coffee cup in its saucer. "What would we do about Buddy?"

"There're lots of places that are calling themselves dog-friendly. We can take him."

"Where do you want to go?"

Alice shrugs, takes a bite of her sandwich, and sits back. The bench seat is so low, she looks like a little kid sitting at the grown-ups table. "Canada? Someplace we can drive to. Montreal?"

"All the more reason to look at a new car. Neither one of our clunkers could handle an eight-hundred-mile drive."

This is fun, this optimistic conversation. It's been so long since they've talked about anything having to do with planning, or adventure, or life beyond being lost parents, that Ed feels like laughing. It might not even be necessary to go on a vacation; it's just a step in a new direction to talk about it. It's a sign to him that Alice is moving out of another stage of her grief. From never leaving her bed to never leaving the house to never leaving

Moodyville, Alice is contemplating a journey out of the country. Ed is fairly certain that she will begin to worry about who will take care of things while they're gone, a train of thought that will eventually derail these happy plans when she considers being absent from the graveside for more than a couple of days. Summer, winter, whatever the season, whatever the weather, Alice Parmalee tends the grave. Chrysanthemums in the fall; impatiens in the summer; greens in the winter. The tulip bulbs poking up in the spring, flanked by daffodils. He's never seen it, but he knows what Alice plants. Sometimes it's the only thing she tells him in a day. Or it was, until Buddy came along.

So, it's quite nice to have her talking about going somewhere else.

Thursday's town newspaper is still on the stand and Ed goes to get one while Alice takes another cup of decaf from Lil. Pushing the empty plates aside, Ed stretches the paper out in front of them and they check through the car ads side by side. The end-of-season clearances are going on, so each of the dealers is touting big savings and decent monthly payments. Maybe even on Ed's fixed income they can afford to do this. They've put some away; money that was meant for college is still sitting there. It seemed wrong to use it for anything else. Taking it would have been tantamount to stealing it from Stacy in the early days following what happened. But now, with Ed out of work, it sits there like a backup plan.

In this little hometown paper the lost-and-found ads are the first classifieds after the paid ads. Lost earrings and cats, found wallets and boots. Alice doesn't want to look, but she finds herself drawn to the column. First ad under the column heading: "Found, small collielike dog. Gray and black, one blue eye, one brown. Near Old Path Road. Call . . ."

It feels like a century ago that she called in that advertisement. Now the object of those few words is a member of the family.

She narrows her eyes, hoping that no one will see it. She wishes that it wasn't the first ad, but was lost among all the other ads for missing sweaters with sentimental attachments and bracelets worthy of rewards. Alice breathes out. If anyone was going to call, they would have by now.

Alice starts to fold up the paper, but Ed pushes it back to the table surface. "We need to look."

She knows what he means, and the old familiar animosity rises. "No, we don't."

Ed ignores her and runs his finger down the lost ads. Alice doesn't watch. She looks out at the car, where Buddy is waiting so patiently for them. He is out of sight, curled up, no doubt, on the middle seat.

"Nothing. No one around here is missing him. We don't have to look ever again, but we had to look now. I couldn't live with myself if I didn't."

"I could."

"But now we don't have to worry about it. Free and clear. We've done what we could."

Ed wraps his arm around her shoulder and Alice lets herself sink in next to him, tucked safely under his arm. "He's our boy now."

The scent of bacon clings to the people as they get into the car. Buddy licks his lips, but tries hard not to look like he's begging. Alice holds out a crumb and he takes it with proper canine etiquette, then finds himself whining for more. Ed usually gives him a whole piece, but Alice wants to parcel it out in bits. After two, she puts the bag away.

Buddy settles into the backseat and begins to enjoy the ride.

The not talking is a good thing. The people in the front seat of the car are gently not talking, but the silence is that of a contented nature. Buddy watches the scenery go by, alert for squirrels, but no longer alert for discord between these people. Not that they have ever raised their voices, or used hard-sounding words, but he knows the difference between tension and relaxation. This is the first time he can recall since his arrival that he hasn't felt the barrier between the two people who take care of him. Buddy is as sensitive a dog as any, and he is familiar with barriers. Justine has no barriers between herself and Candy, or Saundra. But she has barriers between herself and the males who occasionally take up her time. This barrier always made him keep his guard-dog focus on whatever male came to take Justine out of the house, leaving him behind. Or came back into the house. One or two got enough past the barrier that Mack was left on the outside of the bedroom door—but not often. The barrier smelled like distrust; the kind of fear smell a dog that never attaches gives off. That was why he kept himself between Justine and Artie. Justine's distrust was emanating from her skin. He could taste it when he pressed his tongue against the back of her hand.

The barrier he has sensed between Ed and Alice is not distrust. The barrier, diminished today, is fear-aggression. They seem to him to be like those dogs who snap and snarl at everyone because they are confused and uncertain and the only safe thing to do is growl. Even though Ed and Alice don't snap or snarl, or even raise their voices, this underlying current of snappishness is there, and a sensitive dog knows it. They are a little afraid of each other. But not today.

Today, all three of them glide through the scenery, unafraid.

46

The car shopping has been fun, but exhausting. Too many choices and too many hungry car salesmen. They've looked at Toyotas and Fords, Kias and Subarus. At each dealership, Buddy hopped out with them, heeling prettily and sitting like a good boy as the salesman patiently explained the merits of this car or that, this deal or that. With down payment or not. Trade-in or not.

"I'm beat. Let's take the dog for a walk and stretch his legs." Ed snaps his seat belt into place. "I don't think I like any of them any better than this old heap."

"I know. They all look like oversized athletic shoes to me. I just can't picture myself going to Potter's in any one of them. But I think we still need to do it." Alice kisses Buddy's muzzle and points him back into the middle seat. "If we want to go any distance, we need a car."

So the vacation is still on the table. Ed grins and points the minivan in the direction of a state park.

The day is fading into dusk as they get out of the car, but the air is slightly warmer, as if summer isn't quite done. Alice has the bag of bacon crumbles in one hand. Buddy is more interested in those than in stretching his legs, so Alice puts him through his paces, treating him after every command. Sit, stay, heel. "You should work with him, too, so that he knows you give commands, as well." Alice hands the leash and the bag of bacon to Ed.

"Okay, Bud, heel!" Ed trots around with the dog's nose clamped to the side of his knee. He stops. "Down. Stay." Ed lays the leash on the ground and steps backward about four feet. "I bet he can do this without the leash. He knows he's not tied."

"We haven't worked off-leash yet. We're not ready." Alice folds her arms across her middle.

"I think he's ready. Watch this." Ed calls the dog to him, unsnaps the clip, and tosses the leash to Alice. "Buddy, heel!"

Alice covers her mouth with one hand, as if she expects the dog to run off. When he doesn't, when Buddy simply tags along beside Ed, jogging around the pine needle–strewn area, her hand drops as she begins to believe. Ed knows that look, a bird watching her fledgling, a mother watching her child ride without training wheels. It's that good-bye to old concerns, hello to new ones.

Ed stops; the dog stops. Buddy's eyes are riveted on Ed's. He's loving this exercise. Ed fishes another crumble of bacon out of the bag and treats the dog. "Good boy."

Ed tosses the bag of treats to Alice. "Go to Mommy."

As soon as the words leave his mouth, Ed realizes what he has said. He waits to see Alice's reaction. *Mommy*. The *m* word. It's what he called her from the moment they knew that Stacy was coming to the day she died. He hasn't called Alice "Mommy" in seven years, and yet the word came so fluidly to his mouth just now because she has been mommying this dog. He waits, horrified that he may have broken the spell of this better day with an unconscious blunder.

The dog trots to Alice, sits in front of her, herd-dog eyes catching and holding hers. Alice bends slowly from the waist. A strand of hair slides out from under her clip, dangling. She neither praises the dog nor gives him the treat he so clearly expects.

Buddy wiggles. His tail sweeps the pine needles. A soft inquiring woof. *Please?*

Alice holds the last piece of bacon in the tips of her fingers. Buddy takes it gently, his eyes fixed on hers, promising something. Straightening up, Alice looks at her husband. "Tell Daddy it's time for a walk."

47

Everyone is out of the house by five o'clock. Even Paul and his family have gone home. Those who have come back to Adele's house after the service have drifted away, final condolences distributed to Adele, who sits in her living room, taking those sentiments with a royal dignity. I think she looks like she rehearsed for this role. Queen Adele. Or maybe duchess. Maybe only duchess. At any rate, I am left with the cleaning up. I sent Mitch to his hotel. No sense in him hanging around this group of complete strangers. I am meeting him for a drink as soon as I can get away. He's brought his laptop, and I am beyond anxious to get started looking for Mack.

As I'm drying the last platter, adding it to the collection of dishes on the counter that will have to be returned to mystery owners, Adele comes into the kitchen. She stands there watching me, and I can feel her need to comment on how I'm doing the dishes, or where I'm stacking the orphans, or even that I'm making too much noise. She doesn't. She sits in her usual kitchen chair, the one nearest the stove. She's still dressed in her Lord & Taylor outfit, but she has on slippers instead of the good sensible shoes she's worn all day. The slippers are threadbare, the pink terry-cloth faded to something like a washed-out bloodstain, the cloth separating from the foam sole at the edge. She sits and watches and stays silent until I am done with the dishes. I take a last swipe at the wet sink surround, squeeze out the Handi Wipe, and hang it over the faucet.

"Don't leave it there."

Ah. I'd forgotten that faucets weren't for drying; the little towel rack in the pantry cupboard is for drying. Not handy, but the rule. I open the cupboard door and do as I'm told.

"I have to talk to you about your father's will."

I have assumed all along that he would leave everything to Adele. With probably a prize for Paul for being the son he never had. And then I think of how he grabbed Ronnie's shirtfront, and I wonder if maybe he left me a little something, too. A memento.

"He left you the house next door. He insisted. It was your mother's and he wanted you to have it."

I stare at Adele; I'm certain that my mouth is open. "What?"

"I'll tell you the truth; I didn't want him to do that. You don't deserve it; you cut yourself off from us. But he said that's what he wanted."

When I was a little kid, I fell off my bike and knocked the wind out of myself. There was that supreme moment when I felt the air go out, and I thought that I would never inhale again. This is exactly how I feel right now. I can't get a breath. The tips of my fingers are tingling with flight or fight.

A memento. A house. Of my own.

"How do you think you can manage it from Seattle?"

The house. My inheritance. "I don't know. I guess I'll figure that out." *My father provided for me.*

"There's always so much to be done. You have no idea. Painting and repairing the damage done by tenants. Keeping tenants happy. Shoveling sidewalks and mowing lawns." Adele is getting worked up.

"Who takes care of it for you now? You don't mow and you sure don't shovel."

"We have a man."

"Then I'll have that man, too."

"Justine, I'm not sure I can live on your father's pension and Social Security alone. I never worked. Outside, I mean. I took care of you and Paul."

"You took care of Paul. You tolerated me. Mostly."

"I took care of you. Who do you think washed your clothes and cleaned up your messes? Who made sure you had new shoes at the start of the school year? Who fed you? I did, that's who."

"I won't argue that you clothed and fed me, but you never *cared* for me."

Adele fixes a glare on me that would ice over Medusa. "You were a sniveling little girl who refused to let me hold her. I wanted to mother you, but you kicked me. You hit me. You told me I would never be your mother. Do you remember that? Remember?" Adele's icy eyes lock onto mine.

I don't remember any of that. I only remember the disbelief and betrayal of my father in taking up with Mrs. Rose before the flowers on my mother's grave were frostbitten. *He grabbed Ronnie's shirtfront. He defied Adele for me.*

Adele clasps her hands together in an operatic pose. "He needed me to take care of you, but I needed him to love me."

I think I'm going to be sick. "And did he?"

Adele stands up, stretching as tall as she can. "Yes, he did."

My silent father doing as Adele commands—that's what I remember of their relationship. If that's love, then I guess he did love her.

"I wanted to love you, Justine. But you wouldn't let me." This is revisionist history spilling out of her mouth. Adele's version of my life as a foundling.

"I was a bereaved child."

"You were hostile and intractable."

"I believe that I still am. I didn't need you to love me, Adele. I needed my father's love. You deprived me of that."

"How?"

"By making sure every wrong I did and every mistake I made was pointed out. And everything that Paul did got a gold star and was hung on the refrigerator."

"You sound like a child. A jealous child, which you always were."

"Of course I was. I was jealous in the same way that Cinderella was jealous of her stepsisters; they had the unconditional love of their mother's husband and his own flesh and blood served them."

"You never served—"

"Adele, you're being literal. I'm saying that I felt, and feel, like a second-class citizen in this house and you made my father treat me like one. Now he's gone, and I'm done. You'll never have to think about me again. Oh, wait, you probably don't think about me anyway. It won't be a loss."

Adele doesn't say anything to that. She backs down, steps away from me, walks around the small kitchen, pushing canisters back into alignment, testing the countertop for crumbs. "Justine. What are you going to do about the house? I can't live without the rents."

I finally get it. Now, after all these years, Adele needs me. Not for myself—she's already proved that she needs my service, if not my affection—but for the one thing my father, in the end, refused her; the income from the house next door.

Adele leaves me alone in the kitchen, snapping off the overhead light on her way out, as if I'm not standing there, as if I'm going to leave it on and cost her more in an electric bill. Old people get freaky about expenses. The fixed income that they welcome at retirement must feel like bait and switch. Inflation and recession screw up the best of plans. Surely this house is mortgage-free. I have no idea what the rents are from next door, but my guess is that they're substantial enough that Adele and my father have been living comfortably on them since his retirement. Then I think of the yellowed vinyl siding and the neglected yard.

The only window in the kitchen looks out at the big three-decker. I can picture Adele standing in the window, looking over at the house on the day my father came home from the hospital with only his little girl and not his wife. Did her scheming start then, or was she honestly generous, like Diane Santos, with casseroles and kindness? There is nothing more endearing than a man alone with a child. Who could resist? And if the man came with a good job, plus a triple-decker, what woman wouldn't set her cap for him? It made sense, this moving into Adele's house, cramming me into a closet. One more rental unit made available.

Adele is in the living room, sitting on the couch that has been my bedroom for the past week. She isn't doing anything, and I get the impression that she's waiting for me. I come in and sit in the chair opposite her. Her white hair has lost the just-coiffed look and there is a tiny pull in her stocking. In the big cushy couch, she looks like a gnome. I feel the slow cooling of my stoked temper. She looks like what she is, a fragile old lady.

"The reason he wanted that house to go to you was that he thought you needed the stability."

I would gladly give up the "stability" of owning the house next door for one moment when my father opened his arms and held me.

I'm exhausted with the day and this conversation. If I had hoped to slouch out of New Bedford with empty promises to keep in touch, I know now that's impossible. I am forever tied to this woman. "For right now, we'll split the rents."

Adele's expression is more one of victory than of relief and gratitude.

There's no way I'm staying in that house tonight. I call Paul and tell him that his mother is going to be alone unless he or one of his hulking teenagers comes to granny-sit. I rip off my funeral clothes and stuff them into my duffel. My jeans and a plain white T-shirt feel like home to me. I toss on a navy blue fleece vest and run a brush through my hair. I'm out of here. Except that I have no car. I don't think I'm up to stealing Adele's car, even if only for the night. I call a cab and sit on the steps to wait for it. While I wait, I call Mitch. We can indulge in New Bedford's haute cuisine down on the historic waterfront.

48

Fried clams and french fries. That's what we end up with, and they are perfect, even if I have to convince midwesterner Mitch that consuming whole clams, with bellies, is the only proper way to eat the bivalves. Clam strips are akin to fake maple syrup—okay but not right.

Mitch pushes the mess from dinner across the table and sets up his laptop. We sit side by side, hoping to get within range of someone's Wi-Fi. The first thing we do is look at the little video clip again. There he is, my little man, strutting his stuff on some stranger's deck, his open mouth looking like he's smiling, laughing. Enjoying himself. As if he's right at home. I take a big swallow of my Sam Adams, trying to push the lump in my throat down. "What do we do now?"

"Let's check out the local papers, read their lost-and-found ads."

Mitch's fingers fly over the keyboard, scouring the Internet for clues as to Mack's whereabouts. Artie said he'd left him near Exit 8, so we search for newspapers in that geographic area. We find dailies in Springfield and Ludlow, Worcester and Hartford. None of them have a found ad to give me any hope, just sunglasses, bracelets, and a trash barrel.

Out of his black suit and dressed in chinos and an untucked denim shirt, Mitch looks a little more like the guy I hijacked, and I'm beginning to feel like he has a lot of variations: Hell's Angel, Beau Brummell, and now average guy. He taps the keyboard. "Let's put an ad in all of them. Tell me what to say."

"Blue merle Shetland sheepdog with one blue eye and one brown one, missing in area of Exit Eight off the MassPike. Very intelligent. Answers to Mack. Desperately missed by owner. Call . . ." I can't even get my number out before the magnitude of this loss clamps my throat tight.

Mitch pauses in his typing to wrap an arm around my shoulders. "We'll find him."

What I wonder is how I've managed to find him, this white knight. Life is so random. I would have to be a philosopher to even begin to understand how life isn't really lived in the big picture, but moment to moment. The big picture was trying to go east cheaply; the moment was when I decided to hop on the back of a Harley behind a total stranger, panic overruling common sense. A woman alone, and this guy might have turned out to be a mass murderer.

I have no idea if there is something happening here between a single mom with a missing dog and a one-legged violinist, but for right now, it's pretty nice to have his company. I am really not in the market for anything more. I've reached the point in life when the need or desire for a permanent fixture in my bedroom is so diminished, I no longer think it's missing from my life. Still, that arm around my shoulders and the sense of someone else taking care of things is sweet.

Mitch sips at his beer as he patiently fills in all the info for an ad in all the papers. I am suddenly so weary that I can hardly keep my head up. The weight of an entire life believing that my father had turned his back on me has shifted to the weight of knowing that he hadn't. The relief that at least I know that Mack is alive is almost as heavy a burden as worrying about him. New worries have risen. Having seen him, I may never be able to find him. It is certainly better, knowing for certain that he's not dead on the side of the road, but also cruel, in fate's own way, to have him just out of reach.

Just like Tony has been out of reach for the past seven years.

I call the restaurant. I know there's no way my ex-husband is at home on a Sunday morning. Marcone's Grill serves one of the best post-Sunday Mass breakfasts in the area. He'll be there, commanding the troops. This is good for me, because it means the call will be short and to the point and done. Above all, it means I won't have to chance getting his wife on the phone. Anthony, like me, didn't remain celibate. Unlike me, he settled down. One of the very few times Tony went east was to attend the wedding. I put him in the charge of a flight hostess and spent the next two days biting my nails until Anthony put him on the return flight.

The kitchen phone rings four times before a female voice answers with a rough, get-out-of-my-way "Marcone's."

I ask for Anthony. The rough voice on the other end asks the "Who's calling?" question and I have almost no idea what to say. Finally, I just give her my name. It clearly means nothing to this woman, and the phone clatters as she drops it onto the counter. I hear her bellowing for Anthony. "For you!" I notice she doesn't mention who's calling, even though she's got my name. This woman needs to polish her secretarial skills. It's like ambushing Anthony. Very rarely have I ever called him, and this time it's going to be far more difficult than asking for the support check a little early.

"Marcone."

"Anthony, it's Justine"

"Justine, hi. What's wrong?"

Two little words and the floodgates open.

"I just don't know what to do." I can't quite make my mouth say what I've called to say—"Please take him"—but Anthony has figured it out.

"Send him here. I'll take care of him. You've had him all this time, all by yourself."

It's what I know has to happen. But I don't know if it's really the right thing to do. "I don't want to lose him."

"You won't. You're his mother, and you always will be. But a little distance may be just the thing." I remember why I fell for him in the first place, this sensible, sensitive guy. Fleetingly, I wonder what would have happened if I'd stayed with him.

"What will Mary say about this? Shouldn't you at least talk with her?" I realize that I am putting my son into the same position I once suffered, that of stepchild in another woman's home. I feel my knees quake. I am about to change my mind.

"Mary will love having him. Besides, he needs to get to know his half brothers."

The difference is in the blood. Anthony's twins are Tony's blood.

"Just for a little while."

"As long as he wants to stay, Justine, he's welcome." The phone is muffled for a moment as Anthony responds to someone's question. In that space, I feel the last of my anger at Anthony dissolve.

"Anthony, I really appreciate your help."

"You should have asked for it more."

"I didn't want to. I chose to cut the ties, after all."

"Justine, I never meant to be mean to you. I was just so conflicted." This last word sounds so Brooklyn coming out of Anthony's mouth.

"What did we know; we were practically kids."

"Now I have a good business, and a good home. Mary is a great girl. I think Tony will be okay here. I'll put him to work in the kitchen. Who knows, maybe he'll like food service." Anthony's voice is so excited, I have a flash of guilt that I so deliberately kept Tony away from his father.

"He's watched me in the food-service industry long enough; I don't think it has an appeal for him."

"Fair enough. Look, Justine, I'll send you plane fare. He can finish the school year in Seattle and be out here for the summer. How's that?"

It was a good plan, a workable plan. A summer back east, then home to me in the fall. Except that Tony went ballistic.

Mitch has noticed my slump. "You okay?"

"I think I've hit my wall. I'm exhausted."

Which leaves the question of the rest of the night sitting between us.

"I'll take you back to your mother's house."

"Stepmother."

"Step, then. Or not."

It's that little "Or not" that makes me smile. "I really don't want to go back there. I'm done with that house."

"Stay here."

We are back at Mitch's hotel, sitting in the lounge, having a last glass of wine and munching the endless popcorn provided instead of bar peanuts like those at Candy's Place. Mitch leans over. "It's been hard, hasn't it?"

"You don't know the half." I am so tired that I spill out half my life story, only partially edited. I've told him about Mack and our dancing and why I am so desperate to have my dog back. I tell Mitch about leaving home the day after high school graduation and why coming back to New Bedford was supposed to heal that breach, and maybe it has. Because my thoughts have been on the past so much, I tell him about sending my son away when he was sixteen and how that made him so hurt and angry that he estranged himself from me. Mitch hands me his clean handkerchief.

I swallow back the uncontrolled self-pity and ask him to tell me about life with a handicapped plate. He talks of being a normal teenager, then not a normal teenager. About friends who were freaked-out and friends who remained loyal. About being a badass when the mood strikes and the way some music is so divine that he plays without even thinking, just letting the music take charge.

And now we're at that junction where every date eventually arrives—the yes or no moment.

"No expectations, Justine. There are two beds, and I don't think I snore." Mitch tosses this out so casually that it almost seems conceivable that I would share a room with him and not sleep with him.

"What about my expectations?"

Mitch smiles and those blue eyes, just the color of the sky on a bright fall day, light up and he is suddenly quite lovely.

His room is only one floor up, but we take the elevator. I can see us in the mirror that lines the walls. I fit neatly against Mitch's side. My hair is scrambled and I watch myself struggle to fix it. I watch Mitch watching me, so I keep the worry off my face as the questions rise with the elevator.

Do I know what I'm doing? Is this a good idea? Am I simply giving in to all my bad impulses that I have worked so hard to control?

All questions cease when the room door closes behind Mitch and he takes me into his arms in a decidedly not-for-comfort-alone manner. We make love and then I am out cold.

Room-darkening drapes make me think that's it's before dawn when I finally climb out of the deepest sleep I've enjoyed in two weeks—dreamless, cocooned in the comfort of a hotel mattress and surprisingly cushy pillows. The length of a good man beside me, but respectfully on his own side of the bed. I reach for him and can't find him. Sitting up, I hold the sheet to my chest like a ravished virgin and see Mitch sitting at the little table provided by the hotel, thumping away at his laptop, his head moving to something on his iPod. A pair of crutches rests against the other chair. I wake up and smell the coffee. He's been down to the complimentary breakfast and brought up food. On one leg. Amazing man.

Mitch closes his laptop, winds the earphone cords around his iPod, and pushes his chair away from the table. I take that as an invitation. He takes me onto his lap and wraps his arms around me. "Pack your bags, lady, and let's get outta Dodge."

"Do you always talk like someone from the Wild West?"

"That's the Wild Midwest to you."

"Where are we going?"

"To find your dog. Look." Mitch turns the laptop so that I can read what he's found while I've been sleeping. "Found, small collielike dog. Gray and black, one blue eye, one brown. Call . . ."

I nearly weep. "That's got to be him. Where is he?"

"This is the *Moodyville Press*. I'll Google Moodyville; you call the number."

I wonder if the hope on my face will blind Mitch. My hand is shaking as I punch the number. I misdial twice before I get all ten digits right.

"You have reached Ed and Alice Parmalee. Please leave your message . . ."

Her voice. The one on the video, the one that calls my dog "Buddy." Alice. Ed and Alice Parmalee. I know where my dog is.

"Mrs. Parmalee, my name is Justine Meade, and the dog you found"—I actually have to take a breath—"is mine."

49

Deep in the laundry room, Alice hasn't heard the phone ring. Ed is just coming in from getting the Sunday paper, Buddy at his feet, his nose pointed skyward in expectation of a treat. The flashing message light goes unnoticed until it catches Ed's eye as he sits down with a fresh cup of coffee.

"Who the heck is calling on a Sunday morning?"

"Maybe it's someone with a zoning board question. Or it could be Jen, asking if we want any more squash." Alice pours kibble into Buddy's dish, the musical chime of breakfast making him do his little happy hop.

"No, Jen would just leave it on the counter. Anonymously." Ed reaches for the play button.

"My name is Justine Meade, and the dog you found is mine."

The air in the room is suddenly gone, the atmosphere around Alice a vacuum, a void. She reaches for the delete button even before the caller gets to her telephone number, but Ed holds her back. "You can't."

Alice slaps his hand away. Slaps away the good feelings of yesterday, the progress, the fresh air entering her burdened lungs suddenly sucked away by a stranger's voice, a woman claiming their dog as hers, repeating her telephone number twice. It isn't enough to slap away Ed's hands; she wants more—to hurt someone or something. Suddenly, she is pummeling Ed, as if it's his fault.

"Alice, stop it. Enough. I've had enough." Ed moves so quickly away from her that Alice slips, nearly going to the floor. He catches her but holds her away. "This isn't my fault. This is just how life plays out."

"You made me put in the ad."

"We agreed we had to do it."

"We don't have to call her. Finders keepers."

"Alice, that's not how we operate, and you know it. How could you live with yourself?"

"How can I live without Buddy?"

Ed is still holding Alice at a distance, but now he reels her in, holds her close. "She's going to have to prove ownership. We can make it tough."

Alice's tears dampen the front of his shirt and he remembers the first time he held her close. How many years ago? Too many to count. He held Alice in his arms for the first time an hour and a half after they were on their first date. It was the day that Nixon ended the Vietnam War. Everyone was celebrating. The television was on in the pizza place, where they were testing the waters of their acquaintance over pepperoni. The sight of Tricky Dick announcing the cessation of the war that had ruled their young lives was enough for an embrace between strangers. At the end of it, Ed knew that they'd never be strangers again. She fit so perfectly.

Now he holds his wife and wonders if he will ever know her again. Losing Stacy had unhinged her. For a very long time, it seemed like he would never get Alice back from the dark place she had gone. He can't go through that again. Buddy may only be a dog, but this new creature in their lives, this object of their affections, has lightened up the days and made smoother the nights. Buddy isn't a replacement for Stacy. What he has become, in this short time, is a willing receptacle for the flow of love that has been dammed up behind the silence in this house. Even now, the dog stands at attention, his ears turning like radar dishes, his unmatched eyes focused on them. His mouth is a little open, and his breaths are shallow, audible. Like he's worried about them. Like he wants to say something.

Ed keeps Alice tight against his chest as he reaches out to touch the answering machine. He feels her quiver against him, so afraid of hearing that message again.

Ed feels like Michaelangelo's God in the Sistine Chapel, one finger reaching out to change the world. He hits the delete button.

Buddy can't quite figure out how the people went from all relaxed and happy, pouring kibble in the bowl for him and talking to each other, to this, this wounded sound coming from Alice, and the stiff fear-aggressive posture from Ed. He whines a little, trying to get their attention, trying to understand what's going on. Humans are so changeable. You just can't trust them.

Finally, the crisis seems to be over and Alice drops to the floor to pull him into her lap and embrace him so hard that Buddy almost whines. He understands then that she is sad again, and that disappoints him. Alice hasn't been sad for a few days and he's thought his job here was done. Buddy licks her face, tastes the salt from her eyes, and licks again. Then Alice laughs, pushing him off and letting Ed hand her back to her feet. They sit down at the table and he's free to go eat his delayed breakfast.

The people sit in silence, facing each other. He's not sure, but they may be touching hands. He can't see from his low elevation; he'd have to be rude and jump up to see, but he's not that curious about the state of their touching. Things seemed better and now this, this return to the gloom that permeated this house when he first arrived. He's worked hard to be a good guest, and even a good pet, if that's what they needed.

Buddy knows that he needs to break this tense silence with some action. Even a good dog can lie on occasion, and Buddy decides that there is a trespasser—or a squirrel—lurking in the backyard. The rabid barking and growling get the people up from their chairs, and suddenly Buddy is hopeful that for once they'll release him to chase whatever is out there, even if it is only in his imagination. They don't, but they do open the slider, letting him out onto the deck, which Ed has recently gated. He barks some more, then gives up the pretense. The people linger on the deck with him, although they don't sit on the chairs or water the plants. They are talking quietly, and this is better than the silence, so he feels pretty chuffed with himself for getting them to move.

"Hey, Buddy. Go for a ride?"

Buddy barks an enthusiastic yes and dashes in to get his leash.

50

Mitch, the first-chair violinist, doesn't play Vivaldi; he plays Mark Knopfler and Sting. I think he does that for me. We're on the road by nine and, unlike the day I went to find Artie, the drive is smooth sailing—no delays, no traffic, a Sunday, not a busy weekday. We chat. We are quiet with our thoughts. We hold hands every now and then. My heart thumps with excitement every time I think that by the end of the day, I'll have my dog back. I can almost feel the tickle of his fur beneath my chin, the weight of his little thirty-pound body in my arms, the wriggle of his happiness as we are reunited.

My heart thumps when I glance at Mitch, who's tapping out a rhythm on the steering wheel to the percussion-heavy music. I try not to think that he's the first decent guy I've hooked up with in a long time. Maybe forever. I try not to think of it as "hooking up." I try to simply enjoy the feeling. For now. After all, all we have is the now. I know this feeling all too well; the sense of novelty and romance inevitably grows contentious and regretted.

I'll never follow another guy. Not even this one. I learned my lesson the hard way.

Then Mitch takes hold of my hand again and squeezes it gently. Violinist's hands, and they played me last night like a virtuoso.

Before we reach the Pike, I apologize for being on my cell phone in the car, but I have to call Saundra and Candy. I wish that I could get them both on the phone simultaneously, so that Mitch doesn't have to hear my girlie squealing as I breathlessly go over the steps leading to this drive, this moment. I wish he wasn't in the car, because I hate discussing him with my pals. "Yes, he's the guy who got me from Cleveland Heights to Erie . . . well, Conneautville. Why is he here?" I give Mitch a sideways glance. "I don't know. Just is."

Mitch gives me a smile and keeps thumping out rhythms on his steering wheel.

Saundra is far less interested in human relations, just cries and tells me that Sambucca, her husky, sends her love to Mack and can't wait to see him.

The Parmalees haven't called me yet, so I call them again, leaving the same message. I'm starting to get worried, but Mitch won't let me. He shakes his head and says that we'll sit outside their house if we have to.

I shut my phone finally and bask in the warmth of knowing that I am within miles of seeing my dog, of getting him back. I feel myself tearing up and then feel Mitch's hand on mine. I marvel at the warmth of this undeserved friendship.

There is one more call I have to make. I pull the little florist's card out of the pocket of my fleece vest; "In deepest sympathy, Anthony Marcone."

Tony fought with me about being sent to his father. "He doesn't want me. You've always told me that. Why would he want me now?" He begged and pleaded, called me names, but I was obdurate. I couldn't do this alone anymore. I was exhausted with living every day waiting for the next crisis, the next rebellion.

The air between us was charged with resentment and anger

and distrust—on both sides. Anthony's offer was my best chance at being a good parent. Besides, it was only for the summer, a little time to decompress and start fresh in the fall. Mr. Sanchez was right: The boy needed a father. He'd never had anyone to show him what it meant to be a man: be kind, work hard, take pride.

As good as his word, Anthony sent us the money for airfare, and the day after school let out we flew to New York. Watching Tony walk up to his father in that airport arrivals lounge was like watching the young Anthony meet with his adult self. No one could deny that Anthony was Tony's father, and it was enough to break the ice between them. If this was going to work out better than I had hoped, it was also going to break my heart.

I dial my son, who now calls himself Marcone, and, for once, he answers.

"Thanks for the flowers, Tony. They were beautiful. Adele was pleased." The last bit is a lie; Adele never mentioned them, but it would be awful for him to think his expense went unnoticed.

"Sorry about your dad."

"Thanks. He left me the house. The triple-decker."

"Cool."

"I own it. Can you believe that?"

"Will you live there?"

"I don't know. It has tenants already." I could never be the kind of landlord that doesn't renew a lease. But the second-floor tenants are a young married couple; surely they'll be moving in a year or two. I don't ask, "Would you want me to?" I don't want to hear the answer.

"Justine, I don't know how you're going to take this, but Tony wants to stay here." Anthony sounds equally apologetic and pleased.

"I want to hear him tell me that himself." It is the day he's supposed to arrive home. He should be on a plane right now. I have cleaned the apartment like a frenzied housewife and bought every snack food the boy likes. I haven't had but one phone call from him since I left him in Brooklyn, and that one was curt and a request for a CD he left behind.

"Mom. I want to stay here. I can finish school without having to worry about moving again."

"I won't move again; I promise." I haven't told him that I have a new job, a good one at a health clinic. We can start looking for a new place when he gets home. I want to surprise him.

"Yeah, right. Just like the other times."

Tony's sardonic words pierce like a harpoon into the heart of a woman just trying to do the best she can.

Tony never came back to live with me. The next summer, he was too busy working in Marcone's Grill, learning the business, and then he was in college. For spring breaks and holidays, Anthony flew him back to Seattle, but the bond we'd had when Tony was little and still sleeping with his Donald Duck pillow was gone. Tony had finally found the stability he'd needed. A permanence that I had never been able to provide.

Moodyville is one of those forgotten Massachusetts towns, not quite mid-state, not quite the Berkshires. Pretty in a rural way, not a suburban way. Train tracks bisect the country route we find ourselves on, the Albany to Worcester line no doubt. Freight, not passengers. We go over tracks and then, oddly, go under a trestle as the road curls and winds away from the Pike. I feel like I'm on a carnival ride as the road rises and swoops, narrows and straightens. We pass a golf course, a lone foursome playing a midafternoon game. The road flattens out and there are little mill houses lining the slightly wider road, antique duplexes with asbestos shingles and spartan single-family dwellings with narrow porches, all overlooking the road.

We come to a four-way stop. A gas station, a coffee shop, a post office, and a utilitarian brick rectangle that is the town's administration building. Welcome to Moodyville. The coffee shop is open, and I suggest we stop and regroup, which is a euphemism for needing to use a bathroom.

"Maybe there's a phone book in the coffee shop." Mitch pulls into a convenient parking spot and we both climb out, a little stiff from the ride.

Two burly guys sharing a Sunday *Globe* sit at the counter, one stool in between. Mitch and I take a small booth that looks out at the parked cars. The waitress brings coffee and mugs, two menus tucked under her arm.

"Do you have a phone book?"

"Sure." She fishes one out from behind the register and brings it, along with the creamers, on her next trip by our table.

Mitch opens it and quickly finds what he's looking for. "Edward Parmalee, twenty-nine Old Path Road. Same number, and there's only one Parmalee listed in Moodyville."

Suddenly, I'm famished, and we both order the Hungry Man Special. I feel like I'm delaying Christmas with this, but we haven't heard from the Parmalees yet, and I feel for Mitch, who has driven all this way on the strength of one cup of weak hotel coffee.

The waitress is quick with our order and is back in no time with platters of eggs and bacon, then freshens up our coffee.

"Can you give us directions to Old Path Road?"

"Sure. It's easy." She begins to outline a route that has more twists and turns than a video game.

One of the counter denizens chimes in. "Lil, they don't have to go down Creighton; they can take the right at the old mill."

"Either way, they have to end up on Cemetery Road." This is

from the second guy. "You folks going to hike the old path? You can start at the mill if you want."

"No, we're looking for Ed and Alice Parmalee. They found my dog."

"Oh, that's a cute dog. Ed brings him here every morning." Lil drops the check on the table. "I make sure there's a little bacon to take out to him.

I'm quicker than Mitch in grabbing the check. *Ed takes my dog on rides.*

"Ed says Alice is real attached to him. It's helped." The guy on the right-hand stool folds up the paper and spins around to face us.

"Helped with what?" I hand Lil the check and a ten.

The room goes quiet. We are, after all, strangers. Then he shrugs, as if he realizes that what he has to say isn't a secret. "They lost their daughter a few years back. Alice took it pretty hard."

"I'm sorry to hear that. Lost how?"

He clams up again, and I recognize a good old-fashioned New England reticence.

The other guy speaks up. "Drowned. Right there in the mill-pond."

"That's so sad."

"They thought she'd run away."

"How old was she?"

"Fifteen. Right, Lil?"

"Yeah, sophomore."

Lil leans toward me and lowers her voice. "No one likes to say, but it was suicide."

"Jesus. A child?"

She nods and drops the change on the table, where I add another couple bucks to it for a tip. The joy that's been festering under my rib cage all morning is tempered now, diminished a little. I can't help but think that it would have been preferable for the Parmalees' daughter to have run away. They could have survived that. What a tragedy. No wonder Alice has found comfort in Mack. He excels in that.

Mitch slides out of the booth. "Okay, so right past the mill, left onto . . ." He rehearses the directions until everyone in the room is satisfied that we will find Old Path Road and my dog.

I buckle my seat belt before I can say what is on my mind. "It may be hard to get him back from them, if they've gotten that attached. What if they won't give him back?"

Mitch takes my hand. "Justine, they can't keep him. He belongs to you."

The road tucks up again and for a little while follows the slow S-curves of a muddy brown river. We go over a noisy two-lane bridge, and there is the abandoned mill that must have given rise to the little mill houses. There is a millpond behind the brick factory, a spill of river water sliding over the lip. The maple and oak trees on the far side are reflected in the water; I'm sure that in a few weeks it will be a dazzling display of color, but right now it's just a pretty image. And then I remember what the guy in the coffee shop said. It's still a pretty image, but I look away.

I'm on a mission and we keep moving, hunting down the next series of signs that will lead us to the road called Old Path.

They still haven't called me back. It's enough to make me think crazy thoughts.

"Right on Creighton Road." I'm down to the last two turns of this complicated backcountry drive. "Quarter mile, right on Owen Farm Road." We're passing pastures and woodlots, a state park, and empty farm stands. We pass the only commercial building we've seen, a manufacturing plant, but I can't tell what they manufacture.

We're finally on Cemetery Road. We pass the cemetery, one stone pillar flaking white paint and the other scraped to the brick. And just beyond, there it is: Old Path Road. My stomach leaps with excitement. I'm within minutes of getting Mack back.

51

They take the Cutlass because Buddy can sit between them. As they pass the cemetery, for once he doesn't whine, but instead flops down and puts his head in Alice's lap. She strokes his ears gently, thoughtfully, not saying anything to Ed, too much needing to be said.

They take the Pike, then get off on Interstate 91, heading north. Ed seems to have a plan, so Alice watches the scenery go by and lets him be in charge. It takes too much energy even to wonder where they're going. Ed exits at Northampton, asks her if she wants to stop for lunch. She shakes her head no. They continue through town slowly, dodging a constant gauntlet of collegians crossing the wide main street.

It is too much like losing Stacy, and that is a blasphemous thought. How can losing a child in any way be equated to giving up a dog? But the sorrow is there, the same taste of loss. The same weighted limbs and difficulty keeping the breath in her body. She shouldn't have allowed herself to want Buddy. She should have pushed him away. She should have kept Ed away. But Buddy has joined them back together. After being broken shards, cutting each other with every glance, the sense of being cup and saucer again has been good. If Buddy goes, when Buddy goes, what will become of that newly repaired bond?

Their route takes them through the Smith College campus and beyond, past Cooley Dickinson Hospital, until they enter Florence and Alice realizes where they are going—to Look Park. It has been years since they visited the park with its little zoo and the miniature train that circles around it. They spent many a summer Sunday at Look Park, swimming and walking the trails, picnicking on a basket stuffed with their favorite picnic food—cold chicken and potato salad, Jell-O salad, and, at Stacy's request, Ring Dings for dessert. They'd visit the zoo twice, once to say hello and once to say good-bye. A dime bought a handful of feed for the goats. Once one of the goats knocked Stacy down, but she got up, dusted herself off, and announced that the goat was sorry and wouldn't do it again, then asked if she could have more feed.

"Do you remember how Stacy would always call out 'Look! Park!' when we saw the gates?" Ed signals to get in line at the entrance. There are hundreds of cars; even for a spectacular September Sunday, that seems like a lot.

"I remember. She never got tired of the joke."

Ahead of them is a van hauling a small trailer holding a big wicker basket. "Hey, Alice, I think I know what's going on."

"I think you're right."

"The balloon festival. We always promised Stacy that we'd let her go up in the tether ride, just as soon as she got big enough to see over the edge of the basket."

"How come we never did that?"

"Got busy with other things, forgot about it. I don't think we've been here since she was eleven."

They are talking about Stacy. They almost never speak of her. Only the strangled admission of missing her on those days when the grief rises like the immutable tide. Never like this, conversationally.

Ed finds a parking spot on the edge of the field and they sit for a few minutes, watching the balloonists set up. Each group has what seems like acres of silk stretched out on the ground. Oranges, yellows, black, and lime green—the hues are like a giant's spilled paint box. Ed squares his ball cap on his head. "Come on."

Buddy trots along beside Alice, obviously excited to be in a new place. He keeps looking at her to make sure she's there, then puts his nose to the ground to sniff up the myriad scents of new people, dogs, and dropped hot dogs. Ed leads them to a booth advertising tether rides.

"Really, Ed?"

Ed wraps an arm around her shoulders, squeezing her close. "Yes, really. We always said we would, and now we are."

"We said we'd take Stacy."

"And we are."

"What do you mean?"

"We have to believe that she is always with us. Wherever we are, whenever we speak of her, or don't speak of her, she's still with us. She's here because we remember her being here. We'll take her with us on that promised balloon ride because we will both be thinking of her."

Buddy is enjoying himself immensely. This place is laden with new scents. He's greeted two dogs, both very interested in him. Nice guys, also leash-restricted, but not discouraged from saying hi. Buddy thinks that maybe this is a dance place. Even though it is outside, the people and the dogs here all have that special excitement that emanates from people and dogs doing fun things. Alice and Ed are slipping him treats as they wander around. They are touching, and the worry that Alice showed earlier has subsided, although he can still smell it. They stand still for a long time as one of the objects on the ground begins to move. Buddy growls, but the people don't seem afraid, so he stands quietly as they ooh and aah as the thing slowly grows huge, making a constant roar. It is finally upright and a stranger takes Buddy's leash out of Alice's hand. Unbelievably, Ed and Alice climb into the object, which isn't a car and isn't a truck, but it roars with a breathy violence that makes him think of Artie. Buddy locks eyes on Alice, who calls out to him, "Be a good boy."

Gradually, Ed and Alice rise into the air, so high above him that he can't see them anymore. At once, the sense of being lost descends on him and he whines softly, all the while keeping his eyes on the balloon.

Ed and Alice didn't tell him down-stay. Didn't tell him to be quiet. They handed his leash to this stranger and left him. He can't see them, can't smell them, and can't hear them. He is surrounded by these objects with their noise, by strangers and confusion. The nervousness and fear that living with Alice and Ed has made go away suddenly grip him and he can only bark, a sharp volley of panic.

52

We pull up in front of a raised ranch with a two-bay garage. One of the garage doors is open and the bay empty. Now I'm sure that they've run off with my dog. I jump out of the Camry almost before Mitch has come to a stop. I run to the front door, jabbing my finger at the bell over and over. I can hear the chime ringing like Big Ben in miniature. Failing to get anyone's attention, I risk being arrested as an intruder and go into the garage. I bang on the metal door that leads into the house. I try the knob, but, not surprisingly, the door is locked. They may not care about the contents of their garage, but they do lock their doors. I press an ear against it to see if I can hear Mack barking at the sound of my voice.

Mitch catches up with me as I run to the back of the house. "Justine, wait. Calm down."

"You calm down! I want my dog." I scramble up the steps to the deck and grab the handle of the slider. Locked. Cupping my hands around my face, I peer into their living room. Dog toys litter the space—stuffies and squeakies. A chew bone and a fleece pad lie on the couch. But no dog. If Mack was in there, he'd be frantic with excitement. I step back from the window.

Mitch calls up to me. "Justine. This is Jennifer. She's the

Parmalees' neighbor." Mitch is still at the bottom of the stairs, and with him is a young woman, staring up at me like I have two heads.

"Why don't you come down and we'll talk." Jennifer is wearing pink scrubs and white clogs and her tone is pure charge nurse.

"All right." I'm not going to let this stranger prevent me from claiming my dog, but I won't misbehave. "My name is Justine Meade. I saw the Parmalees' ad for a lost dog in the paper. He's mine. I just want him back."

"Buddy's yours, then?"

"Buddy? No. Mack, short for Maksim. Are you going to ask me to prove ownership?"

"I'm not. They might." Jennifer sits down on the second step. "He's been good for them."

"That's the second time someone has said that. I heard about their loss. I'm not unsympathetic, but he's my dog."

"How'd you hear about Stacy?"

Mitch chimes in. "The coffee shop. We stopped for directions."

"Small town. Everybody not only knows everyone else's business but then makes it their business to talk about it." Jennifer gets up. "Come on over to my house for coffee. I don't know where they've gone, but I have Alice's cell phone number. I'll call them."

For the first time since pulling into the driveway, I begin to feel less anxious. Maybe for the first time since Artie left me in Ohio, I can relax. The Parmalees will come home, I will be reunited with Mack, and the whole ugly episode will be over. I will thank them profusely. Now I wish that I could give them a reward, but I can't, not really. I'll send them something from Seattle, a year's worth of coffee maybe. A Christmas card from Mack and me every year.

Jennifer has her back to me as she fiddles with the coffeemaker. "This is going to be very hard on them, on Alice especially. They've been shadow people ever since Stacy died, and

Buddy—I'm sorry, Mack—has been a godsend. Even the fact that they're out for a Sunday drive is a big deal. I guess you must have just missed them."

"I called this morning. When did they leave?"

Jennifer doesn't move for a moment. "A hour, maybe two. What time did you call?"

"Mitch? What time was it?"

"Eight, maybe quarter past."

"I called and they left." The panic bubbles in my gut. "They've taken my dog."

"They wouldn't do that. Maybe it's something else, not a drive."

"Please, just call them now."

Jennifer fishes her cell phone out of her purse, thumbs a number, waits. "Voice mail. Alice must have her phone off."

It is a déjà vu moment. "Try again, please." Does everyone who has my dog keep their phones off?

Jennifer leaves a message. She speaks so quietly, I don't really hear what she says.

"They've doted on him. Ed brings home a new toy practically every day, and he and the dog go to Lil's every morning."

"I know. The waitress told us. She slips him bacon." I sip at the coffee I don't want. Mitch is drumming the table, but when I look at him, he stops.

"Alice is taking him to class to learn how to be a therapy dog." Jennifer spoons a little sugar in her coffee, stirs it gently. "He's a real nice dog. I just . . ."

"What?"

"I don't want to see them regress. Alice is smiling again for the first time in seven years."

Seven years. My child has been gone seven years, too. "Well, I've had him for years, not days. I know how wonderful he is, but they can't be as attached as I am."

"No. Of course not." She taps her spoon against the mug. "Let me call again."

"Thank you." I know about loss. I know about not knowing if your child is safe. But, thank God, I don't know about losing a child to death. I can't imagine how painful that is. A mother's worst nightmare—trumping anything I have suffered.

Jennifer makes the phone call, the look on her face enough to tell me Alice hasn't picked up. She disappears for a minute, coming back holding something. "I'd like you to see this."

It is a small framed picture, a wallet-size school photograph of a girl with blond hair and blue eyes, braces glinting against the photographer's flash. She has a big smile on her face, but her eyes are not smiling. It's as if the photographer said, "Say cheese," and she did, but there is no happiness behind it. It is more of a grimace.

"Stacy?"

"Yes. Her last school picture. She died seven months later."

I stare at the face of an innocent young girl. "Why do you think she did it?"

"No one knows. Alice blamed Ed, because he insisted that they take the psychiatrist's advice and medicate Stacy for her depression. But we don't know why she was depressed in the first place. They did their best with her, and it wasn't easy, them being older parents, but they gave her everything. They loved her entirely."

"So even having love doesn't guarantee happiness."

Mitch takes the little picture out of my hand. "Shit happens. Sometimes you survive it; sometimes you don't."

He's a survivor. And so am I.

53

The balloon rises to the sky, a perfect azure blue sky without a trace of cloud. Alice grips the edge of the basket and looks directly down as the balloon slowly achieves its maximum tethered height. Buddy is standing with his nose pointed skyward. He is a tiny dot on the ground, hardly discernible as a dog; land-bound and diminished.

The propane engine roars intermittently, keeping them aloft. The vivid orange-and-blue zigzags of the balloon itself gently swell above their heads, so that the view is 360 degrees around them, but not above.

Ed puts his arms around her, leaning against her back, his chin on her head. "We aren't going to give him back." He has his lips close to her ear so that she can hear him against the roar.

Alice sighs, glad to feel herself surrounded by her husband. "Yes, we are."

She'd missed Jen's call, coming as it did while she was fumbling for dollars in her pocket to pay for lunch. After listening to the voice message, she shut the phone off. Just a few more minutes, a half hour of being Buddy's family.

As slowly as they ascended, Ed and Alice in their beautiful balloon descend, the tethered balloon reeled in so gently so that the landing is barely significant. In between blasts of the furnace, they can hear Buddy, frantic at their disappearance. He is leaping and barking, fighting against the leash being held by the balloonist's assistant. As they get closer, they see the panic in his eyes, the fear that he has been abandoned.

Ed takes the leash from the assistant and says, "What's the matter, boy? Did you think we'd vanished into thin air?" Ed is kneeling, his face buried in the dog's ruff. "We aren't going anywhere. Don't you worry, fella."

Alice has her cell phone out. It's not fair to keep this dog from his rightful owner any longer.

Ed is still on his knees. Alice reaches out and presses her fingers against him. "Jen? It's Alice." Alice keeps her hand on Ed's back as she listens. "Tell them we'll be home in a couple of hours." Alice snaps her phone shut. "Buddy's owner is with Jen. They're waiting for us."

Ed doesn't speak, and she keeps her hand on him as he gets to his feet. The dog keeps his herd-dog eyes on their faces, looking from one to the other.

Back in the car, Alice fastens her seat belt. "It's all right, Ed. Really." She gathers Buddy up close to her. "We have no choice in the matter." She can imagine the anguish this woman, this Justine, has been enduring. She knows something about loss, oh yes, she does. The feeling is fresh inside her, building up to a deadweight. But this time, she won't blame Ed.

They make their way out of the park and back through Northampton. Ed takes the slower route home, skipping the highway and the Pike, making it a true Sunday drive through a countryside just beginning to show color. Buddy is between them, snoozing contentedly, happy to be back in the car with them.

"Ed, do you think we stop so I can water the mums"—then Alice says something that she's never uttered before—"on Stacy's grave?"

Ed is silent for half a mile. He strokes Buddy's side, curling his fingers into the fur. "Sure."

Buddy keeps his head in Alice's lap, but his back feet are across Ed's. He sighs, happy not to be lost. Reunited with Ed and Alice, riding in their car, going somewhere, going home. Alice tickles the inside of his ear; Ed plays with his feet when he's not gripping the wheel. They are talking quietly, not sadly, but with a little inflection that tells Buddy they aren't fully content. One word keeps coming out of their mouths, each time with a reverential softness: *she.* "When she . . ." "She used to . . ." "Did she ever . . ." "Do you remember how she . . ."

He dozes and has a running dream, waking himself up with twitching. The car has slowed and he feels it making a sharp turn. Sitting up, Buddy yawns broadly. He knows where he is, but it's the first time Ed has ever driven all the way up to the place where Alice likes to go when she brings him here. Usually, Ed stays at the entrance, Buddy's down-stay place. And usually, Alice doesn't let him out of the car.

54

Ed shuts the car off and the engine ticks a few times before anyone moves. "Okay, let's get those chrysanthemums watered." He isn't looking at Alice, because he knows that he can't possibly deserve the look on her face. "Where are the watering cans?"

"Over there." Alice climbs out of the Cutlass, letting Buddy jump out behind her. For once, she doesn't grab his leash.

Ed comes back from the cemetery shed with a can. "Why don't you have one of your own? Why use these?"

"Never gave it much thought." Alice lets Ed fill the can, watches like a mother hen as he drains it over the parched mums.

Ed is careful to water the way Alice wants him to, each one of the four golden mums given an equal share of the water. They are tall and quite bushy, almost, but not quite, obscuring the lettering on the headstone. This is the first time he's seen it, and he is surprised that it doesn't hurt as miserably as he thought it might to look at it. For seven years, he's avoided looking at this rock inscribed with the short life of his only child, as if by putting it in the hard writing of stone, the loss would be made tangible. But in the end, it's just a rock. One that his wife has been carefully tending, making sure no lichen sullies it, no flowers go dead in front of it; that all the major holidays are represented with flags or wreathes, daffodils, or chocolate bunnies. It is Alice's place, her last remaining maternal responsibility. In the end, it is just a rock, and the loss is just the same.

Buddy's eyes are on the pillars. He keeps thinking that he should go and sit there, but he can't remember why that is. It's far more comfortable here, where Ed and Alice bend over the plants. He stands and shakes himself vigorously from nose to tail, circles three times on the soft moss-covered space between the stones. He tucks his nose beneath his tail and continues his nap. This is a pleasant place and he can wait until they are ready to take him home.

55

I am shaken by this story of loss. Shaken mostly because when I examine it beside my own grievances, the Parmalees' loss dwarfs them. I can't get back any of the time I have lost with Tony, but I can do something they will never be able to do: I can call him. I've made it a policy not to bother him, not to impose my maternal neediness on his independence. My calls have purpose. When he calls me, it is usually with equal purpose—a status update, a holiday greeting. We could be former coworkers, not mother and son. I have meticulously nurtured the wound dealt when he left, until it has become a scar. And I sit in the Parmalees' neighbor's house and hold the last school photograph of their lost child and I am filled with regret. No, something more. I feel ashamed.

Mitch sits quietly, watching me. Jennifer has excused herself to finish getting ready for work. The photograph of Stacy is on the table. Abruptly, I pull my phone out of my back pocket and go out onto Jennifer's deck, carefully closing the sliding door behind me.

I just want to hear the sound of his voice.

The phone rings almost four times. Long enough that he can recognize the number and let it go to voice mail. But he doesn't. "Hey, Mom."

"Tony."

Clearly there is something in my voice that warns him. "You okay? What's up?"

He didn't leave me; he left a lousy situation. I have treated him like he chose Anthony over me. He chose a better life, which is all I had ever promised him. An unfulfilled promise.

"I'm fine, but all of this business, you know, with my dad and losing Mack has made me think."

"About what?" Do I imagine that he sounds wary? In our family, grudges are a contact sport.

I am ready to throw in the towel and let my son know, before fate, or God, or luck, decrees that I have run out of time, that I love him. I want to tell my son, a grown man now, that life is too short not to tend to the relationship you care most about. So I just say it. "I love you."

There is a pause, a furry silence between the cell phones.

"And I love you, too, Mom."

We can't impose any longer on the neighbor—she has to report for a shift at the hospital—so I suggest to Mitch that we go find something to do. What I mean is, give Jennifer a head start and then sit in front of the Parmalees' house until they get home. Mitch isn't at all for that. It's a little early for foliage, but we drive around looking at the trees anyway. Then we decide that lunch is a good idea, although I'm too excited and frustrated to do more than move the french fries around on my plate at the lovely little riverside restaurant we find in the next town. I keep my eye on my watch as painfully slow minutes tick away.

"Maybe they're back." I just want to be on Old Path Road. I can't take the chance of not being there when they get home, can't let them think that I'm not coming back for my dog. They'll claim that I deserted him.

"Are you going to eat those?" Mitch nods toward my fries and I am struck with the most perfect déjà vu of my life. Artie's words to me almost exactly.

"Are you going to leave me in the rest room if I take too long?"

Mitch laughs and then pulls a serious face. "No. Never."

I want to say, It's what everyone else does to me. But I don't.

I think Mitch knows he's hit a nerve, because he reaches across the table and strokes a lock of my hair back behind my ear. A tiny gesture of affection and possession, like a mother might do, or a lover.

We climb back into the car and try to find our way back to the Parmalees' house, where I am determined to sit until they reappear with my dog.

"I think you missed it." I twist in my seat and jab my finger at the cockeyed street sign disappearing behind us. We've missed the turn to get back to Old Path Road.

"I think we must have come on Cemetery Road from the wrong direction. I was looking for it on my right." Mitch slows to turn around, using the cemetery driveway. There is a car up ahead of us, in the middle of the road. Mitch throws the car in reverse to back out.

There are exquisite moments in life. When you first see the face of your baby. When a random act means that you meet someone special. When a car stalls and you have a moment to look out the window and see your lost dog.

There he is. Unmistakable. Maksim. My Mack. My dog. He is stretching himself fore and aft, just like he always does after a short nap. Mitch doesn't see what I'm seeing, and I grab his hand, pulling it off the key. "Wait. There he is!" I'm out of the car and running toward Mack.

Buddy stretches out his left hind leg, a little canine balletic flourish at the end of his stretching routine. Ed and Alice are quiet but not sad, and he knows that they'll be getting back into the car in a moment to head home, where he can have a drink of water and another snooze. A car pulls in, but he doesn't know it, and this isn't his property, so Buddy keeps quiet. It is so quiet that the shout startles everyone.

"Mack!"

A voice that he knows. A word that he knows: *Mack!* He always knew Justine would find him here in this down-stay spot. Mack is a blur of silver and black and he rockets toward the sound of his name, launching himself into Justine's arms like a furry ballistic missile.

56

Justine is not what Ed has expected since hearing her voice on the answering machine. She doesn't have fangs or two heads. She is a reasonably attractive woman who is bawling her eyes out while smothering Buddy in her arms. It is obvious that she loves the dog. Obvious that this reunion is perfectly sweet to her, and doubly bitter for him. Even though Alice has said he must be returned, Ed knows that losing Buddy is excruciating for her. How will she survive another loss? "Don't take him. Please." He is mortified at his need.

"Ed, that's enough. The dog belongs to her. We love him, but we don't own him."

She has the dog in her arms like a baby. He is covering her face with kisses. Behind her, a large man in aviator sunglasses stands at a distance. "I know this is hard, believe me. But Mack belongs with me."

"You have no idea." Ed shoves his hands into his pockets. "You have no idea how hard it is."

"Ed. Stop. This isn't the same." Alice wraps her arms around her middle.

"As what?"

"As losing Stacy. He's a dog. We love him, yes. But we knew

this might happen, and we also know that he's going where he belongs. That he will be safe."

Ed yanks his fists out of his pocket and presses them into his eyes. "I don't want to lose you again."

Alice pulls Ed's face down to hers. "You have never lost me. I'm right here." She looks over her shoulder at where Justine and Mitch wait, Buddy still licking Justine's face. "Come back to our house. I have a few things of his you'll want." She lets go of Ed's face. "Give us time to say good-bye."

Buddy is wriggling in Justine's arms and she puts the dog down on the ground but doesn't take the leash. He hits the ground running, barking his sharp little bark, and begins to run around all four of them.

Buddy/Mack wriggles in the ecstatic dance of a happy dog. His Justine did find him, just where he always thought she would. He is very pleased that Alice and Ed thoughtfully hung around today to wait with him for Justine.

But there is something wrong here. Alice and Ed are exuding that grief smell, the aura that never quite goes away but has been neutralized with rides together in the car and holding hands. This scent is fresh and heavier, easily tracked should they disappear.

Mack recognizes that Justine is tense, partly excitement, partly nerves, like a dog that's going for a ride but doesn't know where to. Her posture and Alice's suggest that these females are contending over something.

The people need to be closer together. Justine is standing outside the herd of two that Alice and Ed make up. The man at the distance, who is a stranger, although his scent, even from this space, betokens friend, is also too far away. This arrangement bothers Buddy/Mack, this distance between the people who should be in the same herd because he is responsible for them all.

Buddy/Mack does what good herd dogs do: He begins to eye Justine, fixing his gaze on her until she does what he wants, and she moves a little closer to Ed and Alice. He eyes them. *Stay put, sheep*. He looks back at the stranger and decides that he'll need moving, too. He dashes away from his herd and nips at the man's leg, finding a surprisingly unfleshlike ankle. Still, it works and the man steps forward. A few more nips and he's beside Justine, touching her. Buddy/Mack eyes this for a moment, then judges it a good thing. Then he takes the next step. He begins to circle the herd of four, racing around them, around the headstone, around and around until he is satisfied that he has brought the herd of humans he cares for home.

57

Give us time to say good-bye. How can I say no to that? How could I not understand the need to have closure? My life is full of times I didn't get a chance to say good-bye. To Tony, to my father, to Mack himself. "I'm sorry; I can't."

"Please." She keeps her hand tight on her husband's arm. "It's not far."

Mack has been running around us, his excitement almost like that of a little kid at Christmas.

We open our car doors at the same time. "Mack, in." Panting from his crazy, happy run, Mack looks at me and then at them. The confusion is clear on his face, his little eyebrows giving him a perplexed expression. A question of loyalty.

"Mack, in." He doesn't obey. It can't be that a few weeks without class has turned my award-winning dog into a slacker. He utters a soft whine, and it hits me: Mack needs to say good-bye too.

"It's the right thing to do, Justine." Mitch pats my knee.

"So why do I feel like a villain here? Mack is my dog, my

companion. I do understand how they could get attached, but really, folks, enough is enough."

The Cutlass pulls ahead and we follow. It is too easy to read the lettering on the headstone where they were standing when we arrived. The chrysanthemums are beautiful, but they don't obscure their daughter's name. And the brevity of her life.

"It'll be okay. They're grown-ups." Mitch covers my hand and I bunch my fingers together so that we don't end up holding hands. "Besides, from what you've told me about Mack, you can certainly understand their feelings."

All I understand is that I have Mack fur on my vest and he's in another car, disappearing into a garage bay.

Inside, Alice grabs a grocery bag and starts putting in dog food, Frontline, heartworm pills, three stuffed bears, four squeaky toys, and a bowl decorated with tiny hydrants. She moves quickly, as if the touch of each object burns.

"Really, you don't have to give all this to me."

"What do I want with it?" Her voice has that glottal thickness to it of a woman on the verge of tears. "Ed, will you see what's in the living room?" She sets the bag on the floor, as if the weight of it is too much.

Ed comes back with another chew toy. "This is all I can find." Alice takes it out of his hand and adds it to the plastic bag.

Mack shoves his nose in the bag and hauls out a stuffie, which he begins to thrust at me. I know this game, a gentle tug-of-war, and I grab the end of the toy, pulling hard against his resistance. When I let go, Mack doesn't continue the game with me, but shoves it into Alice's hand. She tugs back, but her eyes are on me. Mack lets go and Alice clutches the toy like a baby.

Mitch stands close by and Mack is sniffing him all over, trying to figure out who this new man is.

We're getting to an awkward moment, and I just want to be gone. "Thank you for all you've done."

"He should go out before you go. Ed, can you take him?"

Ed counters with "You should."

"Both of you, go, take him. We'll wait here." Mitch holds my shoulder, as if he thinks I'm going to chase after them down the back steps.

I really don't want to stand here making small talk with someone whose heart I am clearly breaking, but in the end, Ed and Mitch go out back with Mack. I realize that Alice needs to say something to me.

"He's a wonderful dog. You tell him that for us every day." Alice is a woman who has shed tears in public and is unashamed of shedding them now.

"I will." The dreamed-about joy of this reunion is absent. I am happy and sorry at the same time.

"When we lost our daughter, Ed and I, well, we grew apart. Having Buddy—Mack—has . . ." She pauses, collecting her thoughts. She keeps her eyes on the faceless teddy bear, stroking it. "Helped."

I am not a demonstrative woman, but I hug Alice. We hug each other.

Mack comes bounding back in, tail wagging, overjoyed to see me still here. But there is something different. He seems as overjoyed to see Alice as to see me. As much as I have been frantic over his whereabouts, imagining in my darkest moments the absolute worst, Mack has been with good people.

Mack moves from Alice to Ed, sniffs at Mitch, wags his tail. And then dashes back to me, where he throws himself bodily against my legs, as if asking me to dance.

I send my dog back to the Parmalees so they can give him one last hug.

"You be a good boy. You're going home now." They keep saying the same words over and over, echoing each other, grasping his muzzle and kissing it. "We love you. Don't forget us." Mack gently licks Alice's face in what can only be farewell. Not vigorously like he does when he's excited, but one careful touch, with his ears cast back and his eyes holding hers. He's licked away her tears.

Epilogue

I bury my nose in Mack's fur, inhaling his familiar doggy scent, relishing the feel of his body in my arms. I can't imagine how the Parmalees must feel. Oh yes, I can. It's how I felt when Artie drove away with him. I felt that way when Anthony called to tell me Tony wanted to stay with him permanently, effectively ending my life as a single mom. I felt that way when my father married Adele. I felt that way every time some man made promises that he couldn't keep. Bereft. Grief-stricken. Alone.

Mitch is beside me, his fingers dancing on the steering wheel as a violin concerto blasts out of the speakers. He isn't drumming; he's fingering an imaginary violin. Then his right hand leaves the wheel and strokes Mack, coming to rest against my cheek. I lean into it. He smells of soap, his fingertips hardened by years of violin playing.

I'm going to be making changes again. Once more, I'll uproot myself and begin again. My voyage isn't over, but at least I know what I've been pursuing all these years; my particular white whale is forgiveness. I have forgiven my father, or maybe it's more accurate to say that knowing he did love me has allowed me to let go of the past. I have been forgiven, and that's a sweeter thing.

We are almost to Route 84 on our way to Brooklyn, where Anthony, Mary, and Tony are waiting for us with a Marcone's Grill dinner and a place to sleep. After that, I may say good-bye to Mitch, or I may not. We haven't talked about next steps. My duffel is in his trunk. My dog is in my arms, and wherever I end my voyage, with Mitch or not, my Mack, my dancing dog, will be always be with me.

Ed spots the dog first. It's a little forlorn, its shaggy coat a little unkempt. This one has eyes that match, a deep brown, and he's black, with rusty brown on his muzzle and a full white ruff. Sitting alone in the chain-link run, he greets them with a soft whine and a full body shake. He pokes one paw at the wire and then sits quietly.

It feels like the dog's eyes are on him, waiting for him.

"Go ahead." Alice is beside him, encouraging him.

"You're sure?" Ed doesn't mean about this particular shelter dog, but about doing this at all, taking him on.

"Never more so." Alice takes Ed's hand. "Let's take him home."

Ed nods; he cannot speak for the feeling that he has been graced by an angel, blessing him with a second chance.

Acknowledgments

From conception to delivery—thank you Andrea Cirillo, Annelise Robey, Jane Rotrosen, and, as always, my superlative editor, Jennifer Enderlin. I could never have done this without your guidance, patience, persistence, and razor-sharp insights. This excellent collaboration is what makes a good book potentially a great one.

Thanks, too, for the wonderful support of the entire St. Martin's team: Monica Katz, Joan Higgins, and Paul Hochman, who keep me comfortable with the twenty-first-century way of book promotion; Stephen Lee, John Murphy, Matthew Shear, Kerry Nordling, Anne Marie Tallberg, Carol Edwards, and Ervin Serrano.

For insights into the world of cross-country trucking, I am grateful to Charlie Tucy.

Finally, I couldn't do this without the love and support of my husband, David. Nor would I want to.

1. Justine Meade has bounced around the country a good part of her life. How much of her transient lifestyle do you think is directly attributable to her upbringing and how much is simply who she is?

2. What influence, if any, does the loss of her son have on Justine's devotion to Mack?

3. Justine is one of those women who seem to go from boyfriend to boyfriend. Why do you think she has attachment issues?

4. The Parmalees and Justine have each suffered a loss. Are there parallels between their stories?

5. At which point in the story did you root for one outcome over another, and why? Did you feel that Mack deserved one family over the other?

6. Did Artie get the comeuppance he deserved? Why or why not?

7. In what ways does Mitch earn Justine's trust? When did Mitch earn the trust of the reader?

8. How much about humans' grief, anger, joy, and regret do you think dogs understand? Have you ever had an experience that made you believe dogs know more than we think they know?

9. How did Mack's dancing effect and transform Justine? How did it do so to the Parmalees? What does Mack's dancing represent to each of them? To you?

10. At the end of the book, all three human characters have emerged with new perspectives on their pasts and their lives. What have they learned? And what has Buddy/Mack learned?

For more reading group suggestions, visit www.readinggroupgold.com.

A
Reading
Group
Guide

St. Martin's
Griffin

Turn the page for an excerpt of

A Man of His Own

Prologue

His mother had sheltered him in the nest she'd made in a crawl space under the sagging weight of an old tavern tucked just off the main street of the city that hadn't yet recovered from the Depression. She'd fed him first from her teats, all eight his alone as the only survivor of her brood of five, then from her mouth as she left him for short periods and scavenged for scraps that she would vomit up for him even as she withered from a decent-sized purebred German shepherd to a scabbed scarecrow.

The puppy would never know her history, only that his mother had managed to survive long enough as a stray by falling upon instincts hard-coded in her blood—find shelter, find food, and trust no one—so that when she failed to return to their alleyway nest, he was almost capable of surviving on his own. Almost. What he didn't know about her was that at an earlier time in her life she'd been a show dog. Somewhere miles away, blue ribbons and a silver cup graced a dusty shelf. Not a runaway, but a throwaway when the neighbor's mongrel jumped the backyard breeder's fence.

He stayed in the nest, venturing out only to do his business, lap a little at a puddle of yesterday's rainwater. But his belly began to grumble. Sometimes it had taken her a very long time to return to the nest, so he made do with sucking on the end of his tail, comforting himself, one ear cocked toward the entrance to the blind alley. She'd be back. She always came back. He had no way to know how much time had elapsed except by the extraordinary hunger that refused to be satisfied with tail sucking, and his thirst that was no longer satisfied because the puddle had dried up during the warmth of the day. Hours passed into days and the puppy only knew that his mother was still absent, and without her, he had no strength. What he longed for was to feel her body wrapped around his, to awaken to find her licking him ears to tail, to snuggle up against her warm body and let himself drift into deep sleep.

A noise. The puppy lifted his head, sniffed. A man had come into the narrow alley. His mother had always shied away from people, so he kept himself very still. When the human boldly urinated not three feet from where the pup hid, the odor of it filled the youngster with information. This person was male, this human being had eaten meat and wasn't thirsty. He couldn't help himself; the odor of food wafting out of the skin of this over-warm being drew him to his legs. He didn't consider revealing himself to the human; he just wanted to breathe in the tempting odor, as if by inhaling the scent of pastrami or ham, he'd be filled.

The rain came down and splashed into the hollows gouged out of the worn bricks. The sound of the soft late-summer rain and the earthy scent of refreshed soil confused the puppy. He ran his tongue against the rough brick where a thin layer of moisture trickled toward him. There was no relief in it, only the torment of dissatisfaction. From the splintered access to his mother's carefully chosen nest site, he could see where the puddle he'd licked dry was reforming. Nearly crazed with thirst, the puppy forgot his mother's rules, and dashed out from beneath the building to lap at the new-formed puddle in an ecstasy of relief. And that's when his future was revised.

The sudden insult of big feet against his washboard ribs made him yelp, but something kept him from running back to the shelter of the crawl space. As a dog, a youngster just newly weaned, he didn't have the experience to nip or protest, and being swept up in strong human hands had a calming effect on him. Here was contact. Here was touch. Soft vocalizations unlike his mother's voice, but with her intent. Hey there, little guy. As soothing as her heartbeat.

The puppy made a token protest, and with a wisdom far beyond his mere eight weeks of life, he chose to accept this human's touch, this man's bond.

1

The men's room stinks so badly that Rick walks past it and out the open back door of the tavern. He's in an alley, a brick wall conveniently placed so that he conducts his business in privacy. Today was the last day of play for the Waterbury Comets, and Frederick "Rick" Stanton has just spilled his good news to his teammates. Despite the C-league Comets' losing season, he's pitched well, and in the spring he'll report to the minor-league AA team, the Hartford Bees. It was surprisingly hard to say, and he was a little embarrassed to have gotten choked up, especially when they all raised their beer mugs and toasted his good luck.

He's finally going to be able to say good-bye to cobbled-together amateur teams, and all his years of hard work, from sand-lot to high school to playing in college, have paid off. Sacrificing steady employment in a respectable profession like banking or accounting like his father, in favor of menial jobs he has no compunction about leaving when practice starts up, has been worth it.

Still, he'll miss these guys, the oldest among them the catcher, Foggy Phil Dexter; the youngest, a kid of sixteen who cheerfully takes all their good-natured abuse, lugging most of the equipment, always riding stuck between two bigger players, fetching for the rest of them and enduring persistent razzing about the state of his virginity.

Finishing up, Rick feels the first drops of rain on his bare head. Those few drops are quickly followed by a complete cloudburst, but he stays where he is. It's hot inside, and the cool rain feels good. Rick raises his face to the sky and opens his mouth, taking in the taste of fresh rain. "I'm the luckiest man on earth," he says to the sky, and in that moment, he's pretty certain that he is. Well, he should get back in. Eat another couple sandwiches, toss back one more beer, laugh at a few more tired jokes. The season is over and no curfew tonight.

Thoroughly soaked now, Rick turns around and trips over something, nearly pitching headlong onto the brick pavers. That something yelps.

It's a puppy, and rather than running away after being tripped over, it stays put, and for a hard moment, Rick thinks he may have accidentally killed it with his big feet. In the weak light of the open back door, Rick sees the glint of life in its eyes. "Whoa, fella. Where'd you come from?" Rick squats down and the wet and trembling puppy inserts itself between his knees as if seeking shelter. It sits and rests its muzzle on Rick's leg. As quickly as the cloudburst started, it fades away, the rivulets trickling down the side of the wall, pooling in the interstices between the bricks. "Where're your people, little guy?"

The puppy shakes, spraying Rick with a thousand droplets. Rick scoops it up and heads back into the tavern. In the light he can see it's a male, silvery in color with a darker saddle across narrow shoulders and along ribs that poke out like boned chicken. His ears flop over at entirely different angles, as if they belong to two different puppies. Probably a German shepherd, or at least mostly shepherd. The bartender doesn't say anything when Rick comes in carrying a puppy, so Rick holds him up. "He yours?" The barkeep shakes his head no.

The barkeep's wife swings a new pitcher onto the table and considers the dog on Rick's lap. "Probably got dumped out back. You found him, you keep him. Don't leave him here."

The puppy has settled neatly on Rick's lap, gently taking the bits of meat Rick offers without nipping those important fingers with his sharp teeth. He can't keep a dog, he's living in a boarding house. In nine months he'll be at training camp. In a year, with luck, he'll be pitching for the majors.

"Got to name him if you're keeping him." Dan Lister, their manager, spreads a gob of mustard on his third corned beef sandwich. "How 'bout Spot?"

"Too common. Besides, he doesn't seem to have any spots, and who said anything about me keeping him?" Rick fingers another tiny bite of sandwich into the puppy's mouth.

"Lucky." Foggy has slumped in his chair so that his chin is barely above the edge of the table.

"Well, he is a lucky dog if one of you jamochas keeps him." Rick holds the wriggling fur ball up as if offering the puppy up for auction.

"Darby?" This from the kid.

"Darby?

"I had a dog named Darby. My dad's Irish. It's how they say Derby over there. Darby was a real good dog, never left my father's side all the time he was sick with tuberculosis. We even let him come to the funeral."

The group grows silent. No one had known that the kid was a half-orphan.

"Maybe I'll call him." Rick scratches the puppy under the chin. "What do you think?" The puppy yawns, drops his head, and is instantly asleep. Rick realizes what he's just said. If he names this puppy, how will he ever drop him back in the alley? It's not even fair to keep the dog on his lap, to allow the little thing to accept a few minutes of comfort, let him think that humans are trustworthy. The party will break up soon, and what then? Abandon the tyke to the elements? His first trust in humans to do right by him destroyed, and maybe he'll never trust another human being again. Rick can feel the puppy's beating heart in the palm of his pitching hand. The fluff of baby fur feels like the softest mink of his mother's fur stole as Rick strokes him, lifting the spatula-shaped paws and feeling the thick bones of a puppy with the potential to become a large dog. If he's not hit by a car or starved to death.

Dan Lister pushes away from the table. "I'm done in. Go to bed, gentlemen. I bid you farewell. Keep healthy and see you," he looks at Rick, "most of you, in the spring." The manager presses both hands on the table, suggesting that he's more sober than he is.

The bartender hands Rick a length of string for a leash but Rick carries the ten pounds of soft fur in his arms. Foggy is bumbling into chairs and tables trying to find the front door. "Come on, Phil, throw an arm over my shoulder."

Foggy Phil Dexter gladly slings his arm over Rick's neck and leans into him. "You'll be great. Bees need a good curveball pitcher." His breath is rank with beer and pastrami, but Rick doesn't mind. Phil's been a good friend and taught him a lot about the game. "By God, you'll be in the majors in a year."

"Your mouth to God's ear." Rick bears the weight of the man and the small burden of the puppy as they walk the few blocks to their boarding house.

Everything that he's done has been fed by his lifelong ambition to play for the majors. Rick has never wanted anything else in his life. As a kid he asked Santa for gloves and balls and bats; as a teen, he paid his own way to baseball camp, using the money he earned from a paper route. He never learned to sail, letting his father practically adopt the next-door neighbor's kid to crew for him. Tomorrow he'll head down to his parents' Greenwich home. He wonders if, when he gives them his good news, his extraordinary and long-awaited news, they'll finally respond with some pride and enthusiasm.

The puppy in his hand wriggles himself up and under Rick's chin. Well, so what if they don't. He's a grown man, he's stuck to his plan, and now, at very nearly the last minute, at age twenty-seven, he's finally there. Almost. He doesn't want to be the world's oldest rookie when he finally gets the call to Major League Baseball.

Maybe this will be the last winter keeping fit by any means possible while substitute teaching or doing temporary work at a busy accounting firm. In eight months he'll be back in training, a hardball in his hand, sensitive fingers feeling for the seams, the magic of that perfect throw. The future spools out in front of him: a winning season with the minor-league Bees, then getting the call to the majors. His first appearance in the National League. Rick sees himself doffing his ball cap and waving at cheering fans. He's paid his dues, by God. Forfeited job security and Mary Ann Koble, who didn't want to be a ballplayer's wife.

The puppy yawns, burrows his tail end deeper into the crook of Rick's arm. Why not keep him? He could be a mascot. A lucky charm. A companion on all those miles of roadwork.

There is a church along the way, more beautiful than any other building on this defeated main street; its all-white marble façade glows softly in the newly rain-freshened air. Picked out in gold leaf on the pediment are Latin words: *Gloriam Deo Pax In Terra*.

"Pax. Peace." Rick looks at the puppy in his arms, now sleeping with utter trust in the man carrying him. It's started raining again, a warm drizzle that makes the wet pavement shimmer beneath the sparse street lamps. "I'm the luckiest man on earth."

Pax. The puppy in Rick's arms suddenly wakes. He reaches up with his baby muzzle and his long pink tongue comes out to lick Rick's nose. Pax.